Acknowledgements

The author would first and foremost like to thank Petar Pijanović and Professor Dragoljub Živojinović, the first readers of this novel. He is also indebted to the hundreds of eyewitnesses who were his eyes and ears in the Great War: above all John Reed, Princess Cantacuzène and the journalists of wartime *Politika*, who proved that authors can also write about things they haven't experienced first-hand as long as they are informed about events by good, reliable witnesses.

ALEKSANDAR GATALICA

THE GREAT WAR

Translated from the Serbian by Will Firth

First published in 2014 by
Istros Books
London, United Kingdom
www.istrosbooks.com

© Aleksandar Gatalica, 2014

The right of Aleksandar Gatalica to be identified as the author of this work has
been asserted in accordance with the Copyright, Designs and Patents Act, 1988

Graphic design: Frontispis.hr
Cover photograph courtesy of the Imperial War Museum, London (Q 31930)

ISBN: 978-1-908236203

Printed in England by
CMP (UK), Poole, Dorset
www.cmp-up.com

Education and Culture DG

Culture Programme

This project has been funded with support from the European Commission. This publication
reflects the views only of the author, and the Commission cannot be held responsible for
any use which may be made of the information contained therein.

Contents

The Heroes of this Novel
(by warring countries)

Serbia

DJOKA VELKOVICH, manufacturer of *Idealin*
GAVRA CRNOGORCHEVICH, manufacturer of counterfeit *Idealin*
Major TIHOMIR MIYUSHKOVICH
YANKO and DJURO TANKOSICH, conscripts from Voivodina
Mrs LIR, a lady from Belgrade
PERA STANISAVLEVICH BURA, journalist with *Politika*
ZHIVKA D. SPASICH, seamstress
Dr SVETISLAV SIMONOVICH, doctor to King Peter
King PETER I
Sergeant DIMITRIYE LEKICH, refugee
VLADISLAV PETKOVICH DIS, accursed Serbian poet
Major LYUBOMIR VULOVICH, sentenced to death
Major RADOYICA TATICH, artillery
Dr ARCHIBALD REISS, forensic scientist and writer
ALEXANDER, Crown Prince and later regent
Four heroic lieutenants with pocket watches

Austria-Hungary

MEHMED GRAHO, Sarajevo pathologist
TIBOR VERES, reporter for the *Pester Lloyd*
TIBOR NÉMETH, Hungarian soldier
SVETOZAR BOROEVICH VON BOINA, field marshal
HEINRICH AUFSCHNEIDER, psychoanalyst
BÉLA DURÁNCI, Munich actor
A VON B, spy
MARKO MURK, Croatian volunteer
CHARLES I, the last Austrian emperor
FRANZ HARTMANN, occultist from Munich
HUGO VOLLRATH, theosophist from Munich
KARL BRANDLER-PRACHT, theosophist from Leipzig
ANDOR PRAGER, young pianist

France

JEAN COCTEAU
LUCIEN GUIRAND DE SCEVOLA, scene painter and stage designer
GERMAIN D'ESPARBÈS, soldier
STANISLAW WITKIEWICZ, Polish refugee
GUILLAUME APOLLINAIRE
OLD LIBION, proprietor of the Café de la Rotonde
OLD COMBES, proprietor of the Closerie des Lilas
KIKI DE MONTPARNASSE, volunteer and model
PIERRE ALBERT-BIROT, producer of postcards
FERRY PISANO, war correspondent
Fifty heroes of Verdun
FRITZ JOUBERT DUQUESNE, spy
MATA HARI, spy

United Kingdom

EDWIN MCDERMOTT, bass from Edinburgh
FATHER DONOVAN, Scottish chaplain
OSWALD RAYNER, assassin
FLORRIE FORDE, music-hall singer
SIDNEY REILLY, spy
ANNABEL WALDEN, nurse

Germany

HANS-DIETER HUIS, opera singer
FRITZ KRUPP, Zeppelin bombardier and later pilot
STEFAN HOLM, soldier
LILIAN SMITH (SCHMIDT), music-hall singer
FRITZ HABER, chemist
WALTHER SCHWIEGER, submarine commander
HANS HENZE, right-handed pianist and left-handed poet
PAUL WITTGENSTEIN, left-handed invalid pianist
ALEXANDER WITTEK, architecture student
MANFRED VON RICHTHOFEN, pilot
Fifty heroes of Verdun
ADOLF HITLER, lance corporal of the 16th Bavarian Infantry (List Regiment)

Turkey
MEHMED YILDIZ, Istanbul spice trader
CAM ZULAD BEY, Istanbul policeman

Russia
SERGEI CHESTUKHIN, neurosurgeon
LIZA CHESTUKHINA, Sergei's wife
GRAND DUKE NICHOLAS
SERGEI VORONIN, Menshevik, soldier
BORIS DMITRIEVICH RIZANOV, soldier
VLADIMIR SUKHOMLINOV, Governor-General of Kiev
YEKATERINA SUKHOMLINOVA, Vladimir's wife
COUNT VLADIMIR FREDERIKS, First Secretary of the Court
ILYA EHRENBURG
NICHOLAS II, the last Russian tsar
Tsaritsa ALEXANDRA
KARL RADEK, Bolshevik
YURI YURIEV, acclaimed actor
LEON TROTSKY, Bolshevik negotiator in Brest-Litovsk
A fortune-teller travelling in the trains of the October Revolution

Italy
GIORGIO DE CHIRICO

Note to readers: please be aware that in keeping with the standard practice of the period the novel is set, all Serbian names have been anglicised in order to allow easier pronunciation for the English reader. Major city names remain in the original.

1914
THE YEAR OF THE PATHOLOGIST

Suspects arrested in Sarajevo following the assasination, 1914

PROLOGUE: TWO REVOLVER SHOTS

The Great War began for Dr Mehmed Graho when he was least expecting it, just when he was told that 'two important bodies' would be brought to the mortuary in that June heatwave. But for Dr Graho, hunched and ageing but still hale, with a bald head and prominent flat pate, no bodies were more important than others. All the corpses which came under his knife were waxy pale, with cadaverously gaping mouths, often with eyes which no one had had time to close, or had not dared to, which now bulged and stared away into space, striving with their lifeless pupils to catch one last ray of sun.

But that did not disturb him. Ever since 1874, he had placed his round glasses on his nose, donned his white coat, put on long gloves and begun his work at the Sarajevo mortuary, where he removed hearts from within chests, felt broken ribs for signs of police torture and searched the stomachs of the deceased for swallowed fish bones and the remains of the last meal.

Now the 'important bodies' arrived, and the pathologist still hadn't heard what had happened out in the streets. He didn't know that the Archduke's car had been backing out of Franz Joseph Street and that there, from out of the crowd on the corner near the Croatia Insurance building, a little fellow had fired two revolver shots at the heir to the Austrian throne and the Duchess of Hohenberg. At first, the bodyguards thought the royal couple was unharmed and it looked as if the Archduke had only turned and glanced away in the other direction, to the assembled crowd; the Duchess resembled a doll in a Vienna shop window, and a moment later blood gushed from her noble breast; Franz Ferdinand's mouth also filled with blood, which trickled down the right-hand side of his orderly, black-dyed moustache. Only a little later was it established that the important persons had been hit, and within fifteen minutes the male of the couple had become an 'important body'. Half an hour after that, the important female person hadn't awoken from her state of unconsciousness, lying in the umbrage of the Governor's residence, and she too was declared an 'important body'.

Now the two important bodies had arrived, and no one had told Dr Graho who they were. But one glance at the male corpse's uniform with its breast full of medals and one look at the long, trailing, silk dress of the female body told him who had come under his scalpel.

When he had undressed them and washed their wounds he was told not to extract the bullets from their bodies but just to mix a plaster slurry and make casts of their faces. That is probably why he didn't notice that the Archduke had a small malignant tumour in the oral cavity and that something had been killed together with the lady which could have been a foetus in her womb.

Just put the plaster on their faces and take their masks. And that he did, while shouts out the front of the mortuary mingled with the warm summer wind from the River Milyacka and the distant sound of sobbing. Just a little further away, in the street, a crowd set off to lynch the assassins. Discarded weapons were found beneath the Latin Bridge. In the panic, informants spread various rumours, mixed with copious perversion and lies, while Dr Graho stirred the plaster dust and water in his metal basin to make sure the mixture wouldn't start to set before he applied it to the faces.

First of all, he covered the noblewoman's rounded forehead with the crease in the middle, then her slightly stubby nose with flaring nostrils. He filled the nasal cavity well, spread plaster between the eyelashes and carefully, like an artist, shaped the eyebrows, applying the paste almost lovingly to every hair. This was fitting preparation for the Archduke's countenance and his black, handlebar moustache, which had to be faithfully preserved for posterity and the many bronze castings which—so he imagined—would grace every institution of the Dual Monarchy for decades to come. Was he afraid? Did his nerves show? Did he perhaps feel a little like a demiurge, crafting the posthumous image of what until just half an hour ago was Austria-Hungary's most powerful to-be? Not at all. Dr Graho was one of those people with no loose thoughts buzzing around in their head. He didn't daydream, nor was he plagued by nightmares. The souls of the dead from his day's work didn't haunt him when he closed his eyes at night. If it were otherwise, he wouldn't have been able to become Sarajevo's main pathologist in 1874 and receive deceased Turks and the dead of all three faiths day in, day out.

Nor did his hand tremble now. He modelled the plaster beneath the heir apparent's lower lip, painstakingly shaped the dimple in his clean-shaven chin, covered his eyelids and attentively devoted himself to the moustache. First of all, he removed the tallow which gave it body and then did his very best to ensure that every black moustache hair was given its coat of plaster. When he had finished, two limp, completely naked bodies with white face-masks lay side by side beneath his hands. Now he had only to wait; but then something strange happened.

First one word, then another.

Had someone perhaps come into the mortuary? One of his assistants, or a policeman? He turned around, but there was no one nearby, and the words were coalescing into a whisper. What language was it? At first, he thought it seemed a mixture of many languages: Turkish, Serbian, German and Hungarian, all of which he knew, but they were intermingled with others—Asian, he thought, African, and extinct ones like Aramaic or Hazaragi. But no, he must be fooling himself. This doctor, who never dreamed, sat down quietly on the chair; still unmoved by fright. He looked at the bodies to ensure they weren't moving; yet even if by some chance they did, it wouldn't have surprised him either. When the anima leaves, the body can go wild and twitch in a frenzy. He had seen this back in 1899, when one poor wretch kicked and shuddered almost a whole day after death, as if he had electricity running through him, and very nearly fell from the dissection table. Or take the woman, perhaps in 1904 or—that was it—1905, who seemed to breathe all evening. Her beautiful, youthful breasts, which no child had suckled, rose and fell evenly before the eyes of Dr Graho, as if her dead mouth still drew breath; but it was all a trick of the eye and the doctor later documented the case in a well-received article for a Vienna medical journal.

The Archduke and Duchess could even have embraced and it wouldn't have surprised him. But they were speaking… the words wrested themselves from regional idioms and made their way to him articulately and clearly all in German. He tried to tell where the whisper was coming from and quickly established that it was the mouths beneath the plaster masks which were articulating them. Now he was alarmed. This was far from physiologically predictable and would hardly go towards a convincing lecture before the Imperial Society of Pathologists. Franz Ferdinand and his Duchess were speaking to each other. Dr Graho leaned his ear right up to Franz Ferdinand's mouth, and from beneath the plaster mask he heard one muffled but still discernible word:

'Darling?'

'Yes, my dear?' immediately came the reply from the Duchess.

'Do you see these lands, this forest, whose leaves grow and fall as fast as if the years flew by like minutes?'

In reply, there followed only the Duchess's: 'Are you in pain?'

'A little,' the *important male body* answered. 'And you?'

'No, darling, but there's something firm over my mouth, and it's not the clay of the grave.'

Mehmed Graho recoiled. The plaster casts hadn't yet set on the faces of the royal couple, but at hearing the Duchess's words he set about removing them with trembling hands. He was fortunate that the plaster didn't break because that would certainly have cost him the position he had quietly held ever since Ottoman times. With the two, mercifully intact death-masks in his hands, he looked at the splotchy faces of the wax-pale figures on his table. The lips were moving, he could swear to it now.

'I'm naked,' said the male body.

'I'm ashamed. You know I've never ever been nude before you,' the woman replied.

'But now we're going.'

'Where?'

'Away.'

'What will we leave behind?'

'Grief, a void, our dreams and all our pitiable plans.'

'What will happen?'

'There will be war, the great war we've been preparing for.'

'But without us?'

'Actually, because of us…'

At that moment, a man dashed into the mortuary. He addressed Dr Graho in Turkish:

'Doctor, have you finished? Just in time! The new uniforms are here.' He continued in German: 'My God, how terrible it is to see them naked, and their faces messy with plaster. Wash them quickly now. The court delegation will be arriving any minute. The bodies need to be embalmed and taken by express train to Metkovich harbour, from there to be shipped to Trieste. Come on, doctor, snap out of it! It's not as if they're the first dead bodies you've seen. Once they've stopped breathing, the Archduke and Duchess are just bodies like any others.'

But the voices, and the war, the great war… Dr Graho was about to ask… but he didn't say a word. Dead mouths don't speak after all, he thought, as he handed the plaster casts to the stranger, without knowing if he was a policeman, secret agent, soldier, provocateur, or even one of the assassins. Afterwards everything went the usual mortuary way.

The bodies were dressed, a new coat was quickly put on over the Archduke's breast, new, imitation medals were attached in place of the old, bloodied and bent ones, a new gown almost identical to the silk one in pale apricot was slipped on over the Countess's chest (no one thought of underwear now), and an evening came on just like any other, with that gentle breeze in the valley which cools Sarajevo even in summer.

Dr Graho was on duty in the days that followed. None of the bodies on his table moved and none of them said a word, but 850 km to the north-west the entire Austrian press was firing verbal salvos at the Serbian government and Prime Minister Nikola Pashich, whom German-speaking journalists had always despised. The reporter, Tibor Veres, worked for the Budapest daily *Pester Lloyd*, whose editorial office was housed in a dark, altogether diabolical building on the Pest side of the city, right by the Danube. Veres was an ethnic Hungarian from the border province of Bachka, and since he had a knowledge of Serbian he was entrusted with monitoring the Serbian newspapers. The Great War began for Veres when he read in one of papers: "Vienna, where diligent Serbian businessmen have invested for years, is becoming a bandits' den, and the slander of Austro-Jewish journalists more and more resembles the baying of dogs." Veres flew into a rage. He later admitted to a few colleagues that he was offended not so much as a Hungarian Jew (which he pretended to be) but as a journalist (an exaggeration, because he was an ordinary hack). And over a mug of black beer at the local tavern he snarled: 'I'll get them for this!', and the drunken company took up his words in a boisterous chorus: 'Hurrah, he'll get them for this!'

As a cheap scribbler in the big city, who just yesterday was writing about fires in the buildings of Buda and the chamber pots which some city folk still emptied out of the windows on the heads of passers-by, what could he now do but believe that the exhortation of the jingoistic crowd in the pub put him under some kind of obligation. But to do what? a few days later, the editor gave him a new assignment which struck him as journalistic providence: all the junior staff of the *Pester Lloyd* who didn't have columns of their own—which included young Veres—were given the daily task of writing and sending threatening letters to the Serbian court.

A seemingly futile job; yet not for he who until recently had been reporting on the measles epidemic in the gypsy ghetto on

Margaret Island. The new task demanded loyalty and patriotism, but above all a style of writing adaptable to lampooning. And Veres put his mind to it. He was loyal, and resolute in the extreme. He himself came to believe he was a Hungarian of Israelite faith, with a heightened sense of patriotism. And his style—he had no doubt he'd make the grade. The first letter addressed to H.R.H. Alexander, heir to the Serbian throne, turned out beautifully. Tibor had the impression not of writing it, but of shouting directly at that impertinent prince who had kindled a fire beneath old, civilized Europe. Two sentences in particular were to stick fondly in his memory: 'Stupid swine, you can't even wallow in your own pen,' and 'Son of a polecat, you've fouled your own den with your vile stench'.

When the Serbian press, which he continued to monitor, reported that hundreds of absurd, abusive letters from Pest and Vienna were arriving at the court in Hungarian and German every day, full of the vilest insults to Crown prince Alexander and old King Peter, Veres took that as encouragement to carry on even more resolutely (the editor himself even read one lampoon and told him something like 'you'll make a good capital-city journalist'). But then something strange happened to him, like it did to the pathologist Dr Graho, albeit nothing with quite such Gothic portent as at the Sarajevo mortuary. Tibor simply started to lose control of his words. He couldn't say how it came about.

He began every new letter with an extremely insulting form of address. He'd think up a very impudent characterization of the Serbian king and Serbia as a nation, then develop the idea like a good journalist does, finding shameful examples in history, and in the end embellish it all with thinly veiled threats. When Tibor wanted to show one such letter to the editor and fortunately decided to reread it first, he was greatly surprised. The words he had written seemed to have played games on him, right there on the paper. It was a real free-for-all, a grammatical kingdom without a king. Nouns stole each other's meanings, nor did verbs stay aloof; adjectives and adverbs were right little bandits and contrabandists, like real-life pirates who smuggle booty and slaves. Only numbers and prepositions were partly immune to this supercilious game, the result of which was that everything he wrote ultimately resembled praise of the Serbian Crown prince, rather than an insult to him.

At first, he tried to rewrite the letter, but then he realized it was quite stupid to try and rephrase a panegyric of Serbia when he had actually wanted to write the complete opposite. He decided to change language and switched from Hungarian to German. He dredged up heavy German words from his memory; vocabulary with lumps and bumps and excrescences—words blind and deaf to morality and any vestige of self-consciousness. From this syntactic rubble, picked up off the streets and slapped together with petulant jargon, our little Budapest chronicler would again compose a letter, and once more it seemed quite beautiful, if that can be said of lampoons; but as soon as he had finished, it began to change its meaning before his very eyes and impudently polish itself up. *Gering* (trivial) simply switched to *gerecht* (rightful), and when he wanted to write '*Das war ein dummes Ding*' (that was stupid) it turned out his hand had written '*Jedes Ding hat zwei Seiten*' (everything has two sides) as if he wanted to enter a debate with the impertinent prince rather than defame him. And so it continued. Words which had smacked of devilry and human excretions now seemed to have bathed and doused themselves with perfume. A profanity became an ordinary little reproach, and a reproach morphed into words of acclaim.

He thought this might be because he was writing on thin, journalists' onion-skin paper, so he asked the editor for some thicker stuff. He also changed his fountain pen and swapped blue for black ink, before he was finally relieved of his torment. His hate mail now remained as he intended: a devastating storm with hailstones the size of eggs. The editor liked his letters too, and Tibor thought the secret lay in the paper, pen and black ink. He even felt like kissing his mischievous pen, with which he had gone on to write a whole host of shameless letters to the Serbian court during the summer of 1914. But he didn't know what was happening in the mail.

The sordid letters now realized that they shouldn't change before the eyes of their bloated, sleep-deprived creator; instead, they resolved to change their meaning in the postbox or the luggage van of the Austro-Hungarian mail service, which carried letters all over Europe, including to Serbia. One journalist thus saved his job shortly before mobilization began, and the Serbian court was surprised that among the hundreds of lampoons from Pest there was also the occasional eulogy, and they mistakenly took this as a sign that some common sense still existed in Austria-Hungary.

The Serbian press continued to make a brouhaha and to bandy around insulting language itself, except that the words didn't change in any of the papers in Serbia, and no such glitch ever went to press to skew the meaning of a sentence. Tibor continued to write with his black ink on the new, thicker paper and to monitor the Serbian newspapers. But he only browsed through the first few pages. The advertisements and announcements were of no interest to him, and yet it was precisely these which led to 'an incident' in Belgrade, as *Politika* called it. It all began with a little advertisement which Tibor didn't read. For Djoka Velkovich, a small dealer in shoe polish, the Great War began when he placed a framed advertisement in *Politika*: "Buy German *Idealin* shoe polish! Real *Idealin*, with the shoe on the tin, is made of pure tallow and preserves the leather of your shoes." At the foot of the ad, so as to fill up all the space he had paid for, he added a phrase which would later prove fatal for him: "Beware of imitations for the sake of your footwear."

The ad was printed on the fourth page of *Politika* on the day the front pages wrote "Austria sticks to its blinkered position", "*The Times* varies with Austrian and Pest press" and "Scoop: the assassins Princip and Chabrinovich were Austro-Hungarian citizens", but the small dealer in imported shoe polish didn't read the headlines. Gavra Crnogorchevich, a shoemaker, didn't see the front pages either, but he did note the ad and the phrase "Beware of imitations for the sake of your footwear". It seems Gavra had a bone to pick with Djoka. Once they had both been cobbler's assistants, and people say they even shared a courtyard house belonging to Miya Chikanovich, a nineteenth-century wholesale and retail dealer. Whether shoemaker Crnogorchevich decided to sabotage Velkovich's shoe-polish business out of envy, or due to some old, unsettled accounts, is not known.

They say that Crnogorchevich boasted to his boozy mates in the café Moruna that he hated everything German, especially when it was to do with his trade, and that he didn't see why Serbia should import shoe polish and call it *Idealin* when Serbs could mix tallow and black dye themselves and make a better polish than anything 'the Krauts' could come up with. It was probably this grandstanding in the café—with a refrain very similar to the one which inspired a little journalist in Pest and which the crowd repeated like a salvo: 'Everything of ours is better than the Krauts'!'—which prompted the shoemaker to begin producing an imitation of *Idealin* himself. All he needed was domestic tallow, locally produced dye, a tradesman from Vrchin to make the tins, a shady workman to cast the die for an embossing machine like the one which impressed the design of the hand holding a shoe and the German slogan, 'ist die beste *Idealin*'—and the fake shoe polish came onto the market.

Both versions sold in the grocery stores, so Velkovich and Crnogor-chevich's paths didn't cross at first. But Belgrade was too small a town for this '*Idealin* coexistence' to last for long. Velkovich noticed the counterfeit and it only took him a few days of asking around among shoemakers, coffee-house ruffians and snotty-nosed apprentices to find out who his rival was. He saw red when he heard it was Crnogor-chevich, with whom he had shared a room as a young man and paid for the experience with an empty belly because everything he earned went towards the rent.

He placed one more ad in *Politika*, warning "Mr Crnogorchevich and those who assist him" to withdraw their fake product from the market or else "suffer all manner of sanctions: legal, commercial and personal", but the shoe-polish imposter wasn't to be deterred. Moreover, as a seasoned swindler, he immediately pointed the finger at Velkovich and claimed he was the one selling the bogus *Idealin* and that they should have court-appointed experts examine both products to prove which was genuine. But they were in the midst of the hot summer that followed the Balkan Wars in the south, and it was also the turbulent week when the diplomatic note of the Austrian government was to be delivered by Count Giesl, the Austrian Minister at Belgrade, so initially no one paid much heed to that little dispute.

The sworn rivals considered their next steps, and the first thing they each came up with was to find some heavies to beat up the other and wreck his 'shameful manufactory', but it turned out that hooligans were in short supply. They therefore decided to resolve the matter with a duel! Velkovich and Crnogorchevich agreed to this on the same day as a peculiar aeroplane was seen in the sky above the city; it circled for ten minutes before disappearing back over the Danube into Austria-Hungary in the direction of Visnjica. As there was no tradition of duelling in Belgrade, the two shoemakers scarcely knew all the prepara-tions needed for a proper duel, so they largely went by the kitschy French novels which both of them read, relying on their hazy memory of duels described with the sentiment usual to that kind of pulp.

They scoured the city for pistols and eventually both of them found a Browning (Crnogorchevich a long-barrelled model, Velkovich a short one). Then they set off in search of seconds, and white shirts with lace on their chests and tight breeches à la Count of Monte Cristo, as if they were preparing to get married, not to face death. At roughly this stage, the sensation-hungry press took an interest in the matter and unshaven

Belgrade busybodies turned their attention to it. Partly, at least, it was intended to distract readers from the concern so amply incited by the front pages. The shoemakers were declared to be gentlemen, great masters of their trade and rivals in a contest for an elusive woman's hand, but hardly anyone mentioned that the duel had actually been set over shoe polish.

The press coverage was sufficient for the Belgrade police to also take an interest. It was established that neither Velkovich nor Crnogorchevich had done military service because they had been sent to the rear during the Serbian-Bulgarian War of 1885, so probably neither of them had ever fired a bullet. But the Brownings were itching to be used, and a site had to be found, "just like the fateful battle of the Ottomans and the Serbs found its Kosovo", as one journalist put it. At first, the shoemakers wanted their 'field of honour' to be in Topchider Park, but the Belgrade City Council ordered that there was to be no shooting and killing in that waterlogged wood as it would endanger the peace; the king's nearby summer residence would be steeped in sorrow if he heard of the incident.

The fierce rivals' seconds therefore proposed the nearby hippodrome. It was decided that the duel be held on race day, on the Feast of Saints Peter and Paul, in the week of 29 June according to the old Julian calendar, immediately after the five scheduled races had been run. And so a sizeable crowd gathered, this time less because of the horses than because of humans with the brain of a horse, if that is no insult to gentle ears.

The starting guns were the first to fire: the first consolation race was won by the stallion Gevgelia, while White Rose triumphed in the second consolation race, Greymane crossed the line first in the derby, the jockeys' race was won by the mare Countess and the officers' race, to the bookmakers' surprise, by the yearling Kireta from the same stable. It was getting on for seven in the evening by the time Djoka Velkovich and Gavra Crnogorchevich strode out into the middle of the grassy, sports field, which the race track wound around. At first, everything resembled those heart-rending nineteenth-century novels. The crowd was cheerful and amused. Death, it seemed, would also be vaudevillian. But the doctors at the side had alcohol and balls of cotton ready on their stools, nonetheless. The seconds dressed the death-daring rivals in their white shirts. Both of them really had insisted on lace. The pistols were loaded with just one round and cocked.

The duellers walked back to a distance of one hundred metres and then raised their arms.

At that moment, everything ceased to look like a novel. This was probably because the bloodthirsty crowd roared ever more loudly, and the hand of each shoemaker trembled. Velkovich was unable to even hold up his outstretched left arm, while Crnogorchevich's gun in his right hand jammed and the bullet didn't want to exit the barrel. Now it was Velkovich's turn to fire using his short Browning, and send his adversary to meet his maker if his bullet found its mark. But he hesitated, while the clamour of those who knew they were part of a crowd and wouldn't be to blame for anything afterwards grew and grew. When his fear-blanched forefinger finally pulled the trigger, the cartridge exploded in his hand, bursting the barrel of his pistol and badly scorching the right side of his face. Velkovich collapsed and the doctors came running. In the confusion, the seconds declared Crnogorchevich the victor of the last duel in Belgrade before the Great War.

Fake *Idealin* and its proprietor thus won the day, and a whole month before the war began it was sold in Belgrade as the real McCoy; but shoes in Belgrade, like those in Bosnia, still dried out and warped in the oppressive heat. This made Dr Mehmed Graho resolve to buy a new pair. He dropped in at an old cobbler's in the market place. Once he had bought shoes in Serbian-owned shops, but they were now closed. Their smashed windows were boarded up, and Dr Graho complained that Sarajevo was increasingly becoming a battlefield and a dump—since no one collected the rubbish left behind after demonstrations. He entered the cobbler's shop with that in mind, pointed to a pair of ordinary brown shoes and tried them on. Without an inkling that anything important would happen to him, he focused his attention on buying a pair of new shoes for himself. He was flat-footed and constantly had swollen joints, so not every pair suited him. In fact, he had great difficulty finding the right footwear, and this time, too, he gave up the idea of buying the handsome, perforated brown shoes.

He returned home and set about shaving. First he lathered under his nose, then on his cheeks and finally under his chin. He looked at his face in the mirror, and not as much as a glimmer of the day's events at the mortuary passed through his mind. He made the first stroke with the razor slowly and carefully so as not to cut himself. He'd be on duty in the evening and knew he mustn't look slovenly. He arrived at the mortuary shortly after seven. Several bodies came in that night which didn't interest him. He examined them, carried out two simple autopsies and then sat on the metal chair for a long time, waiting for new work. Nothing happened until morning, and he managed to doze a little.

A LONG HOT SUMMER

Hans-Dieter Huis is singing today!

Maestro Huis is to perform at the Deutsche Oper accompanied by Germany's best master-singers and the orchestra conducted by the great Fritz Knappertsbusch. Huis will sing the role of Don Giovanni in Mozart's opera. All of Berlin is feverish with excitement, and every lime tree in Unter den Linden Street seems to be repeating this refrain. The tickets have long since sold out. It's the talk of the town!

The greatest German baritone hadn't sung this role for more than one and a half decades. This was because he had apparently been something of a Don Juan himself in the previous century, causing one young teacher from Mainz to take poison because of him. He therefore decided not to sing the role of Don Giovanni any more during that overripe nineteenth-century, and he held that promise even longer—right up until 1914.

Now the memory of the tender young teacher had paled, but had it entirely? For maestro Huis, the Great War began when he realized that he felt nothing inside: neither sadness, nor joy, nor any true faith in his art. He was sitting in front of the mirror and doing his make-up without anyone's help when that realization came home to him. He put on the powdered Don Giovanni wig and looked into his already aging face, weary with the scars of many roles. He had played them on stage, played them in life, and now he had to appear before the Berliners—the most demanding audience in the world. Everyone in the auditorium was saying it would be something special, he knew it; he felt the crowd had come to see if his voice would tremble and whether he'd get stuck in the middle of his lines, unable to continue. 'Like an old lion tamer who has to stick his head in the mouth of the beast again,' he muttered to himself and set off for the stage through the side corridors.

The overture was over and the opera began. Donna Anna, Donna Elvira and the peasant girl Zerlina soon fell victim to Don Giovanni's licentiousness, and Hans-Dieter Huis opened his mouth as if he was in the recording studio and singing into the big horn. He didn't feel anything inside—neither joy, nor sadness, nor excitement. When he managed to look into the faces in the first few rows, he noticed that almost all of them were holding opera glasses to their eyes. The opera lovers looked unearthly to him, and he knew they were watching for the slightest twinge on his face, but he didn't remember Elsa from Mainz and didn't know what to think about her suicide because he no longer had any feelings or thoughts about the two of them. He sang like a wind-up toy—by all means brilliantly, but also coldly—and made it through to the end of the opera in that tone. The spirit of the Commendatore enters with an earth-shattering boom (a long-prepared spectacle). Don Giovanni doesn't listen to Leporello's warnings and stays firm when the Commendatore's spirit begins to sing 'Don Giovanni, a cenar teco /m'invitarsi, e son venuto' [You invited me to dine with you, / and I have come'] and drags him away to hell. The closing notes, a satisfied swing of the conductor's baton, and the end of Mozart's opera. A claqueur from the third gallery shouted 'Bravo!' and the audience sprang to their feet. Thirteen bows. Thirteen! That was unseen at the Deutsche Oper, but although the audience clapped loudly maestro Huis knew they were making a din without any real enthusiasm. The greatest German baritone may just have performed, but the petite teacher Elsa from Mainz hadn't gone onto the stage with him, and it was as if everyone had been expecting her. The audience would have applauded a little more and then got up to go home, had not an officer now come onto the stage. He was short and his uniform didn't go with the costumes of the opera, although it matched the costumes of the day. The military man took out a proclamation from the kaiser and read it out with pathos. And yet his voice trembled a little: 'These are dark times for our country. We have been surrounded and are forced to use the sword. God give us strength to wield it as needed and wear it with dignity. To war!'

While the proclamation was being read on stage, Don Giovanni and his cheated lovers, with their smudged make-up, were standing at the side. Someone burst into tears backstage. One man after another rose from his seat in the audience, and on the second gallery it seemed they were trying to sing the national anthem in unison, but the great baritone didn't believe in war and only thought what the reviews would say the next day.

And sure enough, the next day dawned with favourable reviews, but it was a new day for Berlin, a new day for Sarajevo, a new day for Belgrade and a new day for Paris. In Berlin, a performance of the famous Berlin Varieté was broken off. Another officer, long and lanky, took the stage and read out the kaiser's proclamation. And then a third, and a fourth—on all the stages in Germany. In Paris there had already been rumours about mobilization for weeks. People spoke about war not with fear, but with an explosive mixture of romantic and patriotic feelings. Soldiers-to-be imagined themselves as republican grenadiers who were given new uniforms and helmets, and instead of bayonets they stuck irises into their rifles and charged before the eyes of girls seated along the trenches like medieval maidens watching a joust. It seemed that everyone wanted to ready himself for that 'decisive battle'.

At the Café de la Rotonde, a gathering place for artists and aesthetes run by Old Libion, many of the guests had started training and so had stopped drinking. They claimed to be in training, to be sure, but they poured themselves drinks under the table. No one asked for the old cocktails which the painters once used to order for their models; pastis and absinthe weren't in demand, and even Old Libion's sour wine, which had the reputation for giving a bad hangover, was consumed in greatly reduced quantities. Anti-German slogans were to be heard left, right and centre. One voice yelled that 'eau de Cologne' ought to be called 'eau de Louvain'. The fellow at the bar hated everything which came from the Boches and, refusing a new round of drinks 'because it was time to prepare for war', called out loudly, so that Pablo Ruiz Picasso would also hear him, that all the cubists should be stuck on a bayonet because it was a 'filthy Boche art movement'.

But one little man with a sparse moustache sat in the corner of the café and didn't shout anything. He wanted to go to war too. He imagined it as being like one of his poems where verse fought against free poetry on a field of paper and where one rushed at the other with spears raised, but not so violently as to prevent the lyrical battle bringing forth a beautiful poem. That titch's surname was Cocteau. For Jean Cocteau, the Great War began with the serious worry that he could be turned down at the recruitment office for being too thin. Therefore, instead of drinking, he constantly ordered rich and fatty food. Pâté, raisins, fried crab... etc.

When he got home he was sick from so much food, of course. He ran for the toilet and vomited a little on the black-and-white tiles in his haste before reaching the toilet bowl; where, with an immense sense of relief, he ejected what he had consumed. He could identify the remains of the purple crab and the black raisins which stank of the acid of a distressed stomach. But what could he do? Like a Roman patrician who had come back from some great orgy, he realized that his stomach was now empty again and he wouldn't gain a single gramme from what he had eaten at Old Libion's. He went out into the street once more, where Paris's rust-red dust swirled low on his patent-leather shoes and long shadows danced on the walls. He made his way to the neighbouring Café du Dôme and called the waiter, playing the same game as at Old Libion's:

'What would you like, sir?' the waiter asked.

'Please bring me a piece of Gruyère,' the guest said.

'So you'd like dessert?'

'Yes, for starters. Afterwards I'd like half a chicken.'

'Anything else?'

'Yes, I'll have the macaroni.'

'Would you like a steak as well?'

'Yes, but "à l'anglais".'

'All at once?'

'In the order I said.'

The Dôme was significantly quieter than the Rotonde. A former haunt of German artists, it was now empty. No one played billiards at the green felt. The undersized writer wasn't sure of the date—perhaps it was the last day of July 1914, but he smelt war in the air. He called the waiter again and said he had just been joking. He decided to have a light meal because he was coming to realize that it was better to eat five times a day like a frail invalid. After every meal he'd rush home and lie on the bed, on his back, so as to digest the food without vomiting.

Such problems were unknown to most. Although they were artists and hunger had been their constant companion for decades, they had been born strong, with broad shoulders and massive haunches, so they could hardly wait to head to the army supply office in Temple with their recruitment papers to buy all their kit and new steel helmets. For Lucien Guirand de Scevola, a scene painter and stage designer who had recently been praised by the illustrious Apollinaire, the Great War began at the counters in Temple, when he bought himself a complete uniform and then decided to reward himself with a mask against poison gas. They told him it was a supplement to the uniform, a kind of 'war accessory', and that he probably wouldn't need the strange rubber contraption with threateningly protruding little glass cups for eyes, but you never knew. Scevola decided to try on both the uniform and the mask. Even at the counters in Temple everything had to be a bit chic. He went into one of the special cubicles there (at a recruitment office, imagine!), tried on the tunic and tightened the trousers with the belt. He looked at himself in the mirror and was satisfied—he cut a good figure. Then he put on the helmet and foppishly cocked it.

He also decided to try on the mask with the duck-like metal beak for protection against hypothetical poison gases he didn't even know the names of. He took off the helmet, slipped the elastic straps over his head and put the helmet back on, as he was told he'd have to do in the event of a poison-gas attack. He turned to face the mirror and was shocked by how he looked. The first thing he felt was that it was very hard to breathe, and then he suddenly saw stars and visions—so real that he couldn't believe they were just in the dressing-room mirror at the recruitment office. In the depths of the mirror he saw the town of Ypres, although he didn't know it was Ypres. He saw the morning, with swallows flying low over the ground, and he saw a yellowish-green smoke billowing towards a trench. It looked like harmless smoke blown by the wind from a campfire where someone was burning old tyres, and now it enveloped the soldiers like a poisonous cloud. He saw the young men who had no masks; all they could use were white handkerchiefs. Before his eyes the first of them began to fall into the mud of the trenches and writhe in spasms. The others then ran from the trenches, where they were met by enemy fire. The chests of the soldiers heaved in vain and their tongues were covered by a white film; they crawled as if their throats had been cut, while the gaze from their pupils, which floated on bloodshot whites, vanished as if scattered by the savage breath of Aeolus. He, the painter Lucien Guirand de Scevola, wanted to help them but didn't know how.

The next instant he ripped off the mask with the threatening eyeholes. He was back in the yellowish light of the dressing-room lamp in Temple. An impatient soldier knocked on the door of the cubicle and demanded that he finish as he wanted to see himself in uniform too. The soldier swore at Scevola as he went out, but received no reply. To hide the tell-tale tremble of his hands, he put the helmet back on, cocked it like a dandy once again and, now well and truly equipped for war, went to the table where the uniforms were sold. He told the quartermaster he had given up the idea of buying a mask. Besides, he added, his father had pulled a few strings to make sure he'd be a telephonist in the war. The uproar and derision from the assembled new soldiers—those whose faces he had seen when he put on the mask— saw him out into the street and, embarrassed, he rushed to the Rotonde in the hope that his gentle-minded, raggedy painter friends there would smooth his ruffled feathers.

In Belgrade, another man hurried into a café that day. He had a thick moustache and dark eyes beneath drooping eyelids and he cast sharp glances all around. He felt that all of Belgrade knew him, and he wasn't wrong. The victor of the duel at the Belgrade racecourse, the one whose bullet had jammed in the barrel of the unreliable Browning, was now the hero of Dorchol and the other lower-town neighbourhoods all the way to Savamala and Bara Venecia on the banks of the River Sava. The greengrocer's assistants chatted about him while they were carrying their wares and the porters mentioned his name while they waited for late passengers at the railway station, as did all horse-racing aficionados. For Gavra Crnogorchevich, the Great War began in the moment he thought he had finished his personal battle and his counterfeit *Idealin* had vanquished all Krauts.

A merry din rose to meet him at café Moruna. 'To Vienna!' someone called out from the corner, and the crowd cheered: 'To Vienna, to topple Franz Joseph!' Later there came a shout from the back: 'Count Giesl has left, and he'll be followed by the head of every Kraut I find on Teraziye Boulevard', upon which a bunch of young men borrowed the melody of a popular ballad and improvised a ditty: 'Fol-lowed by the head of ev'ry Kraut from Te-ra-ziye.' These shouts made Gavra feel awkward, not because they were roaring a song against Austria—he had already dealt a mortal blow with his *Idealin*, he thought—but because he didn't know what was going on around him, nor had he ever heard of Count Giesl.

If he had caroused less in the previous few days and sold more of his counterfeit *Idealin*, he probably would have thought of lodging an ad in the paper, like every small manufacturer, and then he would have learnt that Austria-Hungary had sent Serbia an ultimatum through its minister Count Wladimir Giesl, demanding that the Serbian government accept and promulgate a pro-Austrian declaration, immediately dissolve the nationalist organization 'Narodna Odbrana' (People's Defence Force), delete all propaganda against Austria-Hungary from school textbooks and public documents, allow the Austrian 'k and k' judiciary to conduct investigations in Serbia, and mete out severe punishment to Major Voya Tankosich and the civil servant Milan Ciganovich, who were involved in the assassination of Archduke Franz Ferdinand, as well as to the negligent border officials in Shabac and Loznica.

On 25 July, by the new Gregorian calendar, when the Serbian govern-ment rejected the ultimatum, Gavra left café Moruna, drunk, at around six in the afternoon. Just a few hundred metres from the door, Regent Alexander Karadjordjevich and his secretary Yankovich, from the Ministry of War, set off for the royal court. At the entrance, they met several ministers who were pained and silent, anxious about what was going to happen. Absorbed in thought himself, Regent Alexander finally broke the silence in the style of Alexander the Great after cutting the Gordian knot, with a terse and abrupt: 'To war then.'

But Gavra Crnogorchevich didn't hear that. He didn't read the papers, so he didn't find out either that mobilization had begun in Serbia. The reserve had been called up and his 1881 year-group was among those ordered to the mobilization offices, the janitor had told him, but, hot-tempered as he was, he pretended not to have heard and just took a loud sip of his strong, black coffee. For a few more days, our duel-winning hero was convinced that his fake *Idealin* would make him rich. He got into a row with several traders who were marketing the real product; and then all of a sudden he disappeared into the blue. No one missed him, and his escapades were soon forgotten because all available ships started to arrive in Belgrade in the first few days after mobilization, and a mass of recruits was flocking to the very same racecourse where the duel had taken place to get their travel papers and set off to their different headquarters and units. Late in the evening on the last day of July by the new calendar, the day Gavra Crnogorchevich disappeared, Field Marshal Radomir Putnik, commander-in-chief of Serbian forces, returned to Serbia on the evening train from the spa in Bad Gleichenberg. The first thing Putnik said when he arrived was: 'At the service of the Fatherland, in health or sickness'; the last thing Gavra Crnogorchevich said when he crossed into Austria and glanced back at Belgrade from the border town of Zemun was: 'This looks mighty bad.'

The same words, *this looks mighty bad*, were also uttered by the Istanbul spice-trader Mehmed Yıldız, but it was 29 July by the new calendar. His elderly lips whispered those words as he sat perched on his red-felt-covered stool in front of his shop, where he had habitually sat for decades. The sounds of the street ebbed and flowed around him—traders calling out their offers, the squeak of wheels and the barking of stray dogs. Yıldız traded in oriental and European spices and his shop was in a beautiful location: right on the waterfront of the Golden Horn, not far from the thick walls of the old palace of

His Majesty the Padishah. Sitting in front of the tubs and panniers, surrounded by the intoxicating smell of his spices in all hues of ochre, brown, green and red, the trader read on the front page of the newspaper *Tanin* that Austria had declared war on Serbia the previous day, 28 July 1914; Russia and France were preparing to declare war on Germany and Austria, and a declaration of war was expected from Great Britain as well. The trader tilted back his fez and blew out a long cloud of smoke. His sole consolation was that his country Turkey was neutral for the time being; even so, he feared the worst and whispered, 'This looks mighty bad'. But he didn't think a trader needed to worry too much about the fate of his country.

Brought up on Nizami's epic romance *Khosrow and Shirin*, while also being a supporter of the true Turkish miniature which rejects the shameful Western laws of perspective, Yıldız Effendi was a true Turk who saw the world not the way it was but the way he wanted to see it. He didn't notice that the Ottoman Empire, still enthralled by the tales of its history and power, was lurching and sinking in the turbulent waters of the twentieth century. He didn't want to acknowledge the signs of decline and the pitiful withering of government. Talaat Bey, the Grand Vizier Haki Pasha, the military commanders Mahmud Şevket Pasha and Mahmud Muhtar Pasha, the ministers Halaciyan Effendi and Noradungian Effendi, and senator Nail Bey—all these personages of Turkish public office were like mythological figures: half medieval, half modern. But since they resembled Yıldız Effendi, he naturally couldn't perceive anything unusual about them. Istanbul itself was decrepit and crumbling, and Byzantine Constantinople was showing ever more often through the debris; but the trader sat down on his stool every morning, gave one of his assistants the sign to start calling out the prices and praising the wares, and opened the noble Koran to read a few lines for the day; he thought what good fortune it was that Sultan Mehmet sat on the throne, a powerful, wise and stern ruler who, just a few streets along from his shop, behind the high walls of old Topkapı Palace, listened to the song of the nightingales which he let out of their golden aviaries into his blossoming courtyard every morning.

One shouldn't blame an old Turk, a man of the nineteenth century, for all that was amiss. He knew that his Sultan became ruler after being released from captivity where he had been held for being mentally un-stable and that all decisions were made by the Young Turk committee; he knew that he probably didn't live in Topkapı, which the sultans had left long ago for fear of tuberculosis and moved to Dolmabahçe Palace, but whenever he said 'Padishah' he would imagine the paradisical garden of the palace not far from his shop; he would see the nightingales and the golden aviaries, feel the defiance and the righteous rage of the believers, and easily fill in the full picture—two-dimensional, of course—which appeared before his eyes as the sole and unverifiable truth. Besides, a motherly sun shone over Istanbul and everything looked different from Budapest, where mobilization was carried out in the first days of August amidst a spell of violent stormy weather: the wind battered the trees in the avenues and the windows of the National Theatre burst, but the glorious Hungarian soldiers-to-be weren't to be frightened by a rainstorm with thunder and hail. The journalist and budding lampoonist Tibor Veres wanted to go to war too, or to be honest he didn't. He said he wanted to, but deep inside he was afraid. He knew that if even a whiff of his fear was detected he'd instantly be pronounced a bad Hungarian, so first of all he boasted to his editor, with whom he had made friends after all those letters sent to the Serbian court, that he was just dying to join the artillery and dreamed at night of firing a machine-gun and hurling out 'a hundred rounds a minute'.

He was also the loudest at the recruitment office. He almost got into a fight there with some smooth-faced striplings from Bátaszék, just for the sake of it—he wanted to show everyone that he was bursting with vigour. But he was much more at home in his skin when they allocated him to a unit behind the lines where his job was to read the letters of prisoners of war. Our old operative's knowledge of Serbian was decisive once again, so Veres left the recruitment office with his travel papers in hand and a pretend tear in the corner of his eye; he set off for the banks of the Danube, to the border town of Zemun.

One very different recruit, his namesake but with the surname Németh, a Hungarian on both sides of the family, was happy that day to be allocated to a reconnaissance detachment. For Tibor Németh, the Great War began when he left the recruitment office with his travel papers in hand and tears of joy in his eyes, exultant that he'd be continuing the heroic Hungarian warrior tradition of both his father's and his mother's side of the family.

Many trains were heading for the front in those few days, carrying cheerful recruits who waved little flags out the windows of their compartments. Tibor Veres set off on the morning troop train to Zemun.

The small-time journalist took along one change of civilian clothes, so his colleagues in the censorship unit wouldn't mock him, and one small suitcase. This travelling bag contained a supply of black ink for three months, which is how long he thought the war would last, a certain amount of paper, and two fountain pens: the disobedient one with the blue ink and the new, obedient one filled with black ink, which produced such lovely German expletives. Tibor Veres thought he looked good in the freshly ironed bluish-grey uniform coat, which he tightened with the belt bearing the inscription 'Königlich ungarisch' on the buckle. He cocked the peaked cap with the badge of Franz Joseph on top and winked to himself. He didn't take a helmet. Tibor Németh also set off to Zemun, but on the evening troop train. He thought he looked good in his freshly ironed bluish-grey uniform coat, which he tightened with the strap with 'Königlich ungarisch' embossed on the buckle. He cocked the peaked cap with the badge of Franz Joseph at the top and smiled at himself. He took a helmet as well. His father had managed to find the money for a gas mask, but he thought it best to save some money so, like Scevola in Paris, he didn't buy a mask. Nor did Németh take any 'civvies' along with him.

The two trains arrived at their destination. Dozens more would set off the next day, and hundreds more throughout Europe. If each of them had drawn a red woollen thread behind them, the blood-red trails would have formed a net covering the Old Continent. Ninety trains alone would leave from Petrograd and Moscow in those few days. The nurse Yelizaveta 'Liza' Chestukhina and her husband, the surgeon Sergei Vasilyevich Chestukhin, would be sitting in one of them. For Liza and Sergei Chestukhin, the Great War began when they took their little daughter Marusya from Moscow to Petrograd to stay with aunt Margarita Nikolaevna because both of them were being sent to the front. Mama and Papa had both been assigned to the hospital train V.M. Purishkevich, and for little Marusya everything seemed like a dream. What was 'the front'? What did a hospital on rails look like, and how did it treat the wounded? How could a person be injured if she wasn't even allowed to fall and hurt her knee? And where was their maid Nastia? Had she gone to the front too?

Questions abounded in the little girl's head, but there was so little time for their farewell in the house on Runovsky Embankment. Marusya remembers her father standing at the end of the room and smoking. He threw restless glances at her and her mother and repeated what sounded like: 'Lizochka dear, don't make her cry now.' But Liza bent over and her thick, copper-coloured hair tumbled down as she whispered to her daughter that she'd bring her back the loveliest Punch puppet, as if she was going on a shopping spree to Paris rather than to war. In the end, her father kissed her goodbye too. His moustache was prickly and he smelt of fine tobacco. Then they left; sooner than they needed to, but not showing any signs of distress.

It was those who remained behind, in Petrograd, Antwerp or Belgrade, who were disturbed. Djoka Velkovich, the loser of the Belgrade duel, lay in the old Vrachar hospital in Belgrade in a bed for the seriously ill. The doctors removed the bandages and gave him a mirror. He saw that his right eye was bulging bizarrely, without the upper eyelid, lashes and brows. All the surrounding skin was as red as a pomegranate. In fact, the whole right half of the trader's face was red; and the doctors worried that something nasty might happen when they told the patient he'd stay that way forever. Finally they told him the truth, but nothing did happen. It was as if Velkovich had come to terms with his appearance the very moment the barrel of his Browning burst at the racecourse. And until the end of that day, he didn't think of leaping out of bed and flinging himself headfirst through the open window of the hospital. Before going to sleep, he thought he ought to have a shave, and he almost smiled at his half-burnt lips. No stubble would grow again on the right-hand side, and he'd easily be able to shave the left-hand side with half the amount of soap. He wanted to call someone before he dozed off, but in the end he didn't. He fell asleep and didn't dream anything.

Neither did Jean Cocteau dream that night. At the twelfth hour, when it was time to go to the recruitment office, he looked in the mirror and saw his protruding ribs and sunken stomach. All the rich and fatty food, the slabs of bread thickly spread with goose-liver pâté and garlic, the whole flocks of partridges and ducks he had eaten, seemed to have done nothing to change his physical appearance. He therefore resolved to take a desperate step that afternoon: he sat down to an abundant meal with an admixture they said wouldn't harm his bowels: ordinary buckshot. Cocteau stirred it into the minced meat on his plate and ate like a man who hadn't eaten in a long time. He set off for the recruitment office with a full stomach. He was a little pale and visibly anxious, but definitely at least two kilos heavier. If only he didn't vomit a minute before stepping on the scales... he left his flat and cut through

the Tuileries Gardens, taking care to choose a route with as little challenging food outlets as possible along the way, which might cause his
stomach to heave. The park was safe: the trees and flowers didn't have
smells which could remind him of food. Then he turned the other way.
Between Place de l'Observatoire and Rue de Vaugirard he saw a few
emaciated people out walking, who, like him, were avoiding all danger
from smells, since there were no restaurants there. Afterwards he took
Rue Férou to Saint-Sulpice, and then went down to the River Seine.
Paris around him was quiet.

Belgrade was also far too quiet at the hour Djoka Velkovich fell
asleep. That evening, Liza and Sergei Chestukhin arrived by train at
the eerily quiet Eastern Front. There they went aboard the armoured
hospital train V.M. Purishkevich. Sergei took charge of the operating
theatre in the third wagon, while Liza changed into a Russian Red
Cross nurse's uniform and put on a starched apron so white that she
thought it would be a shame if it got blood on it. The train stood at
the platform in the town of Bologoyev for some time before moving
off with a jolt. It was headed for Likhoslav, and then on for the border
with accursed East Prussia! With that jolt, all the doctors and nurses
in the train knew that the war had begun for them even before the
first bursts of fire.

Sarajevo was also quiet as night fell on the eve of war. Mehmed Graho
thought about all sorts of things: about regicide, about his Orthodox
Christian ancestry, although he kept that to himself, and about the
generation of his great-great-grandfather who, for him now long ago,
had converted to Islam. He had his own explanation for the war: the
dead had risen up to fight the dead. The end of the last century had
revealed something troubled and rotten, it had consumed people, and
now one batch of humankind was to be purged and replaced with
another. Wars had served that purpose since time immemorial. He
went home that evening after work, undressed and went to bed. He
didn't dream anything, but many others did.

They dreamed beneath Europe's starry, starry summer sky in those
nights: stable boys and gunners, batmen and their officers, and generals
and their chiefs of staff. That night when the armoured hospital train
V.M. Purishkevich headed off from the main platform of Bologoyev
station towards the war zone, the commander-in-chief of Russian
forces on the Eastern Front also dreamed. For Grand Duke Nicholas
Nikolaevich, the generalissimo of the Russian army, the Great War

began when he drifted off into a most unusual dream; he entered a large hall, like a huge underground dance floor, where couples were spinning with wild abandon.

He found it strange that he saw no windows or daylight; the ball in his dream was taking place in some kind of bunker and no one except him seemed to mind. Then all of a sudden, as these things go in dreams, he too felt a desire to dance. He looked around for his wife, the Montenegrin princess Anastasia Petrovich, but she wasn't to be seen. So he decided to take to the dance floor by himself. He discovered that the couples were just men, in the uniforms of the tsar's army. Not a single woman was dancing with the officers, but mostly batmen with their lieutenants, artillery captains with gunners, colonels with orderlies, supply-office chiefs with their grooms.

Now that's what I call a real officer's ball, Grand Duke Nicholas thought and called out for his chief of staff, General Yanushkevich. Who would a commander-in-chief dance with if not with his faithful chief of staff? He just yelled once and there he was, right behind him. They couldn't agree which of them would lead, but then the 'male role' in that dance of men was naturally given to the commander, who now swirled with his partner over the polished parquet of the hall as if bewitched. At first, the steps of his chief of staff were as light and nimble as those of a bar-room dancer, but after a while his response to the long steps and lively turns became ever more sluggish. Yanushkevich was melting away, Nicholas noticed, the smile had disappeared from his face, and soon he could neither dance nor move. The music stopped and the commander-in-chief now saw to his astonishment that he was in a hall with hundreds of clay figures and that he had been dancing with one of them. Every bust had a face, and all of them were dressed in uniforms of stiffened fabric. Then the last stage of his dream began: he was running between the ranks—there were thousands of them in that dance hall now—and he saw that a stream of blood trickled from the clay chest of every one of them. Some seemed to have been pricked with a sewing needle, as there was only a tiny trickle of blood between the buttons of their coats, while others seemed to have a blooming scarlet lily on their breast… and none of them fell. He stood at the parapet of the dance front and it seemed they were all waiting for the music to start again and a *danse macabre* to begin, but at that moment the generalissimo woke up. And he muttered to himself with parched lips: 'A mighty carnage is going to come.'

He called his orderly and asked for a glass of cold water and a compress for his head. It took him half an hour to recover, and then the commander's Spartan mind once again began to think about lines of battle, strategic heights, natural obstacles and weather conditions, as if there had never been people on earth, beneath the sky. He asked that he be brought ordinary soldier's fare from the canteen that day and that his tea in the afternoon be sweetened with saccharin. He didn't allow himself to turn in for the night on the metal camp bed until late. Shortly before morning, Grand Duke Nicholas Nikolaevich, dubbed 'the Iron Duke', realized that this war would be won by the horses, which lugged the machinery of war and the heavy guns. How mighty a power would be which could transport its wartime arsenal by train or even by plane, he thought; he realized this would be impossible for Russia.

But one soldier-to-be did set off to the front by aeroplane. That soldier, however, would never take a gun in hand because he was told in Berlin before he left that Germany had sufficient soldiers to satisfy the Sphinx of war; one needed to think about how to preserve the country's most talented people for the period after the conflict, so there would still be a civilization to speak of when the world war and its tribulations finally ended in German victory. The name of the passenger in that plane leaving for the German-Belgian border was Hans-Dieter Huis. Maestro Huis had been assigned to the staff of General Kluck to organize concerts for the senior officers. Before boarding the plane he was given a pair of leather overalls with a hood, flying goggles and a red scarf—the trademark of German pilots. The plane was captained by flying ace Dietrich Ellerich, who had recently amazed the old, civilized world by flying his plane to an altitude of eitht thousand metres. That day, the squadron included seven other German-manufactured biplanes. Pilots and Zeppelin crews on the ground saw them off with defiant cries of 'To Paris!', and Hans-Dieter Huis, not doubting German victory for a moment, wondered how his pre-war Parisian audience would greet him when he came onto the stage as an invader and sang Mephistopheles from Gounod's *Faust* in German. Yet now, at the beginning of the war, Huis didn't dare to think about what would be after the war. They landed in a strong wind on the grassy strip of the small aerodrome in Evere, north of Brussels. It was a rough landing. He was glad to reach terra firma again, but he didn't want to show his fear. His pale face gave him away. While he was being introduced to several generals from Kluck's staff, he thought that music would reconcile the nations, but he couldn't have imagined that he'd be putting that idea to the test that very same year, at an unexpected moment.

That day, four hundred kilometres to the south, the soldier Jean Cocteau set off to join an aviation unit at the aerodrome in the town of Bussigny. He was assessed at recruitment to be 'malnourished' but was enlisted all the same. He had a very, very nasty time that evening and the next, expelling the undigested buckshot, but he was glad to be still alive and to have become a French soldier. And now he was going to war. But who cared about the war? a uniform and unconfirmed martial glory were much more important. He started daydreaming. He'd return to Paris in the uniform of the victors, enter Café de la Rotonde, wave to Old Libion, and sit down at a table with Picasso.

WAR

There's going to be a big war. The less-than-loquacious owner of the café Casino in Shabac remembered Major Tihomir Miyushkovich for these very words, uttered on the decisive day of his life, Tuesday, 29 July 1914, by the old calendar. Proprietor Kosta and his plump wife Hristina reacted to the insistence that they say something more about the major with the same enthusiasm as if the tax collectors had just knocked on their door: 'Look, that's all we remember about him. Lots of people come here, all different ranks, all sorts of weird and wonderful folk… and we're good people and upright publicans, you know. When we had to pay the tax for street lighting, we were the first in Shabac; when they introduced a duty on music, we took it straight from the street musicians' pay so we could give the government its due.' And the major? They seemed not to remember him, as if they had only passed him in the street, as if he was an apparition or a human shell which didn't have emotions of its own and didn't notice its own suffering or that of others.

There's going to be war again, a great war, Major Tihomir Miyushkovich is said to have muttered on that fateful 29 July 1914, after he'd come from café Casino to the Nine Posts. The owner of that café, a certain Zeyich, a man without children or a woman at the hearth, remembered the major much more clearly and filled his strawy exterior with substance, some of which shone through. 'I hardly remember the major. My memory doesn't serve me all that well, I must admit. But I'm a decent man and orderly in every other regard. When it was time to give the government its due, I never asked questions and haggled. No, my good sir, I demanded that they tax me the most—for the thirty electric light bulbs in the garden. Yes, me… I didn't let anyone leave my place for the unlit streets without a guiding light, be he tipsy or dead-drunk. Now, if you're asking about the major, I'd say he was a nasty fellow: the wars had made him coarse, he was blind with the desire for promotion and had turned his back on his native land, but not before his endless frenzy had cast a pall on his neighbours. The army was his morning and his evening. He drilled his soldiers hard and drove the draught animals to their limits: he whipped horses until they foamed at the mouth, and muscle-bound bulls would tremble when he harnessed them into a team and made them haul a battery to the River Drina. The army was dead scared of him. Granted, he was even-handed, but talk about a hothead, talk about a brute. He broke a soldier's arm or leg every week with his blows. I don't know any more than that. Yes, he dropped in here on that last day of peace in July before the accursed Austrians attacked us. What did he do? He drank, sir, and we don't know anything more than that. After all, I'm a respectable man and publican. When they introduced the tax on music, I said: I'll pay in person for a big band and won't take a penny off the street musicians' baksheesh. That's the kind of man I am.'

There's going to be war again. A great war. These words of the major's were well known to the owner of Shabac's café Amerika, whom some call Munya. And now Munya, a perpetually overtired man with a puffy face and dark circles under his eyes, finally told the whole story about Major Tihomir Miyushkovich. He took what little is known from café Casino, added the strawy substance with a shine from the Nine Posts, daubed the straw with soil and breathed life into it after what he heard in his café, Amerika. 'Yes, I remember the major and that decisive day in his life. It was Tuesday, 29 July 1914 by our calendar. It was the last day of peace for many: for us publicans, for our guests, for Shabac and for Serbia. You know, there are some people who sail through the decades and arrive, crying or laughing, at end of their life—and then founder on that last, quiet day. The major's whole life passed in front of him in one day, in one afternoon, even. That's what happened to him, from what I've heard and what I personally saw. You say he was hot-headed? That he thrashed the draught animals and belted the men? Maybe he did. They say that the army was his morning and the troops were his evening. For sure, there are officers like that. But between the morning and the evening the sun comes out and God draws it across the sky. The major's sun was his wife Ruzha. She washed him, she ironed him. She moved with him time and time again, from headquarters to command post, from hilltop to outpost, until they finally settled down in Shabac two years before the wars began. He was promoted to major and became commanding officer of the 2 Battalion of the Combined Drina Reserve Division, and she became the major's wife. Everything was easier in town, and when the washing, sewing and shopping was done the major's wife had a lot more time. But she didn't use it for herself. She didn't go out or dress showily. She didn't make eyes at anyone—until that last day.

'The war must have had a part in that, sir. On the fated day, the major first went to café Casino. I'm surprised that Kosta, the owner, doesn't remember, because I know that Ruzha went there the first time and asked the major for his ring. "Your fingers have got thicker, Tiho," she said to him, "the ring is galling you. Let me have it widened so it doesn't rub and hurt when war comes again." I'm surprised Kosta didn't hear that, but I know the major was already quite drunk and sent her away without giving her the ring. Later in the afternoon, when he was well under the influence, he went to the Nine Posts. Soon after he'd gone in, Ruzha turned up at the door there too. She didn't berate her husband for drinking or insist on taking him home. She knew as well as he did that war would come the next day and flatten anything that was less than sturdy. It was just the ring she wanted. She wanted to have it widened here at a craftsman's, who was a Vlach. She just needed the ring for an hour or two. No longer. The major didn't give her the ring or take it off his finger, but he hugged his Ruzha. He gave her the tenderest of kisses, even though behind those lips stood the sharp teeth and the voice which the army feared like the plague. And as he fondled her flaxen hair she just repeated: the ring, the ring.

'He had her thrown out. Soon the musicians dashed in and wanted to sing a little more so that people would get teary. They claimed they were from the famous Cicvarich family of performers, which of course was a lie. They started to sing, and the major sang with them. He sang "Shabac Girl", "When the Nightingale Calls" and "I Sold My Horse Blackie", and he drank and drank like the parched earth, and still he hadn't had enough. He paid for the music and went out into the street, his shirt half open and his hair ruffled. He staggered but didn't fall—he took care not to dirty his uniform because it was sacred to him. As he lurched along, he cursed and swore. He was angry, sir, but at whom? a white-hot fury flashed from his eyes but couldn't burn anyone now except himself. He came into my café, ordered more blood-red wine. He asked where the music was. The door opened, but it wasn't a band pretending to be descendants of the Cicvarichs, but Ruzha again. She didn't ask for the ring now but took it off her drunken husband herself. She said she'd bring it back after he'd had another drink or two. To take it to the Vlach, an excellent craftsman, just to have it widened a little. And she repeated: "The Vlach, an excellent craftsman, just to have it widened a little... have it widened... widened...".

'And so she went, like a harbinger of doom. Afterwards we learnt that a fickle-minded young officer was passing through Shabac, a child of rich parents. He wore an elegant, grey-blue reserve officer's uniform;

one to be worn every day, not one to die in. He was driving to the front in his father's open car and I don't know how he noticed Ruzha, the major's wife. One glance beyond the limousine's footboard was enough. He invited her to get in and took her for a drive around Shabac. They went into a wood by the River Sava and tossed a friendly salute to every guard, while he kept saying that forests always reminded him of Beethoven's *Pastoral Symphony*, which beautifully imitates the chirping of birds! What birds, you may ask? War was drawing close, and that rake wanted a woman for one afternoon. Ruzha, like a moth drawn to a fatal flame, probably wanted to kiss one last time. After returning from "Beethoven's forest" he promised her his estate, a title and money; he told her stories about leaving Serbia and escaping the war. He promised her a flight to freedom... but she wasn't free; she was still someone's wife. The cavalier in the ironed coat persisted, and the last bastion of the major's wife's repute soon crumbled. Finally she saw the pledge of fidelity—her entire former life—as being embodied in her wedding ring, which she now took off and flung into the Sava as they spoke. Now there was only the major's ring left, that anchor and her last fetter.'

'The adulteress had been to café Casino, but the major had had her thrown out. Then she went to the Nine Posts, but still she didn't get the pledge of her fidelity. They say that she and her new flame—the seducer and the moth—drove along behind the major quietly, in second gear so he wouldn't hear them, to see which café he'd go into next. So when he came in here, like I said, Ruzha came in after him. She no longer begged him now. She took the ring. I went after her and saw her get into a big car. She giggled and tossed back her open, sandy-blond hair. Later I heard she also threw the major's ring into the river before driving away to the south. When some guys came running into the café and said "The major's wife threw the ring in the river!", the major sobered up in the blink of an eye. Not a trace of wine remained on his face. Like an orderly soldier, he looked first of all at his uniform. He smoothed it out with his hands, tightened his belt and tucked his trouser legs into the top of his boots. He called the servant boy to bring some shoe polish, and while the boy was shining his boots he rested his fingers together. He didn't look at anyone and didn't ask anything. The boy finished. "How much do I owe you, Munya?" he asked and paid the bill. "July is almost over, and in August we'll be going to war," he said and went out through the café's garden. You know the rest.'

History knows the rest, too. The second last day of July came. It was a hot day. The wheat had been harvested, but the corn stood horseman-high in the fields. On Wednesday, 30 July by the old calendar and 12 August by the new, Austria-Hungary's Balkan army was set in motion across the choppy River Drina and through the tall corn which almost overarched it that year.

The Great War had begun.

The Austro-Hungarian 5th Army under the command of General Frank attacked across the Drina along the line of Bijeljina–Zvornik–Priboj–Brčko. The 6th Army, under General Potiorek, moved from the Vlasenica–Rogatica–Kalinovik–Sarajevo area, while the 2nd Army, under General von Böhm-Ermolli, entered Serbian territory from the north, from Syrmia and Banat. The Austro-Hungarian command concentrated the bulk of its forces on the Drina and decided on a strategic thrust here, at Serbia's north-west. This somewhat surprised the Serbian Supreme Command, which reacted by turning its forces ninety degrees and rushing from the north to defend the western border. The chief battle took place in the Cer mountain range, but to finish the story about the major without his wedding ring it is more important to describe his brief, brave showing on the field of battle.

The 2nd Battalion of the Drina Division went into combat three times in those two fateful days, and each time Major Tihomir Miyushkovich was pale, clean, washed and resolute. He plunged into battle the first time near Tekerish when the Austro-Hungarian 21 *Landwehr* Division attacked the Combined Serbian Division, including the 2nd Battalion under his command. Then in the engagement near Beli Kamen, which ended at Begluk. A third time then sufficed to cut short a life which, to tell the truth, had already ended in café Amerika in Shabac on 29 July 1914 by the old calendar. The decree decorating Major Tihomir Miyushkovich and posthumously promoting him to lieutenant colonel was announced in *Politika* once it resumed publication immediately after the Battle of Cer. The decree was read by everyone in Shabac except one woman, who no one ever heard of again—whether she was alive or dead, happy or unhappy. Her name was Ruzha, and that's all that was known about her.

Were the survivors the lucky ones, or did the wounded envy the dead? Perhaps the corpse-strewn hills of the Cer mountain range and the blood-red River Yadar had an answer. Many of the wounded fell back across the Drina, which became a roaring grave for both armies. Doctors at the field hospitals removed bullets from the wounded in the hope of saving their legs, and sawed legs in the pitiful hope of saving heads.

There was just such an Austro-Hungarian hospital in narrow, river-bound Zvornik, and one of its surgeons was a certain Mehmed Graho. Everyone skilled with the scalpel was needed for the war, so our pathologist, who since 1874 had mixed with the dead, donned the uniform of a Bosnian infantry regiment, stuck a crimson fez on his head and set about saving the living. But his hands, it seemed, were made only for the mortuary. The grievously wounded soldiers brought back from the River Yadar strangely melted away and died beneath his knife. He did the same work as other surgeons. The operation would go well, but when everything was done Graho would feel a chill behind his back, as if death had come to visit him, and he watched as he lost the soldier. He tried with all his strength to bring the wounded man back from death's door, but most often in vain.

So much killing and dying was going on in those days that hardly anyone noticed that a doctor of death was at work in the hospital in Zvornik. But Mehmed Graho was certain it was him. He tried once again, then a second time, ten times, and still all the men died on him. 'It seems I was made not to heal, but to kill,' he said to himself and, if it was his lot to kill, he set about selecting the most severely maimed soldiers and those he least liked the look of in order to finish them off. His rationale was that if he took the wounded who were beyond all hope, it would be harder for anyone to notice that almost every patient died on his operating table. And so he chose them, one after another. He repented, prayed and begged Allah, but in vain. He wanted to give up, but he knew he'd be court-martialled if he refused to work. Men screamed like a monstrous choir all day in the chaos of the army hospital in Zvornik, and there was no one he could complain to or ask to be relieved of his duties as the doctor of death.

He had no choice but to kill the soldiers, so he almost reconciled himself to his hideous role. He read a selection of verses from the Koran and told himself that desperate certainty was better than uncertain hope. He walked among the stretchers lying in front of the hospital in files and rows like the graves of a military cemetery and said: 'Him, him, and him here—to me.' Then he strove and struggled to help them, but they all died. He'd go out into the courtyard again and speak in an indifferent voice: 'Him, him, and him there—to me.'

What Dr Graho didn't know was that there, on the banks of the Drina, death was claiming what it left alive elsewhere. As if by some enigmatic geometry of death, one and a half thousand kilometres to the east, in the hospital train V.M. Purishkevich, the neurosurgeon Sergei Vasilyevich Chestukhin witnessed the wondrous recovery of his soldiers after the initial battles in East Prussia. Young men were brought in with their heads split open, with bullets in parts of their brain which ought to make them vegetables, or corpses, but that was mostly avoided. The other doctors noticed that miracles were occurring in the third wagon and each of them, as soon as he had rested a little after his shift, came in to watch Dr Chestukhin operate. The healing hands of the doctor adeptly extracted bullets from the heads of soldiers, reconnected shattered pieces of skull and sewed wounds which had bled so badly that there seemed to be no stitch able to hold them. The men lay on his table for ten minutes longer, and then life returned to their eyes even in the most hopeless of cases; after several such remarkable operations the assembled Russian doctors broke into applause.

Yet there was just one strange thing about these patients. The soldiers brought to the hospital train had been peasants before the war, or menials on the estates of the gentry, who had never seen anything of the world beyond their willow groves and little rivers. A large number of those who miraculously survived now began speaking German while still unconscious. First they would whisper 'Hilfe, hilfe!', then some of them would launch into whole monologues in that language they had never learnt and would talk about things they simply could not know about, uneducated as they were. Dr Chestukhin's wife, the red-haired nurse Liza Nikolaevna Chestukhina, heard many of these monologues in German while bandaging the wounded men's heads after the operations and could find no answer to this mystery. But since she knew German she understood the erudite talk of the muzhiks.

She didn't want to bother her husband with what she heard, but since he kept sending her miraculously saved men and future experts in German from the third wagon, she started to listen attentively to these 'wonder wounded'. One boy, whose medical card stated that he was a farmhand from Yasnaya Polyana, the former estate of Count Leo Tolstoy, talked about Goethe for an entire afternoon. It was a kind of trance and he couldn't open his eyes under the bandages, but he said: 'Als Goethe im August 1831 mit dem noch fehlenden vierten Akt den zweiten Teil seines *Faust* abgeschlossen hat, sagt er zu Eckermann: "Mein ferneres Leben, kann ich nunmehr als reines Geschenk ansehen, und es ist jetzt im Grunde ganz einerlei, ob und was ich noch etwa tue." [When Goethe finished the fourth act of *Faust* in August 1831, thus completing the second part of the work, he said to Eckermann: 'What remains to me of life I may now regard as a free gift, and it really matters little what I do, or whether I do anything.'] Two beds further along, a badly mangled soldier recited poems by Schiller, which Liza had learnt as a girl. Then he spoke loudly, as if on stage, and it turned out to be part of the poem 'The Ideal and Life': "Wenn, das Tote bildend zu beseelen / Mit dem Stoff sich zu vermählen / Tatenvoll der Genius entbrennt, / Da, da spanne sich des Fleisses Nerve, / Und beharrlich ringend unterwerfe / Der Gedanke sich das Element." ["When, through dead stone to breathe a soul of light / With the dull matter to unite / the kindling genius, some great sculptor glows; / Behold him straining, every nerve intent / Behold how, o'er the subject element."]

Liza thought there might have been a mix-up with the wounded: a battlefield is chaotic, and perhaps the Russian stretcher-bearers had brought back educated German soldiers as well. She waited for them to wake up, whereupon the 'German speakers' successively died: some after one, others after two days of tirelessly mouthing German verse, or simply individual German words. A few of them did wake up out of their coma, however, and when she asked them who they were, she realized they really were ignorant Russian peasants and semi-skilled artisans. Liza asked them if they had ever learnt German, but they didn't know what to say and just kept repeating how much they hated 'the Krauts'.

And so time passed, but Sergei's wounded didn't speak German for long. It only happened for the first few days after the Battle of Cer in faraway Serbia, when students and poets were dying under the hand of the pathologist Mehmed Graho and their souls migrated east for a brief while along some imponderable transversal, in the invisible barques of the dead, into the split heads of Russian farmworkers. Already towards the end of August 1914, esteemed 'Dr Sergei' no longer managed to save as many soldiers after the victorious battles of Stallupönen and Gumbinnen. The heroes who survived the operation and were moved to the care of his wife Liza no longer spoke at all, in Russian or German; they groaned in the language known and shared by all wounded soldiers in Europe.

Men groaned in the same language and died in the same language—in east and west. In the region of Alsace-Lorraine on the Western Front many young Frenchmen had cheerfully plunged into the first border battles, convinced that one shot, one shout and one charge would resolve everything. Waiters rushed into battle together with the artists they served, who had just recently 'avoided alcohol so as to better prepare for war'. Light-headed as they were, they thought it wouldn't take much, not much at all, for everything to be over and done with, and what a shame it was that their sweethearts weren't there to watch them after seeing them off in Paris with unforgettable cheers and sticking flowers in the barrels of their rifles; flowers which each of the men now wore under his shirt like a shrivelled rosebud.

Everything was different to how the soldiers had imagined it. The recklessness of senior and mid-level commanders in the border battles in north-western France saw that the flower of young French manhood and their officers perished in the last days of August 1914. Death trawled and netted big fish, not stopping even when the catch was so heavy that it could hardly be dragged from the field of death. For the junior officer Germain D'Esparbès, the Great War began when he wrote a letter to his superior commander after the great slaughter in Alsace-Lorraine:

I think the work of the French Red Cross is simply disgraceful. I woke up near the town of Lunéville to find myself in a sea of dead soldiers and spent three whole days with them. Nothing unusual, I hear you say. But I wish to describe to you those three terrible days, which passed before one of our Red Cross crews finally found me. I commit these lines to paper in the deepest conviction that I am about to lose my mind, so I need to write quickly, however illegible that makes my handwriting even for me.

I woke up at dawn in a wood beside a road. At first I was unable to move, so I tensely felt myself all over with my right hand: first my left arm, then one leg and the other. On realizing that I hadn't been blown apart by a shell, I passed my hands over my belly and shoulders and licked my forefinger and thumb. By the taste of dust on my fingers I realized I had no blood on my coat, so I probably hadn't picked up a Hun bullet. Oh, how I rejoiced at that moment, but I shouldn't have! I lay there until afternoon on top of something soft, only hard and uneven in a few places, so I thought it a mound covered with grass. I was unable to move much or swing my arms; if I had been, I would have realized that the mound was not one of earth and grass but of the dead bodies of my poor comrades.

It wasn't until the next day that I realized where I was and what I had been lying on; that was to be my second day spent among the dead. I jumped up fresh and almost healthy that morning—I think it was the last day of August—when, oh my God, I saw the carnage. There were dead as far as my eyes could see. In many places they lay one on top of another, entwined and entangled, and completely covered the ground like human humus which monstrous plants of war were to germinate from. I found some of the soldiers in a sitting position, with their eyes open, seeming to me to be still alive. I rushed to one and then to another in the hope that they would answer, but in vain. The grim reaper must have cut them down so abruptly that the life hadn't managed to flee from their eyes, and so they sat, and the occasional one almost defied gravity by still leaning against a tree or a worn-out old nag. Two comrades, with their arms around each other, had crawled into death in a patch of wild strawberries. The blood on their faces mingled with the juice of the strawberries they seemed to have eaten with their last strength before they expired.

I started shouting and calling for help, but no one from the Red Cross came that second day either. What a poor wretch I was, whom an evil demiurge had condemned to life. I wanted to run away and escape, but where could I have gone when there was an endless tangle of corpses all around, and it seemed to me that not even a whole day's running in the summer sun would have led me to anything new—except to the next trench full of dead soldiers. That's why I stayed where I was. Straining my senses, I summoned all my presence of mind. I thought it would be much harder for them to come to my aid if I wandered about rather than staying put. I still don't know if it was the right decision.

On that second day among the dead, I identified a plot of bodies I'd be able to put in some kind of order. I set about disentangling the bodies of these comrades and cleaning their wounds as best I could. I sat them up or at least had them reclining, like in a Roman theatre. It must have been about a hundred corpses I repositioned in this way, maybe more. Towards evening, I wanted to see who they were, so I took out each one's identity card and read their particulars. Jacques Tali, student; Michel Moriac, wholesaler; Zbigniew Zborowski, member of the Foreign Legion. I was still perhaps the man I had been before the war until I got to know them and looked each one in the face. At that instant, they ceased to be unknown heroes. I thought about what they would have gone on to do if they had survived the attack near Lunéville. Tali would have become a famous curator of the Autumn Salon; Moriac would have made a fortune dealing *in vinegar; Zborowski would have become Polish ambassador to France. But like this? Like this they were simply dead, but certainly not silent.*

Before the day was over, my reason definitely began to leave me. That's right, I heard them talking. I answered them and even began to argue with them, although I was still aware that everything was coming from my mouth—their voices and mine. I took a real liking to some of the comrades, to others not so much, and when I woke up on the third day I pulled the ones up to me who I'd become especially close with. On that third day we had a kind of group session, but the conversation didn't hold us for long. I discovered a deck of cards in the pocket of one of my best friends, the wholesaler Moriac. Decency restrained me for a while, but the terrible loneliness drove me to do what I'm about to describe with a shudder of shame.

I sat my comrades in a circle and started playing Lorum *with them. I shuffled the cards and dealt them first to one fellow, then to a second, a third, a fourth and lastly, myself. I moved their hands and fingers, which by now were stiff, so they could hold their cards, and then the game began. I'd play my card and set off around the circle. There was no cheating; I didn't abuse my role. Everyone would play a card, and whoever had the best hand would win the round. Then I'd deal again and start off around the circle once more. Another game for my comrades and me.*

The Red Cross found me in the middle of a round I was set to win and sent me to Metz for a regimen of therapy, and then on to Paris. Please treat all that I've written as the complete truth and take whatever steps necessary so that our medics make it to the survivors faster and don't consider it futile to search among hundreds of bodies to find one who still has breath in his lungs. If they had noticed me on the first day I would have remained who I was, but now I've become someone else, a different person who I'm frightened of and who will forever be foreign to me.

Thus wrote Germain D'Esparbès, though hardly anyone was likely to have read the young officer's letter at the time. At the beginning of the Great War, the Germans concentrated the bulk of their army in the west, on their borders with France and Belgium, based on the strategic plan of first defeating France and then transferring their forces to the east to reckon with Russia. Since the defences along France's eastern border from Belfort to Verdun were considered impregnable, the German Supreme Command deployed the larger part of its forces on the right flank along the Aachen-Metz line, in the spirit of the old

Schlieffen Plan from the nineteenth century. At first, war seemed some way away because Germany only requested 'free passage' through Belgium. Since Belgium declined, and since Britain sided with the brave Belgian King Albert and his people, Germany set General Kluck's and Bülow's armies in motion. They advanced through Belgium like a mower through a wheatfield, and as early as 24 August 1914, the German cavalry entered Brussels—the first city on the wartime tour of Hans-Dieter Huis, the great German baritone.

Fêted Huis arrived in Brussels together with the staff of Kluck's 1st Army. Cheerful cavalrymen stood by their animals' sweat-glistening necks and sang 'Die Wacht am Rhein' and 'Deutschland über Alles', and for Huis this was all a little absurd. But he didn't think of laughing out loud. The next day he was to hold a concert, and he alone knew how much effort it had taken to find an accompanist among the Belgian POWs, and afterwards to locate a badly scratched Bechstein grand in the deserted city. Then there was no one far and wide to tune it, and the instrument with its open lid bared its strings at him like a shameless nude. An old fellow finally arrived in Brussels to tune the piano, a full three days later, so the concert for the senior officers in the City Hall couldn't take place until the end of the week. Maestro Huis chose the repertoire himself. He didn't think of singing arias by composers from enemy peoples; he didn't dare to sing the aria from Gounod's *Faust* or from *Boris Godunov*, which he liked so much, because the former was in French and the latter in Russian. He thought it best to stick to Mozart, with the occasional aria by Rossini or Verdi (the Italians were still neutral). The concert began at exactly five minutes past eight. Only for a moment did he waver and think he should perhaps have changed from his uniform into a concert tailcoat. He decided to remain a soldier because he thought he'd be performing to ordinary soldiers, but he was surprised when he saw many officers with ladies in the audience. The generals of the 1st and 2nd Armies, Kluck and Bülow, were unable to attend due to the victorious campaign, he was told, which had seen the Belgians thrown back to the North Sea coast and the French to the very outskirts of Paris. Instead, this first concert in 'liberated Brussels' was attended by their chiefs of staff, who were great admirers of Huis's art. Perhaps he was a little affronted that no top generals were present, but he went out onto the stage and sang. Two or three times he had to stop and clear his throat, but for the German officers who missed opera so much the performance was of great satisfaction. The generals came up to him after the concert with tears in their eyes and told him he had brought a piece of civilization to that terrible war. Just then, he realized who the ladies were. They were Belgian and Dutch prostitutes, women who never leave a sinking ship and are satisfied as long as their clients are happy. They too congratulated him and giggled loudly, praising him in bad German, and Huis felt very awkward. Not so much due to those ladies in their worn dresses as because of his singing. 'I was well out of tune. God, how long has it been since I've performed? That concert at the Deutsche Oper in Berlin was the last!' With these thoughts he departed Brussels and set off after Kluck's army as if he was a quartermaster supplying them not with beans and chewing tobacco but with stocks of opera songs. That's why the German generals were so grateful and looked so happy each time.

Not all generals were so lucky as to have such moments of serenity. The Austrian general Oskar Potiorek had to regroup his routed forces after the disastrous Battle of Cer. The pandemonium on the Serbian Front lasted several days. Wrathful Serbs crossed the turbid River Sava and occupied the territory between the Sava and the Danube in southern Syrmia for several days, burning the stubble-fields and empty lands along the Danube. The unbearable stench could be smelt in Zemun, and soldiers and civilians went about with handkerchiefs over their faces. Those several days saw the rise and fall of Tibor Veres, the Budapest journalist who specialized in offensive letters.

Veres had come to Zemun full of his own importance, and now he could hardly bridle his anger.

Veres's disobedient fountain pen with the blue ink arrived in Zemun too, hardly able to bridle its rage that the censor was no longer writing with it, while the obedient one, with black ink in its chamber, was full of its own importance now that Veres was writing with it exclusively.

From the very first day, however, Veres performed the mind-numbing work of censorship, so it wasn't clear why the fountain pen with the black ink was so proud. Like a gold prospector, he had to read a hundred letters to come across just one where he found something significant. One soldier wrote to his mother about how cold he was and that he missed her corn-bread (how trivial!). Another complained that he hadn't had a proper night's sleep for a fortnight and that the worst thing about war wasn't the bullets or the hand-to-hand combat but the lack of sleep (not completely irrelevant but a fact already known to the upper echelons). A third wrote to his beloved that when men killed each other they didn't make human sounds but grunted and groaned like cattle who know nothing of humanity (an example of the declining morale of the Serbian forces!).

On the second day in Zemun, Tibor's blue pen was already bored. And although it was writing all day, his black pen quickly became bored too.

Tibor's life in Zemun, however, became interesting in those five days. He was billeted to an elderly Serb woman who had formerly run a guest house by the Danube together with her daughter. A large flag of the Dual Monarchy now fluttered in front of the house in the lower Gardosh neighbourhood, and mother and daughter took pride in having sewn it themselves. Tibor had it good in the former guest house. Small and beardless though he was, he felt that the daughter took an interest in him from the first morning when she served him the meagre breakfast and started a conversation in her broken Hungarian. Just when he thought the Great War would turn out to be a boon for him, and that he'd perhaps even marry in Zemun, his own small private war began, one which would end fatally for him. And everything started as a miniscule problem, like when you feel the first stab of pain in a tooth, which is white and healthy looking but full of caries inside.

On the third day in Zemun, Veres's black fountain pen became increasingly disobedient. Again he wrote with the one, and left the other lying on the paper. He wanted to report that he had read a soldier's letter home about the poor prospects of the Serbian army recovering after the Battle of Cer, but it turned out that he had written—with his own hand and in the black ink which had been obedient until then—that the prospects of the Serbian army soon returning to battle-readiness were very good! He had already encountered this problem at the *Pester Lloyd* editorial office, so this time, too, he waged war with the pens and paper as if they were his only enemies. He decided to punish the recalcitrant new pen with the black ink, which he had glorified until just recently, and return to the old one (which he had rejected in Pest for the better one with black ink). And all seemed well at first. The disobedient Pest pen became the obedient Zemun one; but the once obedient black fountain pen from Pest had no intention of backing down and, with thoughts as black as the ink which were its lifeblood, began to plot its revenge.

Veres didn't notice anything at first. For the whole fourth day of his brave censorial war-making he wrote precisely what he wanted—in blue ink; but the pen with black ink revealed its vengeful nature for the first time by furtively discharging its entire fill of ink into Veres's bag. The censor cursed it and decided to no longer take it with him to the City Hall building where he worked. He left the gutted pen with its stained nib on his bedside table. His fifth and last day in Zemun dawned.

Veres worked arduously on the fifth day, too.

His black fountain pen thirsted for vengeance all day long.

That night, what had been festering had to come out. When the assiduous censor returned from work after nine in the evening and was good-nighted without any supper by the devoted but mystified Serb ladies, the fountain pen was ready and waiting for him on the bedside table. Tibor had a wash at the porcelain basin and fell into bed, groaning with fatigue. He didn't dream anything that fifth night in Zemun, and only at first light did he suddenly turn over, like a person who wheels round after having been caught unawares from behind. He grasped his chest for a moment, gurgled and went limp. No one was there to witness his death.

The Great War ended for Tibor Veres when the attentive mother and daughter found him with the fountain pen sticking in his chest. The perfidious stylus had somehow risen up and, like an abandoned mistress, taken revenge on Tibor Veres, killing him with a last stab, although it broke its own spine, or rather its nib, in the process. No one at the coroner's office thought that the censor—such a modest and retiring fellow—could have killed himself, especially in such a theatrical way. The mother and daughter were therefore in hot water, but they were saved by their Hungarian bloodline on the maternal side and the connections in Pest which they immediately used to avoid any adverse consequences for the killing of a Hungarian non-commissioned officer. After five days and five nights of warring, Veres was buried in chaotic circumstancess behind the guest house, in the Zemun cemetery beneath John Hunyadi Tower, with the briefest of military honours. There was no time for a longer service because Zemun fell the very next day, after the three-day Syrmian offensive by Serbian forces. The new army immediately began questioning Serbian residents in their houses, and Veres's death even turned out to be of benefit for the mother and daughter from the Gardosh neighbourhood, who could now claim that they had begrudgingly put up with a Hungarian spy in their guest house for five days and then liquidated him. The Serbs honoured them in word alone because there was no time for anything more in the scant four days of Serbian-controlled Zemun in 1914.

There was no time for congratulatory speeches and the awarding of medals on the outskirts of Paris either. After the fall of Brussels and Antwerp, Kluck's 1st and Bülow's 2nd German Army crossed into the north of France without difficulty. The kaiser's army took Sedan and St Quentin and advanced swiftly towards Paris. A blackout was ordered in the streets of the City of Light. One morning, proclamations appeared in the squares. General Gallieni, the military commander of Paris, alerted Parisians to the danger of the city being besieged and appealed to them to evacuate, but Paris was already empty. All who had got wind of war and didn't want to smell gunpowder had already left: for America like Georges Braque and the cubist painters, for the Côte d'Azur like the former petty gentry and disinherited counts, for Latin America, Spain or London like many foreigners who had considered Paris their home until 1 September 1914. The declaration of a possible siege turned the ongoing flow from the city into an exodus.

The police issued new orders: all public places had to be closed by nine. The city no longer resembled that merry metropolis of bohemians and spivs. One September morning, the student Stanislaw Witkiewicz was woken by a terrible racket. He jumped out of bed and ran out onto the terrace of the small Hotel Scribe to see what was causing it. The sounds of powerful motors were coming from Boulevard Haussmann, where an endless line of cars was taking troops to the north. In that monstrous column were classy models adorned with French flags, sports cars hastily converted into armoured cars and the requisitioned camionettes of various wineries—and all of them were hurrying north. Horrified by what he saw, the young Pole groaned. For Stanislaw Witkiewicz, the Great War began when he thought the Parisian garrison was fleeing and General Gallieni was surrendering the city to the Prussians. What was the young fellow doing on the terrace of the shabby hotel anyway? Why wasn't he with the troops in the north or with the conceited, cowardly artists in the south of the country? He wasn't in the north because he had been turned down by the Foreign Legion recruitment office for having a heart murmur; he hadn't skipped off to the south because he was a waverer like every Pole and still wished to help his new fatherland, France. He imagined himself as a doctor performing an operation; he imagined driving an ambulance with only one hand because the other had been amputated in a heroic battle, and he lived on those illusions for all of August 1914 while he eked out an existence by helping at the Rotonde and eating the leftovers from the plates he was brought to wash up.

Now the end had come, he felt. Paris was deserted and he no longer knew anyone. Rue de la Paix, where before the war you could see all the peoples of the world, was empty the next day. Silence reigned, an eerie silence: no creaking omnibuses, no cars blowing their horns, no clatter of horse's hooves. Most of the restaurants were closed, and in the streets the wind played with the remains of clothing, crumpled-up greasy paper which failed to interest even the stray dogs, and newspapers still touting the great successes of General Joffre's forces in Alsace-Lorraine. And then he felt hunger overcome him. A nourished man chooses one of the masks from the arsenal we call life, he said to himself, but a hungry man has only the face of hunger. He had to do something. The metal shutters on all the shops were drawn down and it was hard to force them in the daytime, so he decided to use the curfew. He set off on forays to the ghostly, deserted apartment buildings at nine in the evening when the curfew sirens sounded. He would cut through the side streets to avoid the patrols. At Place de l'Opéra he would break through the gate of one of the buildings and quickly ascend the stairs. Night by night he learnt to judge by the size of apartments' front doors, or by the value of their brass door handles, which of them would have the most food left in its pantry.

Then he would eat from others' plates, as he had done recently at the Rotonde. He entered the apartments of prominent Parisians and found what the fugitives had left behind. The taste of mould and sour red wine didn't bother him. He needed to eat and drink, and as a man of good manners Stanislaw would set the table in the new apartment every night, don the owner's housecoat with initials monogrammed on the breast pocket, light his candles in the candelabra and sit beneath his portrait. Then he'd eat the crumbs from his hosts' table. The goose-liver pâté and crab which the poet Jean Cocteau had once gorged himself with were no longer edible, but the cured meats, preserves and hard cheeses were by all means palatable in the days when Paris darkened its streets and the entrances of its metro stations.

One night, Stanislaw set his sights on a splendid apartment occupying the whole first floor of a proud building adjoining the Tuileries Gardens, but he had no idea that he would find not only food, clothing, copper candlesticks and his own little romantic supper ritual—but also the woman of his life. Just as he was sitting down at the table, he heard something rustle. He thought it might be the rats, which, like him, had also remained in Paris, but he was mistaken.

No sooner had he put the first bite in his mouth than the barrel of a pistol emerged from the bedroom, followed by two frightened eyes belonging to a young woman in a nightie.

'What are you doing here?' she asked.

'Having dinner,' Stanislaw answered simply and continued to eat ravenously.

'Why are you eating here?'

'Because I found food here, and now I've found you,' Stanislaw added between mouthfuls and proffered her a seat at the table.

The girl sat down next to him. She told him she was sick, which is why she couldn't leave Paris, and that she would starve if he ate up the food the apartment's owners had left, for whom she had worked as a maid. First Stanislaw calmed her, then he took her in his arms. To begin with, they ate up all the food left behind by the girl's employers; then our thief, like a real man, decided to go in search of food for himself and his companion. Every evening after midnight, he came back to the apartment at the end of the Tuileries Gardens with whatever he had found that evening. First they would eat; afterwards they told each other about their trivial lives; and in the end they kissed. Her breath had the taste of sour fruit which puckers the mouth. That love could not resemble the Parisian romances from the stage of the Comédie-Française. She smelt of penury and had just one seasoning: the smell of disease.

The girl was melting away, had a hacking cough and was constantly changing dark red handkerchiefs. But she longed for life. After their meal, she would undress before Stanislaw, and he in his passion was soon naked before her. His lover had dark circles under her eyes, two dangling things which hung from her diseased chest in place of breasts, and long, thin legs, whose muscles barely covered the bones. But it was war, the Great War, and it seemed to Stanislaw that he and she were the last people in the world.

And they made love like those last people. They rolled, groaned, coughed and exchanged the smells of sweat and their less than pleasant bodily secretions, but they were in seventh heaven. Their relationship lasted a whole week and they both knew it wouldn't be longer, but ceremony had to be upheld. At nine, when the sirens wailed, Stanislaw ran out of the little Hotel Scribe and off into the night and the curfew. He broke into apartments like a righteous thief, bagged food and rushed to the Tuileries Gardens. At midnight his beloved would be waiting for him in 47 Rue de Rivoli, in an open silken dress, with ribs that stood out beneath her breasts, as seductive as a dried haddock. When they sat down at the table to eat, everything smelt of blood. After satisfying their hunger with their one and only meal of the day, they'd shift to the batiste sheets, from which they no longer bothered to wipe the traces of blood.

On the fourth day, after several frenzied copulations, Stanislaw told the girl that no one had ever satisfied him like her. On the fifth day, he told her he would never leave her. On the sixth day, Stanislaw Witkiewicz promised he would make her Mrs Witkiewicz when that terrible war was over, but even as he spoke those two words, 'Mrs Witkiewicz', he knew he was lying. Mrs Witkiewicz said she knew she would be cured of tuberculosis as soon as the war ended and they found better care and a little warm, kindly sun from the south, which she expected that coming winter. And as she spoke those two words, 'coming winter', she knew she was lying.

That love came to an end on 13 September 1914, the day the newspaper boys began selling papers on the streets of Paris again and shouting: "Great Battle of the Marne. Gallieni transfers Parisian garrison to the front and strikes the enemy. Kluck's army on the retreat." That was the first major Allied victory on the Western Front. Exploiting the large gap between Kluck's and Bülow's armies, General Joffre made a risky manoeuvre and divided the allied forces into three parts. The left and right flanks were composed of French forces, and in the middle, south of the bloody River Marne, along a line between Lagny and Signy-Signets, was the British Expeditionary Force. Pouring into the gap, the British failed to engage the enemy, but the pincers managed to seize the Germans and the battle was won. With that victory, life began to return to the city.

Patrols soon made the rounds of the Paris apartments to which the home comers would return. One of these found Mr and Mrs Witkiewicz in bed, both splashed with blood. At first glance it looked like just another of the ritual suicides of married couples, but then they saw that the shamelessly naked woman was dead and the shockingly nude man was alive. When he regained his senses, Stanislaw learnt that he had become a 'widower' and was accused of murdering 'Mrs Witkiewicz'. They gave him a choice: either to be mobilized into the Foreign Legion at once, or to be shot. He chose the former. No one asked him now if he had a heart murmur and he was sent directly to help bring the newly formed French 9th Army up to strength.

The prominent Parisians returned to their apartments. Many of them didn't notice the missing food and decorations which Stanislaw had stolen for his beloved. The owners of the apartment in Rue de Rivoli were horrified to hear that 'the girl' who had cleaned for them had died in their bed. They didn't know that the cleaning girl had found the love of her life and had even become 'Mrs Witkiewicz' on that last night in evacuated Paris, but they hurried to purchase a new bed and scrub down the walls. Others cleaned their apartments and buildings too, but Paris on the streets looked completely different to Paris from the air. That was the Paris which one German Zeppelin crew member was painstakingly watching on an almost nightly basis. After the Battle of the Marne, the Germans withdrew to a line behind Reims and the soon-bloody River Aisne, but their Zeppelins continued to blitz the French capital.

Those first bomber pilots, among them the one-time artist Fritz Krupp, were bold and adventurous airmen. The bombs in the Zeppelin were stacked one on top of another. The crew consisted of a pilot, a machine-gunner and a bombardier. The latter, unprotected, climbed down into a gondola suspended beneath the giant craft as it flew over Paris. The winds over the Seine would ruffle his hair as he withdrew the priming pins and heaved thirty-kilo bombs over the side of the gondola to plummet down onto the roofs of the city. Each time he dropped a bomb, the Zeppelin would lurch, the pilot would step on the gas, and the flames far below and the column of black smoke would mark where the Zeppelin had been. Anti-aircraft shells whined erratically around the crew, but there were only occasional puffs of smoke from explosions because the artillery still couldn't raise their guns' barrels at a steep enough angle, so the lumbering balloon filled with thirty two thousand cubic metres of helium now looked like a robust creature ruling the heights.

For the Zeppelin bombardier Fritz Krupp, the Great War began when he realized he had always hated Paris, even before the war while he still thought he loved it. He had studied painting in France under the great Gustave Moreau back in the nineteenth century, a century he intended to stay in as a painter. Krupp didn't approve of anything that happened in the art scene after 1900. He even took up residence in Paris, but his canvases—so he thought—emanated the harmony of the young Ingres. Krupp's classmates André Derain and Paul Cézanne were not of the same mind, however, and as of 1903 they painted with pure colours like 'wild animals'. Then there was that Picasso and a whole crowd of hungry and impertinent blue-collar artists.

Fritz himself had painted several works 'à la Cipriano Ruiz de Picasso' in 1908 and also created a few like Cézanne, and he felt that—if he only wanted to—he would be able to outstrip both of them in their daubings, which were devoid of composition, proportion and harmony. How impertinent they were, in spite of that, and how they ignored him. They started to bother him wherever he went: at the gallery in Rue La Fayette, in Boulevard Voltaire, and when he was using the same prostitutes and worried about catching syphilis. But, despite all this, he didn't leave Paris. In time, he became their walking shadow and was always somewhere in the same galleries, in the same cafés, but never at the same tables. When Picasso and the poet Max Jacob moved into a little, lice-infested flat in Boulevard de Clichy, he found a similar one (with bedbugs instead of lice) not far from there, in one of the steep streets leading down from the Basilica of the Sacré Coeur; when Picasso moved to Rue Ravignan, to the famous 'Bateau-Lavoir' building, Fritz was again close by, having suddenly felt the need to move a little further up Montmartre himself; when Picasso crossed the Seine and moved to Montparnasse, Fritz also decided discreetly to change his address so as be closer to the ateliers near the abattoir in Rue de Vaugirard.

And he saw it all, there in Montparnasse. The once proud pavilions of the 1900 Exposition Universelle had been turned into dismal dwellings for hundreds of 'ingenious painters' from the east. These shacks now housed aspiring Italians with guitars and a song on their lips, reclusive Jews from the east, Poles with a weakness for alcohol and tears when they were drunk, Belgians with incorrigibly provincial views—all this was little short of loathsome to Fritz. Why he had found himself a flat near Hôpital Vaugirard he couldn't say, because he didn't dare to admit to himself that he was following Picasso.

Then the Great War began. He was mobilized into the *Luftwaffe* and trained as a Zeppelin bombardier. Finally the day came which he had longed for: he was sent to bomb Paris. But Sergeant Fritz perplexed his crew. They went on raids every third night, and since the bombardier had the best view of the targets and ground fire because he was the one putting his life on the line, the crew had to follow his directions and go along with his choice of targets. The Zeppelin's orders were to follow the course of the Seine and strike at district offices, government buildings and Les Invalides. In exceptional circumstances—if they encountered heavy enemy fire and contrary winds—the payload could be dropped in other places.

Fritz exploited this loophole and directed his airship LZ-37 to tactically dubious destinations. First he had the vessel make for Montmartre, and there, night after night, he took aim at Boulevard de Clichy, the steep cobblestone streets around Sacré Coeur, and Rue La Fayette, where there were no targets of military significance. But there were targets here of importance for the would-be painter Fritz Krupp. Picasso's compatriot Mañach had let him stay in a room on Boulevard de Clichy in 1901. Then, in 1903, the painter of the smutty *Les Demoiselles d'Avignon* (that was Krupp's opinion of the canvas, which he dubbed 'The Brothel') moved to Boulevard Voltaire, and finally in 1904 to the most noted address in Rue Ravignan, the 'Bateau-Lavoir'. That building was completely insignificant for German High Command, but not for the history of modern painting, so the Zeppelin bombardier endeavoured to find it and destroy it by his own hand.

Now, in 1914, it seemed the hour of reckoning had finally come: the chance for him to get back at the colours on the pictures of his classmates Cézanne and Derain, at the indecent figures on Picasso's canvasses, and at the uncouth repute of the hobo hack painters from the east. Paris was his! The whole night belonged to him! He just needed to take good aim at the 'Bateau-Lavoir'... but it wasn't easy to locate and destroy an ordinary, two-storey thatched cabin on the steep terrain of Montmartre, especially since strong winds were always blowing above that hill. Therefore he often reluctantly agreed for the Zeppelin to turn south. The target? Montparnasse, of course. *En route*, Fritz threw the odd bomb at the government buildings by the Seine, just so he'd have something to report to his superiors, and then he demanded that the LZ-37 continue south. 'To Montmartre!' he shouted from the gondola. Here Fritz mercilessly rained bombs down on the painters' colony La Ruche in Rue du Maine, where the ateliers of the itinerant professors of painting were, and on the colony Falguière where Modigliani worked.

What he actually ended up hitting is a different story. The bombs mostly fell into the brambles and weeds between the buildings, but up in the sky it all looked otherwise to Fritz. Every night he felt he had put a spanner in the works of modern painting and levelled its rakish habitats, so he always returned to base in La Fère satisfied and wrote a report on the sortie in the operations log, describing the great damage inflicted on the enemy although there was virtually none. That was one painter-bombardier's idea of fighting the war. But he wasn't the only one who badly assessed the impact of his dangerous actions. The Russian generals on the Eastern Front also thought that their armies were now very well positioned after their initial victories in East Prussia and that the hour had come to re-ignite old disputes from the beginning of the century. The Germans took advantage of this. After the first defeats, General Prittwitz was replaced by the experienced Field Marshal Paul von Hindenburg at the side of the young General Ludendorff. These two generals, who would turn the tide of German fortunes on the Eastern Front, met for the first time at Hanover railway station. From there they immediately set off for the Front. They could hardly wait for an opportunity to mount a military response, and they were given it.

The German offensive was made possible by the personal antipathy between the Russian generals. Several years earlier, the commander of the 2nd Russian Army, Alexander Samsonov, had openly criticized General Rennenkampf, the commander of the 1st Army, and a quarrel ensued between them. When a gap developed between the two Russian armies in 1914, Rennenkampf was in no hurry to fill it and man the unoccupied hills and fields of East Prussia. By the time he realized the Germans' true intentions, it was too late and he could no longer come to the aid of Samsonov's 2nd Army. He set his army in motion, but on 30 August 1914 he was still seventy kilometres from Tannenberg, bogged down near Königsberg, where Immanuel Kant rested peacefully in his grave. It was hard to counter the Germans. The Russians transported their weaponry using draught animals, while the German army was already making full use of the rail network.

Like in a game of chess, the debacle at Tannenberg had its logical consequence in the Battle of the Masurian Lakes and the near collapse of the Russian forces in 1914, causing more wounded to arrive at the hospital train V.M. Purishkevich than could be taken in and operated on. There were times when the train stood out on the track, defended only by the escorting armoured train, which had two open anti-aircraft wagons. Already in the second half of September, the Germans began using their frighteningly fast two-seat Aviatik B.I planes in East Prussia. There was one such attack which Liza would never forget. When the alarm sounded in the train, she and the walking wounded dashed to huddle on the track beneath the train, but in the middle of the attack she heard that one of the wounded was calling for help under a nearby tree. She didn't think of Marusya, who she had left behind in Petrograd, when she ran out towards that young man. Her flowing, coppery-red hair got showered with dirt. She shot angry glances with her eyes the colour of sepia, and she cursed and shook her fists at the enemy planes. 'Damn Huns! Damn, bloody Huns!' she screamed at the top of her voice as she crawled, to give herself courage. She hauled the wounded man back, dragging him with her hands and teeth. One of the planes fired large-calibre cannon rounds commonly known as 'suitcases', but the 'luggage' missed them that time. Liza's mouth was full of soil and her clothes were torn and rent when she reached the life-saving shelter between the wheels of the train.

Two days later, she was decorated by General Samsonov with the Cross of St George. For the occasion, Lizochka put on the clean-est uniform she could find: a grey skirt with a white blouse and an apron with a large red cross. The medal seemed to match her beauty and copper hair; her husband and the other doctors smiled, and the wounded gave her souvenirs for little Marusya: iron spoons shaped from fragments of the 'suitcases' while they were still hot. Only one thing didn't fit the occasion: Liza couldn't find a single white apron without bloodstains on it.

Not everyone immediately encountered blood close-up, like Lizochka. Things were particularly festive in Belgium in those October days. The kaiser's birthday was celebrated on 20 October. Every building was decked with flags, and Zeppelins plied the sky like big cumuli when the kaiser arrived in Antwerp, accompanied by the Crown prince and the oldest general. Young Prince Friedrich Wilhelm III still looked the dandy. He drove up in an open car, on the seat next to the driver, with a cocked hat. It seemed he didn't yet know what war was, and he chattered away at dinner.

Neither had Jean Cocteau, that scrawny fellow who needed to gorge himself with buckshot so as to be enlisted, found out yet what war was about. In fact, his involvement in the Great War ended up being very much as he had hoped. To begin with, they sent him to an aviation unit near Bussigny. After a surprise enemy breakthrough, he was sent back to the Parisian army supply office, ultimately to be transferred to the medical corps under the command of Étienne de Beaumont. The war looked like a lark to him. He was posted in the vicinity of Bussigny again, which made him happy because he had come to love that little town during his first posting of the war. He didn't mind being woken in the mornings by the thunder of guns. That Monday he had time to write. No landscape is more magnificent than the azure sky with shrapnel bursting around the aircraft, he thought. He noted down this image and wondered a little about whether to replace 'aircraft' (it sounded like a dated, Blériot-ish contraption) with the more modern 'plane' or the romantic 'Zeppelin'. He left the word 'aircraft' and decided to trim his nails. If only he had a sweetheart to send a poignant farewell letter to, he thought, together with the ten nail-clippings. Should he send them to Picasso? No, that would be too theatrical and he would take it the wrong way. And besides, to what address? Picasso wasn't in Montparnasse any more. Some said he was in Spain, others claimed he was searching for his roots—in the middle of the Great War, of all times!—in the little town of Sori by the Ligurian Sea, where his mother supposedly hailed from. Others again swore he was passing the time in Cannes on the sunny coast of the Mediterranean, which smelt of rosemary and laurel, not of war.

Djoka Velkovich also trimmed his nails that day. No one had told him that he would be discharged from hospital, but he was already dreaming of joining the Serbian armed forces, who were awaiting a new enemy offensive like a locust plague they couldn't escape. The doctors, however, didn't let him go. He was still running a high temperature, and the skin on the right side of his face looked raw and weepy, covered by a web of taut capillaries. Soldiering in the dusty fields would be fatal for him, given his unhealed wounds, so the Front would have to wait. But there were some for whom the Front didn't wait. After being mobilized into the Foreign Legion, Stanislaw Witkiewicz was given brief, basic military training in the rear. He learnt to crawl, shoot and withdraw. He bayoneted several sacks of potatoes mixed with cherries. The potatoes were supposed to be like the bowels of enemy soldiers, and the cherries their blood: Quite enough for any newly-fledged soldier, or was it?

The following letter from a German soldier ought to be a warning to every military command. He wrote home to Heidelberg, and due to the negligence of the censor the letter made it through to his family as if it was any other piece of mail.

LETTERS OF LIFE AND DEATH

Dear parents, if only you knew how much I miss our Heidelberg, wrote the German soldier Stefan Holm, for whom the Great War began with an unexpected friendship, in fact a real, bashful, male love at the front. *The whistle of shells and even death itself in all its repulsiveness are not the worst thing in the trenches, but the lack of sleep. We sleep little, always with one eye open, forever on our guard. But whenever Morpheus takes me away down the intoxicating river in his barque and offers me a shred of deceptive sleep, I dream of our crimson River Neckar and the castle on the hill, of our university and the long-bearded professors, who in my younger days still hadn't heard of the inhumanity of the most civilized nations of Europe.*

I don't know if this letter will make it past the censors, but I feel an urge to tell you about the most terrible experience of my life. You will have read in the papers about us starting triumphantly, gripping Paris itself in a vice, but then Joffre repaid us pushing us back from the Marne, even as far north as the accursed River Aisne. Here both we and the French fought and tried to surround the enemy by curling around their flanks. We became preoccupied with our right flank, and they with their left. And none of that—neither the retreating nor the attacking—was any different to the usual battlefield operations until the moment we ended up with a large number of prisoners on our hands. They were mostly French, but there were also some recruits from the Foreign Legion. No one knew what to do with them, as we still didn't have prisoner-of-war camps, and we were slightly surprised by the order that each of us be given one POW to 'look after' there at our positions. My comrades, simple soldiers already steeped in blood and with hardly any education, immediately began treating their prisoners as servants, and worse: as dogs. The mature men of forty from the Landwehr *reserve weren't much better, nor were the officers of the Uhlan cavalry unit a little further along from us.*

Not only did the French have to wash their underwear, darn their socks and fit bullets into their cartridge belts, but they had to put up with insults and beatings, as well as address their masters with pretentious titles such as 'Your Countship' or 'Your Excellence'. That was, of course, ridiculous and sad at the same time, and, seeing as I couldn't help the others, I decided to at least relate to my prisoner as a human being. You know me, dear parents—I don't have the heart to hate. I took a liking to a Pole by the name of Stanislaw Witkiewicz. It turned out that he spoke German and was familiar with our great minds, Goethe and Schiller, because he had studied in Paris before the war.

You can imagine what good friends we became. I'd sometimes yell at him, too, and make him clean my boots, but he knew I was only doing it so we wouldn't look suspicious. When things were quiet, we'd talk at length, recite poetry to each other and pledge that our camaraderie would continue after the war. But those vows of post-war friendship were easily made. We had only that one week of autumn on French soil to spend together. I told him about you, about home and Heidelberg, and about German science, which will entwine with that of Oxford and the Sorbonne one day to end this terrible war. He confided in me that he had betrothed and married a beautiful young woman in Paris during the blackout and siege. He spoke of her as a nymph: with pure, pearl-like skin, long flaxen hair and eyes as blue as the lagoons of warm seas. His description of her was so vivid that I fell in love with Mrs Witkiewicz on the spot and was greatly saddened when he told me a few days before we parted forever that his beloved was no more—she now slept among the stars and he was a widower.

I mourned with him but also hoped that his solitude would strengthen our friendship; the two of us could become a symbol of a new and different Europe, a Europe of friends, not of enemies. I imagined our first meeting after the war: I arrive by coach at the far end of Lazienki Park in Warsaw. I get out, pay the coachman, and Stanislaw runs towards me elated yet relaxed, his hair tossed by the afternoon breeze. I too spread my arms to embrace him, a dear friend I haven't seen for so long, much too long; and all at once the senseless charging and killing and dying are gone, and the German and Polish and French. All that remains is friendship—a friendship I thought would last forever. But how could I have known, dear parents, that it would end just a few days later?

I found out on 15 September that the end was nigh, but I didn't tell my dear Polish friend until the last moment. There was to be a heavy artillery barrage and aerial bombing to destroy the enemy positions, to be followed by an irrepressible assault of our massed cavalry and infantry. When the hour came for the charge, each German soldier was to push his prisoner out in front of him as a human shield and expose him to 'friendly fire' from the French lines. I couldn't believe it. My comrades-in-arms, those rude 'uhlans', now simply went wild at the news. Bruises and black eyes were harmless compared to the injuries which the masters now inflicted on those poor wretches in the last few days. They only made sure not to maim them so badly that they'd be unable to walk in front of them when the whistle blew.

When the whistle blew…the prospect of that day haunted me with a mixture of horror and revulsion which war raises to the throat of every civilized man. My good Pole noticed that something was going on at our positions and asked me anxiously what it was about, and I, like a good doctor of death who spares his patient the news of his impending demise, didn't tell him the truth. On the last day of our friendship I looked at him tenderly, but I realized I couldn't help him. On the afternoon of 17 September, the artillery fell silent. The order came to tie ourselves to our prisoners with rope and stand them in front of us, facing away. At that, a screaming and shrieking began. My Pole burst into tears too, and I used the occasion to hug and kiss him for the last time.

Then dozens of sergeant's whistles sounded all at once. We jumped out over the breastwork. The French tied in front of us screamed inhumanly, almost squealing like swine, in fact. My comrades prodded them with their bayonets, swore at them and drove them like cattle. Some of the French called out and tried to warn their compatriots not to shoot, others persistently shouted things in French so the other side would see that a line of Frenchmen was moving towards them. But salvos resounded from a range of about one hundred metres and began cutting swathes through the line of prisoners. We were under orders to run with them as far as we could, to cut the rope connecting us as soon as they were hit, and to stay lying there. I had spent the whole night pondering what would be best for me and my Pole: for us to hang back and try to save his neck through hesitation, or to charge out ahead of the others and get him killed before he suffered too much. I decided on the latter.

I caressed him one last time before the charge, and at the sound of the whistle I started running as fast as my legs, or rather our legs, would carry us. I thought for one last time that we were tied together and ready to die together, the way it should be, like in Plato's Feast. I planned to cut the rope as ordered when he was hit, but instead of falling to the ground I'd continue the charge and collect some French bullets myself. But it didn't turn out that way. For Stanislaw Witkiewicz, the Great War ended fifty metres across no man's land when the first friendly French bullet struck him just above the heart. For me, the war is still going on. I admit that I only briefly considered uttering a cry for both of us and continuing the advance. How far? Another twenty or thirty metres maybe, in a futile

67

attempt to reach the French lines. But I didn't do it. Coward that I was, I hit the ground, having got the furthest of all my comrades. I managed to look and saw the field littered with dead Frenchmen like discarded old sacks. The faces of my comrades were panic-stricken, and mine probably was too. The sergeants screamed: 'Look at Stefan, you stupid rabble, look how far he's got!' And they made the others advance to reach me.

It was all over in the evening. We achieved a small breakthrough in our section of the front (I'm not allowed to tell you where it is). Instead of a meal of Dutch cheeses, which our army supply office had been constantly feeding us, we now found tins of French meat called 'Madagascar' along with garlic left behind by the enemy. We ate that meat with zest, like the greatest delicacy, until someone told us it had been rumoured among the French that the tins contained not beef but monkey meat. We were disgusted and threw away the remainders, leaving the 'Madagascar' monkey meals for the French, since we knew they'd be taking back the trenches the next day. They quietly and hurriedly collected the dead they themselves had riddled with bullets. Our commanders swore they'd take the positions again, and yesterday I was awarded the Iron Cross. Me—the biggest coward, who was afraid to die even when his friend was cut down by a hail of lead! My only consolation is that Stanislaw Witkiewicz earned the medal. In my eyes, he is the only Pole from the French Foreign Legion to be decorated with the German Iron Cross, 2nd Class.

I'm ashamed to write to you about my weaknesses, but the shame would be much greater if anyone could look into my heart, where he would see only ice. Esteemed Father and Mother, my dearest parents, I beg you to pardon my weaknesses and commend my soul to God, who saw all of this but did nothing to stop the carnage...

Farewell. Your son Stefan (still alive, for the time being).

* * *

Our positions,

I know where they are but won't write it because the censor will black it out anyway.

Dear Father and Mother,

This war is hilarious one moment and tragic the next. I didn't tell you in my earlier letters that we've invented a new form of warfare. We and the Boches now consolidate our positions by digging deep holes which we crawl into like moles. It all began when we suffered terrible losses from just one machine-gun fired by a single dug-in uhlan machine-gunner. Each little entrenched position like that was able to halt our advance north of the Aisne for several days.

It seems both we and they got the idea that you can hold a position with trenches for much longer, so for a day or two both we and they threw aside our rifles and took up spades and shovels. At first, we dug holes for a short stay, shallow like soldiers' graves, which we were convinced we'd soon fill with our own bodies. Then we started joining those holes into trenches, passages and redoubts, and in the end we made a whole little city four metres down. All the moles in France must have envied us. In places we had aisles ten metres wide and almost fifty metres long. In the narrow parts we'd excavate a few steps and observe the enemy through trench binoculars, but we saw nothing except occasional shovelfuls of earth flying up out of their trenches and making little mounds on the surface.

At first, the men complained at having to dig in. The sickly started to cough from the damp which crept from the ground, but soon we made friends with the rats in the trenches and even had little houses where friendly smoke rose from chimneys. That little degree of comfort and civilization quickly inclined the soldiers to laugh and joke. As a pre-war entertainer, I was given the honour of naming the broader tracts of the trenches and decided to name them after our greatest hotels. We therefore had a Hotel Ritz, Hotel Lutetia and Hotel Cécil. The opening of the Ritz was a wonderful, festive affair until its abrupt end. I must admit I set the tone of that travesty. Our first guests had to be our most corpulent comrade and 'his sweetheart'. The sweetheart was played by a short lance corporal who I'd got to know before the war when he was involved in my production of Jarry's ribald stage play Ubu Cuckolded. *We dressed up that little comedian to be the woman and the huge soldier to be the gentleman. He even found a lorgnette which he stuck on his nose, and 'her' underpants were padded up with French newspapers to such an extent* that the men just whooped and whistled at her. We organized waiter's livery for the two of us and waited on the first guests.

'It's so hot today, sweetie, although the summer is long past,' the hulking fellow began, acting the gentleman who enters the hotel with his lady. 'It's so hot, darling, a glass of champagne would be just spiffing,' the lance corporal said in a squeaky voice like a woman, to the cheers and hoots of laughter of all the assembled soldiers. 'Please take a seat, madam, sir,' I replied and sat them at an ordinary wooden table in our Ritz, but they had to pretend it was the most luxurious hotel salon, and I must admit they played their roles most convincingly through until the end. We had organized a bottle of real champagne. The gentleman inquired who was playing at the 'Hotel Ritz' today, and his eyes lit up when I told him it was the Parisian Garrison Officers' Band. 'May I?' I asked, once the bottle had been opened. 'Oh yes, yes,' he replied and added: 'I'm democratic, you know. However much champagne you pour me, my wife is to get the same. Two fingers for me and two fingers for her.' (He showed two vertical fingers for his glass, meaning it would be filled to the top, and two horizontal fingers for hers, so only the bottom would be covered.) 'Don't you be condescending with me,' she hissed, and just at that moment a 'coal box'—a shell from a long-range howitzer—came down and exploded right on top of the Hotel Ritz, in other words our trench. When the black smoke had dispersed and we spat the dirt out of our mouths, we saw that our lady and gentleman, the first guests of the Hotel Ritz, were dead. The glasses had remained intact and the champagne, which they hadn't managed to sip, wasn't even spilt. Only they were no more. For the two first actors in the French trenches, the Great War began and ended with the shortest flash drama in the broad trench named 'Hotel Ritz'.

That's how things are in this war. I've all but forgotten my first guests now. I have no more tears, and there's no one more for me to mourn. I'm sick of myself already and almost regret not having taken the role of the gentleman instead of playing the waiter. Sometimes I can just remember that little lance-corporal actor of mine, who played his last role in our trench. Then I sigh and say to myself: this world is a botched job, slapped together in an off moment when the Creator either didn't know what he was doing or wasn't in control of himself.

Best wishes,

Your son Lucien Guirand de Scevola (still alive, for the time being)

* * *

Cannes, 28 October 1914

  Dear Zoë, love of my life,

  By the benevolence of our righteous Republic I've been given one month's rest and recuperation in the south after spending over two months in Hôpital Vaugirard in Montparnasse, which was bombed like crazy by German Zeppelins every second or third night, contrary to the Geneva Convention and any sane logic. Since I didn't have any injuries of the body but, after three days spent with the dead in Lunéville only wounds of the soul, manifested in a constant twitching of my right eye, I practically became an assistant to the hospital staff.

  In the evenings, when the sirens sounded, I'd join them and help haul the moribund patients down into the cellar. No one looked to see who was taking whom, we just grabbed the first ones we were ordered to. That gave me the chance to play God a little. You'll be amazed at my words, but you should realize that I'm no longer the man you knew and loved. May the true God grant that you still love me after this letter and after the Great War, whose end cannot be glimpsed. Let me return to Hôpital Vaugirard. I'm not sure if I should be writing you this, but I hold that even in these changed circumstances, where I don't know if I'm still in control of myself, I should continue to be sincere with you; what is left of my sanity tells me that true love can only be based on openness. The painful truth must therefore come out.

  The hospital took the most serious cases from the battles on the Marne and Aisne, and many of them didn't look much different to butterfly cocoons in their cobwebby beds. They weren't alive, but neither had they taken up oars in the galley of the dead, and the doctors were forbidden from practicing euthanasia. But I overheard the hospital staff complaining that the moribunds were using up iodine and morphine which could help a wounded man who still had a spark of hope in his eye... at that moment I decided to help them. With a clean conscience, my dear Zoë, and without a trace of spite. Every evening, when the sirens sounded and those accursed Zeppelins bore down on our hospital, I chose a patient who I'd decided to relieve of his suffering. I made that choice like a God come down to Earth: without mercy and hesitation. But since I was only a man I swallowed my shame and abhorrence and hid them inside me, consoling myself that not even my victims' faces were visible beneath all the layers of turban on their heads. And so, freed of any pangs of conscience, I'd choose one of them and start dragging him towards the cellar. En route I'd twist his neck, yank him so roughly that he'd expire by himself, or let him go crashing down the stairs like a decrepit Egyptian mummy. All that went unnoticed in the rush and confusion, and it's not that I wasn't circumspect. To start with, I killed one a week, then two. But when I realized that I not only wouldn't be discovered but also had the tacit consent of the doctors, I decided to relieve one incurable invalid of his life every evening when the siren sounded. After all, the dead must be spoken to in the language of the dead. Cum mortuis in lingua mortua.

So I stayed on at Hôpital Vaugirard for two months longer. My medical card said I was in a stable but critical condition, but in reality the doctors only kept me because they saw me as a sad tool for doing what they weren't allowed to do. They wrote that I first had nervous and then digestive problems, and that I had eventually begun to sleepwalk. They thought up all sorts of things just to keep me on for as long as possible. Finally they saw me off with tears in their eyes, and I felt I'd been saved because in my final days there I felt I'd become a prisoner in the hospital and feared that the role of executioner was mine forever. I left by train for Marseille and changed there for Nice. The southern sun bathed me and purged me with its warmth, and for a day or two I even thought I'd overcome my torment, but now I feel I'm in its grip again.

My dear Zoë, the faces of those I righteously killed don't come back to me because I never saw them through those dead butterfly cocoons, like I say. I still think I carried out the task, which was intended for me. But am I deluding myself? I don't know what is good and what is bad any more, but I don't think any living creature will need rationalizations like that after this war. You are all I still love. I send you my tenderest greetings and beg you to ask Nana to come to the coast again and join me in my sorrow.

Your Germain D'Esparbès.

THE FIRST WARTIME CHRISTMAS

Thus wrote one French doctor of death, while Mehmed Graho, once the Austrian doctor of death, was promoted. He became head of death and also received the rank of colonel of the Medical Corps. He didn't earn this senior position through success as an army surgeon but by using his connections in Sarajevo; he arranged that an order be sent to the hospital in Zvornik stipulating that the doctor of death was to be appointed head of death. With Graho now out of the operating theatre, the many wounded men lying in files and rows in the courtyard of Zvornik's Imperial Lyceum like discarded piles of overripe pomegranates and melons, could heave a sigh of relief.

Mehmed Graho continued to go out into the courtyard, but his words 'Him, him, and him—to me' no longer had the same ominous ring as after the Austrian defeat at the Battle of Cer. At first, things on the Balkan Front had gone much better militarily. The army of the Dual Monarchy had seized Serbia in a pincer movement and the capitulation of the recalcitrant neighbour had been in sight. But heavy fighting had developed at the River Drina, which had accepted and carried downstream all the fruits of strife; like the Styx and Cocytus, it took lives away to the insulted River Sava and also to the Danube, that freshwater monarch which heaped a human cargo without name and origin on its deep bed.

There were those who survived this time, too. Head physician Graho again faced a growing mass of wounded, and he passed them on to his surgeons, who pruned them like saplings. And still no one noticed that the hospital in Zvornik had a far higher death rate on the operating table than the collection points in Tuzla, Mostar and Trebinye. But it was war, the Great War, in which a human life was worth less than one word from a general, so no one remarked the poor record of the hospital in Zvornik.

Nor did anyone take any notice when the Istanbul spice trader Mehmed Yıldız realized his beloved Turkey was going to enter the war. Effendi had no family and thought of the young assistants and apprentices in his spice shop as his own sons, but he didn't tell them when he learnt that Turkey would be going to war. That day too, 28 October 1914, he got into the tram at the railway station below Topkapı Palace, which took him up the hill to the Aya Sofya, where, as a good Muslim, he prayed at dawn every morning surrounded by a hundred other, mainly, elderly men. He noticed there were no more young men at all in the rows of bowing, shoeless believers because the army had been mobilized and many Rumelian Turks were now 'under arms', waiting with clenched teeth somewhere in the Caucasus, but at morning prayer he still hoped for peace and progress in the Padishah's righteous land. After prayer, he thought of going down to the shop on foot, but fine snow from the Bosporus made him catch the tram again. It seemed very early for snow. As the aged vehicle descended the slope by the Golden Horn, creaking and ringing, and circuited the mighty walls of the Sultan's domain, the effendi thought about the snow and how surprised the Sultan's nightingales would be when he let them out of their aviaries to fly in his celestial garden that morning after first prayer.

Mehmed Yıldız had been brought up on Nizami's epic *Khosrow and Shirin*. He was a defender of the true Turkish miniature, which never departed from the canon of two-dimensionality. Now he arrived at his shop. It was slightly after seven. He looked to see if his assistants had prayed and then gave a sign for the calling out of the day's prices to begin. He opened the newspaper. Sitting in front of his shop, surrounded by the spices which smelt as pungent that morning as ever, he read on the front page of *Tanin* that the Turkish government was in crisis. The Minister of Public Works, General Mahmud Pasha, had tendered his resignation, as had the Minister of Commerce and Agriculture, Suleyman Effendi, and the Minister of Postal and Telegraph Services, Oskan Effendi. The Minister of the Navy, Djemal Pasha, and the Minister of Education, Djenan Pasha, temporarily took charge of the portfolios without ministers. It didn't sadden him to read that Suleyman, a Syrian Catholic, had withdrawn from the government (he'd never trusted him), nor that Oskan, a damned Armenian, had resigned (he was an intruder here), but when he read that his childhood friend, the righteous Mahmud Pasha, had also left the government, he muttered to himself: 'This looks mighty bad.' Still, he continued to hope without foundation that the trumpets of war would bypass the Golden Horn and his righteous and stern Padishah.

But then he raised his eyes from the newspaper, and what he saw numbed him. No one knew that Yıldız Effendi played a little game every day, just for himself, like when Westerners open a game of patience. That day too, the orange and red spices were competing on sale against the yellowish, green and brown ones. A victory of the former was a bad sign and a victory of the latter a good one for that day, but the battle was always closely fought and only the experienced eye of the trader could tell which spices carried the day and how he, following those signs, would act until evening prayer. Now he folded *Tanin* together and his jaw dropped. He wasn't even able to utter his 'This looks mighty bad', because he saw the signs of impending misfortune in all their blatancy. For the trader in oriental spices Mehmed Yıldız, the Great War began when he realized that the red and vermillion spices were outselling the others by such an overwhelming margin on 28 October 1914 that his boys were already glancing his way, mutely calling on their master to replenish the stocks from the large storeroom beneath the bridge, to which he alone had a key.

The next day, 29 October, Turkey entered the Great War. Those half medieval, half modern people celebrated in the streets on the opposite side of the Golden Horn. The coachmen took passengers to all three parts of the city for free. No toll was charged on the bridge that day. One beardless lad even jumped off Galata Tower with improvised, wax-coated wings and tried to fly like a moth over the windy Bosporus, but he crashed into the ground and died of his injuries the same evening.

Just one week after the red spices had won a crushing victory over the browns in Istanbul, another beardless lad by the name of Tibor Németh was to be the first Austro-Hungarian soldier to enter evacuated Belgrade. After the Serbian defeats on the Rivers Drina and Sava, an acute shortage of ammunition had forced the Serbian command to order the army's withdrawal to reserve positions along the line Varovnica–Kosmay–Rudnik–Gornyi Milanovac–Ovchar–Kablar Gorge. So the army withdrew from cities like Shabac, Valyevo, Uzhice and even Belgrade. The last train to set off south for Nish with refugees, who had returned to the capital for their winter clothing, left from the main platform of the station with a whistle on 26 October by the old calendar, or 8 November by the new.

'It's not my fault!' General Zhivoyin Mishich thundered into the receiver of the field telephone. 'What can I do if my men are exhausted and the capital is located on the border where there should only be a customs post?'

And so Belgrade was evacuated. The first Austro-Hungarian scouts crossed the Danube into the city in silence. When this advance party set off cautiously towards the low-lying quarters of the city, they were met only by starving bitches with protruding ribs and shrivelled teats hanging between their legs. The reconnaissance battalion had the task of going from house to house and checking if any defenders remained in the deserted flats; if so, they were to be killed immediately. Németh's comrades shouted 'All clear'. And he thought it was too, at first. But when he entered a commercial building in Dubrovnik Street, someone fired a shot at him. Private Németh couldn't tell who it was. He thought he saw a man with long sideburns and a kippah in the reception room of that building, but it wasn't really a man but a phantasm, half real and half transparent, through which he could see the *bergère* from where the shot was fired.

The bullet was certainly real enough. It whistled past his ear and made a hole in the wall above his head, but when Németh thrust his bayonet at the illusion of the Jewish trader he only impaled the empty *bergère*, which spilt its hemp stuffing at his feet like bowels and threw out springs like bones. The proud soldier didn't know what to think, but he wasn't afraid. He continued to comb the streets of Belgrade, while all around him more and more ghosts were abroad. They flitted across the streets like shadows, and many were watching him, pressed up against the small Turkish windows. In Yovanova Street two small boys, their bodies transparent like the Jew's had been, ran past him and hit him without warning, one on each side. He felt a pain and fired a few shots, but the bullets passed right through the boys, and he started running after them. He didn't know why. He should just have shouted 'All clear' and let them bolt off like mountain goats, but his perseverance was to be the end of him—his fatal error. The boys passed from courtyard to courtyard, jumping fences and ditches. From Yovanova Street they crossed to Yevremova Street, and then suddenly turned and ran through the park and on towards King Peter Street. He looked into that deserted, grand avenue: tall buildings loomed on both sides of the street and seemed to be leaning inwards, towards him, as if conspiring to collapse on top of him. But the proud Hungarian soldier wasn't afraid now either. Where had those little brats got to? Finally he spotted them again, just before they disappeared into a strange building, its facade tiled with green majolica.

He dashed after them into the entrance. He smelt the odour of sticky sweat and thought he'd never catch up with them, encumbered as he was with all his equipment and carrying his rifle with bayonet affixed, but they knew he was slow and never got so far ahead that he'd lose sight of their fleeting heels. So it was that they lured him into an apartment. Tibor followed them in, panting, and set foot in a large drawing room. He didn't manage to turn around and almost didn't realize that he was killed—the apparition of a huge, semi-transparent woman fired a bullet from a hunting rifle. She was evidently the mother of the two small boys. Now she had killed a Hungarian soldier without a twinge of conscience. She caressed her two sons and all three of them vanished. The Great War ended for Tibor Németh when he was shot by one of the dead women of Belgrade, one of those who died in 1914, taking her own life after both her sons drowned in the Danube.

So ended the military career of a soldier who betrayed the family line by not entering the pantheon of the brave. But Belgrade took no notice of its ghosts, just as Paris was unaware of its spectres near the Tuileries Gardens; and did Istanbul did not save the young fellow who launched off Galata Tower like a bird with waxed paper wings and bars for flapping them.

The wings of the new planes were not much more robust than the flimsy ones of the unfortunate young Turk because the first aircraft were completely unarmoured, with a fuselage made of wooden ribs like a boat. The former Zeppelin bombardier Fritz Krupp was familiarized with the functioning of a plane in just three days. He was instructed how to move the flaps, operate the tail rudder and fire the machine-gun in flight. After those three November days, he was transferred from the Zeppelin unit to an aircraft squadron, and his new superior praised the planes as deadly new fighting machines which would win the war. That made the former Zeppelin bombardier feel good. In fact, he was full of himself. The same day as Tibor Németh, whom he never met, was killed, Krupp was already enjoying delusions of grandeur: he imagined himself with a red scarf around his neck, shooting at French planes and being decorated as an air-ace. He ate well that evening and even went out after dinner with a Belgian woman who swore she wasn't a prostitute. The town of La Fère, where he was stationed, was empty. The streets were deserted in La Fère just as they were in Belgrade, even several days after Austrian troops had entered the city.

Then civilians began to arrive in occupied Belgrade. Half human and half animal, they had hidden from the war, and as troublemakers they didn't conceal their moral depravity. Now they hoped for fun, quick gain or simply adventure. One such renegade was Gavra Crnogorche-vich, the hot-tempered victor of the last duel in Belgrade before the Great War, a ruffian who evaded mobilization and disappeared into the blue with the words 'This looks mighty bad'. Now he came back from wherever he had been and really hit the town. In deserted Belgrade, the November trees shed whatever last leaves they still had, while Gavra shed what few moral scruples he still had from before the war.

Relieved of any great contemplation, he swiftly found himself an occupation. He didn't think of selling his *Idealin* shoe polish to the occupiers but quickly gathered a team of 'his women', who were actually prostitutes—the only people not to have left the city. He killed two interlopers for deluding his 'good women', thus demonstrating to his reluctantly smiling harem what would happen to them if they tried to leave him or do business on their own. Then he began offering them out for hire, but he encountered an unexpected problem. The military command which was soon established in the city didn't ban prostitution, but the Austrian and Hungarian officers were reluctant at first to get into bed with whores. The war had just begun, and many of those who abstained in those chilly November days had brought with them not only their kit but also a ballast of morality, although they would soon cast it off. Those who became rapists later that year now still saw themselves as family men, and the pimp Gavra Crnogorchevich realized that his public houses in Yevremova and Strahinyicha Bana Streets had to be wrapped in a new guise.

A family one, of course.

He found respectable clothes for his ladies and dressed himself in the best pre-war suit lifted from Prime Minister Pashich's house in Theatre Street. He brought in a few tables and cast clean white sheets of silk damask over some of them and green felt from a gambling hall over others. The older prostitutes began to play the role of mothers, and he, of course, was the father. The young ones—there were seven or eight of them, one more dissolute than the other—became their daughters, and the two public houses were dubbed 'open Serbian homes'. Now business really began to flourish. The house in Strahinyicha Bana Street was mostly frequented by junior officers, so Gavra sent the uglier prostitutes there, while Yevremova Street drew the cream of the occupiers, headed by the commander of the city, Colonel Schwarz, and including Baron Stork and Lieutenant Colonel Otto Gelinek, who was not only a customer of Gavra's houses but also purveyed them with luxury victuals. 'The family' took care of everything in the houses. Both of them had a mother (who also prostituted herself when it got busy), an aunt and several daughters, but Gavra Crnogorchevich was the father of both.

Like a real bigamist, he went to and fro between the establishments, collecting the takings and checking the health of his protégées, who had to service up to ten johns a day. Almost playfully, he embellished the charade with a different suit for each house, different silken dressing gowns and even a false beard which he added to his black-dyed moustache, but only when introducing himself as father of the more elegant 'open Serbian house' in Yevremova Street.

And the money 'came in shitloads' (Gavra's expression) during the thirteen days of the occupation. All this time, the other unfortunate from the last Belgrade duel hung around in the old hospital in Vrachar. Not that Djoka Velkovich couldn't have fled from Belgrade along with so many others, nor was he left behind like some of the incurably ill. Djoka decided to stay on at the hospital, which he had got to know well and now hid in, waiting for new doctors to come and heal him of his freakishness. When Colonel Graho and his Austro-Hungarian medical corps entered the hospital in Vrachar, Djoka prudently emerged from the cellar. He thought he'd be caught immediately, but no one noticed him because there were so many patients and so few doctors. He nudged a moaning, wounded man aside and shared the bed with him. His bedmate didn't complain; after all, it was nothing unusual for two soldiers to share the same bed, so no one paid any attention to the Serbian patient. Djoka was slightly annoyed by the bustle as well as the smell of carbolic acid and congealed blood; nor did he understand German or Hungarian. But in time he got used to everything. No one treated the red-and-white patient, but he was given a little food like all the others. He didn't think of going into town, so running into Gavra the pimp and challenging him to another duel could be ruled out. He was happy with his situation, which was a rare blessing, considering that virtually no one was satisfied with their circumstances.

For Sergei Voronin, the Great War began and ended when he thought he could introduce rank-and-file democracy into his platoon, which was manning the defences of Warsaw. This came at a time when the pendulum of war on the Eastern Front had again swung the Russians' way. The Russian army had defeated the Germans in the Battle of

Galicia near Lviv and broken the enemy offensive. The Russians pushed the front forwards by over a hundred kilometres, all the way to the wolfish peaks of the Carpathian Mountains. The Polish city of Przemysl was under siege by the Russian 8th Army far behind the front line, but the German defenders held on valiantly like the Ilians of legend. Przemysl became a name on the lips of every Austrian and German soldier. This was why the Germans tried to shift the Front back to the east and take Warsaw. But the Russians gained the upper hand in the battle on the gleaming River Vistula. After this victory, quarrels re-emerged in the Russian general staff. Their supreme command could not agree how to capitalize on the most recent successes. The 'Iron Duke' was in favour of an offensive on the open ground of East Prussia, while Chief of Staff Mikhail Alexeyev proposed an offensive in the wool-carding region of Silesia. Either icy plains or woollen yarn.

At that time, the Germans intercepted Russian encoded messages about the proposed invasion of Silesia. Hindenburg hoped to repeat the success of the Battle of Tannenberg by striking the Russians in the flank as they moved on Silesia. And so the Battle of Lódz began, and with it the harsh Transcarpathian winter. The troops of General Pavel Plekhava's Russian 5th Army were force-marched from southern Silesia towards Lódz—students of Petrograd University and peasants from the estates near Staraya Rusa covered a Herculean one hundred and twenty kilometres in two days in temperatures of minus ten. And after those terrible two days they still had the strength to mount a surprise attack on the right flank of General August von Mackensen's German 9th Army. The Germans retreated, but they continued to threaten Lódz up until December 1914.

The sky above Lódz was red in those days, and the night seemed never to come due to the constant blaze of heavy guns, but things were different in Warsaw, where General Nikolai Ruzsky commanded the army group charged with the defence of the city. While Russians were dying, like fish caught in a net, near Lódz, Warsaw was behind the lines for several weeks. And it was at this time that one sergeant tried to introduce rank-and-file democracy into his platoon. Sergei Voronin was a socialist. He had a small sterling-silver locket holding Plekhanov's picture on the left and Lenin's on the right. The left-hand side was the reason for him being in uniform, because Plekhanov had called on all Mensheviks to respond to the call-up and join the fight against the 'accursed Krauts'. The right-hand side of the medallion was responsible for the idea which Voronin tried to institute in icy Warsaw in the first days of December—one he claimed would decide the Great War.

He resolved to break the chain of command. The goal of this minor military reform was for his platoon of forty men to issue its own commands and reach decisions in the style of an ideal grass-roots council. But this state, which Sergei termed 'consummate soldierly conscience', could not be attained overnight. The transition from the 'imperialist-hierarchical' form of command to a 'collectivist' one (Sergei's expressions) lasted a week. That week saw both the rise and the shameful fall of that idea, but it was far from the mind of the socialist sergeant that everything would take place so quickly. First of all, he spoke of his intentions with his deputy platoon commander. Once he had won him over, he tried hard to persuade the group commanders. On the third day, he set up the original rotating-system of command in which it fell to each soldier to be the platoon's commanding officer for one hour. He didn't reserve any privileges for himself: in forty-two hours he was sergeant for one hour, and not one minute longer. Everything went smoothly at first, but then Sergei noticed that his forty or so Russians included a few blockheads who shouldn't be entrusted with command for even one hour, so he developed a two-tiered, and afterwards an even more complicated three-tiered rotating system of command.

In Warsaw, where there was no fighting, all this remained a game and went unnoticed for surprisingly long—six whole days. But then soldiers of the other platoons started to pick up on a strange thing: Sergei's men not only strutted around their sector like peacocks but also soon came to enjoy commanding and kept giving each other orders which there was no one to carry out. Ultimately they upgraded the three-tiered system and instituted 'order exchanges': I order you to do this and you carry it out; you order me to do that and I carry it out in return. Commanding thus became a kind of swap; Sergei vehemently opposed this at party meetings of the platoon on the second-last day of his reform, but to no avail. The most enterprising soldiers found a way of imposing their will amidst that chaos. They began remembering each other's orders, and in the end they were trading them like shares. A lop-eared mathematics student came off best: he swiftly converted these fluctuations to figures and soon became the proprietor of the greatest number of orders owed to him by the others. On the last day he thus became the informal leader of the detachment of forty-two presumptious commanders.

Who knows where all this would have led had Sergei not been arrested, brought before a court-martial, summarily sentenced and shot. His soldiers escaped the firing squad, but they were now given the most inveterate old sergeant as platoon commander, a man of fifty-four, steeled back in the Russian-Turkish War of 1878. He alone gave orders, and everyone else had to obey. Half the men received bruises from his blows, and three of the most persistent had their arms broken by the old sergeant. Thus the necessary 'imperialist discipline' was restored in the 2nd Platoon, 3rd Company, 5th Battalion of the army group defending Warsaw just before the fighting began, and everyone soon forgot Sergei.

But unforgettable events occurred at the railway station in Nish, Serbia, and were publicized in *Politika* on 18 November by the Julian calendar. This news, delivered to the paper's offices in Belgrade by special mail, was from a lady fondly known as Mrs Danica, the founder of the 'Serbian Blue Cross', an organization for the welfare of draught animals at the front, and the first woman from Shabac to learn English. Mrs Danica wrote:

I found the little railway station in Nish full to overflowing with troops, villagers and women. They had all been sitting on the ground for hours and waiting for the hospital train. Then the whistle of an engine was heard and everyone headed to the main platform. To our surprise, smart and tidy-looking prisoners-of-war started to emerge from the train, and we lost heart. They were Austrian soldiers, and everyone would have looked at them with contempt if one of them had not suddenly leaned out the window and shouted excitedly: 'Djuro, Djuro!' a Serbian soldier on the platform wheeled around, ran up to the soldier in the blue Austrian uniform, who had now hopped out of the train, and embraced him. They were Yanko and Djuro Tankosich, brothers from the same village in Syrmia, where the Great War had begun with both the Austrian and Serbian armies mobilizing able-bodied men. Brother Djuro was able to escape the Austrian's mobilizers in August 1914 but they caught Yanko, and consequently the brothers fought against one another up until the moment when the 'Austrian' seized the opportunity to surrender. Now he was willing to change into a Serbian uniform and wear our *Shaykacha* cap.

The meeting of the brothers was a touching event. They both cried and hugged each other as if they were two bodies with the same soul. Those standing closest to them heard them promise each other that they'd never be separated again, in life or death. We applauded them as they embraced, and an elderly man with a long, grey beard instructed that the brothers' wish be respected. The gentleman spoke with such authority that those around him immediately obeyed. When I took a second glance, I realized he was none other than the Prime Minister, Mr Pashich, who was waiting for the train along with everyone else.

The train for the Prime Minister didn't arrive, and Yanko and Djuro soon went off into town, arm in arm. Their song resounded through the streets and was picked up first of all by gypsy brass bands, then successively by merry fellows in the cafés and debauchees of every variety, finally to be sung by the whole town, and the Tankosich brothers from Syrmia were its luminaries.

Thus wrote the first member of the Serbian Blue Cross. The same lady was also a correspondent for the first issue of *Politika* to come out after the victory in the Battle of Kolubara on 8 December by the old calendar. If the previous story had been penned to song and celebration, this one was awash with tears. It read:

I recently reported in *Politika* on the meeting of two brothers. Now I owe readers the end of the story. I concluded my previous letter about Yanko and Djuro Tankosich with the song which all of Nish was soon singing. But a new sun rose—a bleak, winter sun—and Sunday 19 November was a very different day. The two brothers went to army headquarters to request that they both be enlisted in the 1st Company, 4th Battalion of the 7th Reserve Regiment of the Serbian army, which was Djuro's unit. This time, too, they set off arm in arm, with a smile on their lips and convinced that their sufferings were over. But things turned out differently.

The recruitment service viewed Yanko with suspicion.

'Why didn't you desert straight away, like Djuro did? Instead, you fought at the Drina and killed who knows how many Serbs, and now you want to wash your hands clean,' they challenged him.

Young Yanko swore in vain that he had been in the medical corps, served under a certain Dr Mehmed Graho in Zvornik, and never fired a shot at his Serb compatriots. They detained him at the army supply office, and his brother Djuro fell into despondency. The officers responsible said to Djuro:

'It's only for a few days, and he's not under arrest. We're just detaining him because there are all sorts of Czech and Slovak riff-raff around who speak our language and claim to be Serbs, when in fact they're Austrian spies.'

'But... but that's my little brother Yanko. I've known him since he was just this big. Why a security check when you have my word?'

Djuro pleaded and swore by his wounds received at the River Yadar, but the officers were bureaucratically intransigent.

'No, no, he's to stay in for a little longer. But we need every man who can hold a rifle, now that the decisive battle is brewing, so you can rest assured that we'll release him when the twelfth hour comes.'

And the twelfth hour arrived. Djuro's 7th Reserve Regiment had rested and now received orders to set off from Nish for the decisive battle on the slopes of Mount Suvobor. Djuro requested permission to leave the unit for an hour and went back to the army supply office's lock-up.

'The twelfth hour has come! We're going to the battle on Mount Suvobor. Please let my brother free so we can fight and die for Serbia together,' he begged, but the officers remained hard-hearted.

'The information on Yanko still hasn't arrived,' they said. Then Djuro requested to see his brother one more time before they were separated. His wish was granted. Downcast and gloomy, he entered the cell. It stank of his brother's urine because there was no toilet. He felt sick, and he saw red. Hugging his brother, he turned him the other way and took out a hand grenade: 'The documents on Yanko have now arrived... release my brother!'

When they saw the grenade, everyone took cover. Djuro and Yanko now set off for the station, where the troop trains were leaving for the front, along the same streets where they had sung with the assembled populace two weeks earlier. Our tireless Prime Minister was no longer on the platform, and if he had been I'm sure he would have resolved the whole matter immediately. Yanko and Djuro arrived at the station with an armed squad of military police hot on their heels and just itching to kill them as deserters. They would have been executed right there and then, had not Major Djuro Sharac and his Chetniks happened to be on the same platform; and they sided with the brothers. Impetuous as they always were, these staunch fighters had heard of the two brothers from Syrmia, immediately recognized them and formed a ring around them. 'If you want the Tankosichs, you'll have to kill us first!' they shouted at the military police. Armed though they were, the MPs realized they'd have to make a ruckus in the middle of the station, and in view of all the civilians standing nearby they decided to back off.

The brothers got into a wagon, sullen-faced. Djuro's trembling hands only just managed to replace the pin of his grenade. His captain of the 1st Company told him that they were going into battle now, but when they returned he was going to have them both tried. The brothers glanced at each other, determined not to go before any court martial. As soon as the first evening came, and with it the first battle in the vale on 3 December, both Djuro and Yanko fell in a frantic charge beneath Mount Suvobor, running and holding each other's hand like little girls. And that is how the Great War ended for them.

84

Now, I don't know what to say about this story, which I was told just the way it happened, but I do know that I have a moral duty to propose to the High Command, through this article, that the Tankosich brothers be posthumously decorated—not put on trial. May Serbian medals for bravery be sent to their poor mother in Syrmia when the Great War ends.

But the Tankosichs were never decorated because of the enthusiasm which engulfed people's souls, and everyone slept just an hour or two so as not to miss the days of victory celebrations after the Battle of Kolubara. Old King Peter hurried to Belgrade to enter the capital together with the first troops. Jubilant crowds tried to stop the royal car, but he didn't mind. He passed the damaged royal court, and the car drove over the flag of the Dual Monarchy, the first symbolic trophy of the war, as it lay in the mud. Many a strange thing was found in the recaptured city, but the soldiers of the 13th 'Hayduk Velko' Regiment were particularly stunned by what they discovered in one elegant house. The Austrians had been preparing to celebrate Christmas by their calendar, and two houses in Strahinyicha Bana and Yevremova Streets were found to have substantial stores of luxury goods: huge quantities of roasted coffee, chocolate, liqueurs, sweets, biscuits, sardines, sultanas and various delicacies which ordinary soldiers had never heard of and the commanders ordered them not to try. But soldiers being soldiers, they started helping themselves to the sweets, until they noticed that frightened eyes were watching them from hiding.

They found a group of strange women in the house, embracing and intertwined like denizens of a snake-pit, with dishevelled hair, pale thighs and smudged make-up around swollen eyelids. All of them claimed to have been raped several times a day and said they had been driven to whoredom by a certain Gavra Crnogorchevich. He had put on a charade of being their father but in reality he was a cruel brothel boss. When asked where Gavra was now and if he had fled with the Austrian army, the women only said they didn't know but thought he was probably still in Belgrade.

That saw the start of a wholesale search for Gavra in lower Dorchol. Houses and deserted flats were peered into, but the ghosts of dead Belgraders could now rest peacefully in their graves and none of them fired on the liberators. In any case, Gavra was caught after just a few houses had been searched.

At his trial, which was brief because there was neither time nor desire for more, he claimed to have been 'forced' and 'blackmailed by a certain Otto Gelinek' and to have 'had no choice'. The High Military Court condemned him to death nevertheless. As the sentence was being pronounced, his dry lips beneath the still well-groomed, black-dyed moustache just murmured, 'Looks like this is it'. On his last night, he couldn't sleep. He got up, called the guards and asked for a cigarette. They just gave him a butt, from which he took three passionate drags. As he took the first, he remembered his victory in the duel; as he took the second, the boonful days during the brief occupation of Belgrade appeared before his eyes. As he took the third, he decided to flee to America. He tried to bribe the guards with a pile of the occupier's banknotes extracted from the lining of his frock coat, which they had been sewn into, but it didn't work. He fell asleep and didn't dream anything until morning. They woke him at five o'clock and offered him the last sacrament. He was shot that day together with three other unscrupulous traders imprisoned in the environs of Belgrade and in Smederevo. For Gavra Crnogorchevich, the Great War ended before the firing squad on the sandy river bank below Vishnyica, with thousands of German marks still sewn into the lining of his coat; they became soaked after his body splashed dully into the shallow water of the Sava. 'If only I had *Idealin* here to polish my messy shoes,' was the last thing Gavra Crnogorchevich thought.

'If only I had my helpers here, whom I love as my own sons,' Mehmed Yıldız thought as he called out the prices of his wares by himself. A small boy, no more than eight years old, was by his side. His five strapping apprentices and young assistants had been called up into the Turkish army and each sent to a different part of the world, where his empire defended the rising and setting of the sun. The eldest—the red-headed one, who cheated so adroitly at the scales, just so much that his master was satisfied and the customers didn't complain—had been posted to Thrace. His black-haired brother with the slight birthmark on his forehead, who would dispel their weariness with a song in the evenings, had been deployed to the Caucasus. The third apprentice, his dear beanpole with the infectious smile which dispersed all their worries, had been sent to Palestine. Yıldız Effendi also had two young assistants, and they had also been recruited because they were born in 1895 and 1897 respectively. The one was almost a man, but the other still very much a child. In that way he was deprived of the brightest young employee he had ever had, his newly-fledged bookkeeper, who had been sent to Mesopotamia. And even his youngest assistant, an urchin from the house next door, had been mobilized for the Turkish army in Arabia. That was a particularly hard blow for the old spice trader. Did the Sublime Porte really need children in this war?

And so Yıldız Effendi was left all by himself. True, the neighbour had loaned him his youngest son—the brother of the red-headed and the black-haired apprentices—so he would at least have someone to help out, but that was just to keep an old promise; the gesture in no way suited the circumstances because a boy of eight was unable to lift weights, take responsibility or yell out prices. After two days, he told the boy: 'Off you go home, son,' and stood behind the counter alone. The streets of Istanbul were now deserted. Occasionally a Muslim woman from a good home, with a violet veil, would call in, but that was a rare occurrence. 'What silence, what silence,' the trader muttered, with ample time to look around. Over in one of the traditional porched houses, looking in through the window, he could see a servant rolling out lengths of wallpaper. Through a gap between two other houses he glimpsed the Bosporus gleaming like a shed snakeskin.

Yıldız Effendi slept very, very little at night. He would wake up with a start and call one of his apprentices. One day one of them was gone, the next—a second, the third—a third, the fourth—a fourth, the fifth—a fifth, and on the sixth day all of them had disappeared together. At four in the morning he went down to the storeroom by the Golden Horn and fetched new stocks of red spices. Before dawn he went by tram to prayers at the Aya Sofya, so as to open the shop by himself before seven. He called out the prices, hardly got round to reading a few lines from the noble Koran, and saw himself as the last old-fashioned Turk. He didn't play his little game with the spices any more. The red ones were outselling the browns and greens by such an overwhelming margin every day that the trader lost all hope that any hour would be good.

The great singer Hans-Dieter Huis, too, had completely given up hope. The concert he held in occupied Brussels now appeared to him as the last memento of a dying civilization. In the meantime he had seen hunger, retreat and death. They called on him to sing at the deathbed of two German princes who paid with their heads in Holland and France. That was the hardest thing the maestro had ever done. The Prince of Schaumburg-Lippe had already given up the ghost when they called him, so his singing at the catafalque was in fact a requiem, but the Prince of Meiningen still gave signs of life when they rushed the singer to him in an ambulance. The Prince requested hoarsely that he sing Bach's arias, and he, without knowing why himself, started singing a Bach canon, which was ridiculous and almost impossible for one voice. He'd begin with the higher notes like a tenor and then lower his trembling voice to the deeper notes, while it seemed to him that someone was mutedly intoning the other voice in a cold tenor. No, that wasn't the prince singing in the hour of his death because he scarcely had the strength to breathe. He heard, yes he clearly heard Death singing the upper register of a canon for two voices with him. And then the prince died. Be-medalled officers who had been waiting for the prince's death now came in, saying to each other, 'It's over now', and rudely shoved Huis out of the room. As he was leaving, he saw a doctor going in with a metal basin of plaster solution to make the prince's death mask.

Some other be-medalled officers later sent him down to the cellar with a few polite words. There he sat at a table with two old men who only spoke French. He tried to exchange a few words with them and learnt that they were the owners of the house which had been turned into a German army headquarters, where the prince had breathed his last. The men told him defiantly that the house had been in their family for three hundred years up until 23 September 1914, and then they asked him if it had been him singing on the upper floor. He affirmed that it had, and told them his name, at which they jumped up and started kissing his hand. They had twice heard him in Paris, they said, but for maestro Huis this was so wretched and strange that he didn't know whether to burst into tears or reprove the old men who were kissing him. Civilization had thus survived, he thought, but it had been driven underground, into cellars, and was so old that it would expire before the end of the Great War.

Such thoughts preoccupied him for the next two weeks as he was carted from venue to venue behind the lines and made to sing like a wind-up doll. But hadn't he admitted to himself that he no longer felt anything and had no faith in his art any more? Was it not then irrelevant where he sang and who gave the orders? Therefore he reluctantly agreed to these battlefield assignments. They drove him around, introduced him to the superior officers, and he performed. His last scheduled event of 1914 was on Christmas Eve at the supreme command headquarters near Lens, where he was to sing for Prince Friedrich Wilhelm, heir to the German throne and titular commander of the German 5th Army. They told him that the great Theodora von Stade would be performing with him. The Crown prince welcomed the singers as if it was the seventeenth century, not the twentieth. He said he was glad they had come to his estate, and the generals clustered around him exchanged anxious glances. Then the door was closed behind the singers. The prince was their only listener. Theodora began to sing the upper part in a clear and unimpaired voice, but when the second voice was called for, Hans-Dieter Huis cleared his throat with that 'front-line cough' of a malnourished man of broken health. The prince raised an eyebrow, looked at them with tear-filled eyes, and the old man at the cembalo played the first chords of the Sanctus from Bach's *Mass in B minor* again. Theodora finished the opening, and Huis replied beautifully. The prince gazed at them both with strange, voracious eyes. He smiled happily, but with a hint of desperation, as if he was on the verge of a nervous breakdown. At the end of the short, a cappella concert, he too enthused about them having brought a little civilization into that terrible war, repeating almost word for word what his generals used to say when Huis finished a concert. That embittered the maestro. His thoughts were far from dinner. He took the opportunity of asking His Majesty to allow him to visit some units from Berlin at the front, which was just a few kilometres away. 'Our soldiers need a song for Christmas too,' he said, and the Crown prince immediately filled out a permit for him and arranged transport.

In the trenches near Avion, which smelt like graveyard loam, he was met by the members of the 93rd Division, each of whom was an opera buff. He recognized many staff from the Deutsche Oper among them. Now they were tired soldiers with lice in their hair, their cheeks ruddy from the cold and noses red from alcohol. 'Sing für sie,' the tenor from the Opera choir encouraged him, who had first called 'hurrah' when Huis appeared. But what could he sing when he no longer believed in song? Something German? Bach? In the end, it was the men who decided. '*Don Giovanni, Don Giovanni!*' they shouted in unison, and he began to the sing the aria 'Fin ch'han dal vino'. He began in Italian: 'Fin ch'han dal vino / calda la testa / una gran festa / fa' preparar' ['For a carousal / Where all is madness, / Where all is gladness, / Do thou prepare'], and then continued in German: 'Triffst du auf dem Platz /

Einige Mädchen, / bemüh dich, auch sie / noch mitzubringen.' ['Maids that are pretty, / Dames that are witty, / All to my castle / Bid them repair.'] As he sang, he saw that something unusual was happening. The soldiers moved him. This was no longer the threatening audience with opera glasses before their eyes, and his voice began to come from the depths of his breast, where he had kept his artist's soul locked away for so many years. He remembered Elsa from Mainz and finally let his unhappy soul come out on that Christmas Eve; and he drank in the starry night air and sang as he hadn't sung in a decade and a half. He grabbed one of the Christmas trees and began to climb the steps in the side of the trench up to the open ground between the German, French and Scottish lines. They cautioned him that just that day it had been impossible to even fetch the wounded, who still lay there with snow-dusted cheeks and eyebrows and cried for help.

But in vain: Huis trod those steps and made it into no man's land. His song was heard well into the enemy trenches, but one Scottish soldier from the Scottish 92nd Division realized better than the others that only the great Hans-Dieter Huis could sing Don Giovanni like that. It was Edwin McDermott, a bass from Edinburgh and Huis's constant companion in the role of Leporello whenever Huis performed in Scotland. The Scottish soldier waited for the end of the aria, then he too leapt out of his trench and began to sing Leporello's aria in reply: 'Madamina, il catalogo è questo / delle belle che amò il padron mio, /un catalogo egli è che fatt'io, / osservate, leggete con me.' ['My dear lady, this is a list / Of the beauties my master has loved, / a list which I have compiled. / Observe, read along with me.']

The two singers now started walking towards one another. At one hundred metres, Huis and McDermott saw and recognized each other. They both smiled and could see the radiance in each others' eyes. For Huis, it was as if his beloved Elsa from Mainz was striding there hand in hand with him. All at once, everything took on meaning. Leporello sang ever more loudly: 'In Italia sei cento e quaranta, / in Almagna due cento etrent'una, / cento in Francia, in Turchia novant'una.' ['In Italy, six hundred and forty, / In Germany, two hundred and thirty-one, / a hundred in France, / In Turkey, ninety-one.']

No sooner had the two old friends and associates embraced, when a cry resounded. From the French positions, someone started to sing like the Commendatore: 'Don Giovanni, a cenar teco / m'invitarsi, e son venuto.' ['Don Giovanni, you invited me to dine with you, /

90

And I have come.'] Immediately afterwards there was a burst of fire. Leporello had only just looked into smiling Don Giovanni's face, when he began to stagger and fall. His burly body protected Huis from the bullets of the wrathful singer in the French trenches, whose shots had evidently been meant for the great German baritone, not for the Scottish singer.

Instead of Don Giovanni, it was his faithful servant Leporello who lost his life in that field of fire. The Great War thus began and ended for the celebrated Scottish bass when he decided to reply to maestro Huis's song and join in the first wartime opera of 1914. As soon as the Scotsman fell, there was a shout. German soldiers raced out to haul Huis back to the trench, but he refused to be separated from McDermott. He cried, and how he cried: for Elsa, and now also for Edwin from Edinburgh. He almost choked from sobbing when they finally dragged him back to the German trenches.

The name of Leporello's killer was never revealed, not least because the sad event set a chain of unexpectedly positive events in motion at the front near Avion. As if the Messiah had fallen, the death of the Scottish soldier led to the start of negotiations and then a Christmas-Eve truce between the companies of the German 93rd Division, the Scottish 92nd Division and the French 26th Brigade. A Scottish priest, Father Donovan, held a midnight Mass for a thousand men, and on Christmas Day they buried all the dead who had long lain uncollected between the trenches. The pipers played *Flowers of the Forest* at McDermott's funeral and Huis sang at his friend's shallow grave; he swore it was the last time he had sung Mozart's *Don Giovanni*.

THE TYPHUS SITUATION

The infected feel a growing inner disquiet, which rapidly deepens into a draining sense of despair. At the same time, they are overwhelmed by mental exhaustion. This spreads to the muscles and tendons as well as to all internal organs, not least to the stomach, which rejects all food with revulsion. There is a strong need to sleep, but despite great fatigue, sleep is fitful and shallow, full of fear and not at all refreshing. The infected have severe headaches; their mind is dull and confused, as if wrapped in mists and pervaded with dizziness. They feel an ill-defined pain in all their limbs. There are periodic nosebleeds for no apparent reason. That is how the disease begins.

This introduction describes the state many Belgraders were in when a typhus epidemic broke out towards the end of December 1914. The Serbian papers wrote with undisguised, malicious joy about the mass outbreak of measles in Hungary and cholera in Austria; but the Serbian typhus was passed over in silence. The disease started at the banks of the Danube and the low-lying parts of the city, at the pools and by-channels which collected the water turbid with blood and human decay; the ailing Drina brought these with its waves and infected the already sickly Sava, which in turn passed on the illness to the irresolute and horrified Danube. Weary swamp herons and frogs in the shallows were the first to feel that something was way out of order, but they were unable to carry any warning to the people carousing in cafés and celebrating the second expulsion of the Krauts from Serbia with the same cheerful songs as at the beginning of the Great War.

The first typhus sufferers blamed the café owners and sour wine for their bad and restless sleep and the constant headaches, which didn't subside from morning till late evening. Then fires were seen, over beyond Bara Venecia; people thought it was Gypsies who had returned to their dugouts and wooden hovels with the liberators and were burning off old rags. But in fact it was health officials silently incinerating the infected clothing of the first victims; they wanted to postpone declaring an epidemic so the enemy wouldn't find out and exploit the outbreak to their advantage.

At that time, the first people to come down with typhus fell into bed. It was absurd the way they now blamed their wanton and dissolute company for the sad state they were in. Their teeth chattered; black pustules the size of lentils came out on their chests and abdomens. Dizziness became ever more pronounced, and their teeth and gums were covered in a blackish, resinous scum. Even when wails and invocations began to be heard from many houses, there was no official admission that an epidemic of typhus had broken out in Serbia.

So it was that typhus made its way to Belgrade and swept on to Shabac, Smederevo, Loznica, Valyevo, and all the way to Uzhice and the recently liberated territories in the south; it was like a horseman on a furious steed with steaming nostrils, but its pounding hoofs remained unheard even in the deepest silence. The disease spread like a weed in a neglected garden and soon the hospitals were full of typhus cases being tended by nurses of the Serbian Red Cross, who then fell ill themselves. They were treated by doctors of all ranks, who also fell ill. Doctors from Greece and Britain came to the aid of their Serbian colleagues, only to come down with typhus themselves. Disease thus carried off those whom the battles had forgotten.

One small shoe-polish dealer was among those infected with typhus. For Djoka Velkovich, the Great War ended when he inanely directed a last, watery gaze at the calendar for the New Year, on which he saw a Serbian soldier with '1915' on his back crushing an Austrian soldier with '1914' on his chest. The Serb had the resolute countenance of Saint George, victor in the Battles of Cer and Kolubara, while the Austrian gazed up from the ground, like a sordid snake ready to deliver one last desperate bite.

At the twelfth hour, the last breath left the chest of Djoka Velkovich as gently as a feather which drifts off from an empty pillow. It was the New Year 1915 by the Julian calendar.

The same day, by the same calendar, the 'Iron Duke' Nicholas Nikolaevich reluctantly celebrated New Year's Eve at Russian army headquarters. He spoke little, drank little and looked down at his quarrelling generals. He went to bed early and apologized, saying he had a headache.

On New Year's Eve by the Julian calendar, Sergei Chestukhin and his wife Liza found themselves in Riga, on the north-easternmost stretch of the front. After the time of victory came a time of defeat, but Sergei had managed to buy some Königsberg amber for his Lizochka on the black market, a piece of incomparable beauty with an interned bee in the centre. She turned it in her hands. The Baltic gold gleamed like the honey of that petrified bee, like her copper-bearing hair bathed in the sun. 'It would have been better if supreme command had given me Marusya for the New Year,' the heroic nurse said and burst into tears, defiantly wiping those pearls from her cheeks as they rolled from her eyes the colour of sepia.

The greatest German baritone, Hans-Dieter Huis, couldn't remember how he saw in the New Year 1915. But that was nothing unusual, because many soldiers later couldn't say where they had been during the celebrations and New Year's break.

The writer Jean Cocteau returned to Paris on leave. He arrived in the City of Light like a real wartime popinjay: in an ironed and scented uniform with a crimson helmet. Everyone at the Rotonde and the Dôme was meant to see how he had 'gone to war in style' in 1914. He couldn't find Picasso.

Lucien Guirand de Scevola spent New Year's Eve beside a radio-telegraph. He had read in *Le Parisien* the same day that wireless telegraphers had specific occupational illnesses like a straining of the right forefinger, which they used to type Morse code with; after all the horrific wounds he had seen, he could only laugh about this one as he saw in the first night of the New Year.

Germain D'Esparbès spent New Year's Eve writing yet another despondent letter which began with 'Dearest Zoë' and ended with 'Tell Nana I'm not a monster. I'm still waiting for you, but with a loaded pistol at my side.'

Fritz Krupp spent New Year's Eve sitting in a prototype of a plane, the Aviatik B.I. He fell in love with it as if it were a woman, and could hardly wait to fly and attack Paris with it in 1915. He fondled the machine-gun and said to himself: 'I'll kill you, Picasso, I'm telling you.'

Like maestro Huis, Private Stefan Holm also couldn't remember where and with whom he saw in the New Year 1915.

Yıldız Effendi couldn't help but be amazed that the streets of Istanbul were so deserted. Shoppers were few and far between, starving dogs wandered the streets, and on the opposite side of the Golden Horn someone was always lighting fires, whose acrid smoke crept across the water to enter his nostrils, even here on his side of the estuary. On the day of the infidel New Year he didn't even think it was a special date.

On 1 January by the new Gregorian calendar, a wave of cold descended on the whole of Europe. On 1 January by the Julian calendar, an oily sun rose and fought against the low, waxen clouds on the horizon. On the Eastern Front, the German, Austrian and Russian armies fortified their positions from Riga to Chernivtsi; on the Western Front, the French, British and German armies dug in from Ostend to Mulhouse; on the Southern Front, Austria readied itself for a new attack on Serbia—and everyone thought this was the beginning of the last year of a war which was to end all wars.

Mehmed Graho the pathologist, on whose table the Great War had begun, was perhaps the only one who thought otherwise. He scratched the little patch of grey hair on the back of his head and counted on his thick fingers like a child: thirty days, no, forty-two days in Zvornik, multiplied by at least nine moribunds a day, and then at least a hundred more in Belgrade, minus the one or two every day who pulled through. He had been responsible for five hundred deaths at the very least, and then there were all the other doctors of death, generalissimos of death and chemists of death. 'No, the great calamity is still to come,' he muttered, without much of a guilty conscience.

Graho spent the New Year of the boisterous Catholics, and later that of the quiet Orthodox, at home in Sarajevo, and neither of them meant much to him. What was much more important to him was that he managed to find a pair of shoes his size which didn't pinch his swollen feet on either side. 'Bravo,' he said to himself, and thus ended the year of one pathologist.

1915
THE YEAR OF
THE TRADER

The pianist Paul Wittgenstein before one of
his concerts for the left hand, 1919

THE SMELL OF SNOW AND FOREBODINGS OF DOOM

In Istanbul you need to stay for six days if you're a traveller, six weeks if you're a Westerner wanting to see only the good face of Turkey, six years if you're an infidel trader from Beirut or Alexandria and want to make a quick and easy fortune, six decades if you're a trader and believer who intends to stay on in Istanbul, six centuries for you and your descendants if you wish to merge with the cobblestones, wood, waters and lifeblood of this city on the water, and six millenniums if you're the Padishah, ruler of the righteous.

Thus went a popular saying which Mehmed Yıldız, the trader in oriental spices, often repeated in tearooms and in the company of idle coachmen. He himself had almost reached the tally of six decades on the streets of the great city. That's right, he calculated, unfolding his thick fingers to count the decades on them like a child. In 1917, it would be sixty years since he took his father's place. His father Husrev Yıldız, a manufacturer and trader in fur apparel, moved from Izmir to the capital in the golden times following the reforms of Mahmud II and opened a furrier's workshop with an attached boutique, which would become famous among the Jewish traders in Galata. At that time Mehmed was attending *rushdi*—Islamic middle school—and his mother lay dying, but that didn't prevent his father from staying at work from dawn until dusk. He offered his wares like a prophet, not a trader. He had a separate stand for every kind of fur. With his body inclined like the Sultan's wine taster, his head slightly bowed, he would pronounce 'bison' with relish as he showed a customer the fine bovine fur; now, bent at the waist like a Western flunkey, he spoke the word 'sable' with a ring of importance as if he was saying 'sailed the seven seas' and held up his produce, always emphasising its quality; and later, bent almost double in deference, he would mincingly pronounce 'ermine' and invite his clients to the back room of the workshop to bargain over a glass of well-stewed mint tea.

Business flourished, yet Husrev Yıldız was ever more alone, and never himself but someone else. When his wife died of tuberculosis, leaving his son Mehmed crippled with grief, the father didn't shed a tear but withdrew into his storeroom in the Haseki area and the very next day was offering sable again just like a Jewish merchant. That is how

Mehmed Yıldız learnt early in life that there are Turks who find their place and know themselves, and others who wrench themselves out of their culture. The former stay put and wait for the tides of time to either break against them or crush them. The latter go away to study Western medicine, only to realize it is the enemy of humanity; they go away to become Westerners beneath the street lights of Rome and Paris, and learn to understand that Europe is the enemy of Islam; they fall in love with revolution and then see that the more radical its promises are, the further their fulfilment is postponed into the distant future, and the promises thus grotesquely dwindle. The 'Westerners' become disillusioned and return, but alas, they cannot go back to their beds because the mould which was made for them has long since shattered.

That is what the trader Mehmed Yıldız most feared: becoming like those others, resembling his father who presented everything in a false light and said it was good for business because furriers sold not goods, he claimed, but dreams and status. The son therefore sold his father's fur business without regret as soon as Husrev Yıldız had his first stroke a few years later and in 1857, without reconsidering, left the Jewish quarter; he descended the icy marble of the Camondo Stairs for the last time and put Galata behind him. He set up a spice shop below Topkapı Palace using the money gained from liquidating the fur business, but still he felt threatened by his father's business lies and falsehoods—as if they could be passed on to him through the air or by blood. For that reason, he wanted only to be a Turk and only to love his helpers. Finally, it seemed to him that he had everything and that he had fused with his matrix, but then the Great War came on the threshold of his seventy-sixth year and sixth decade of trading in Istanbul and threatened to make him one of those others who have to leave the Bosporus after so long and start a homeless life without form and identity. Still, he hoped it wouldn't come to that. Each of his assistants was now in the army but the fronts were all still quiet. If only that winter of his ill temper would pass, which here too, at the gate to Asia, held the threat of snow and low temperatures. The forecast said it would be minus five even by the water, and the wind from Anatolia brought the smell of snow mixed with forebodings of doom.

The Serbian press did not report whether the temperature in Istanbul fell below zero. But in Belgrade, to be sure, everything froze: iron became sheathed in ice, the mighty walls of Kalemegdan fortress congealed to icy rock, and the ground was frozen too solid to even to dig a grave for a dead cat. It was January 1915, the peaceful lull after the slaughter of a whole generation at the River Drina and Mount Suvobor. The impetuous bands of carousing ruffians who had celebrated liberation in December 1914 had long since come down with typhus and been decimated, and the winter wind from the Danube and Sava had stolen the mirth from their lips and turned it to morbid moans. Those who were still healthy—neither happy nor sad—went outdoors wrapped in rags. And the smoke from charities' portable stoves seemed to turn waxen and freeze above the heads of the volunteers who offered passers-by weak, but mercifully hot tea.

'What a terrible winter,' *Politika* reporter Pera Stanisavlevich Bura would announce from the door as he tossed his foppish, battered bowler hat onto the hall stand, cast off his frozen-stiff coat and laid aside the decrepit black umbrella he used as defence against the fine snow, which in such cold weather was hardly able to fall.

'Hey Bura, did that plucked chicken of an umbrella shield you from the snow?' the brash journalists called out, and Bura replied with a good-natured smile. He was one of those people who were happy all day long. He himself didn't know why. For him, even the Great War began on a day he found especially beautiful. It is a fact that some people are born happy and always look on the bright side of things. This minor journalist of the Belgrade paper was one such person.

Maybe it was precisely because of Bura's merry disposition that the editor let him write a column called "While They Were Here: Notes from Thirteen Days' Occupation". The aim of this amusing but cynical column was to present a range of anecdotes from the shifty, shady side of Serbia during the almost two weeks of Austrian occupation of Belgrade in 1914, and Bura took the task very seriously. He went into grocery shops, chatted with tough little Dorchol ladies with black-haired warts on their faces, and listened to the gossip of the leisurely world. His colleagues claimed he even spoke with the animals and knew how the occupation had been for every cart-pulling ox in front of the railway station. But these slights couldn't dent his spirit, and Bura became a household name. People read and enjoyed his stories: about the shrewd young clerk from the Palilula neighbourhood who found a way of getting back at the Austrians; about the superstitious Croatian in the uniform of the empire who was bucked by his horse at the corner of King Alexander and King Milutin Streets; and about the incredible bravery of a wounded Serb soldier who hid in different houses and then had the courage to steal an Austrian uniform and stroll the streets and drink wine with the occupiers as if he was one of them.

The editor concealed from Bura how popular he had become so he wouldn't 'get a swollen head', but the cheerful journalist returned to his little house in Savamala, content with life. Bura was not what you call handsome: he had just a little hair around the ears, his face was tipped forwards as if someone had pulled his nose and twisted it out of shape while he was still inside his mother, and his forehead was a sea of wrinkles. Not to mention the creases around his eyebrows and eyes. But Bura was happy despite his less-than-attractive appearance. Besides, he was a 'peaceful journalist', not a rabble-rouser or a noise-maker. He lived with his elderly mother and his wife, Stana, with whom he had no children. It seemed nothing could disturb the harmony of that home, to which Bura brought everyday cheer. Contrary to Serbian customs, his mother didn't quarrel with her daughter-in-law, and both of them loved Bura. But then typhus moved into the journalist's house. First his mother came down with the disease and very soon died. She was buried the same day as Bura's column fielded the pieces "The Nightmares of Herr Schwarz, Administrator of Belgrade" and "Arbod the Clerk Protects Skadarska Street". Bura didn't descend into sadness because of his mother. 'She was old—as long as she had a good death,' he said to himself, still cheerful in spite of the loss.

But two weeks later, Bura's wife also fell ill. She had a raging fever and her once pearl-like teeth were covered in a black scum. She suffered greatly and in the end just sank into the pillow and directed her last glance towards her husband. She was buried the same day as the popular journalist's pieces "With Russia Behind Us" and "The Waiter From Café Macedonia" went to press. Bura stood by the shallow grave, which the undertakers had scarcely managed to scrape, and burst into tears. He wept bitterly as if he had been abandoned—as if he was his wife's son, not her husband. He returned home and thought that his innate cheer would see him through, but the empty house where every step echoed made something in Bura snap.

His colleagues didn't perceive any change at first. He skilfully hid his intentions and outwardly remained the 'cheerful Bura' they knew, and he edited the "While They Were Here" column for a little longer. But after a while the people around him began to notice he was changing from the good-natured shrimp of a man into a rude and ambitious journalist quite unlike his former self.

He soon demanded of the editor-in-chief that he be promoted, and he laid claim to the editorial column. He said he had made a name for himself through his regular column and now wanted to follow the adversities of the enemy: hunger, contagions and fiscal ruin. The editor had no objections. Moreover, he took to the idea immediately: an embittered journalist was just the right person to chart the enemy's woes. That is how Bura was promoted to editorial writer. From that day on, he went to the quay on the River Sava every morning and was given the imperial and royal press of the 'k and k' monarchy from lads who reeked of coal dust from the holds of barges. They only ever exchanged a few quick words, but not because it was still so cold in Belgrade. A mild change had come from the south and wet snow now fell on the bare heads of the couriers. Bura and his informants were in haste: the boys because they were risking their lives by delivering him newspapers in German and Hungarian, and Bura because he found no time to be affable towards them. He paid them and took the papers without a single word and without the slightest sign of mirth on his once jolly face.

Afterwards, he wrote about things he hadn't read in the enemy's papers: that Germany was on the verge of bankruptcy, that famine was ravaging the villages in northern Hungary, and that desertion from the Austrian army in the east had reached such proportions that Russia would soon be sending trainloads of Serbs to Serbia. The editor became very fond of Bura and considered that life's adversities had steeled him into being a great journalist. But he misjudged his jolly editorialist.

Bura was in fact greatly upset and despondent to the point of despair that not one Serbian newspaper was saying a word about the typhus epidemic which had cut down his family. He devised a little intrigue and executed it audaciously in his front-page editorial in *Politika*. He heard that cholera had broken out in Austria-Hungary and proposed to report on it regularly. Needless to say, the proposal was accepted without opposition, just as the counter-proposals about reporting on typhus in Serbia had been rejected out of hand. 'Cholera' thus became the most common word on the front page of *Politika* in early January 1915, but in Bura's pieces it was really just another name for typhus. And so the once merry Bura, who used to speak in confidence with the oxen at the railway station, devised his own plan. He had constant access to the secret figures about typhus in Serbia and devised a way of publishing them.

He looked at the list of counties in Croatia, which was part of the Dual Monarchy, and paired up each of them with a Serbian district. The county of Syrmia in Croatia played the role of the Morava district in Serbia, the county of Pozhega was actually the Levach district, Karlovac county corresponded to Machva district, Sisak county to Shumadiya, and so on. Zagreb, of course, represented the Serbian capital Belgrade. The main city of each county was then given a 'twin city' in Serbia, and in this way Bura was able to begin publishing the number of cases and fatalities from the Serbian typhus epidemic on the front page of *Politika*—under the guise of diligently tallying the number of cholera cases in Croatia. Now he just needed to make his 'code book' public. He was preoccupied with the idea of producing an anonymous leaflet, but he abandoned the idea because he knew he would quickly be caught, and there was no need for that. Several of his most vocal colleagues spread the story by word of mouth, and now all readers could easily inform themselves about the 'illicit' typhus situation in Serbia.

People from the Morava district followed the 'cholera situation' in the Croatian county of Syrmia. If they had relatives in Chachak, they looked to see how many 'cholera cases' there were in the Croatian regional centre of Tovarnik, and if they were interested in Ivanjica, they kept an eye on the figures which *Politika* published for the town of Shid in eastern Croatia. Belgraders were well informed thanks to the details on the "development of cholera in Zagreb", so it is easy to see how this trickery managed to go undiscovered for months. Neither politicians nor journalists had an ear for the people who bought *Politika* and repeated 'God bless you, Bura'. Secret agents were dispatched but failed to find a lead, so 'Bura's bulletin' was able to come out for another ten days, up until the moment when the journalist himself started to feel the first signs of typhus. First he felt exhausted, then he lost his appetite. That didn't worry him in the beginning because, small and thin as he was, he hardly ate anyway. But then Bura began to get drowsy. He came in with puffy cheeks and dark circles under his eyes and published his bulletin for the day, which he considered a crucial task. The editor suggested he take a few days off, but Bura declined. He started to feel a pain in his limbs and then, just as he was finishing the list for the next day with his last strength, the number of "cholera victims in Zagreb" rose from 1,512 to 1,513.

The 1,513th victim of typhus in Belgrade was a journalist, the formerly merry fellow with his trademark broken, black umbrella, Pera Stanisavlevich Bura. His death meant the abrupt end of the bulletins on cholera in Austria-Hungary, but for a long time readers retold strange stories about 'Bura's code book', whose secret neither amateur informers nor professional Belgrade spies had been able to crack. That is how the Great War ended for the 1,513th victim of typhus in Belgrade on 16 January 1915, by the old calendar.

The Great War ended that same day for one apprentice in the distant Caucasus, but his guardian, Effendi Mehmed Yıldız, would not find out until later, the day a large fire broke out in Istanbul's Emirgân neighbourhood. It was fated that the trader hear bad news during the fire. Fires were an inseparable part of the five-century history of Istanbul and the people of the city always had to be prepared for their wooden houses by the Bosporus and all their property to fall prey to the flames. In spite of that, or maybe precisely for that reason, fires remained an unavoidable fact of social life, and when a fire broke out hundreds of closet pyromaniacs—children, women, the idle and the elderly, and even pashas—gathered to watch the sparks flying into sky and to catch a whiff of the pungent smoke wafting to their nostrils from the charred beech-wood.

It was the beginning of February 1915 when the paint factory caught fire. The effendi heard about the blaze shortly after evening prayer, so he too, the old Istanbuler, rushed to see the red and blue flames licking the sky above the roof of the factory. He ran to the quay to grab onto a departing barge, and soon he was on the opposite side of the Golden Horn. A crowd quickly gathered in the lanes leading to the factory. The agitation of the throng, which stared at the fire and flames as they devoured the adjoining wooden houses, did not bring a tear to the trader's eye or draw a sigh from his mouth. The acquiescence with fate and the Turkish acceptance of whatever befell one in life, overcame him.. But then a distant acquaintance worked his way up to Yıldız through the crowd. Whether he was a business partner or a rival, a man of note or a good-for-nothing—he couldn't remember.

'Yıldız Effendi, you're sure to have heard of the collapse of our army in the Caucasus,' the man said to him. It was a fitting moment to say such a thing. No one would have dared to utter such words in the street under normal circumstances because every Turk seemed to have a constant 'companion', be he in the café or talking shop, on the square or in his own neighbourhood. That fellow was usually moustachioed, stocky and inconspicuous; he listened to the musicians, drank soda water without ordering coffee, strolled along past the shops or tested overripe fruit with his fingers, while in fact he was following everyone and listened to everything. Yıldız Effendi also informed himself about matters in silence, without exchanging thoughts with anyone, just as he had learnt to read between the lines when perusing his *Tanin*. He had been overjoyed when he heard of the victory at Miyandul and the capture of almost the entire region of Azerbaijan, but the fortunes of war had turned against the Turkish cause. The Russian army had pushed back the Turkish forces—that could be seen in the phrases "retreating to more secure positions" and "relinquishing the strategically superfluous Azerbaijani bases". Then came the most terrible day for the Caucasus army: the Battle of Karaguy, and one day later the engagement at Ostip.

No one had been killed; the Turkish side had hardly suffered any casualties at all—that was what his *Tanin* said, but on the streets people were beginning to jostle and pass one another pieces of paper with the names of the dead. No one had yet come up to him, but the effendi was painfully aware that he had someone close to his heart in the Caucasus. He tried to turn his mind from it. As people in the Orient know, rumours are like flighty dancers. They come swirling up to everyone who has to be told good news, and they are borne on an even faster storm when there is bad news to be conveyed. That is why he usually retired to his red-felt-covered stool, and when he went to watch the blaze at the paint factory in Emirgân it was like going to meet his fate.

That stranger came up to him and said loudly: 'Yıldız Effendi, you're sure to have heard that your apprentice Şefket was killed at the Battle of Ostip in the Caucasus. Russian Cossack cavalry cut down three hundred of our fleeing infantrymen. They caught up with him and chopped him in half as he ran, from shoulder to groin. They say that his separate halves went on hopping by themselves for another ten metres before they both sagged and sank to the ground.' Once he had spoken these words, the stranger vanished back into the crowd. Who was he? How could it be that a random person watching a fire at a paint factory brought him such news, like a walking bulletin from military headquarters? But Yıldız Effendi barely thought about it. Spreading news like this was typical of wartime Turkey. He didn't even think about having heard the rumour from that obscure man, of whose face he had only seen one eye, with a scar on his right brow and a lock of black hair. No, it had been the ethereal herald, that singer beloved of Allah, who in the shape of a virgin with fluttering veils brought bad news faster than good. She had chosen a stranger to speak and convey to him what had to be said.

Şefket, his black-haired apprentice who used to dispel their weariness with a song in the evenings, was dead. Yıldız Effendi didn't think of checking the news; there was no one to ask. The news had reached him and he could be sure it was true. He simply stood there, without bursting into tears, and after a few moments he turned and went back to the shop. He thought of the words he should use to deliver the news to Şefket's father but then realized that Allah's Pheme was sure to have made it to all who were dear to Şefket on her rounds of Istanbul that night, so there was no need for him to wear down the soles of his shoes and interfere in her herald work, as bitter as wormwood. Şefket's father certainly knew by now, as did Şefket's red-headed brother now stationed in Thrace, who had cheated so adroitly at the scales before the war. The eight-year-old brother who had been sent to Yıldız Effendi as a replacement for the two robust apprentices under arms also knew everything. Everyone knew. Şefket was dead. And to think he had died so shamefully, like a wild animal cut in half by a Cossack sabre out in some God-forsaken steppe.

The city of Ostip didn't know that one part of the old spice trader died that night. Four of his assistants were still in the Great War, and he fervently prayed to the Saviour for their redemption, now that he could only beg that dear Şefket enter the Garden of Heaven. The next morning, however, everything in the trader's life was the same again: the way it should and must be. His alarm clock rang. He got up. He caught the tram to the Aya Sofya. After prayers, he walked down the hill. He gave a whistle by the thick walls of the palace to see if one of the Padishah's olive-green nightingales would pop out its head, and then he opened up the shop. He laid down the prices for the day and began to call them out and haggle boldly as if that one part of him hadn't been snuffed out. He was surprised at himself for a moment and thought the alarm clock must be to blame: it rang every morning and announced the day which had to happen.

The inexorable new day was also announced by one rather unusual alarm clock: it rang at the French positions at exactly ten o'clock every morning and soon became the subject of comprehensive study by the German command. Its regular ringing in the French trenches north-east of Vic-sur-Aisne began shortly after the brief celebration of New Year's Eve 1915. At first, the German officers thought the alarm clock was announcing something: an artillery barrage, an infantry charge or flares, but it was hard to establish its purpose because it rang at ten in the morning on days when there was movement on the French side and on also days when there wasn't.

That should have been reason enough to put aside this eccentricity of trench warfare but, the army being the army, it began to spin yarns about the French alarm clock. To begin with, rumours spread that every ringing portended the death of at least one German soldier, which could have been true almost every day despite it being relatively quiet on that part of the front; later, word spread down the trenches that the alarm clock was meant to disable German weapons; finally, the alarm clock was reputed to be the cause of disease among the troops and even delays in the delivery of food. In order to prevent this, sergeants spoke with captains, who in turn approached company, battalion and brigade commanders. 'The case of the alarm clock' even came to the attention of the corps commander, but no action was taken.

Then the soldiers in the German trenches came up with an idea. They ordered a small company of alarm clocks from home, and their pugnacious Prussian wives sent them little wooden cuckoo clocks. The men suspended the clocks from the beams supporting the sides of the trenches so their pendulums could move freely and keep their mechanisms working. The cuckoos were 'throttled' every hour on the hour by holding shut the clocks' little trapdoors. Only at ten in the morning were they all allowed to cuckoo in chorus from the German lines. This bit of tit-for-tat could not disconcert the robust French alarm clock, whose ringing overwhelmed the choir of German cuckoos and thrust the kaiser's soldiers even deeper into misery.

Four hundred kilometres further west, on the same Western Front, no one thought of winding up an alarm clock. At the positions near the French town of Avion, everyone was still talking about the first wartime opera which had ended in the death of the great baritone Edwin McDermott from Edinburgh, and about Hans-Dieter Huis, who had sung so beautifully from the German side, and about a Christmas Eve when all men became brothers who could no longer shoot at each other. Other German soldiers were now facing the Scottish 92nd Division and the French 26th Brigade, sniping at them with clenched teeth and a hostile gaze whenever they stuck their heads up over the top of the trench.

New Year's Eve near Avion had led to a real flurry of investigations on both sides. Never before had so many generals converged on a simple French property. Soldiers of all three armies were accused of high treason for having gathered beneath Father Donovan's cross on Christmas Eve. Arrests followed, and ultimately executions. Father Donovan was also put on the list of those to be shot, but in 1915 no one yet dared to execute a priest for high treason, so the chaplain was pardoned.

Both warring sides realized that the soldiers who had knelt together beneath the cross would not be able to fire at each other any more. Everyone was therefore waiting to see which side would be first to relocate those men. After two days of hesitation, the Germans made a move: the soldiers of the 93rd Division were transferred in livestock wagons to the east, to the future slaughterhouse by the Masurian Lakes. Other Germans now came up to face the Scottish and French troops and began to hate them with a vengeance, when they heard what had happened. That ire satisfied the generals, who were chauffeured back to their headquarters in high-roofed black automobiles.

Everything seemed to return to normal at the front near Avion. Flares burst in the night sky like sinister fireworks, German artillery pounded the allied positions from a nearby coppice, and long-range French 75mm guns never neglected to reply. On 5 February 1915, the order was given for the assault. Although the French artillery had pummelled the enemy positions for three days, the Fritzes surprised everyone by meeting the attackers with a steady hail of fire. The Scottish soldiers quickly withdrew. The more lightly wounded managed to roll their way back to the trench, while those further away quickly stopped groaning and fine snow began to cover them like a shroud. Night fell, but Father Donovan couldn't get to sleep. Later, long after midnight, he talked with a wounded man who was crying for help out in no man's land. Why did he talk with him instead of helping straight away? Why didn't he haul him into the trench? British precision was the reason. Scottish regiments, like all others in the British army, were equipped with hooked poles six ells (twelve feet) long, for hauling wounded men from no man's land. It was considered that longer poles would break and also that dragging men further than six ells would cause such severe bleeding that hauling them back into the trench was pointless.

That is why Father Donovan had a hooked pole of six ells beside him that night. Not an inch longer.

The young man who was moaning so frightfully and begging for help was about ten ells away.

This is the conversation which took place between the pastor and his lamb that night.

'Father Donovan, I'm going to die! My right side hurts terribly. I'm holding my hand against it so it doesn't bleed. Help me. Help me, by God.'

'Grab hold of the pole, my son. I'm flinging it to you. There, can you see it?'

'It's so dark, Father. I'm dying. I can't see a thing.'

'Wait for a flare... there's one, hear it hiss. Can you see the pole now?'

'Aye, Father, but I can't reach it. It's too far—a good four ells. Damn Sassenach measurements! Why does a pole have to be just six ells long?'

'Take it slowly, my son, It's only four ells away. That's nothing.'

'I can't, Father, I'm bleeding. I'm leaking all over the place. All I can see is mist, and my head is spinning. Help me, Father, you're our pastor and there's no other God except Our Father.'

'Who are you? Tell me something about yourself. You know me, but I don't know you. '

'My name's Hamilton... John Hamilton. I was born in Glasgow in 1893. I'm studying mathematics... I have a brother and a sister. She married away to England. I love the afternoons. What am I talking about? I love the gloaming in Glasgow. I used to be a sportsman. I love the smell of old Chippendale furniture. One little table...'

'Go on, my child.'

'There was a little table I especially loved as a boy. My mother served tea and quince jam on it. I'll never forget the smell of black tea and Mother's hand putting a teaspoon of sweet quince in my mouth. And then dark fell, like this now. But I was a child then, Father. I was healthy, not disfigured like now. Mother laid me in starched bedlinen and stroked my head. Poor Mother, when she hears I've died. Like this.'

'What's your mother's name and her maiden name?'

'Rebecca. Rebecca Sutton.'

'In the name of God the Father, it seems we're related. My name is Donovan Sutton, and your mother must be a distant niece of mine. My son, you mustn't die. We're of the same blood, of the Montgomery clan.'

'Save me then, Father... Uncle, if you can. Find a longer pole or come up out of the trench.'

'I tried that, but a German had me in his sights. He very nearly killed me. '

'I heard the bullet. So what now? We're back at square one. I'm ten ells from the trench, and you have a pole of six.'

'Tell me some more about yourself.'

'I can't, Father. I'm thinking now what a short distance that is for one life. Four ells! Four ells is the length of the bar in Arta pub in Albion Street. The tapman needed just three seconds to push a pint of dark ale to a guest sitting four ells away. And a Scottish vinegar fly—it needs less than a second to fly four ells.'

'That isn't going to get us anywhere, laddy, or bring you any closer to the pole of six ells. Tell me about yourself.'

'What can I say. I was a top student. I was being considered for an assistant's post at the university, but I loved sport. As soon as I finished classes I'd jog to the old sports ground at Hampden Park and practice for football and running. Oh, I was a great sportsman, may God be my witness. I could run a hundred yards in 10.3 seconds. I hoped to surpass the record holders Williams and Kelly, but I couldn't get below ten seconds. Did you know, Father, that a runner needs one hundred and ten steps to run a good hundred-yard dash? One step more and the result will be worse. He needs three steps to run four ells. Three steps, Father Donovan! Just a year ago I would have run that distance in less than a second. One second! And now it hurts so much I can't drag myself to a six-ell pole.'

'Let's talk about sport a bit more. We British invented it, whatever our French allies say. You were a footballer too. Which position did you play?'

'I was... ah, it hurts... I was centre forward.'

'Oho, the one nobody's supposed to see, who's not even supposed to really play, but just taps in the ball.'

'Aye. When they told my trainer I was "nowhere on the pitch" but still scored a goal, he said that if people didn't understand... if they didn't understand the role of centre forward they should watch Chinese ping-pong instead. The centre forward... I can't laugh now... the centre forward is meant to go unseen, to lull the opponents' defence, and then to bite like a snake, or rather to knock the ball into the goal. He doesn't have to do much. He just has to... just has to put that ball in.'

'Come on now, my son, let's score a goal against the Germans.'

'It hurts, damn it hurts.'

'What distance is it easiest to miss the goal from?'

'From the edge of the goal area, Father, from four ells... That's right, it's easiest to miss the goal from just four ells away.'

'I've heard that before, but I can't believe it. How is it possible that he misses from four?'

'The posts and the crossbar are too close. You think: I'll just tap in the ball and Bob's your uncle. But no damn way... pardon me, Father—it's not like that. If you kick the ball properly it sails off over the bar; and if you bother to aim it goes past the post. All you need to do is close your eyes and boot the ball any which way. That's the only way to make it go in.'

'Come on then, we can do that too. Close your eyes and imagine you're in the opponents' box. Don't think about the wound. Push your body like it's that ball. Any old way. If you try and get up properly you'll be too high and the German sniper, who's awake tonight specially for us, will get you; and if you try to aim for the pole I've pushed out you'll miss it in this starless night. You've only got one chance. Let go with the hand that's holding your belly wound, close your eyes, and reach out with both hands.'

'I can't, Father, you're talking to a dead man.'

'Oh yes you can, by all that's holy. Yes you can! The Spartans at Thermopylae were also "dead", and look how many dead Persians there were at the end of the day. I'll sing a hymn to the Lord, and you dig your nails into the ground. Remember the motto of the Montgomerys: *Garde bien*! The night is dark. Crawl straight ahead, not to the left or right. Come on, my son, that's it: That's your blood, I can smell it, but you still have enough to live, and you're young: That's it. O Scottish centre forward, the enemy can't see you, and you're netting us a goal. Come on... great is our *Eaglais na h-Alba*, great is our church, and great is our God. Push, my son... grab the pole. That's it. Now hold on, I'm pulling you. Forget about the bloody trail you're leaving. All your blood will come back. You'll be prized and praised for every drop of it. Pipers awake! Medics, to me! We've got a wounded man here. You're alive, my son. You'll shoot goals against German teams when this terrible war is over!'

Suffice to say that only this 'Pipers awake! Medics, to me!' went down in history. The whole preceding conversation remained between Father

Donovan and his distant relative John Hamilton; but one wounded man was saved. Many others didn't survive the night between 5 and 6 February 1915, but the generals in the rear seemed not to care about the casualties. The commanders-in-chief leaned over their topographic maps of the fronts, and they showed only elevations, lines and little crosses which didn't multiply the lives of the soldiers on the ground, but took them away. Twenty-six soldiers were killed near Avion that night. Nineteen were mortally wounded and died where they fell. Seven died of their wounds fifty ells and more from the Scottish trenches. Only one wounded man ten ells away was saved, but Hans-Dieter Huis knew nothing about that.

Huis returned to Berlin, a city now filled with the intoxicating aroma of disinfectant mixed with the persistent smell of coagulated blood. His favourite street, Unter den Linden, was deserted, just as the soul of the great singer lay forsaken, now forever. He was determined never to sing again, regardless of the pressure on him and despite all expectations. Some knew what had happened to him in northern France, others didn't. But no one was prepared to excuse his weakness, because that was the easiest way of concealing one's own. They tolerated his silence for two days, no longer, and then he was ordered to the Ministry of War. He was received by an aged general with a monumental, silver Kaiser Wilhelm moustache, who had most probably fought in the Franco-Prussian War.

'Perhaps you do not appreciate that our country is experiencing a tragic lack of the saltpetre needed for producing gunpowder,' the tall, aged officer began his speech, which remained unintelligible to Huis. 'We used to import saltpetre from Scandinavia, in case you didn't know, but the enemy has now closed the marine supply route. You are also perhaps unaware that this country lacks sufficient supplies of copper, lead, zinc and foodstuffs. You have probably heard of the order to economize on rubber and only to use cars in cases of emergency. But that is no concern of yours. You, maestro, are withholding from this country what it needs as much as copper and saltpetre. You refuse to give it song. Why did you reject the planned tour of Poland?'

Only towards the end of this speech did Huis realize what the man was getting at, although the connection between saltpetre and his voice seemed tenuous. He thought of lying and using his sick throat and weak health as a pretext, but then he remembered the two old Frenchmen penned up in the cellar and it became clear to him once more that civilization would be forever lost after the Great War, and that in the end even his audiences would be gone. Why then lie?

'Mr... General, sir, I can't sing any more. I had an experience, something not worth relating, which took the voice from my throat and the breath from my lungs. I am an artist.'

'An artist? You're not an artist —' shouted the nervous mouth beneath the silver moustache, 'you're a soldier, Huis!'

It annoyed the maestro to be addressed only by his surname, as if he was being interrogated, but he had no intention of giving in.

'I've told you, General sir, and I'll say it again: my throat no longer obeys me. I try to sing, but only a wheeze comes out. When I can sing again, you and my audiences will be the first to know.'

Night was falling. The evening star stood out in the clear winter sky above the Berlin plain when the great pre-war baritone Hans-Dieter Huis came out onto Friedrichstrasse. There he was surprised by a sight he hadn't attached any importance to before: all around him were women. Women worked on the trams and drove cars, women wheeled carts and swept the streets, and women smiled as they stood at the entrances of empty pubs. He was in an unfamiliar female world, he thought, like the last man who couldn't fight, because his only weapon—his fine voice—had failed him.

The Great War was over for him. He would withdraw into the provinces in the north, to his parents' city of L. on the Baltic coast, like he did when he was a child. He could start all over again and teach young people to sing and prepare them for the new world, if there was going to be one.

'There will be no more wartime performances,' he said to himself as he put his hat on, but he was mistaken.

THE MAN WHO DID EVERYTHING TWICE

His name was Wilhelm Albert Wlodzimierz Apolinary de Kostrowicki and he had eyelashes the shape of commas. He was the *enfant terrible* of the Paris art scene; no one could drink as much at Old Libion's Rotonde or knock back as many glasses at Old Combes's Closerie des Lilas. Or perhaps only Amedeo Modigliani. From this wealth of experience, he wrote the poetry collection *Alcools*. But now Wilhelm Albert Wlodzimierz Apolinary de Kostrowicki wanted to go to war.

As a Polish Italian, he intended to enlist in the Foreign Legion. He set off for Rue Saint-Dominique with a heavy step. It was late afternoon one Tuesday when he got there, , and he was not alone. A crush of sweaty foreigners was besieging the Foreign Legion recruitment office. For Guillaume Apollinaire, the Great War began when he was told that the Legion was already at full strength. What? Didn't the war need every King Ubu who wanted to lose his head for France? But no, the Foreign Legion only took in the number of recruits it required. Afterwards, he went to the army supply office in Temple, for doubting Wlodzimierz wanted to buy a uniform after all. And a gas mask. Everyone's money was good, and they sold him an overcoat, trousers, tunic and a peaked army cap, which he would later turn into a wartime adornment.

He was angry at not being allowed to enlist straight away, and railed against Romain Rolland for 'becoming German'. He went out into the street yelling 'Bloody Boches!' and claimed that the Germans had printed his poems but not paid him a single mark. At the Closerie des Lilas, he no longer drank as much. The price of a glass of pastis rose to six sous. When he left the café he saw young men cursing and swearing at those who they said just 'guzzled for the glorious war'. He wanted to shout to them that he wanted to go to war too, but he swallowed his words. He thought they wouldn't understand him, but certainly not because his French was poor.

A month later he wanted to clarify a few things and went down to the district offices. He claimed he loved France. The bureaucracy saw that differently. He was born in Rome and his mother was of Polish extraction. Why such an awkwardly long name? Wlodzimierz might be a fine name, but who had a name like that in Poland? Did he know a single other Wlodzimierz? He didn't. Perhaps he had invented it. But Albert was just fine. After all, the courageous Belgian king was called Albert. Apolinary, in turn, sounded more like the name of a dog to them. But his first name Wilhelm aroused the greatest suspicion. Wasn't that the name of the German kaiser? The circumstances required that everything be given careful consideration.

Apolinary therefore went to Nice. The Mediterranean sun shone there and knew nothing of the war in the north. And the traitorous sun would warm his treacherous evasion of the war. In those days, the poet forgot his pre-war muse, Marie Laurencin. She had left for Spain without a word, neglecting even to return her ring. Talk about faithless! It transpired that she had actually eloped with a so-called painter, Otto von Wätjen, and married him six weeks later. So now the poet sought a new sweetheart. Desperately. On the train from Marseille he saw a candidate—a beauty with long eyelashes which cast shadows on her rainbow-coloured eyes. But at the station their paths diverged, and they separated.

The choice then fell on Louise de Coligny-Châtillon. She asked him to call her Lou. He asked her to call him Gui. Lou pretended to be a nurse, he a volunteer in the Great War. She was really just an ordinary floozie: her every gaze exuded lust, like a bayonet glinting atop every rifle, and he was already her 'life-long servant'. He wanted a relationship to the limit. He demanded nine days of wild copulation. She wanted something more distanced. More platonic. For nine days they went to 'Chinese' opium dens together, run by refugees who tried desperately to play the part of orientals, since Chinese people were in short supply. The opium pipe was lit and they were laid down on the couch. They blew out puffs of smoke. Artificial paradises, like cemeteries of broken hopes, descended on their eyes. Then on their limbs; and finally penetrated to the bone.

Lou and Gui. They smoked opium. They made love. With abandon. Nine days and nine nights.

A few weeks later, the recruitment office called for the would-be soldier Wilhelm Albert Wlodzimierz Apolinary de Kostrowicki. They sent him to Nîmes for training although the origins of his names had still not been unravelled. 1914 had gnawed away a whole generation, and in 1915 the Foreign Legion needed even those called Wilhelm. Apolinary quickly became accustomed to barrack life. He learnt to ride, and his arse ached from the saddle. He suffered from diarrhoea. Being penniless was difficult, but he didn't complain about becoming a candidate for non-commissioned officer. All he really missed, more and more, were those nine days. And nine nights. He wanted Lou. He wrote her shameless letters, reminding her that they had made love in the 69 position from the *Kama Sutra*. He asked her to be bawdy in her letters too and demanded that she pluck out a few of her pubic hairs and send them to him. At first she refused. He insisted again. When the letter with the hairs finally arrived, Gui froze. The hairs lay in the folds of the paper. He had imagined them in a chaotic mound like the mons pubis; instead, they stuck to a blot of blue ink in the middle of the paper, and right at the words 'I only want you' they had formed themselves into a cross. They were undoubtedly Lou's pubic hairs: they smelt of those nine days. And nine nights. But they were flattened and clung together to form a cross. Like on a tombstone. There was nothing for it—the poet broke up with Lou. He didn't want her to be his grave-digger. Now Guillaume Apollinaire was looking for a new sweetheart.

On the other side of the front, amongst the German soldiers, many also dreamed of their sweethearts. Stefan Holm's unit was transferred in livestock wagons to the Eastern Front to fill the gaps in the thinned ranks of the relatively new German 9th Army. As soon as they arrived near the army positions in East Prussia, they were met by the northern-European winter. The mercury fell to more than thirty below zero, and many soldiers got rid of their lice and bedbugs simply by shivering for two hours in the icy air. Then they would comb out their scurf and pick the frozen vermin out of their pants. In the town of Braunsberg, where Stefan's unit rested in the building of the local lyceum, he found a button in his pocket which had belonged to Stanislaw Witkiewicz, the unfortunate Pole whom he had had to tie up and drive out in front of him, exposing him to the 'friendly fire' of the French in a futile attack in 1914. He burst into tears when he saw it, remembering vividly the moment when it had fallen off. He also recalled that he had promised to sew it on for him as soon as he found a piece of thread and a needle. But he found neither thread nor needle. The whistle blew. The order came, and any recalcitrance was punished by firing squad.

Holm was later decorated with the Iron Cross, 2nd Class. Oh, what an irony that he now wore it, with ostensible pride, on the left breast of his coat. Yet the problem of the button remained, and he decided to keep it for a few more days. Then they were transferred to positions east of the Masurian Lakes. They weren't told anything, but the soldiers knew a great battle was brewing because several days of complete silence ensued and stocks of food kept arriving for them. Like the others, Stefan had nothing to do while they waited for the fighting to begin. And so he thought about what to do with the button. Then he had an idea: he would sew it on exactly where the Iron Cross was pinned, but from the inside. The button would thus be the metaphysical basis for the cross, the foundation for the medal to stand forth—the medal they had both received when they were tied together like Plato's two halves of one being. And so he began to ask up and down the trench, for a needle and thread but his rather rough-hewn comrades laughed in his face, coughing between two drags of a cigarette. One soldier from Frankfurt finally produced a little sewing set, which his mother had packed for him and now he gave Stefan a threaded needle as if he was secretly handing him a loaded gun. Stefan then found himself a quiet spot and, in the same place as the cross, but on the inside, sewed on Witkiewicz's brass button with the emblem of the French Republic. It chafed him at first, but he got used to it. Now his dear Polish friend was with him again. But he didn't have long to ponder the button and the cross being reunited because on 8 February 1915 the second, winter Battle of the Masurian Lakes began.

Biale Lake, long Augustów Lake and hundreds of smaller ones would soon witness something their waters had never seen. Despite the extreme cold, the German 8th Army under the command of Otto von Below began a surprise attack in the middle of a snowstorm on 8 February. The offensive headed towards the gorges of Wylkowyszki and Elk. The Russians suffered heavy casualties and retreated one hundred and twenty kilometres, with the greatest losses being sustained by the Russian 20th Corps. In the forests near Augustów Lake, the German 10th Army encircled almost one hundred thousand Russian soldiers who were under the command of General Bulgakov.

Although the thermometer read minus thirty-eight, the Russians' defence did not flag. But soon the only road from Sierpc to Plock was cut off and hunger visited itself upon the Russian 20th Corps. First they ate up the stocks of food, then they caught all the little animals they could find in the forest, and in the end they searched for moles' burrows opened up by shelling; they pulled out the little critters, skinned them and ate them alive before they went cold and stiff. On the tenth day of the encirclement, the soldiers peeled bark off trees for want of food. The ground was all churned up but there was no more food to be found. The steely sky brought no salvation; a distant, hazy sun topped with a cap of blue seemed to be laughing at the Russian troops caught in this pocket . None of them knew that their impending defeat was being covered up; they didn't hear the Prime Minister, Ivan Goremykin, who declared in the Duma to shouts of 'hurrah' three days after the encirclement: 'Now that the favourable outcome of the war is becoming ever clearer, nothing more can shake the Russian people's deep faith in final victory. Our heroic army is stronger than ever before, in spite of its losses.' If anyone had bothered to ask the heroic 20th Corps out in the Polish forests to verify the Prime Minister's last sentence, the men would only have agreed that the losses were greater than ever before. It became colder by the day, and in the second week of the siege many a soldier began to think seriously about cannibalism. And maybe the men really would have begun eating their dead comrades if they hadn't been beaten to the frozen corpses by half-savage dogs from the thickets of the forest, which echoed at night to terrible, endless concerts of barking and howling.

Several days before the final collapse, one common soldier decided to arrange a feast with his comrades of 12th Platoon, despite the adverse conditions. The Great War had begun for Boris Dmitrievich Rizanov when he left home with his kitbag and took along his favourite book, *Satyricon*, by the liberated Roman slave Petronius Arbiter. It was no coincidence that Rizanov had this particular book with him. In his life before the Great War, when he himself had felt the fear mixed with determination of the masses on Nevsky Prospekt, Boris had studied classics. He could quote Sophocles and knew by heart the closing words spoken by Socrates at his trial, an hour before he drank the black milk of hemlock in front of his students. Shortly before the beginning of the Great War, Boris read 'Trimalchio's Banquet' from *Satyricon* in Latin and decided he would translate it. That is why he took it along with him, hoping for free time between occasional marches and taking pot-shots at a distant enemy. But he didn't have any free time, for there was plenty of marching, shooting and slaughtering of the enemy. Soon he told himself he had become a butcher and stopped being a philologist.

He would use both his philological inclinations and his aptitude as a butcher to put on a real Trimalchio's feast in northern Europe, just one day before the final collapse of the Russian pocket by the Masurian Lakes. Before he launched into the role of rich Trimalchio, Rizanov, like a proper patrician, invited his starving comrades and their officers to be his guests. To introduce them to the idea, he hurriedly translated and read out aloud a part of Petronius' work: "'A brilliant feast,' we all cheered and cried, and servants came and draped our couches with special covers, each embroidered from end to end with hunting scenes—nets, and beaters with spears lying in ambush. Then came servants with a tray, on which we saw a wild sow of enormous size, and from her tusks hung two baskets woven from palm leaves: one filled with sweet Syrian dates, the other holding dry Egyptian dates. The slave who stepped up to carve was a huge fellow with a big beard. He took out his hunting knife and made a savage slash at the sow's flanks. She brought forth roast sucking-pigs, and when in turn the giant slashed open these, dozens of thrushes came fluttering out!"

Boris, it must be said, did not translate Petronius all that faithfully, but it was what came next which most interested his comrades. At the risk of being picked off by a Kraut sniper, Boris Rizanov and two other men had dragged up a huge carcass of a horse from a nearby copse. It had probably died a fortnight earlier, but it was warmed up and then stuffed there in the wood. The roasting of the animal lasted until late at night, and the soldiers broke trees and brought up armfuls and armfuls of black wood for the great fire with a song on their lips. No one knew how that poor draught horse could have survived the soldiers' frenzy for food, but it seemed that Rizanov had kept it buried in the ground, so the raw meat smelt of the Polish earth; not that anyone turned up their nose at it. When the hours of turning and roasting the stuffed beast were over, Boris-Trimalchio stuck something he called a 'liberty cap' on the poor gee-gee's head (although none of his comrades knew what that was) and chose a Russian giant to make a slash at its flanks. The meat smelled a little, but the guests were armed with the best seasoning known—ravenous hunger.

Great was their surprise when out of the horse's belly, as stuffing, there came two scrawny tykes, whose ribs stood out even when they were roasted, and a bitch with limp and wrinkled teats—but that was not all. Relishing the role of Trimalchio, Rizanov had the dogs cut open too. Finely minced meat came out of them, like a mixture made of pluck. In different circumstances and at a different time, everyone would have gazed in wonder, but there by the Masurian Lakes in the early hours of the day when the Russian enclave was about to fall, each man cheered and fell upon the roast. A crowd formed, a crush, and neither Boris nor his giant who cut open the meal were able to share it out in a way worthy of Trimalchio's banquet. The horse stuffed with dogs, which in turn were stuffed with a fine ragout, was seized in a jiffy. Only its large ribs, one bulging eye and the odd bloody stain were left beside the extinguished fire, like the aftermath of a bacchanalia, when someone finally had the courage to ask the great chef what the exquisite pluck had been inside the sinewy bitch and her two mates.

Rizanov dithered for a long time and made excuses, eventually passing it off as a secret recipe. He changed the topic and tried to make everyone laugh. But his friends, who like real Romans had all vomited after the feast from eating so much meat on a empty stomach, did not give up. 'Come on, Boris Dmitrievich,' one of them badgered him, 'tell us what that super-tender meat was in the bitch's belly. Didn't you secretly mince up some moles or polecats, perhaps?' the Russian Trimalchio refused to answer until noon, and just when he felt he was cornered and had to come clean, a German artillery barrage began and ushered in the collapse of the Russian 20th Corps. Bullets whistled like thrushes, and several of the large shells dubbed 'coal boxes' exploded above the improvized patrician court, where the famished Russians had devoured the stuffed horse. It was all over that afternoon. One hundred thousand Russian soldiers surrendered to the Germans, and Boris didn't have to reveal his secret.

In the wooden shed near Königsberg, where the Russian prisoners were first held by the Germans, Boris Dmitrievich thought once or twice more of telling his fellow POWs that they had feasted on their dead comrades, but all the survivors had more pressing things to worry about, and the men who had been at 'Trimalchio's Banquet' cherished its memory so much that the philologist cum butcher saw no reason to spoil their reminiscences, which, after all, are the only things one lives on in captivity.

The sad but heroic fate of the Russian 20th Corps was immediately reported to the commander-in-chief of Russian forces, Grand Duke Nicholas. The duke's tents lay somewhere in the coniferous forests between Grodno and Bialystok, where, rather than quartering in a cosy requisitioned house, he forced himself, his favourite chief of staff General Yanushkevich and most of the senior officers to bivouac even though is was minus thirty degrees. It was here that the generalissimo of the Russian army received daily reports and issued orders to the commanders of the army; he ate in his tent and drank his black tea sweetened with saccharin. He was horribly cold himself, but he didn't want to show his subordinates so much as a single twitch of cold on his face (do not understand this sentence). Instead, he tried to imagine he was in his log-cabin dacha, or rather in the attached Russian bathhouse, pouring a thin stream of water over burning fir logs so that it vaporized to form a pleasant steam to make him sweat. He left his tent every morning, enormous as he was, naked to the waist, and rubbed himself with snow. Then he would sit on a tree stump and stare into the distance. It didn't bother him that it had been minus twenty-five and grew a degree colder every day, going down to minus thirty-eight on 25 February 1915. Only those standing closest could see that he was holding something indiscernible in his hand, gripping it by the handle. The duke tipped it as if he was pouring it drop by drop onto the enamelled, almost dry snow; but what it was remained a mystery even for his closest staff. Then he would smile a vague smile in the direction of the forests where one hundred thousand of his soldiers were trapped, or turn his head and direct his gaze to the north-east as if, from his enormous height as a colossus, his eagle eyes could glimpse the capital far in the distance with the ice-bound delta of the River Neva, the Hermitage, the court and the grand balcony, from which Tsar Nicholas had called out 'hurraaah' six times and roused his people for the Great War.

Then he stood up and went with a heavy sigh to put on his uniform. Something had to be done. One hundred thousand men were trapped, but the Russian armies regrouped and began a counter-offensive in the Osowiec area and on the roads to Przemysl and Plonsk. Every morning, the duke took a 'steam bath' in front of his tent. He sweated at thirty below zero and came out wrapped in a towel. He felt the ritual helped the Russian troops. One day they reported to him that attacks along the left bank of the Vistula had been repulsed, the next, that troops were advancing near Witkowice and south of the River Rawka, and the third, that a major offensive had been stopped in its tracks near Bolinek. Finally, it was reported that the hard nut of the Przemysl fortress had been cracked after withstanding a siege of almost a year, like ancient Troy. Only then did the duke stop bathing out in the gleaming snow, and the harsh winter finally loosened its grip.

This mild change in the weather did not please one general on the opposite warring-side. It annoyed him that the Battle of the Masurian Lakes hadn't been turned into a resounding success for his army, and he was distressed that the ironclad city of Przemysl had fallen.

That general's name was Svetozar Boroevich von Boina. Everything about this officer said he was interested solely in war. Neither his bearing nor his look were suggestive of a spirited man but only an extremely disciplined one. His small, dogged eyes could focus on one spot on his counterpart's face with such icy persistence that all generals and even the emperor himself lowered their gaze before him. Svetozar Boroevich was a descendant of Serbs from the borderlands between Austria-Hungary and the Ottoman Empire, a child of the Banovina Border Regiment, in which his father Adam Boroevich had served. He had been brought up by the army more than by his mother Stana, with the simple and resolute frontiersmen giving him milk from their canteens, and this was bound to make a soldier of him; how could it have been otherwise. He had had a lightning career. In 1905, Boroevich was raised to the Hungarian nobility and bestowed the title 'von Boina'. He had already become a general in the Austro-Hungarian army back in the brilliant nineteenth century. After 'defeating' the units of German Kaiser Wilhelm in joint manoeuvres in Bosnia before the Great War, he was raised to the rank of field marshal.

Svetozar von Boina mixed with many, but few really knew him because he believed that, in the end, a commander must be a loner. Therefore hardly anyone realized that Boina did everything twice. This was perhaps not so strange because two men were joined inside him: an Orthodox heart beat in time with that of an Austrian soldier devoted exclusively to the imperial crown. One Serbian word overpowered the German one in his mind, and a few distant images of his parents' modest house in the border province were incompatible with the sights of the royal court where he usually stayed. Therefore the field marshal had everything in duplicate. He had two orderlies. His staff was never just in one city—he divided his staff officers between two places. So it was that in the Battle of the Masurian Lakes he commanded from two different positions. Boina had two horses, two uniforms, two rows of medals (all imitations, because he always kept the real ones at home) and two pairs of army boots, which he polished in the evenings himself.

What was so strange about this was that Svetozar Boroevich never wore one pair of boots and then the other, never rode both horses, and never wore both uniforms with the same rows of imitation medals. One pair of boots, one horse and one coat were for the other Svetozar who dwelt in the depths of his bitter soul, who could not die and therefore had to live. One horse, one pair of boots and one field marshal's uniform were reserved for him. That other Svetozar, who was actually the first and original Boroevich, was only a phantasm—without frame, feet or the desire to ride—but still had to have everything at his disposal.

He was like that in war, too. It verged on a miracle—as only he knew—that no one had noticed his schizophrenic streak and that it hadn't hindered him in his great career in the service of his country. Boina thought he had simply been lucky. On manoeuvres, he would always have two goals and had to choose between them; he always sent the army in one of two equally good directions at the last minute. It worked like that year after year. His dividedness had been put to the severest test in the previous year of the war when, as commander of the 6th Corps, he was ordered to liberate the besieged fortress of Przemysl.

Why was Przemysl so important? That little town was a symbol of German tenacity and bravery. During the Russian offensive in Galicia, the Russians were victorious in the Battle of Galicia fought near Lviv; they pushed the front back one hundred and sixty kilometres all the way to the Carpathians. Przemysl fortress held out like an island in a Russian sea until 28 September 1914. The defence of the town, which was shaped like an eagle's nest and manned by a hundred thousand penned-up German soldiers, thus became of great importance for the Central Powers. What was more, this 'German Troy' was on the lips of every Austrian and German soldier, and the commander charged with the defence of the city, Hermann Kusmanek, was proudly referred to as 'the German Priam'. That's why it was so important to hold Przemysl and bring up all the forces needed to support the defenders. A people so enamoured of the Classics couldn't afford to allow its Troy to fall.

The enemy was of a different mind. The commander of the Russian 3rd Army, Radko Dimitriev, began the siege of Przemysl on 24 September 1914. Dimitriev did not have enough siege artillery but ordered an attack on the citadel nevertheless, before the Austrians had a chance to relieve Przemysl. For three days, the Russians incessantly attacked that German Troy, like the allied Greek crews of yore, and gained nothing. Forty thousand human lives were sacrificed on the altar.

Then Field Marshal Boroevich was ordered to break through and liberate Przemysl with his Austrian 6th Corps, on the wave of Hindenburg's offensive. The order came from commander-in-chief Hindenburg and, as an orderly soldier, Boroevich took his two sets of staff officers, two horses, two pairs of boots and two coats with him into battle. He didn't now go in two different directions and in two columns because all German roads led to Przemysl. Even so, Boina hesitated. It seemed to him that there were two Przemysls in the same place: the real one and a false one. If he liberated the real one, everything would end triumphantly; but if he liberated the false one the fortunes of war would be a chimera lasting only a week or two. Which route should he take? Naturally, he chose the road from Kraków towards Lviv.

He delivered a savage blow to the enemy, and General Dimitriev withdrew across the River San on 11 October 1914. Boroevich rode into the city like a sultan returning from a triumphant campaign to India. There were neither women nor children in the city, so soldiers took on their roles instead. The streets of Przemysl were strewn with rose petals, and officers threw confetti made of shredded enemy-leaflets from the windows. A large flag was draped from the church steeple to the ringing of all the bells. The horse he rode and the other he led by the reins didn't shy but stepped gracefully like Arab thoroughbreds devoted to the padishah, and Boina smiled. But he thought it was all too beautiful to be true, and soon doubt began to gnaw at him that he had perhaps liberated the wrong Przemysl. The crowds and smiling faces were just figments of his vanity as a general.

And the real Przemysl? It was like an invisible metaphysical essence somewhere beneath the dizzily ebullient, headlessly euphoric city; it suffered and groaned in its transcendence and, all alone, continued to fire away at the real, remorseless enemy. If that was true, the liberation of Przemysl wouldn't last long…

And, to his sorrow, he was right.

Hindenburg was defeated in the Battle of the Vistula River and broke off his thrust towards Warsaw on 31 October 1914. Boroevich therefore withdrew from the River San. The Russian 11th Army under the command of Andrei Selivanov now undertook a second siege of Przemysl. Selivanov did not order frontal attacks on the stubborn, besieged garrison but decided to starve the defenders into submission instead. All the German soldiers sang the glory of that Troy, to no avail, and like Cassandras predicted its repeated liberation.

Boina alone knew that all this was happening because of him. He had liberated the wrong Przemysl, which is why in February 1915, after the indecisive Battle of the Masurian Lakes, he desperately sought permission from superior command to be allowed to liberate the real Przemysl. He emphasized that he knew the difference now and would be able to find the way to the real besieged city, but it was too late. The order to launch a new attack didn't come. Vienna had been warned in a confidential dispatch that the field marshal was on the verge of a nervous breakdown, and so Svetozar Boroevich von Boina, the descendant of the Serbian frontiersmen, was sent on R&R to Bad Gleichenberg, the same spa which the Serbian Field Marshal Radomir Putnik had set off from at the beginning of the Great War. Putnik had left the spa with only one uniform and coat. They allowed Boina to bring along everything of his: two adjutants, two horses, two coats and two pairs of shiny, spick-and-span high boots. *Omnia mea mecum porto*, the field marshal said to himself when he saw he had everything together, and still he set off for the spa reluctantly.

Omnia mea mecum porto, Sergei Chestukhin also repeated to himself when he took his Liza from the terrible winter of eastern Silesia to the slightly milder but still sub-zero Petrograd. During the Battle of the Masurian Lakes, Lizochka had been hit in the head by shrapnel. She was immediately brought to his wagon and his knife. There was no time to wait for anyone else, and no one could operate on her better than the celebrated Dr Chestukhin. So Sergei shaved his wife's copper hair around the wound, opened the top of the skull and removed the pieces of shrapnel from the soft grey-tissue. He staunched the bleeding, returned the piece of skull as if he was putting back the lid on a child's wooden toy box, and sat down by his wife's bed. When she opened her eyes the colour of sepia and looked at him, there was no man gladder than him; when she spoke, there was no man sadder. None of Liza's vital functions were impaired, but her prattle and choice of words now made her strangely similar to their small daughter Marusya.

The entire staff of the hospital train V.M. Purishkevich gathered to see them off when they left for home. In the house on Runovsky Embankment there was no child happier than Marusya when she saw her mother again, alive. Liza hugged her and completely immersed her in her flowing copper hair. Then she showed Marusya all the presents she had brought from the Front as promised, and the two of them sat in the corner and played like two little sisters. The maid Nastia, aunt Margarita and Sergei regarded them god-like from above, while mother and daughter, now strangely similar, were devoted to each other down to the last little puerile secret.

In his thoughts, Sergei returned to the operation. He opened the top of the skull, staunched the bleeding, removed the fragments of shrapnel, checked all the vital functions of Lizochka's brain, closed the top of the skull, and she woke up like one of his miraculously saved wounded. And then all over again: he opened the roof of Liza's skull etc. Where had he gone wrong? With these thoughts he returned to the front, but without Liza at his side Sergei would never be the same again.

WAR AND THE SEXES

Yekaterina Viktorovna Goshkevich looked like Hera: with her ox-eyes, her enormous 'opera singer' breasts and bulging nipples which stood out even through her blouse and vest, she was hot stuff. Although she had graduated from engineering school, she showed her 'civic spirit' by taking on a job in a Kiev solicitor's office even back in the nineteenth century. Here she was noticed by the placid landowner Butovich, who promptly wedded her. In order for Yekaterina Viktorovna to become his 'Katenka', he had to agree to a number of conditions: that she continue working, stay living in Kiev, and not to have to move to his estates. They therefore lived separately and only saw each other on weekends and went to the occasional performance at the Solovtsov Theatre, and this gave Hera sufficient time to search for her Zeus in the city.

At the Solovtsov Theatre, during a performance of Dostoevsky's *Poor Folk*, she was espied in the second gallery by the Governor-General of Kiev, Vladimir Alexandrovich Sukhomlinov. He was allowing his opera glasses to wander—out of boredom, of course—and when he bent his neck enough he caught sight of her. He noticed her breasts first of all ('Good God!'), then the nipples (again: 'Good God!'), and ultimately the ox-eyed gaze of her blue eyes (once more a drawn-out, whispered 'Good God!'). That was in 1904, or the year after. The governor-general was almost sixty at the time and the solicitor's assistant still in the flower of her youth at thirty, but that didn't stop them from swiftly agreeing. She worked? No problem. Married? Even less. The governor-general cut an imposing figure: his face was bloated like a balloon with a thin, twirled moustache attached, and he had thick reddish eyebrows, which he combed upwards every morning. His deep voice and the smell of black tobacco in his mouth rounded off the picture. He skilfully concealed his hair of the same reddish colour, which now only sprouted around his ears, beneath his hat. All in all, he emanated a sense of danger. Hera had thus found her Kievan Zeus, but just like in Greek mythology the rest of the story didn't go smoothly.

The reclusive landowner Butovich loved his wife and wouldn't let her go quite so easily. Instead, he clenched his teeth and sent her away to his estate in Silka, near Poltava, placing her beneath the watchful eye of a servant. This infuriated the red-headed governor-general, who immediately decided on a 'frontal attack' to liberate Silka, until he was handed a confidential note which smacked of transgression. This upset him so much that he immediately received the Austrian consul Franz Altschuler, who introduced himself as an old friend of Yekaterina's and presented him with a plan. Not every nuisance of a landowner required that one had to 'call in the cavalry', he said. (The governor-general was a cavalry commander and author of several textbooks on the role of cavalry in modern warfare.) A wife could file for divorce, providing there was proof of her husband's infidelity, and it so happened that a French governess, a certain Mademoiselle Gaston, was employed in the Butovichs' household. One simply needed to spread a rumour in Kiev that Mademoiselle Gaston was the landowner's lover, and then the divorce would be a matter of course. And who would spread the rumours? None better than the foreign citizen Altschuler.

The dastardly act was promptly done. All of Kiev turned its opera glasses towards the second gallery—in malicious glee, of course—and looked there for Yekaterina 'Sukhomlinova', as they were already calling her, but the box was empty. When Mademoiselle Gaston heard she was involved in a scandal, she hurriedly packed one little case and fled to Paris. Sukhomlinov and Altschuler sent a shady and very dangerous man on her trail, a certain Dmitri Bogrov, who was not only adept with weapons but also an expert on the Parisian dregs of fallen souls who end up at the Mont de Piété pawnshop. Bogrov's mission was to find Mademoiselle Gaston and offer her a tidy sum, but she surprised everyone by rejecting the money and requesting an official medical examination, which established that she was a virgin.

When Sukhomlinov heard this he didn't know what to do. 'What? a thirty-year-old French woman—a virgin? That's impossible!' he declared. The scandal had already mounted an invisible steed and swiftly ridden to the capital, and the tsar had been informed of everything. What could the cavalry general do other than appeal to the monarch, who for some reason seemed to quite like him? The circumstances, too, required the tsar's judgement. Since the rumours concerned such an important military figure, French diplomacy immediately sided with Mademoiselle Gaston, so there was no choice but for Tsar Nicholas II to quickly cut the Gordian knot. 'Ms Gaston is perhaps a virgin in France, but not in Russia,' he said in his own unmistakable style. That was the signal for the obsequious landowner Butovich to sign Yekaterina Viktorovna's divorce papers right away.

Now she could triumphantly return to her box in the second gallery at the Solovtsov Theatre, and was thereafter always accompanied by her second husband. She never took off her black *chapeau*, and he always wore his fur hat so no one would see the sizeable bald patch atop his knobbly yet seemingly distended skull. It was the anything but tranquil year of 1905, but for them it was one of the loveliest. They moved to the capital and began building a house in the charming neighbourhood near the Church of the Saviour on Spilled Blood, but Mrs Sukhomlinova soon revealed her true, imperious nature as the wife of a general. Not only did the subordinate officers and orderlies now have two superiors, not only did her circle of friends immediately join the general's clique of confidants, and not only did the Austrian consul Franz Altschuler become the dearest dinner guest, but ox-eyed Yekaterina also decided on alterations to the plans for the new house. So it was that madam's boudoir was connected by a door to the general's study where he, as commander-in-chief of the Russian cavalry, received confidential visits; at the same time, a door in the opposite wall of the boudoir connected it to the parlour.

The dastardly act was complete. With much celebration, song and dance, and a jaunt in a beautifully adorned troika-sleigh across the frozen Neva, the Sukhomlinovs moved into their new house in February 1906, and the years of luxury began. Both of them fondly remembered 1909; they visited Capri for the first time in 1911 and also saw Pompeii; in 1912, she received the tsar's permission to attend manoeuvres of Russia's land forces and they almost went so far as to make her a general's uniform of her own, adorned with same row of medals as her husband wore. But people age, even if they do live in the lap of luxury. She developed an ever more massive chest over the years, and he had ever more red hair, albeit only around the ears. Hera softened her nipples with Parisian creams so they wouldn't be so visible; he took on an unkempt look, and before he knew it he had two red horns like a real Zeus. The dearest household friend remained the Austrian Altschuler. The general seemed to love him more than the others, ever since the days when they were involved in that little plot, although he also lauded and extolled the others who had helped him on that occasion.

Altschuler was the most influential of all the envoys of foreign embassies in Petrograd and Tsarskoye Selo. He came to see the Sukhomlinovs on Wednesdays, Fridays and Saturdays one week, and

Mondays, Thursdays and Sundays the next. He became so much at home there that the general felt he could hear his voice even on days he hadn't said he was coming. That happened for the first time when they had just moved into the house. He had received an important military deputation in his study, and Yekaterina was in her boudoir, when he had the distinct impression that he heard Altschuler behind his back somewhere between two of his replies. But what could he do? He became a little nervous, but Hera found a way of stopping Zeus' ears better than Ulysses did for his sailors. She bared her breasts for him, and other voluptuous tracts, put two pillows under her belly, lay on her stomach and let him have fun with her bare bottom. After that, Sukhomlinov kept hearing Altschuler's voice, but he no longer paid any attention to it, and if he did, it was only so as to occasionally see the buttocks of Yekaterina Viktorovna. The envoy therefore continued to visit them unhindered and every time brought presents from Vienna. Whenever the general said: 'How can I ever thank you?' Altschuler replied: 'The debt of gratitude is entirely mine.'

It all went smoothly and completely unimpeded: Altschuler would enter the boudoir through the one door, eavesdrop on what Sukhomlinov was saying through the other, and leave quietly through the first door again, planting a passionate kiss on Yekaterina's pouted lips on the way. Everything went swimmingly until that 'most influential envoy' vanished on the last day of July 1914. Before long, Germany and Austria-Hungary declared war on Russia. Sukhomlinov, the minister of war, cursed Altschuler as a 'Viennese bastard'. At last he would no longer have to hear the tinny drone of his voice, nor accept his tawdry presents, which had never meant much to him anyway. His wife was of a different mind, however, and she no longer even thought of baring her chest and her plump behind for her red-haired goat. Now she herself listened through the boudoir door, slightly ajar, to what her husband said, and then attempted to deliver the information to the Austrians.

Yet the plan was absurd, because she had kept the door ajar all those years out of tenderness, not in order to spy herself, and now, in the middle of the Great War, she didn't know what to listen for, what to sift out and who to report it to. 1915 came, and by now Yekaterina had accumulated a confused mass of information through the door of the boudoir. It didn't occur to her that much of it became 'stale' within just a few days, forgetting her time as an assistant in a solicitor's office. So she was left with the dilemma of what to do with her 'archive'.

Who could she give it to? The embassies of the warring countries were closed, and proper spies naturally avoided working with the ox-eyed general's wife, which further dented her self-esteem.

After defeat in the Battle of the Masurian Lakes was narrowly avoided, hard times came for the minister of war. 'Iron Duke' Nicholas Nikolaevich ordered from the front that Sukhomlinov be replaced as a matter of urgency, and the tsaritsa wrote to the tsar to warn him that Sukhomlinov would be moving against 'Our Friend' (Rasputin), which was one more nail in his coffin. This once powerful and dangerous man was brought down not by an ordinary Petersburg intrigue, however, but by a tip-off which came by circuitous route from the enemy in Vienna. The presumptious 'boudoir spy' Yekaterina Viktorovna had most incautiously begun leaving letters for Altschuler with friends, their friends and their friends' friends, in which she enclosed various lists from the Russian Army supreme command without understanding their worth; that booming espionage drum had to be silenced immediately so that the real Austrian spies on the banks of the Neva would again be able to distinguish reliable information from junk. The denunciation arrived via the double agent Viktor Bedny but was actually sent by a military intelligence officer code-named 'Man of God'.

Not until many years after the war did it come to light that Franz Altschuler was behind that code name. Only a handful knew at the time the affair broke. Sukhomlinov was relieved of his post. A press statement announced the formation of a commission of inquiry "to investigate the former minister's role in supplying the army". General Nikolai Petrov, member of the State Council, was appointed to chair that commission, but that is of no importance for this story. After the fiasco of their joint careers, Zeus Sukhomlinov and Hera Sukhomlinova were... But what does that matter? Perhaps their fate, too, is of no significance in this tale about the war because the masses are only interested in glossy life-stories and days of guillotining. Who cares what happens to a head that falls into the basket and where the decapitated body is carted away to afterwards.

The decapitated body is of course taken to a mortuary, but it was hardly likely that the body of Vladimir Alexandrovich Sukhomlinov would end up on the table of Mehmed Graho in Sarajevo, especially since the case of the Russian minister of war was hushed up and no one touched a single reddish hair on his head around his ears, so for many people it wasn't even a proper story. Neither could the Sarajevo pathologist's last days in 1915 be turned into any kind of story—except perhaps in his own head.

After the crushing defeat of the Austrian army at Mount Suvobor, Graho too hastily withdrew with his staff from the old hospital in Yatagan Mala in Belgrade, where he had settled-in nicely. He returned to Sarajevo and found the first signs of cholera in the population, forcing him to team up with the epidemiologists. The events left him speechless. He became infected himself and died two weeks later. The superstitious would say it was because he used up his year in playing doctor of death. The less credulous would look at the pathologist's last words, which might tell us how he became that so-called doctor of death. But Graho didn't utter any last words. A nurse was the only person nearby. He didn't even manage to wear in the new shoes he had bought on the eve of 1915.

Yet the story of the death of our doctor of death could go something like this, based on the information that remains about the man: the pathologist who was the first to examine the corpse of Archduke Franz Ferdinand and the flaccid body of the Duchess of Hohenberg breathed his last in the midst of a magnificent reverie. Before dying, he fell in love with the nurse caring for him. When the disease was well advanced and his once corpulent, well-fed body began to lose a litre of fluid per hour, Mehmed Graho imagined he was very handsome. He dreamed up a picture of himself and presented himself as such to the attending nurse. On the third day, the skin hung limply from his chest and sides, and his nipples sagged like the udder of a skinny cow. In his imagination, however, Mehmed Graho was ever more good-looking. In a flight of madness between two deliriums he convinced himself that he was irresistible. Why else would the same nurse keep leaning over him so devotedly and wiping his forehead with white gauze?

He died at a moment when the whole room reeked of his excrement, just when he appeared on his inner perceptive horizon as a paragon of manliness, clad like a Syrian prince from the Arabian Nights, and was intent on declaring his love for the nurse. But his words failed and he succumbed. The body bound in his shrivelled, almost parchment-like dry skin was infectious, and the grave-diggers immediately took it to the cemetery in Bare for cremation. All that remained of Mehmed Graho was a pair of broad, orthopaedic shoes and a pocket watch. No one came to claim them because the pathologist had no family. The shoes were given to the Austro-Hungarian Red Cross, and the watch was sent to the front for a soldier to wear.

What became of that pocket watch sent to the Great War is not known, but yet another timepiece, on the Western Front, caused no end of confusion. It was the alarm clock which rang at the French positions near Vic-sur-Aisne at exactly ten o'clock each morning. When even all the cuckoo clocks sent from Prussia were unable to drown it out, one German soldier began calling out to the French across no man's land. He was a student who knew their language. No one dared to lift his head up over top of the trench, so this conversation in murdered French and butchered German lasted for days. But even after that, no one understood why the alarm clock rang, up until the day when a ceasefire was agreed and the wounded had to be collected from everywhere they lay. The student volunteered to leave the trench together with the stretcher-bearers. But, unlike them, he didn't start going up to the frozen bodies of his comrades; he went straight over to see the French. Foreign faces gazed at him with suspicion but bore a remarkable resemblance to his own. Students or grocers, painters or mechanics—all of them now had war imprinted in their eyes and had come to resemble each other like identical twin brothers. But those brothers were there for the business of killing, and only one day was allowed to be different. That day, the German student sought an explanation for the alarm clock ringing at ten o'clock—and found it.

It was so simple that he couldn't believe it at first. The alarm clock sounded because one lieutenant of the French 86th Regiment had promised his wife in the city of Touraine that he would let her know he was still alive by ringing the alarm clock at the same time every day. In return, she wound up another alarm clock so that it rang at the same time to tell her beloved husband she was still true to him. The German soldier returned to his trench and started to laugh. And he laughed long and loud, thinking of all those stories, forebodings and the dozens of Prussian clocks with their belligerent cuckoos. His comrades had to wait quite a while for him to stop his uncontrollable laughter, which almost made him choke, and tell them why the alarm clock rang precisely at ten. The other soldiers didn't find it so funny, especially those who had written to their wives asking for clocks of their own. The alarm clock continued to ring, only now it wasn't an ominous sign in the German trenches but more like a ten o'clock gun firing to give the exact time, and both warring sides long set their watches by the French lieutenant's alarm clock.

No one knows whether the alarm clock in Touraine rang with the same regularity, every day at ten. If someone had walked through the streets and asked the townsfolk if they had heard of the alarm clock, many would probably have said they knew nothing. In those wartime days in Touraine, people spoke a lot more about the war of two lady wine merchants who upheld the fame of their husbands' wineries and supplied the wine for two famous cafés in the capital: the Rotonde and the Closerie des Lilas. Although this war began in Touraine, it didn't actually take its course in this little town where Rabelais and Descartes were born, but in Paris, where two publicans took to the warpath: Old Libion, who ran the artists' hang-out Rotonde, and Old Combes, proprietor of the artists' tavern Closerie des Lilas.

It all began because of bad wine, and as such the 'winery war' started in Touraine. But it would have remained a small, local conflict of two amazonian wine merchants, had not two old men got involved. Victor Libion was proud of his café La Coupole, but he was particularly fond of the Rotonde, which he had set up in 1910 on the corner of the Boulevards du Montparnasse and Raspail. Libion, who was portly and a bit of a boor, bought a hole-in-the-wall café here and turned it into a meeting place for artists. This was where people started their drinking, and before the Great War they also finished it here. Victor Libion never liked competition, so he naturally viewed Old Combes with suspicion. The latter, in turn, didn't like the former and claimed that the 'so-called gentleman' served stale food and sour wine, and that people only went to Old Libion's after they had had a good meal and tanked up at his café. Old Combes didn't conceal that the Rotonde had much greater turnover and that there was infinitely more garbage left there after the guests in the mornings, but he stuck to his story: people came to his place to eat and drink, and then the drunken 'bohemian loafers' went to Libion's, well sloshed, to tell cheery tales which attracted greenhorns from the provinces and transatlantic bumpkins who thought they would become painters as soon as they heard a single joke of Picasso's or joined in a punch-up on the terrace of the Rotonde.

The conflict between the two café owners simmered like this up until the really big fracas broke out, the Great War. Then it seemed both of them would relent because the Rotonde and the Closerie des Lilas would soon run out of guests. But things turned out differently: the vagabonds, cowards, armchair patriots, cripples and draft-exempted were not so disheartened that they stopped going to Old Libion's.

If the truth be known, they became significantly fewer in number and garbage swirled between the empty tables on the terrace of the Rotonde, but the number of guests dropped by half at both cafés, so the proportion remained the same. At least until the day a guest was found dead at the Rotonde.

Just like that, at a table. He hadn't had much to eat and hadn't drunk to excess, Old Libion later claimed. Nor could the proprietor recall him having done anything out of the ordinary. He had been sitting alone. He hadn't started a quarrel with anyone, peed at the table, raved or waited for the opportunity to read out a manifesto. Nor had he spoken with a strange accent when he ordered, although it would later be established that the dead man had been impersonating a poet from Belgium. That wasn't important for the coroner's inquest. He had been exempted from military service, so at first no one suspected the murder could be connected with military espionage. But the deadly-boring fellow was dead, that much was clear, and a murder investigation had to be carried out, war or no war. Therefore the wretch was sent to the mortuary to have the contents of his stomach examined. When the pathologists cut him open, a fountain of coagulated plonk and remnants of undigested food shot out of him like from a wineskin. Wine is wine, they thought at first, but then they discovered traces of hydrochloric acid, and some other less-than-nutritious additives were also present.

That was a good lead for the inquest. Where did Old Libion get the wine from? From Touraine. From whom? From cheerful Madame Marion, whose husband had twice been decorated for bravery in the battles of the Marne and the Aisne. Good, her husband was an innocent hero, but she herself? The winery was immediately closed and Old Libion banned from opening for a week. No one was happier now than Old Combes! That stupid brood of painters and poets, those self-certified geniuses, immediately switched to his Closerie des Lilas, and it seemed clear who was going to come out on top in the war of the café owners. But misfortune is seldom selective: one ordinary day, when Old Combes was just about getting used to the throng, a guest was found dead at a table in his café too. The man hadn't eaten or drunk much, nor was he strange in any way; unsurprisingly, he was an errant genius from Lithuania, actually a Jew by the name of Abraham Safin. The fact of him being a Jew was unimportant for the inquest. He had been exempted from military service, so no link with military matters was seen in his case either. This second man was now taken to the same morgue to be a still life on the neighbouring dissection table. He also received a toe-tag. When they cut him open, bad wine shot out of this poor wretch too. The wine was not taken to be just wine now, since the sample was shown to contain formic acid.

Once again, the trail led to Touraine, namely to a small winery run by Madame Lilly, another very independent woman and wife of war hero, although her husband had been killed in the border battles in the Ardennes. This second winery was closed, too, and Old Combes was also ordered to close his café for a week. You should have seen Old Libion's face now! It had taken two days for a guest to die at the Closerie des Lilas as well, and the upshot was that Old Libion could open his place two days before his rival. He just needed to find another winery. But that wasn't quite so simple because the café owners' war had spread to Touraine, too. Amazonian Madame Marion up and took a bus to Paris to tell Old Libion 'in a friendly way' that she would immediately claim all the money he had been owing her for years if he dared to change wineries. What could the café owner do but give credence to what she said: that her wine was 'as pure as a tear'. They went to the police station together; Marion dressed as a *femme fatale* with a hat topped with feathers, a floor-length black dress with a deep slit, and seductive fishnet stockings. She crossed her legs and then burst into tears. She said that her wine matured in oaken barrels for thirty months, and that she only added as much sugar as the regulations of the Third Republic permitted. They tested the wine on location in Touraine and found nothing suspicious, so business could return to usual at the Rotonde.

It was almost exactly the same with the Closerie des Lilas, except that Old Combes was in the role of Old Libion, of course, and Madame Lily in the role of Madame Marion. They too went to the police station, but in this sketch complete with crying and posing she played the distressed widow, not the *femme fatale*. Nothing unusual was found in her cellars either, so the Closerie des Lilas was reopened. But the two old publicans were cunning and wanted to hedge their bets. Take Old Libion: for all he knew, a guest could go to his rival's café, drink a glass of poisoned wine there, and then call in at his place before the harmful substances began to take effect; he would order a glass and then collapse at the table. Old Combes thought the same, so both café owners introduced subscription cards. Whoever subscribed at Old Libion's could no longer go to Old Combes's. There were, of course, people who tried to get cards for both places, but in vain. There are many times you can go to the left and to the right, but there comes a day when you must choose to go either left or right. That day came, and one thing was clear: whoever now died at Old Libion's would die from his wine only, and anyone who collapsed at Old Combes's would kick the bucket due to his wine alone. Things were tense in Touraine, too. The two amazonic wine merchants almost got into a scuff in the street and accused each other of being 'poisoners'. Each of them continued to deliver wine to Paris, but now they personally accompanied the demijohns and casks all the way from the winery to the capital.

Despite the universal caution, an unpleasant air of suspense prevailed. Which of the two café owners would the next guest die on? As it happened, it was neither. The police exposed a pro-German fanatic who had killed the poet de Gros and the painter Abraham Safin. He had no criminal record and was not known to the police. He said he had poisoned the wine on the way from Touraine to Paris. He held no grudge against the men he had killed, but he wasn't sorry for the two wretches and saw no harm done to art because both of them had been arrogant upstarts. Although a Frenchman, the poisoner was incensed about the French attitude towards the Germans and the Café du Dôme, their former meeting-place, which now gaped empty. He was angry about the disgraceful sale of pictures from the galleries of German collectors and the headlines in the magazine *Paris-Midi*. Irate about all these things, he had intended to carry out poisonings in other cafés too, but fortunately he was caught shortly before all the café owners in Paris introduced passes for their locals and the 'local conflict' of the two café owners grew into a Paris-wide war.

The poisoner was arrested. Our two proprietors tore up their passes. One day, Old Libion visited Old Combes and they clinked glasses with his wine, and the next day Combes returned the visit and tried Libion's vino. They both agreed that their wine was sour and could make for a nasty hangover in the morning but was nothing to die from. The situation simmered down in Touraine too, and no one was happier in the end than the boozers.

And so drink was able to claim many more lives—even that of Jean Cocteau, who at the time was on another spell of leave in Paris. He too had a bite to eat and a glass of wine or two at Old Libion's, but luckily there were none of the 'added acids' in his glass. That was rather unlikely, to tell the truth, because 'the poet of war' did not hang around at the Rotonde all day this time, having been informed that he wouldn't see Picasso there. Besides, this member of the medical corps under the command of Étienne de Beaumont had come to attend to a different matter. Food at the front was poor—that was almost an understatement—and, being his unit's former quartermaster, he was in Paris to go to the canning factory which supplied French troops with the 'Madagascar' cured meat famed among soldiers at the front. He had also heard stories about the cans containing monkey meat instead of beef, but that didn't concern him. He wanted to have something else put in the tins, so he found a way of befriending a seedy girl who was a kind of local orphan-girl of pre-war Montparnasse.

They called her Kiki de Montparnasse, and she was a girl of a woman. She was no stranger to love, even before the Great War, but the three or four freckles on either side of her nose, her cropped black hair and plump, prickly legs made her look like a lustful, virgin schoolgirl holding out for her first man. Kiki wore a men's hat, a patched coat and shoes a few sizes too big for her. Since 1914 she had worked at a factory canning food for soldiers at the front. She had got to know Cocteau before the war in the circles of the painter Chaim Soutine. Now the cavalier with the crimson helmet called on her and reminded her of that cheerful company. Together they recalled the pre-war jokes of the many artists, and the cavalier claimed every single one of them had been his. Did Cocteau like Kiki and therefore woo her? Not at all. Crafty little tarts weren't his sort. He just wanted to use her; and she him.

She was short of money, and he needed better meals because he had begun to feel his ribs again—even through his overcoat. So Cocteau procured Provençal goose-liver pâté, red caviar (he thought it was Russian, but in fact it was Baltic), pinkish crabs (without shell) and other luxury food, which he asked Kiki to conceal and conserve in the familiar 'Madagascar' tins at his expense. It was not a difficult task for her; Kiki operated a canning machine and just needed a few days to sneak in his food and then hand the tins of special rations to the gratified soldier. Cocteau couldn't go back to the front flaunting upper-class titbits, could he? This way it was better camouflaged than any mortar position. Cocteau returned to the war with a whole bundle of tins, and for a long while he secretly relished his stocks of 'monkey meat'. 'Look, that could hardly be beef, could it?' he'd say to his comrades and show them the rosy lobster meat. 'Huh, that's monkey business,' they'd reply, while others would shout: 'No, magpie business!'

Cocteau never found out what magpies had to do with it, but it is a known fact that magpies like to steal shiny objects, and bands of Belgian magpies made off with the shaving mirrors of many soldiers on the Western Front. One 'thieving magpie' got up to similar antics in London. That 'bird' was a stunningly beautiful woman, the vaudeville singer Lilian 'Lilly' Smith. On more than one occasion, she had roused a whole senior officers' mess to sing 'It's a Long Way to Tipperary' with her in unison. Refined and affable, Lilly had polished cheeks like a porcelain doll and sleek, well-groomed black hair gathered up into a bun. Two large eyes with lacquered pupils stood out on her face, but the most captivating thing about her was her self-confident and authoritative mezzo-soprano.

Lilly was rich in wartime terms. The vaudeville shows she performed in earned her a substantial income. She had a soft spot for soldiers of the British Expeditionary Force leaving to be killed on the Continent, so for a slightly reduced fee she gladly accepted invitations to sing at their send-offs, even if part of the agreement was to give one hundred soldiers a 'goodbye kiss' at the end.

Despite being invited to every social event, Lilly led a secluded life in a house in the country with 'Uncle'. This was a bony man, folded in two at the middle like a waiter, with crooked yellow teeth and a monocle on a silver chain. No one knew what Uncle did. No one knew what Lilly actually did. No one knew that her mother was a German and that her real name was Lilian Schmidt, and that Uncle wasn't her uncle but relayed the intelligence collected by Lilly in Britain from Dover to Calais, from where it was forwarded to Germany. No one found out because Lilly was circumspect. She didn't giggle loudly in the company of senior officers; she didn't throw herself at the next best senile general, perhaps a hero of the French-Prussian war, who kissed her hand; she didn't sing 'It's a Long Way to Tipperary' just like that. Like a proper magpie, she sought a man who really shone and found him in Major Lanoe George Hawker, the first commander of the Royal Flying Corps.

In retrospect, everything looked like a real wartime romance. The major went on dangerous missions off the eastern coasts of England and to France, and returned with a whole clutch of information for his sweetheart. Lilian relayed figures, locations, sorties, routes, gross tonnages and the composition of convoys. She worked long hours and had already earned the German Iron Cross, 1st Class, when everything went wrong. The equilateral triangle between her, the major and Uncle was skewed by the appearance of a lover called Scarlet Rose in the major's life. When she discovered this, Magpie couldn't believe she had been supplanted by an ordinary rose, even if this Rose was herself a singer. How could the lass's rustic soprano with uncultivated coloratura compare with the dignified, even patriotic mezzo-soprano of Lilly Smith, she asked herself. There was nothing for it but for Lilly to take revenge and get the major back for at least two reasons: because of her wounded pride as a woman, and because of the professional pride of a spy.

And Lilly probably would have made that first injudicious move of her career, had not members of the British intelligence service knocked on her door. They told her that Scarlet Rose was a German spy whom they had had under observation for a long time. They offered Magpie the opportunity to co-operate and promised her a knighthood if she helped them. Lilly froze, but then quickly composed herself and thought two things: how nice it was that they had found another spy instead of her, and how splendid it would be to be called *Dame Lilian Smith*. So she readily agreed to become a double agent. And the others at a meeting of the small 'wartime staff' (Uncle, Lilly, the gardener and the maid) gave their approval that evening.

Major Lanoe George Hawker now had two wartime sweethearts, two houses and two pairs of attentive ears listening, but with Lilly he seemed to be increasingly perturbed. He was no longer in the mood to talk about battles and didn't tell her about any military plans. They went out like two stuffed owls to the Scott's Arms, and every evening, when he was tanked up, she had to sing 'It's a Long Way to Tipperary' for him. Afterwards the two owls went to bed, but even in his sleep the male bird wouldn't hoot anything.

What conclusion did the seasoned operative Lilian Schmidt come to about this new state of affairs? She knew that real information was not flowing across Scarlet Rose's bed because she knew she wasn't a German spy, obviously, but she seems to have been convinced that real male fluids were nevertheless being spilled there. Therefore she resolved to stand in her way. That was presumably what the British intelligence service expected of her. She told the SIS officers that she was close to getting the major to reveal to her the role of Scarlet Rose, but she already had a plan of her own. This time she didn't share it with her little staff, although she should have. Lilian Schmidt decided to make Scarlet Rose a spy. But how? Persuasion? Recruitment? No, simply by framing her. One evening she went to the Savoy, where Scarlet Rose was singing, and planted her own German code book on her.

Then she made sure that Uncle immediately changed the codes. She informed the SIS men that they would find absolute proof of Scarlet Rose's spying in her possession. All she then had to do was wait. Less than one day later, several high-roofed black automobiles drew up in front of an ordinary country house. The rain poured down on the flat British landscape, and the nervous wipers could hardly clear the water from the glass. Several men in wet bowler hats got out of the cars, but there was no royal envoy between them bringing word of Lilly's knighthood. The first to enter was Major Lanoe George Hawker in his damp dress uniform, which didn't surprise her. After him came the two men from British military intelligence, wet to the skin, and that didn't unsettle her either, but a real surprise was in store for her when behind them—dry, as if there was no deluge outside—the counter-intelligence officer Scarlet Rose strode triumphantly into the sitting room, holding her German code book. Lightning flashed low on the horizon on the way to Hayes, the major's medals gleamed, the code book glinted, Uncle's monocle fell out and cast a gleam on the side of the car—and the career of the 'thieving magpie' was over.

The end of Lilian Smith's successful singing career did not go unnoticed. The management of the Empire Music Hall's variety show first instructed that 'Cancelled' tape be stuck over her posters, followed by 'Singer ill'; finally, without much ado, they just wrote '"Long Way to Tipperary" show dropped from the repertory'. Some English families in their cramped flats on Fulham Road near Edith Grove remembered Lilly Smith with her resonant voice for a while, but she was soon forgotten because people don't remember heroes, let alone singer-spies.

On 11 April 1915, Lilian Schmidt was exchanged for three British spies. On 12 April, Lilly was awarded her Iron Cross.

THE FATHER OF ALL GOTHIC DOCTORS

'Herr Doktor?'

'I was just on the phone to my wife…'

'Herr Doktor, you'll appreciate this is an urgent matter.'

The man who entered the large room where three generals were waiting was Fritz Haber. Dr Fritz Haber. He glanced around and back as if trying to follow the invisible footsteps of someone who had already walked the long way from the tall door to the solid wooden table by the window. Fritz Haber was a small, bald-headed man: his stooped, rheumatic body was crowned by a large head with a skull which would definitely have been of interest to lobotomists. He wore a small, framed lorgnette fastened by a spring to his short, stubby nose. Two broad, tearful eyes looked out from beneath the glasses, concealing a far from delicate gaze.

Fritz Haber was a leading chemist and founder of the Kaiser Wilhelm Institute for Physical Chemistry and Electrochemistry. Haber had once been a Jew, but that is of no significance for this story, although quite a tale could be written about his conversion to Christianity. His place of birth was Wroclaw—or Breslau, as the Germans called it—in Poland. He was born into the family of that city's most prominent textile merchant. His mother died when he was still young, but none of that would be important for this story had Haber not been predestined to be a chemist. Even as a boy, he set up a small laboratory at home. Later he duxed his degree in Heidelberg, topped his postgraduate class at the University of Berlin and became the youngest lecturer at the University of Karlsruhe, only to move back to Berlin in 1911 to found the Kaiser Wilhelm Institute of Chemistry in the capital.

This bent dwarf of a man would not have been able to achieve all this without a devoted wife. Fritz always emphasized that the best decision he made in his life was to marry Clara Immerwahr, a young chemist who sacrificed her career for her husband and was an enthusiastic admirer of his work. They married in 1901 and were very happy together. They were both delighted when their son Hermann came along in 1902. He was a good baby, quiet and accustomed from an early age to the acrid smells from the chemical laboratory, so Clara was always able to be of service to her Fritz. Who stood behind Dr Haber when he announced the Haber-Weiss reaction? Who translated his work from German into English? Who was happiest when Haber and Carl Bosch succeeded in synthesizing ammonia? Who went with him to negotiations at the BASF plant, where the first large, high-pressure reactor was made operational? Clara Immerwahr, of course, the faithful Clara who wrote that a female chemist is happiest when she supports the great work of her chemist husband.

'Herr Doktor?'

The man who entered the large room where three generals were waiting was Fritz Haber. He set off over the creaking parquet with careful steps. His body topped by the large head rocked from side to side. He stared away above the heads of the generals into the Berlin trees he could see through the window. It was the beginning of April, and after the terrible winter of 1915 the trees of the northern German plain were budding and flowering proudly as if spring would efface all the wounds of winter.

'My wife phoned. She was hysterical and didn't know what she was saying.'

'Herr Doktor, you'll appreciate this is a matter of the utmost strategic interest and cannot wait for the recovery of your wife.'

But the Great War came, and Fritz very soon showed the face of an avowed German nationalist. He thought a chemist had to be a soldier and put himself at the service of his nation. He considered it the privilege of an educated soldier to be able to kill hundreds with one blow instead of just a few. His wife was not of the same mind and begged him to stop. But all her imploring was in vain. The moment he showed Clara an ordinary piece of white paper with a simple formula on it in the summer of 1914, Fritz lost his faithful wife who had served him devotedly for thirteen years. It amounted to a farewell message, written not with letters but as a formula, as befitted chemists. Clara read it and understood as quickly as someone reads a parting *Aufwiedersehen*. Fritz's theory simply stated $C \times t = K$. 'C' stood for the concentration of poisonous gas, 't' for the interval of time and 'K' for the constant, the denominator for death.

Dr Haber had established that a lower concentration of deadly gas over a longer time had the same effect as a larger concentration over a short period of exposure. In both cases the only constant, marked 'K', was death. Clara couldn't believe it. She tried one last time to dissuade her husband. She cried. Science must not be put at the service of death but only of life, she appealed. In vain. Fritz just turned his back and took his formula to the general staff. He and his associates in the first German 'gas unit', the future Nobel Prize winners Otto Hahn and Gustav Hertz, needed a year to determine the best mixture of deadly gas. He decided on chlorine, an old chemical friend who had nearly killed him and his family in 1907. Now his job was to incite that 'old friend' to become a merciless killer.

He didn't want to stop. He wasn't ashamed and didn't feel any guilt, and he thought he could go on without Clara. But her? She fell into deep despondency, a chasm of silence which not even their son Hermann could rouse her from. Fritz Haber therefore sent them to Karlsruhe, where they couldn't bother him and constantly remind him of himself.

'Herr Doktor, are you with us?'

The man who had entered the large room went up to the big table by the window and leaned over a map of the Western Front.

'My wife, my Clara... she's seriously ill.'

'Herr Doktor, let us proceed. Today is 19 April 1915. Are we fully prepared to move to a higher level of chemical warfare?'

'General sir –,' Fritz Haber started, and then needed a few moments to compose himself, 'from a chemical point of view we are in a state of readiness. We will use chlorine gas, also known as bertholite. Chlorine spreads quickly in the air and is deadly for whoever inhales it because it forms hydrochloric acid when it comes in contact with the mucous membrane of the lungs.'

'Alright, alright, this isn't a chemistry lesson. Are we prepared from a military angle?'

'The gas has been produced in ample quantities at the IG Farben works, put into cylinders and taken to the Western Front.'

'Where is the best place to attack?'

'The meteorologists inform me that best place to strike will be in the part of the front near the town of Ypres. The prevailing winds are from the Atlantic, and the favourable terrain turns them south towards enemy positions. Since it is spring and the weather is changeable, we just need to determine the most suitable day.'

'And who is facing us there?'

'I've been informed, sir, that a few Frenchmen from the Home Reserve are in that part of the front but that the forces there largely consist of colonial troops from Morocco and Algeria.'

'Excellent. If a few Frenchmen are killed there will be less of that supposedly civilized people to defy us, and no one cares about those savages. It's up to you, doctor, to blow the whistle and give the signal to attack. You have supreme command's authorization. Leave for Belgium immediately and send us good news from there.'

'At once, sir.'

'Don't forget what our kaiser said when we entered this war: "We have been surrounded and are forced to use the sword. God give us strength to wield it as needed and wear it with dignity."'

'I'll do my best, sir.'

Fritz Haber left the room, and the generals simply replaced one set of maps with another. The chemist departed that same night. He arrived at the front the next morning, 20 April, and was met by one of the worst rains he had ever seen. After waiting three days for a favourable weather forecast, he decided to attack on 22 April. His dry mouth didn't whisper anything when he gave the signal and the chlorine was ordered to attack, but five hundred kilometres to the south-east another dry mouth repeated: 'God save us.' They were the lips of his wife, Clara Immerwahr.

Not long after Haber's wife uttered those words, the chlorine was released towards positions near Gravenstafel, not far from Ypres, held by the French 45th Home Reserve Division and the 78th Colonial Division. It was five in the afternoon. Flocks of birds perched on the branches, anxious about what was going to happen. The lids of 5,730 cylinders were unscrewed and the southerly winds blew the greenish-yellow gas towards the enemy. The gas was silent. It went on tiptoe. The chlorine only needed a few minutes to cover the space between the trenches. It was immune to bullets and artillery shells. The first soldiers who inhaled it noticed a metallic taste in their mouth. Thousands then sobbed in pain and doubled up in the mud of their trenches. Life quickly ebbed from the eyes of those poor wretches from Morocco and Algeria. Some fell immediately; others fled in panic into no-man's-land, where they were met by the waiting German artillery. Birds from the anxious flocks perching on the branches now fell down dead on top of the men, and before long almost all the soldiers in that seven-kilometre section of the front, who had not even been given the opportunity to buy a mask, were dead.

Success seemed complete, but then the wind changed direction for a short time and many of the German soldiers who had operated Haber's cylinders now became victims of 'friendly gas'. It was all over in less than half an hour. The confusion on both sides was so great that after Haber's all-clear the Germans were unable to enter the gap in the front near Ypres made by the new and formidable German soldier chlorine, alias bertholite.

The gas seemed to disperse—all except one cloud, hardly more than a puff.

That misty ball of chlorine started on its journey: it floated from Ypres to Lille, from Lille to Mons and from Mons to Charleroi. That cloud of chlorine from Ypres then seemed to disappear somewhere between Charleroi and St Quentin, but there it was again and continued on resolutely towards Sedan, and from there towards Metz. The poisonous cumulus entered Germany at Saarbrücken and, neither slowed nor scattered by the north-German winds, continued on through the Palatinate Forest straight towards Karlsruhe. Driven by the high air-currents along the Rhine, it sank towards the ground and flitted past Bad Bergzabern and Oberhausen. When it passed Lake Knielingen and was near Karlsruhe, it only needed a few minutes to find the house of the chemist of death, Fritz Haber, at the very moment when the doctor's wife Clara went out into the garden.

She had a suicidal look and her husband's pistol in her hand, but she didn't manage to use it. That last cloud of chlorine from Ypres dissipated above the garden and enveloped it in a strange, yellowish-green fog. The first thing Clara noticed was a smell of pepper mixed with that of pineapple. Then she had that metallic taste in her mouth. As a chemist, she immediately realized it was chlorine. She tried to raise her hand and point the barrel of her husband's pistol at her heart, but it was too late. The bertholite quickly came in contact with the mucous membrane of her lungs, reacted, and she fell to the ground writhing, her tongue sticking out like that of a dying animal and hanging to the side between her once beautiful lips. A moment later, the wife of the chemist of death was dead and the poisonous gas dissipated like a consummate murderer; it mingled with the fresh air over Karlsruhe and vanished forever, leaving no trace for the investigators.

The death of the wife of the great patriot Fritz Haber was kept secret. A proper inquest was never conducted, although the body of the poor woman was left in the house the whole day. The chemist-of-death visited Karlsruhe the next day. He saw what his beautiful wife Clara had died from so agonizingly—there was no overlooking it—yet he just turned and left for the Eastern Front, where a first deadly chlorine attack was to be loosed on the Russians. A soldier mustn't cry about the loss of loved ones because in wartime he is wedded solely to his homeland.

That is what Fritz Haber thought in icy eastern Europe when he was informed that the kaiser had awarded him the rank of captain, a unique distinction for a scientist of his standing.

Had a certain German soldier had a modicum of shame, the strange events which saw him join the list of aviators missing in action would probably never have happened. Fritz Krupp was one of the first German pilots to test the new German warplane Aviatik B.I and even saw in the New Year 1915 sitting in it, fondling the machine-gun and muttering to himself: 'I'll kill you, Picasso, I'm telling you.' But the first German planes were two-seaters, so for his unflinching intentions he needed to find a worthy sympathizer who shared his hatred for Pablo Ruiz Picasso, that luminary of all modern painters. He asked around to see if any of the young pilots knew anything about modern art, but it turned out he was the only painter among the airmen in his unit.

After a while he therefore chose a stripling, an apprentice house-painter from a small town, and immediately set about 'educating' him. He began with shocking stories about Paris, 'that perfumed cloaca', continued with tales of modern painters whose every painting was 'a trip to a witches' Sabbath to kiss the devil's arse', and fleshed out the nascent hatred of everything modern with Gothic tales about Pablo Picasso, whom he portrayed as a moral freak and artistic shark, an unparalleled Beelzebub who flayed painters alive, purloined their ideas and sucked out their souls. He succeeded in making him so abhorrent, that the poor boy could hardly wait to head for Paris to kill that 'greatest enemy of the Germans'.

But the German command only assigned reconnaissance tasks to the new short-range aircraft, so Fritz requested that he and his small, malicious gunner be transferred to the first German long-haul plane, the LVG C.II. When that was finally approved, he felt like an albatross. The plane had a heart-shaped tail, an enormous wingspan, a significantly more powerful Mercedes motor, and much greater speed and range. No one could have imagined that Fritz and his cynical assistant, so mighty in the air, would soon fall and vanish from the firmament. The most important thing about the plane for Fritz was that it could fly to Paris, but his happiness did not last for long. No one was sadder than Fritz when he heard that Pablo Ruiz was not in Paris at all but, like every coward, was lounging around on the Côte d'Azur and seducing the ladies with his bear-like, Spanish charm. He almost burst into tears at the thought of Pablo Ruiz being out of his range, but he curbed his emotions so that his apprentice, who now almost revered him as a saint, would see nothing of his weakness.

He then changed his plan and resolved to fly to the Côte d'Azur. He would go to the end of the world if he had to, even if all the monsters from edge of the universe awaited him there. That's what aviator Krupp thought, and everything he imagined would soon come true. It was early May when he was tasked with flying far behind enemy lines and making aerial photographs of French supply routes. This was an opportunity too good to let slip. He clambered into the plane with his evil apprentice, who was now growing a thin moustache like him, started to walk with the same broad-legged swagger, smacked his lips and imitated him in everything he did. One glance at each other was enough to make the joint decision to fly directly to the south. They both knew they wouldn't be coming back, but they were prepared to fall into enemy hands just so as to bomb Cannes and environs. Besides, they would be the first German airmen to drop bombs on the Côte d'Azur, which would make them famous, even if they had to spend years in captivity beneath the kindly southern sun waiting for German victory. But the friendly sun did not warm them because something went amiss in the very first hour after take-off. They were sure they were flying south, avoiding the usual routes of British and French fighter planes, which at that time were still rare. They didn't photograph any lines of communication and trains because they had no intention of performing the set task and returning to base, but headed in their big white bird straight for Marseille and on, to the sea.

Fresh on their mission, the two men merrily sang 'Die Wacht am Rhein' and the 'Song of Hate against England', while cultivated French landscapes glided past beneath them. Or so they thought. They were convinced they could see grapevines and the green humps of homely, rolling hills, and they thought they would soon spot the Mediterranean, but then everything abruptly began to resemble a nightmare. Fritz Krupp and his cynical assistant didn't see water when they should have, although their instruments showed they were flying straight for the Mediterranean. Wide vineyards alternated with fields of waving red poppies for several long hours as if the Europe beneath them had increased to a monstrous size. Their fuel was rapidly running out. Where was the sea and the Côte d'Azur, where they hoped to deliver their load of bombs and finally foil the plans of the greatest swindler and pseudo-painter of all time?

Finally water came into view. They knew they had to loop to the left. There was not a single enemy plane in the sky—no one expected them so far behind enemy lines. But what a strange coast… it didn't look at all like the broad gulf and pleasant beaches of the Mare Adriatica. Instead, jagged rocks reared up sharply, as if they were flying between the stalactites of a giant cave, and waves beat savagely against those inhuman, caramelized landscapes as if trying to smite them with every blow. The two German airmen were frightened. They banked to the left, but then the land disappeared behind them without warning. Instead of the coastline staying on their left, there was suddenly deep water all around them. Their one hope was that they would soon be able to take their bearings from the stars, but they flew on for hours over deep waters of a strange greenish colour, with the sun constantly at the apex of the sky, as if it was eternal noon.

Ten hours after take-off, Fritz had to acknowledge that they were hopelessly lost and in less than a minute would crash into the now crimson water, which looked more like molten jewels than the sea. They spoke no great words but simply waited for the end, and still the plane flew on. The needle showed that there was no more fuel, but the propeller of the LVG C.II kept turning. That gave them hope. After craning their necks to survey the sky several times, they saw something huge coming towards them: a squadron of the strangest flying craft they had ever seen. Like beetles, with wings which swung back as they flew at great speed, the huge warplanes closing in on them were ten times bigger than the largest German plane of 1915. Fritz and his assistant reached for their guns and fired a few rounds at the giant enemy. The cruisers replied with rays of light which passed through their plane without leaving any holes, just as their machine-gun bullets could do no harm to those incredible airships. The skirmish was indecisive and the enemies passed each other by, each continuing in the same direction as before. The German pilots were glad to have survived that first clash, but then they realized they were no longer in control of their plane. Without fuel, and flying blind, the plane could now only go straight ahead at a constant height. They weren't going to crash, it seemed, but nor were they able to land.

After three days in flight, they finally realized that they were prisoners trapped in the fuselage of their plane flying at a good 130 kmph and that they would never come down. They resigned themselves to the fact that they were heading towards their fate and that nothing more could frighten them. But then, on the fourth day, they met a fleet a thousand times greater than the first one they had seen. Enormous aircraft as huge as uprooted mountains were now plying the sky. Their LVG C.II, with the black cross on the tips of its wings, was so small that they didn't even notice it as it passed clean through their formation. Nor did the German airmen think of shooting again, because these mountains in flight couldn't be French or British, and it was as clear as day that chattering German machine-guns wouldn't affect them.

On the fifth day, hunger took over in the nose of the plane. Both the pilot and the co-pilot fell into despair at the deep, green water rippling beneath them without end and the midday sun shining without respite overhead. For the last time before they fainted from hunger, they encountered such a huge aircraft that they felt that they had a whole planet beneath them, and another above them. Then they lost consciousness and fell into a sugar coma. Soon afterwards the two pilots died. Their LVG C.II continued to furrow the sky, but that is no longer part of the history of the Great War: the plane finally crashed in southern Patagonia and created considerable panic among the natives and gauchos, who had never even heard of the Great War.

In Old Europe, Fritz Krupp and Dietrich Strunk were declared missing in action. They were the first crew to be lost in the new planes which, like chemical warfare, were meant to turn the course of the war decisively in Germany's favour. But the war in the air continued and the days of the flying aces were ahead. Planes and Zeppelins fought air-battles near Dunkirk and off the eastern coasts of England. One of those Zeppelins, commanded by Captain Karl Linnarz, took off on 20 April 1915 from an aerodrome north of Brussels. In complete silence, it made its way to London unnoticed. The first bomb on the British capital was dropped from the basket beneath the cabin, and it was followed by thousands of leaflets. The explosion caused some minor damage by the Thames, but the leaflets were a challenge even for British composure. They read: 'You damned English, we are coming to either destroy you or cure you. Signed: Linnarz.' Since it had come in silence, the Zeppelin also flew away unobserved, while down on the ground fire engines began to wail through the streets of London, although nothing was ablaze in the city. The firemen gathered up the leaflets, removed them from monuments and grabbed them out of the hands of passers-by. Still, thousands of them ended up in the pockets of travellers and so made it not only to Salisbury and other nearby cities, as well as further north and even to Scotland. But by evening, everything had calmed down and the rain was turning the last of Captain Linnarz's shameful proclamations to papier-mâché.

Rain set in that night in Istanbul, too, forcing Yıldız Effendi to move all his spices into the dry. He lugged them into the shop with his fez pulled down over his ears and managed to get them all inside in good time. Since no customers came, he even started a hushed conversation with the deserted shop and its contents. He thought the war could be ended in its second year with the help of the traders and merchants. He even went so far as to loudly ask the red spices what price they wanted so they would start selling less than the brown and green spices. There was no reply, or perhaps the reply for the red and orange spices came from the rain beating persistently against the dilapidated tile roof of his shop. Drop by drop, life by life, the rain seemed to be saying, there was hardly anything here to be traded.

It was also pouring rain in Bad Gleichenberg, where General Boroevich von Boina was recuperating. The spa resembled an enormous hotel complex from better times, when German families came here on holiday, convinced that nothing could dispel the idyll. Here the broken field marshal from the Eastern Front was given a large apartment with a terrace overlooking the spa's promenade. He entered the room as a commander, but as soon as the door closed behind him he slumped into the armchair like a crushed man. The suitcases he had put down gaped at him, and the sun slanted in through the venetian blinds on only one of his half-closed eyes. In that room, Boina began his arduous recovery. He no longer spoke of the two Przemysls—neither the false one he had captured, nor the real one he couldn't reach. He just smiled at the friendly doctors, who prescribed him medicines he found strange, and kept an eye on all his things, which were still double. Every morning he discussed the schedule of the day with his two adjutants, as if he were still at the front, and painstakingly polished his two pairs of boots. Two coats hung in the wardrobe along with two shiny, black-plumed helmets.

At the stroke of noon, the general would go down to the dining room ceremonially dressed in his ironed uniform and wearing a black-plumed metal helmet. Everyone saw him, but he didn't mix with anyone.

It was wartime, and he considered that he belonged at one of the fronts, but how was he to know which was the right one? When, after more than a week, the medicines showed little effect, a young intern doctor from the spa volunteered to devote himself to the field marshal. They struck up a friendly rapport. He tried to behave as if he were his son. After two luncheons together, he admitted that he wasn't a patient, but a doctor. Seven more were needed for Boina to invite him up to his apartment.

In the large sitting room there, the doctor could hardly fail to notice that everything of the general's was in duplicate but that he only ever wore one; there were reserve things meant for the spirits of the past—pieces of clothing which were ironed, polished, washed and put away ready for use but never saw the light of day. He immediately realized that for Boina to tread the path of recovery he would have to persuade the great man to begin wearing those 'reserve things' too. The young doctor was not surprised when the field marshal rejected the idea, but he knew this was the beginning of Boroevich's Sisyphean rise on the rocky terrain of schizophrenia, which would end either in his discharge from the sanatorium or in the complete ruin of one of the Dual Monarchy's most brilliant officers.

Every day at noon, the doctor and his illustrious patient lunched together. The general in his dress uniform, the doctor in a smart, chequered jacket with a fine linen belt around his waist. The doctor quickly learnt to distinguish the twin boots, twin sets of medals, twin uniforms and twin helmets. He needed twelve more midday meals to prompt Boina to put on the pair of tall boots he had never worn. This was utterly new for the general. He sweated, dithered and threw aside the boots meant for the Serbian Orthodox Boroevich, only to put them on in the end. As soon as he had pulled them up, an evanescent image of life came back to him. He remembered his mother and a certain Serbian lullaby, which no one had sung to him for almost half a century. The general burst into tears in his apartment, but he didn't want to show that weakness before the young doctor, who praised him when he saw the 'ostracized boots' on him at lunch.

'Now we've set off on a long march,' said the doctor, who smelt of skin cream. 'It will be a thorny road, a harsh and stony one, but we must stick to it till the end.' And Boroevich did. When he donned the uniform which for years had been meant for his childhood phantasm, he remembered his grandfather's prickly moustache; when he put on the unworn helmet for the first time, he smelt the frankincense in the small church in Boina... he cried, bawled and tore at his chest, and he had just enough presence of mind not to uglify his face, because that would have given him away at lunch where he still went outwardly composed, orderly and with soldierly punctuality. But the doctor knew that the field marshal's process of recovery would only be concluded when he stopped dividing the food on his plate into two halves and eating only the half closest to him—not a forkful more. Five more lunches were needed to persuade him that they 'cross into enemy territory' and 'requisition' a little food from there (he intentionally used military expressions), and when Boina managed that too he was able to report for duty again at the high command.

Was he cured? No, but he was able to serve the monarchy once more. As soon as he arrived back at the Eastern Front, he asked for two horses, two batmen and two chiefs of staff, but now he made a point of using both horses, both batmen and both chiefs of staff in the conviction that this perspective would prevent any errors of judgement and, when everything was viewed binocularly, enable him to choose the correct military objectives. On 20 April 1915, Boroevich was sent to the Italian Front because lady spies more successful than Lilian Schmidt had reported that Italy would soon be entering the war as an enemy of Austria-Hungary. Boina thus became commander of the Isonzo Front. He located his headquarters north of the River Piave, wore his pairs of boots alternately, rode his horses one in the morning and the other in the afternoon, and was convinced that he had left all his problems behind him.

Things were quiet on the future Italian Front at first, but the field marshal knew a great battle was brewing at the other end of Europe because he had to sign an order for all the ships under his command, anchored at Fiume and Pola, to sail for the Aegean Sea. There they were to intercept the British and French fleets, which on 25 April 1915 began an invasion of the southern, Asian end of the Dardanelles, on the Gallipoli peninsula, not far from the place the Turks call Çanakkale. The story told by these ill-considered landings, whose ultimate goal was to capture Yıldız Effendi's Istanbul, only concerned Boina insomuch as he was needed for signing the order. It had a lot more to do with bootlaces.

Among soldiers, there were two common ways of doing up boots: one with the lace divided into two unequal lengths and parallel lacing along just the longer side, from the lowest to the highest hole of the boot, and another with the lace divided into two equal lengths and crossing at right angles from left to right and right to left. Only one shoe-cleaner from Trieste with a face as dark as brown shoe polish, who only came along when a stiff breeze was blowing from the first quadrant of the sea, knew twenty-four more ways of lacing; but he only revealed his secrets to the retarded children at the home, who were thrilled beyond measure. Soldiers in the Great War tied up their boots now this way, now that, and coincidence had it that five Australian and five Turkish soldiers became the eyelets, through which the joker of fate pulled the long lace that was the Gallipoli Campaign.

It all began with the landings. Once the Allied ships had picked up their human cargo—the men who would go ashore on Turkish soil—and managed to avoid the traps set in the deep waters off the Dardenelles, the invasion could begin. The objective in the mind of Winston Churchill, First Lord of the Admiralty, was to crush Turkish resistance there and march on to Istanbul like in medieval times, when the Crusaders liberated Constantinople. But six Turkish divisions at Çanakkale under the command of Esad Pasha and Vehip Pasha were of a different mind. The Turks had prepared well, dug in artillery and infantry, and like real Ilians, here near the site of Troy, waited for the attack of the modern-day Achaeans. They weren't deterred by months of daily bombardment from the sea or the arrival of the amassed sea-farers. Aeolus scattered the thick smoke from their ships, leaving them fully exposed, and so the British 29th Division, the Australian and New Zealand Army Corps and the French Oriental Expeditionary Corps were met by withering fire. Soon the sandy beaches were littered with bodies like a freshly cut harvest.

But the attackers made it up to the grass and rocky slopes and quickly dug themselves shallow trenches south-east of Anzac Cove, and then, on 1 May 1915, an exchange of rifle fire began and chance started to do up its bootlace. First, it was pulled through from the Australian to the Turkish side of the lines near Chunuk Bair. A soldier of the 2nd Company, 1st Battalion of the 9th Turkish Division, Esad Saledin, suddenly smelt horses in the middle of the exchange of fire. A moment later, a picture appeared to him, as vivid as only a vision could be: he was in the Australian outback speaking English, breaking in horses, drinking coffee by the fire and, for sport, grabbing horseshoes from the top of posts at the gallop. That gilder from southern Turkey smelt and felt all this although he had never ridden or owned a horse. He looked at the palms of his hands, and before his very eyes they became strangely furrowed as if he had just let go of reins. A second later, a bullet from the Australian side passed through the head of Esad Saledin the gilder. This projectile was fired from a range of several hundred metres from Rhododendron Ridge by Graham Dow, a stable boy and horse breeder from South Australia. Chance determined that all his experience from the time before the deadly shot would be passed to his Turkish victim, and so the bootlace passed through its first two holes.

Now it had to go back from the Turkish to the Australian side. Liaison officer Peter R. House had been yelling all day and was now completely hoarse. For this reason he was unable to yell in surprise or confide in anyone that he suddenly acquired all the experience of a Turkish smuggler of gold coins. It became clear to him all at once: how the fake gold coins were made in Italy, how peasants were cheated into buying them, and what could be bought with them. All of a sudden Peter R. House saw Izmir as his native city, and smelt the smells of tallow and saffron as if they had impregnated his shirt collar back when he was child. When he sniffed his hands, he realized they smelt like the copper used in imitation Ottoman gold coins. He wanted to share this unexpected knowledge with the soldiers around him, but before he could reach out his hand he was dead. Chance had pulled the lace through from the Turkish to the Australian side. The bullet which killed House was fired from the rifle of Cevdet Baraklı, an Izmir black marketeer and maker of fake gold jewellery and coins.

The next eyelet for the ominous bootlace was pulled through from the Australian to the Turkish side. The third victim of this Gallipoli lacing was, appropriately, a poor shoemaker by the name of Koca Umur. Koca's legs started to jiggle of their own accord, although he had never as much as run over the bridge of the Golden Horn. He looked down at his poor legs and suddenly realized he was a sprinter. He caught a glimpse of Perth, as if it was his home city, and saw the Australian national championship in the hundred-yard race. He even smelled the red dust strewn on the lanes of the track. Just as he realized he had crossed the line ahead of his greatest rival from Sydney. He was fatally wounded by a bullet fired by Simon Hatings, the Australian national champion in the hundred-yard race held in Perth, 1913.

Philip Hershaw was the next. He saw himself as a Turkish shoemaker from the town of Abydos, not far from the positions in the Dardanelles, who was so poor that he took out his two imitation gold coins every evening and looked at them as if they were holy. And, to his surprise, Hershaw began to repeat to himself in Turkish: 'With these I can buy a good hunting falcon with a cage and a glove, or ten dozen rounds of fresh bread; I can pay a dervish labourer from Tabriz for a month, or buy three grave-plots, and the coffins too.' Then he stopped, because at the same instant his life was snuffed out. Hershaw was killed by the penniless shoemaker Şefik Kutluer, who had never as much as trodden on another's shadow. Four soldiers were dead, but two holes remained to complete the deadly act. A shot still had to be fired from the Australian side; and that was performed by Sergeant Rodney Kellow.

The bullet was intended for an ordinary apprentice from a shop for European and oriental spices, who considered Effendi Mehmed Yıldız his second father and mentioned him every evening in his prayers. That red-headed apprentice's name was Orhan Fişkeçi. He had a swarthy younger brother recruited into the army in the Caucasus, who he heard had been cut down by Russian Cossacks. Now, before he too became someone else and was shot dead, he thought back once again to his real life with Effendi Yıldız and to cheating so adroitly at the scales, just so much that his master was satisfied and the customers wouldn't complain. He laughed out loud, and the next moment, without warning, he became Rodney Kellow, a solicitor from Canberra. Suddenly he was able to cite various articles of the British Empire's penal code almost off by heart, and in English... and then a bullet bored right through him, just below his left eye. Orhan Fişkeçi was dead, and with his death chance had finished lacing up its boot and tied a knot. A lace in the form of a bullet passed from stable boy Graham Dow to Esad Saledin; from the counterfeiter Cevdet Baraklı to Peter R. House; from the sprinter Simon Hatings to Koca Umur; from the impoverished shoemaker Şefik Kutluer to Philip Hershaw, and finally from the Canberra solicitor Rodney Kellow to Yıldız's eldest apprentice, Orhan Fişkeçi. Five living soldiers: five dead soldiers. Çanakkale Savaşları or the Battle of Çanakkale, as the Turks called their first and only major victory in the Great War, thus did up one of the war's many boots. The attackers of Gallipoli never made it to Istanbul, but rumours about the dead of Çanakkale certainly did.

Now there was no longer any joy or great expectation. Still, *Tanin*, which the spice trader Mehmed Yıldız bought a copy of that morning too, gave a romanticized account of victory in the First Battle of Çanakkale.

It was two-dimensional, the way everything was meant to be in Turkish history: the attackers came from the sea, and we met them on the beaches and the rugged slopes. They attempted to charge and were cut down. The righteous triumphed. The infidels sowed the ground with their own bodies so they would sprout with weeds and become the homes of snakes. The correspondent from Gallipoli made it sound as if no Turk could be killed in that holy war of the righteous against the wrong, but a chill crept over Effendi Mehmed's heart because he knew there were no fell dragons which could simply be put to the sword without devouring a martyr or two first. What had become of his oldest apprentice, Orhan?

Who could he ask? No one, of course. As long as no rumours reached him, everything was alright. The battle was very large and many souls departed for the bosom of Allah. But no rumours reached him. It would be best not to go out and meet them. He closed the shop for several days because the rain over the Bosporus was relentless, and there were no customers anyway. With a sheet beneath his knees, he prayed to Allah on his small terrace. He kept the door closed but was under no illusion: if rumour wants to reach us, it will make its way through a gate with five locks. And so it was this time, too.

There was no fire this time, and no stranger came up to speak to him. Instead, Yıldız had a bad dream, in which Orhan appeared. His red-headed apprentice laughed in his face and bit a gold coin in front of him to show that it was fake. When the spice trader woke up, he took the Koran and began searching for the word *hazen* (melancholy). He decided to prepare himself so that Orhan's death would not catch him unprepared as Şefket's had. He found the word spelt as *huzn* in two verses and *hazen* in three others. The year in which the uncle of the Prophet Mohammed, Abu Talib, and his wife Khadiya died is called 'Senettul huzn' (Year of Melancholy), he read, and he thought of preparing himself for the impending deaths in his family.

When he finally found out that Orhan was dead, there was nothing which could really comfort him. The body of his beloved apprentice was supposed to be brought home the following week. Now at least there were earthly remains to bury. But how could he wait those three long days until Orhan was finally wrapped in green cloth? He would withdraw deep into himself, far away from people, and quench another part of the embers which smouldered and maintained his elderly life. Now only the youngest of the Fişkeçi brothers remained, the eight-year-old boy who was sent to his shop as a gesture and only stayed one day. What would that eight-year-old-old think? Both his older brothers had given their life for the Padishah. Why yes, he should be proud; that eight-year-old boy should go out into the streets of Istanbul and sing. Yıldız knew that he should take him in his old arms and proudly head to the Padishah's new palace. Yet he knew he was no longer capable of that. He could only die. But he wouldn't, no, because he had three more apprentices on distant frontiers, watching and waiting to defend Turkey from the infidels who were pressing the country from land and sea, invading his two-dimensional world along evil old routes. 'To the dogs with them,' he muttered to himself and then began to shout: 'Filthy dogs! Curs!'

He had to keep living for his three young apprentices. He had to pray to Allah, and once again he read the verses with the words *hazen* and *huzn*.

BEST WISHES FROM HELL

I'm sorry, sir, but you don't know the man you're talking about, so it's easy for you to just call him 'the butcher of Kinsale'. Unlike you, I knew Captain-Lieutenant Walther Schwieger quite well. It's strange that all of what you say is true, but the way you say it is unacceptable because you never met that great submarine captain and unhappy man. You don't seem to know, for example, that all seafarers who come from the coast resemble one another, while each mariner from the mainland has only himself as a model. Walther Schwieger came from a Berlin-Frankfurt 'landlubber' family. I spent most of my childhood with him. We went to school together; he was top of the class, and I... wasn't exactly second.

We went on board the submarine U-14 together on the day the war began. We were the last to swim to the surface of the mercurial sea when we lost that first vessel at dawn on 15 December 1914, immediately after leaving the Baltic. After a brief questioning, the captain was given a new underwater shark, the U-20, which would later sink the RMS Lusitania. That's right, I remember that day as clearly as if it was yesterday: people screaming for help as they drowned—and were cruelly ground—in the mad vortex of the sinking ship out at sea. It was twenty kilometres west of the Irish coast, off the Old Head of Kinsale.

Yes, sir, for all your astuteness you overlook or don't wish to see that the sinking of the Lusitania was a terrible tragedy, in which they all had their part: Dock 54 in New York, from where the ship started on its fatal voyage on 1 May 1915; Captain Daniel Dow, who steered the ship towards Liverpool; and all of the 1,255 passengers on board. Don't tell me they didn't know she was a dual-purpose vessel: on the outside the RMS Lusitania, a merchant ship, but on the inside the AMC Lusitania—a warship in disguise. Naturally you know, and don't deny, that in 1913 the British Admiralty ordered that the section of large passenger ships beneath the main deck, which usually remained empty and served as a buoyancy chamber in the event of water penetrating the lower decks, be unsealed and equipped with a rotating cannon. This could 'magically appear' on the main deck within just a few minutes, right next to the first-class passengers wrapped in blankets and watching the last rays of the sun drowning in the ocean. And of course you known that all of the 120 Canadians who drowned were actually soldiers in mufti, but you have a new argument already.

Yes, I know what your reply will be, and you'll even be right in the interpretation of that intrigue. The catastrophe of the Lusitania was caused by forces on both sides of the Atlantic. It's true that the illuminati had their fingers in it. Captain Daniel Dow was one of them, there were quite a few illuminati in the Admiralty, just like on Capitol Hill, and my unfortunate friend Captain-Lieutenant Schwieger was one of them too—how's that for an admission? They were all in collusion in some way and it was in their joint interest to draw America into the war. And it's even true that a torpedo was consciously fired at that target, and the ship was lumbering straight into our ambush, as vulnerable as a fat lady swimming—but how wrong you are when you claim that the illuminati plot my poor friend was involved in was the decisive factor, and you go so far as to speculate about a meeting in the lovely Indian summer of 1913 between Captain Dow, Captain-Lieutenant Schwieger and the First Lord of the Admiralty, Winston Churchill!

Would it surprise you to learn that the Lusitania was actually sunk by sea serpents two kilometres long and abominable giant octopuses from the depths of the sea? a ludicrous idea? Never mind. But remember this: I am a reliable eyewitness who spent fifteen years together with Walther Schwieger, four of them deep under the sea. It all began back when we were cadets at naval academy in the Free City of Lübeck. Hallucinations? The cramped conditions in which the first submariners lived and waged war? The near nervous breakdowns of the top of the class? All this together probably caused Captain-Lieutenant Schwieger to begin having visions as real as life itself. Even our first submarine, the U-14, was trailed by enormous serpents, megalodons with huge maws, and legendary giant octopuses, the captain said. I, too, felt I was beginning to hear their sneaking, their knocking and scraping against the hull of our submarine and their faraway shrieking and tittering like the giggle of old women—but you're right, I never saw a single one of those monsters. Schwieger did.

He claimed they were our cruel, infernal allies—that they were on our side and we dared not anger them. And when our U-20 calmly sailed out to sea on 30 April 1915 and submerged off the westernmost German port of Emden, the captain claimed that the beasts set off behind us. Don't laugh, sir. They were there, I swear to you. Ask any of the other crew members from the U-20, and they'll confirm that the shuddering sobs, eerie singing and dreadful cries from the salty depths told of their proximity, even though they were invisible to us. But we couldn't summon them, or assuage them. Only the captain could do that. I have to tell you that the captain, the one you call 'the butcher of Kinsale', couldn't reconcile himself to having to contact them, but he did it in the end because it would have been mad to ignore the alliance with such mighty creatures. 'We are now heading to embrace our fate, and we have to do what is expected of us above the water and under the water,' he told me, and I realized we were heading for some spectacular sinking.

And so we were. We travelled the North Sea for half a day. Then we rounded the northern coast of Scotland, and three days after setting out we arrived at our destination: Twenty kilometres from the Old Head of Kinsale. There we stopped. I confirm what you say—we were waiting solely for the Lusitania. But you don't know what happened in those four days during which we waited for the 'innocent' merchant ship to arrive at the place where we had set the ambush. For safety reasons, we only surfaced briefly to replenish our supplies of oxygen. And while we were under water, the captain was engaged in a veritable war with those aquatic beasts. He was on the verge of giving up, cheating the 'landlubbers' and not sinking the Lusitania after all, but that displeased the sea creatures. No one apart from me was allowed to enter the captain's cabin, and whenever I brought him a meal he would suddenly fall silent and then tell me, as if I was au fait with the 'negotiations': 'It's no good, the sea serpents have decided: the ship has to be sunk.' One day, and then the next. I swear to you, their screams were becoming ever louder, and the captain's replies ever shriller and more embittered, so you'll understand why all the crew members of the U-20 were terrified and longing for the day when it would be over.

Then the day came. It was Friday, 7 May. Shortly after noon, we spotted a floating mountain of metal approaching from the west. One torpedo launched from seven hundred metres meant the end of the Lusitania. Five minutes after the hit, the ammunition stored under deck exploded, so I can say with some certainty that that detonation didn't derive from our second torpedo. For seven minutes after that, the passengers screamed. They tried to lower the lifeboats for four more minutes.. Eighteen minutes after the encounter with the U-20, the Lusitania plunged into the infernal depths and took more than a thousand lives down with it into the silence, to feed that colony of colossal sea denizens. When the ship reached the bed and became prey to the monsters, only the screams for help and the cries of the few survivors remained on the surface. 'Now the people above and the sea serpents below are satisfied,' Captain-Lieutenant Walther Schwieger said coldly, pale as if he had been wrestling for days with an unseen enemy.

The scene on the surface was terrible, by any account. The propeller blades, still turning, were chopping bodies in half; they smashed lifeboats and flung people ten metres through the air as if they were spitting out cherry stones; a severed human head was riding on a life jacket; but we retracted the periscope and returned to our home port. In Berlin, the 'land-lubber' Walther Schwieger was decorated with the Iron Cross, 1st Class and promoted to the rank of Captain-Lieutenant. And now, my good sir, you are the first to have learnt the full truth about the sinking of the Lusitania.

* * *

Ferrara, 23 May 1915

Dear Mother,

The fierce heat has come on early this year in Ferrara. The hemp harvest is drawing to a close in the fields surrounded by the old arms of the river and the swamps full of fetid water, so I'm writing to you as I hide from people who simply go wild at this time and display their lustful nature. I'm hurrying to send you these lines because I know you'll hear the rumour that my nerves have given way and I've become mentally ill. Please don't worry—I feigned a nervous breakdown and met a friendly army doctor, a major, who had me moved to a sanatorium near Ferrara. The convalescent home was once a Benedictine abbey with a small cloistered atrium and a host of passageways and secluded chambers, which has given me the opportunity to return to colours and produce a few large paintings with metaphysical passages and abandoned dummies caught up in long shadows ascending the walls like spiders.

But imagine what happened here. An audacious, uneducated man barged into my life. His manner was just like his name: Karlo Rota. The rotter proclaimed himself a painter and, without asking me—even my epigone. Wherever I went, he followed at my heels and painted the same things as me, and did all this with mind-boggling impudence and sans gêne. He was a man without moderation in his actions or scruples in his intentions, and all his work was barer and bleaker than my paintings. His dummies were ragged and inside out, as if an evil demiurge had cruelly ripped out their hemp stuffing, springs and threads, and on some canvases they eventually even began to bleed. When I asked him why he did that, he said the devil had told him to do it. What a cheap excuse for an untalented dauber! And I wouldn't have given a damn about such nonsense,

163

had he not claimed that his paintings announced that war was coming to Italy too and that he was in collusion with the future victims of the war, whom he represented as butchered dummies. I didn't take that seriously either, until I heard today that our country has entered the Great War.

What is to come, I don't know. I do know that Karlo Rota spared me his presence and so-called friendship this very evening. He ran away, taking his paintings with him, and is being hunted as a deserter. Please write, and don't buy a ticket to Ferrara just now. Maybe things won't all turn out like on the canvases of that painfully untalented painter.

Your devoted son,
Giorgio de Chirico

* * *

Mogilev
Stavka – Tsarist General Staff
1 September 1915

Monsieur l'Ambassadeur,
As you know, I am no longer a young man. At seventy-six, I have seen both the last century and this, and things both fair and foul; I have tasted both the sweet and the bitter, have touched soft flesh and stuck my hands in the nettles. I therefore ask you to please not take what I am going to write to you lightly, and to let it remain just between us: c'est pour nous deux. You have lived in my country for long enough to realize that Russia is awash with the occult and mystical, that our church is an island of Christian Orthodoxy in a sea of raging unbelievers, that the people here are violently excessive, and that the black forces from hell can find their way straight to the heart of even the most steadfast and justice-loving man. Unrest is therefore our ally, hysterical visionariness our future, and dull-witted brutalities are the roadside monuments of our history.

I am writing this to you as a confirmed believer and patriot who cannot allow anyone to beat his breast and claim to have obligated the tsar's family more than me. It is precisely concerning the future of the Romanovs that I am writing to you, a Westerner, and please do hesitate to warn me if you find I am exaggerating. You are sure to have been informed that the emperor dismissed the Generalissimo, Grand Duke Nicholas Nikolaevich, on 25 August / 8 September (New Style) and, despite the opposition of almost everyone devoted to the throne, made himself commander of all his armies on land and sea. I am sure you know that our 'Iron Duke' took the news as only a Christian can. If I may cite him, he said to the new Minister of War, General Polivanov: 'Thank God that the emperor has relieved me of a task which has completely consumed me.' But that was not the opinion of his wife Anastasia and her fury-like sister Milica, the wife of Nicholas's brother, Grand Duke Peter Nikolaevich.

You probably know about those two Montenegrin princesses, or witches. Forgive me for using such undiplomatic language. No one dares to look those two 'black pearls' in the eyes: newts' eyes and frogs' toes fall out of their pockets, and the air around them smells of magical, ethereal oils. The two bitter sisters were galled by the news that the duke had been relieved of his post and sent to the Caucasus with his faithful chief of staff, General Yanushkevich. 'And this after such suffering?' they are said to have hissed. 'After sleeping in a tent by the Masurian Lakes at minus thirty?' As furious as Medeas, they demanded to be allowed to see their husbands, but neither Nicholas nor Peter were in a position to receive them because Peter was still in Moscow, while Nicholas left without delay for Tbilisi. And that is why I am so bold as to believe they have begun a "great war" of their own from their residence in Kiev, like two Baba Yagas. Why do I claim this? The sequence of strange events which unfolded here leads me to think this, but the little town of Mogilev is not to blame, nor the fact that so many important people were all here in one place—practically in just a few houses on two main streets intersecting at a sharp angle.

First of all, something strange happened to the court major-domo, Voyeyko, who began to stammer and became eccentric. You know him, I'm sure: he is the devoted, taciturn old fellow who only speaks when he must, or when he is asked. He, of all people, now began to spew forth love quatrains and terza rima, loud and garbled. After him, strange perturbations were manifested by the ever restrained Admiral Konstantin Nilov, who started reciting Shakespeare's sonnets, which he knew by heart, instead of going about his usual duties. He walked about the stately house, muttering Sonnet 18 to himself in Russian: 'Shall I compare thee to a summer's day? / Thou art more lovely and more temperate: / Rough winds do shake the darling buds of May, / And summer's lease hath all too short a date.'

The Germans had taken all of Lithuania and cut the railway line connecting Vilnius with Daugavpils and Pskov with Petrograd, and it was not long before a right love-struckness took hold of Mogilev like in one of Shakespeare's comedies. The climax came when Grand Duke Sergei

Mikhailovich arrived at the Stavka together with his stunningly beautiful friend Matilda Kshesinskaya, the prima ballerina of the Mariinsky Theatre of St Petersburg. A narrow face, pronounced eastern cheekbones, piercing sapphire eyes and a beauty mark on her face... It was as if everyone's heart had suddenly been shot through. Admiral Nilov went swimming in Lake Pechora every day so Matilda might see he was still strong, like a strapping lad. I've heard that Voyeyko, without warning, went up to ask the ballerina's hand and knelt before her naked, though I'm not sure I want to believe it.

But the worst thing was that the brothers, the Grand Dukes Georgi and Sergei Mikhailovich, fell out over Miss Kshesinskaya. The artillery thus struck a blow at the cavalry (Georgi was in charge of the artillery, Sergei of the cavalry). Then the aviation got involved too, when the third brother, Grand Duke Alexander Mikhailovich, also declared his love for that femme fatale, and a world war of lovers was set to begin. Matilda didn't know what to do. She requested an audience with the tsar, with whom she had also once been in a sentimental relationship. But ask as she might, she was not allowed to see him. It was the tsar's custom to take tea at five in the afternoon, and no one dared utter a word about love-struckness, at least until the brothers armed themselves and even vied with Shakespeare in the cruelty of the letters they wrote to each other. Rumours spread about duels and about the beautiful prima ballerina having disappeared from Mogilev—and just when the tension was almost palpable it suddenly stopped.

Voyeyko, the court major-domo, doesn't remember falling to his knees, naked, and offering to marry Matilda; Nilov no longer recites Shakespeare and bathes in the cold waters of the lake in a striped bathing suit; Georgi Mikhailovich has returned to artillery matters; Alexander Mikhailovich now ignores the ballerina; Grand Duke Sergei Mikhailovich has retained his sweetheart after leading her through the eye of that storm, and everything has returned to wartime reality. The Russian army is no longer retreating. Our forces have even gone on the counter-offensive on the right bank of the River Styr, along the line Derazhnya–Olit–Nizhne. May God grant that the tsar's command be triumphant. But was that week of amorous pandemonium enough to satisfy Anastasia and Milica, those two servants of hell? Or will they unleash more chaos? Please write, chide me if you must, and counsel me.

Minister of the Court, Count Vladimir Frederiks

Dear Herr Doktor Schnebel,

You know that having a son without the use of his arms is far from easy. It's not the nursing or the hard work of teaching him that is hardest, but having to see that handsome face combined with his helpless hands which cannot pick up anything or do any normal human task, not even button up his own shirt. My son Hans is one such patient, but God is my witness of how grateful I am that Hans has gifts in return for what he lacks. That lovely face, and our piercing, northern blue eyes—every girl would desire him, and maybe he would even have gone to war if it weren't for his two useless arms, which since childhood have hung down beside his trunk like the branches of a withered tree.

Oh, how many nights did I lie awake crying, but that is over now by some strange miracle. No, Hans hasn't found a marriageable girl, being as he is, but strength has unexpectedly begun to return to his arms. Imagine! Those muscles, once like deflated balloons, are now flushed with blood; colour has come back to the deathly-pale skin; and my poor son began first of all to wave with his arms, then to write first letters and to do much, much more. But what at first was a source of indescribable joy has since come to rather concern me.

Maybe his long years of waiting are to blame for it all: the feeling that you're handsome and well built, quite a stunner, a real man in every way, but no one wants you because wherever you go people react with a mixture of compassion and revulsion, which pushes you ever further from all society and any satisfaction. But to cut a long story short: after twenty years of waiting, blood began to flow through the veins of Hans's arms. I immediately notified you and also our friend Dr Ingelthorp, who, to be sure, said the process could stop again, but we took no notice. Who was happier than the two of us. Hans has been without a father since he was eight, and I have no one other than him.

Within two days, Hans was able to do up a button, after a week he was eating soup by himself, and within a month he could thread a needle. We danced and sang, but then his gloomy feelings began. Why couldn't he simply be happy? I don't know. He began to confide in me. First, he claimed his arms weren't his own (Dr Ingelthorp recommended I ignore that), and afterwards he said he would soon tell me whose the left was, and whose the right. Before long, he triumphantly came out with the 'news'. I was dumbfounded. His left arm had belonged to the French poet

Blaise Cendrars, he said, and his reborn right was that of our famous pianist Paul Wittgenstein. How did these arms become Hans's? He claimed that the right arm was amputated from Private Wittgenstein after the abortive siege of Warsaw on 1 March 1915 (you see, he knew the exact date). The wounded pianist was taken prisoner by the Russians, and the Russian doctors amputated his hopelessly mangled right arm; according to Hans, the pianist sat by his bedside and sobbed as all the music came back to him which he had played with it, and would no longer be able to. The left arm was amputated from a certain Private Cendrars (again an exact date: 7 October 1915) and then became the possession of my son.

I tried to joke about it and find a logical flaw in the tale of boy who had never left his home town, never listened to Wittgenstein, as far as I know, and, like me, had never heard of Cendrars. I asked him why the pianist's right arm had waited from March to November—what had it been waiting for? The left arm, he answered. Where had the right arm waited? In hell, he said. I immediately wrote and told Dr Ingelthorp, of course, and he replied that the story would be easy to confirm: one just needed to check up on the fate of the soldier cum pianist Paul Wittgenstein. The doctor and I both made inquiries, and we found out that the pianist really had lost his right arm. What a misfortune for the musician, and what a boon for my son! But how could that be? 'It just is,' my Hans replied. 'I'll prove it as soon as I get a bit more used to the hand. I'll play the piano, which I never practiced and never even learnt.'

Afterwards we went through the 'Blaise Cendrars period'. Who was that? What did he do? I found out everything in detail from the mouth of my son. I won't bother you now with the whole life story of an enemy. Suffice to say, Cendrars was a destitute poet—a weasely sort of man. His real name was Frédéric Sauser, and he wasn't even French. Even so, he was shooting at us. I'll skip most of the biography of that small-time poet to tell you one important detail: it seems that Hans has acquired not only the arm but also all the memory and emotions of its owner. Just imagine what he said to me: a year of fighting for his adopted Fatherland aroused the war poet in Cendrars, but later his confidence began to crumble when he apparently saw the way generals offhandedly send soldiers to their deaths yet seek ease and luxury for themselves. This is what Hans says he learnt from Cendrars—a picture as vivid as reality itself: troops enter the town of Chantilly, where Commander-in-Chief Joffre and his generals have their headquarters. The great general doesn't want to be disturbed by the harsh pounding of infantry boots passing through the streets, so he orders that tons and tons of hay be spread in the streets to preserve the quiet he says he needs for his strategic deliberations.

There is no way of us verifying this because it is behind enemy lines, but how could Hans know all that when he has no idea who Joffre is, nor where the little French town of Chantilly is? That's why I'm very worried instead of simply being happy. Hans has promised poetry in French and his first concert for the right hand in just a week or two. Please come and pay us a visit, Dr Schnebel. It would make me feel much better. If things turn out well, I'll be the happiest and the most unhappy mother in the world. If they don't, I'll be the most unhappy and the happiest mother in the world.

Yours respectfully,
An anxious mother, Amanda Henze

* * *

Dear Zoë, love of my life,

You haven't come. You weren't allowed to—Nana didn't let you. You were afraid to come and see the monster who played cards with the dead near Lunéville in 1914 and callously killed hopeless patients in Hôpital Vaugirard in Montparnasse. You didn't believe you could rouse and nurture the man in me again. I don't blame you. You're probably right. And now, farewell. I am going to hell. The first step: I take the pistol. The second: I put a bullet in the barrel. The third: I close.

Your Germain D'Esparbès

DEFENCE AND ULTIMATE COLLAPSE

Behind each announcement in a newspaper is a story. Shortly before the Central Powers decided to deal the death blow to Serbia in October 1915 and the heavy shelling of Belgrade with mortars and Big Berthas began on 6 October, the last issue of *Politika*—printed in the city on 11 September 1915 (by the old calendar)—published one of many missing-person announcements. At the bottom of the fourth page of the thin edition it read: "Where is Mrs Lir, who used to live alone in number 3 Valpinska Street in Belgrade? If anyone knows anything about her whereabouts, please write to Karlo Saradal, c/o Bank of Prague, Chupriya branch." Hardly anyone took note of this announcement printed in nonpareil, and the people in the town of Chupriya say that Karlo Saradal did not receive any messages in the days that followed. But how could he have? The bank clerk left for the Front the same day as he placed the announcement, while the Bank of Prague closed its doors in the middle of October and compensated savers by distributing shares signed by the manager.

Still, maybe someone was able to get in touch with the worried nephew about his aunt from Valpinska Street in Belgrade. But how could they have, when no one at all had seen Mrs Lir in the days leading up to the ultimate collapse? She was last noticed at the beginning of September 1915 (by the old calendar) in the tailor shop of Zhivka D. Spasich in 22 Dunavska Street, at the moment she drew the curtain of the changing cubicle to try on a garment she had had let out and mended. Only the assistant was in the shop when something happened which the seamstress had unfortunately already seen: instead of Mrs Lir, a different woman appeared in the cubicle: with dishevelled hair, bedraggled appearance and scratched arms. This person did not as much as ask 'Where am I?' like the previous one, but just ran out and drowned herself in a pond in Robiyash Garden.

It wasn't always the case that the changing booth took one woman in behind the curtain and spat out another, but the assistant still had an aversion to it. Whenever she could, she suggested to customers that they change in the corner next to the sewing machine or behind her substantial frame so they wouldn't have to go into the changing room, but Mrs Lir was ashamed of her frayed petticoat, which she hadn't had altered, so she pulled the curtain closed behind her. Then she vanished into a different time like the confectioner Nataliya Babich, Anka Milichevich the pensioner, Yelka Chavich the baker and Mileva Voivodich the cab driver before her. By some strange interplay of time and circumstance, the space behind the curtain in 22 Dunavska Street wore people out on ephemeral visits to the years to come and sent them back to the present haggard and bewildered, condemning these slaves of a better future to spend a day or two, a month or two, or their whole life in wormwood-bitter 1915 and the years that followed. That is what happened to Mrs Lir. And that is why no one replied to Karlo Saradal's announcement or those of relatives searching for other previous visitors to the changing room in Zhivka D. Spasich's tailor shop.

At first, Mrs Lir was quite taken with 1937, where chance had randomly cast her. It was peacetime, and a soft, warm September, with people wearing strange suits and driving unusual cars. She briskly walked up the hill from the Danube and saw a large church being built on the near side of Tashmaydan Park, once the Turkish cemetery. At first she didn't know where to go, dowdily dressed as she was in her mended traditional skirt embroidered with silver thread, but the very next day she found a gentleman who began to woo her and buy her everything she needed. She went out onto Teraziye Boulevard and saw how Belgrade would look in twenty-two years' time. Everything appealed to her, and she even started to like the regent, Prince Paul. And just as Mrs Lir thought how blissfully easy it was to forget her nephew Karlo and the whole arduous past, she suddenly fell back into her 1915—into the same booth behind the same curtain in 22 Dunavska Street, which has since been demolished.

She went out into the street in the late afternoon of 6 October, and the sky was red and livid blue as if the sun had been maltreating it all day. Bewildered people were running past her, skirting the huge holes made by shrapnel, and shouting to each other as if she wasn't there. She tried to tell them to stop and that there was no reason to worry, that in 1937 everyone would be happy, the sweets would be bigger, the cars larger and the gentlemen more courteous, but who could listen to the Belgrade Cassandra when the ultimate collapse of the capital was all about them. She spent that night alone, and on the morning of 7 October hell unfolded its wings. Now she didn't know where to go either. She started to run through downtown Dorchol.

She saw the desperate defence of Belgrade and could hardly believe it was real. All along the Danube quay down to the sawmill and the Prometna Banka, Serbian soldiers were offering resistance under the command of a madly brave, paunchy major with a long black moustache drooping into his mouth. The major, already hoarse, was yelling at the top of his voice and berating, cursing and encouraging the men at the same time—as if they were dogs one moment and people the next. The enemy emerged from the turbid river, mud-covered attackers like river monsters, who with gritted teeth captured the railway embankment, Ada Ciganliya Island, Robiyash Gardens on the outskirts and, like uninvited guests, took table after table of the Sharan restaurant. The major's men pulled back, and then at noon the Belgrade gendarmes charged the enemy. They were literally mowed down by those invaders from the river's sludge. It was little short of a massacre. Mrs Lir knew she had to console the bewildered people she met. Once again, she tried to tell them not to fret; they may be leaving their city with the enemy at their heels, but they would return and Belgrade would be more beautiful than before; a magnificent church would be raised at the edge of the former cemetery, and the sky above would be broader and smell of a childhood autumn.

She went from street to street, threading her way through destroyed houses, and again reached the small square near café Yasenica. Soldiers were standing there, lined up in three rows—more dead than alive—their rifles adorned with flowers from the nearby flower shop. She saw the pot-bellied major with the moustache and wanted to go up to him. She thought she would tell him there was no need to yell, that the people would make everything whole again and reward the defenders for all their efforts. But the Belgrade Cassandra was pushed aside and the major shouted to his men: 'At 15:00 hours sharp the enemy must be smashed and swept away by your mighty charge, by your grenades and bayonets. The honour of Belgrade, our capital, must be upheld. Soldiers! Heroes! The supreme command has struck our regiment from the records. Our regiment has been sacrificed for the glory of Belgrade and the Fatherland. You need no longer fear for your lives. They no longer exist. And now: forwards, to glory! For king and country! Long live the king, long live Belgrade!' And the soldiers moved off with a song whose ribs were all broken, with a heroism which had long since overcome all fear of death. Death had become a reality, to which they were reconciled.

It was 7 October, the day before the fall of Belgrade. And then the bloody 8 October came, the indifferent 9 and the dull 10 October. The Serbian army had evacuated Belgrade, a city located right on the border where other nations would have only built a watchtower, and now continued its great retreat. When the 2nd Bulgarian Army reached the River Vardar and entered the Kachanik Gorge on 26 October, cutting off the Serbian retreat south, the rain set in. It rained when rumours came that the folk hero Prince Marko had appeared near Pirot riding his skewbald charger Sharac and brandishing his golden sword. It rained when Hannah Hardy called on Annabel Walden and the other British nurses to leave Kraguyevac and head south. It rained when they arrived in Kosovska Mitrovica with dishevelled hair, like Hecuba and her daughters. It rained when the last officer of the Serbian 4th Regiment, Major Radoyica Tatich, left mud-bound Knyazhevac, retreating before superior enemy forces. It rained when King Peter told his troops near Djer on 27 October that he would stay with them and fight until final victory, or complete defeat. It rained when the king noted in his diary in Ribarska Banya, one day later: 'I hope the God of the Serbs still has a surprise in store for us.' It rained when the old Serbian king visited the positions of Colonel Milivoy Andjelkovich Kayafa near Lepa Voda on 31 October. When the royal train set off towards Kruševac—a terrible rain fell. When General Zhivkovich reported that the Germans had taken Kralyevo—a heavy rain broke. When the Morava Division, like a company of phantoms vanguarded by raucous copper trumpets, set off from Kosovo to defend a piece of Macedonia or join the river of refugees—a leaden rain poured. When Ribarska Banya fell on 11 November—the rain fell without let-up. When the remnants of the victorious Serbian army of 1914 huddled in the valley near Priština—the rain turned to sleet. When the royal family dined with its generals in the Fatherland for the last time and the silence was heavier than any words—the sleet turned to snow.

Then they all started towards Prizren and further, deep into uncertain Albania. A last liturgy and a last glance at the friendly landscape. The first station on this hardest of all roads was Lum-Kullë. The sides of the road were littered with field trains, cabs, guns, discarded breechblocks of cannons, cars with their doors pulled off, men with a suicidal look, and draught animals blind with hunger and thirst. Old King Peter was accompanied by Colonel Kosta Knezhevich, the court major-domo, adjutant Djukanovich, cavalry Captain Milun Tadich, who travelled one day ahead of the king, and finally the king's physician, Dr Svetislav Simonovich, who was inseparable from his umbrella. Everyone asked themselves what the long black umbrella was good for amidst the rocky terrain of Albania, in the incessant snow with sharp little flakes which crept under one's collar like bedbugs, but Dr Simonovich didn't explain much. He never used his big British umbrella to defend himself against the blasts of snow, nor did he swing it like a man of leisure, yet he was never to be seen without it. He set off into Albania with the umbrella and carried it all the way to Tirana.

The doctor was faster than the others and lighter than them too, although he had to lug thirty kilos of the king's medicines and dressings through Albania. But he had his umbrella. When no one was watching, Dr Simonovich would open the brolly and carefully arrange everything on his lap: the dressings, wooden boxes, ointments in glass jars, syringes and oval-shaped metal, surgical bowls. Then he closed it, fastened it with a band and clasp, and the umbrella would 'swallow' the whole load with only a slight bulge to be seen. The thirty kilos of medicines and related materials were reduced to a lump no larger than a nugget of gold and weighing just a hundred grams, until he opened the umbrella again. The doctor didn't understand how it worked, but he thanked his lucky stars that it lessened his load in that Calvary through Albania[1]. So he went from Lum-Kullë to Spas, and on to the towns of Fletë, Pukë and Fushë-Arrëz. He watched his old king suffering and others straggling, saw frozen soldiers by the wayside and came across Field Marshal Putnik's sedan chair, which was so small that it looked like a kind of box—while he had no problems of his own. He didn't tell anyone because they could get suspicious, so he grimaced and grumbled a little and always made sure to arrive in a new town before or a little after the others.

In Fletë, he dashed breathless into the caravanserai before the king's escort, and when he opened the umbrella he was almost caught by the commander of the provisional army base there, Zhivoyin 'Eiffel' Pavlovich. In Fushë-Arrëz, the king was received by a dozen of Esad Pasha's soldiers, and several of the Albanians rubbed their eyes when the doctor's truly remarkable umbrella accidentally came open and

---

1 After a dramatic retreat from Prizren (Kosovo) to the Adriatic coast through the hostile Albanian highlands, during which over 100,000 Serbs died of cold and hunger, the remnants of the army were ferried to Corfu by the Allies in early 1916.

the thirty kilos of medical supplies dropped out. The king's group reached the town of Leshë on 5 December 1915 at around eleven, and it was only thanks to Captain Murat Zmiyanovich that the secret was not discovered. In Shëngjin and Fushë-Krujë the medicines were 'unpacked' without incident, and finally the little convoy arrived in Tirana.

In the old Italian hotel where the king's suite was located, Dr Simonovich opened the umbrella as before, not suspecting anything. No, he couldn't have noticed that his wondrous 'carry brolly' had become lighter on the way to their final destination or that the load was different in some way; after all, it was condensed into a spot the size of a nugget of gold. He was therefore most surprised to find completely different medicines when he opened it. Instead of heavy little red-glass jars, long syringes, needles arranged in tins and crystalline blocks of various salts, the doctor saw neatly ordered phials in unusual transparent sheets, and tiny little jars and syringes made of some kind of lightweight, transparent glass. He was frightened: he closed the umbrella and opened it again. The new medicines were still there—they had truly replaced the old ones. What should he do with them? With doctorly discernment he opened one phial and sniffed at the powder inside (the smell was reminiscent of mould), he also examined the minuscule syringes, but he was most amazed by the hair-fine needles neatly ordered in a flexible covering of another kind of transparent material unknown to him.

Maybe these medicines were far more effective than those he had taken along with him; perhaps they would be better for treating old King Peter's ailments, but Dr Simonovich had no way of testing them, so he disposed of them without any pangs of conscience. Through various medical connections in Tirana he was able to reacquire the thirty kilos of conventional medicines and medical supplies. He didn't say a word to the king. He no longer hid the medicines in his umbrella, nor did he ever find out that he had discarded valuable antibiotics, medicines for high blood pressure, antidepressants, powerful analgesics and a small supply of aspirin.

Would a doctor on the opposite side in the war, Heinrich Aufschneider, have been able to recognize these medicines? Probably not, and not only due to him being a Viennese psychoanalyst, but because he was also a child of his age. He was a sergeant in the medical corps of the Austro-Hungarian army. In the thirteen days of the first occupation of

Belgrade in 1914, he too was a guest at Gavra Crnogorchevich's 'friendly Serbian house'. He was a soldier who had not yet seen a downfall—his own and others'—but still had the need to soothe his conscience and console himself by pretending to believe he was entering relationships with Gavra Crnogorchevich's 'daughters' there in occupied Serbia. He remembered that house well: the entrance was through a pigsty, and then there was an open sewer to be jumped; but when the prospective visitor opened the door, his astonished eyes were met with the spectacle of a real, slicked-up 'diplomatic club', with a number of thick-legged women whom the head of the household openly kissed and called 'my daughters'. This psychoanalyst got to know his host Gavra well in the space of those thirteen days in 1914: he was a man who seemed cruel and crude on the outside, and inside fatalistically certain that business would soon be over and he would meet a tragic end.

He was the first of the 'dead-end people', as Dr Aufschneider later came to call his protégés. When he entered Belgrade again one year later, in 1915, the psychoanalyst saw many dead-end people. He was given the task of accompanying a priest on his final visits to men sentenced to death, and this was a totally new experience for the psychoanalyst. He decided to write a paper about it and send it to the inner circle of psychoanalysts. The men condemned to death, he noticed, reduced their whole life to the few days remaining before the noose and began to live it like a new, three-day existence in which they had an urge to do something they had never done in their ordinary life, unbounded by the death sentence. Men who had never learnt to read asked for books or newspapers; others started painting; some took up smoking; others used the time to swear about the kaiser all day long; others again refused food and prepared themselves to leave for the afterlife on an empty stomach—and all of them were convinced they could do what came into their heads in those three or four days because nothing worse than the death penalty could happen to them.

A few weeks later, the doctor gave his work in progress the title 'The Psychology of the Man Sentenced to Death'. He completed it with ease and provided several dozen examples of men hung in Belgrade. He added photographs of the men on death row and was convinced he had to show the paper to the other psychoanalysts. Although he had applied for and received several days' leave, he didn't set off straight away because the entire army had to wait for Kaiser Wilhelm, who was coming to take a walk in Belgrade's Kalemegdan fortress—the first

German ruler since Barbarossa to glance down at the mouth of the Sava into the Danube beneath windy and spiteful Belgrade.

As soon as the kaiser was gone again, the doctor of the men sentenced to death immediately packed and boarded the first hospital train departing Belgrade railway station for the north. Setting off on this trip to find his fellow psychoanalysts, one after another, was to be the beginning of Dr Heinrich Aufschneider's personal drama. There would be no such story to tell if the doctor had not felt a sense of guilt deep in the dregs of his soul and if he had not been far more frightened than his men on death row. That was nothing out of the ordinary, any psychoanalyst could have told him, but what was about to happen on his peregrination through wartime Europe would become the subject of a paper written after the Great War by one of Freud's closest collaborators, Karl Abraham, albeit only as an extension of an earlier article from the 'totemic phase' of 1913.

The psychoanalyst Aufschneider was to become the centre of a tragic case of totemic identification. But what tormented the Vienna psycho-analyst so much that made him totemistically identify with death? Back in 1913, the psychoanalysis congress was held in Basel and each of the delegates of this mortally ill movement had to decide whom to vote for: Freud or Jung. Aufschneider gave his vote to the 'disobedient son Jung', but afterwards changed his mind. He never forgave himself for rising up against 'father Freud', however briefly, and for temporarily trusting Jung and allowing himself to be enchanted like an impressionable youth. He sought an appointment with the professor and Freud forgave him, but did Heinrich Aufschneider forgive himself?

The Great War came and the artillery barrage drowned out all thoughts, except perhaps those we conceal deep inside. But as soon as the operations on the Balkan Front ended, Aufschneider applied for leave, grabbed his paper and set off on his journey—a fatal voyage he should never have made. Later everything would be documented in detail. To begin with, he took 'The Psychology of the Man Sentenced to Death' to show to Freud's close associate, Sándor Ferenczi. Having totemistically identified with his guilt, and now inducing diseases in himself, Aufschneider suffered a perforation of the duodenum while visiting Ferenczi among the Hungarian hussars. He agonized and vomited and was miserable, but he put up with the terrible pain and continued his pilgrimage: to see the next member of Freud's com-mittee, Max Eitingon. There it was established that he had a chronic inflammation of the prostate gland (with suspicion of cancer) and was put to bed on doctor's orders. But the patient signed his own discharge papers and made it clear to Eitingon and the other doctors that he had to continue his journey. So it was that Aufschneider 'found his way'—as Freud's third confidant, Karl Abraham, wrote with a dash of unpsychoanalytical pathos—to see him at the military hospital in Olsztyn, East Prussia. Here the patient ought to have rested. Dr Abraham immediately confirmed the existing ailments and began conducting psychotherapy on him, suspecting from the start that these were totemic diseases, which a patient comes down with of their own, hidden volition. But the diseases were genuine and Dr Abraham trembled with excitement at the possibility of discovering a new link in the chain of psychological possibilities of a patient burdened by guilt; it would be the first recorded clinical case of someone falling ill of their own accord.

He told none of this to his colleague and patient Aufschneider but tried to keep him in bed and on his analyst's couch for as long as possible. Once he had documented two diseases—a perforation of the duodenum (he termed it 'Ferenczi's disease') and chronic prostatitis ('Eitingon's disease)—and then diagnosed a third, cirrhosis of the liver, which the patient had developed while visiting him ('Abraham's disease'), the patient was allowed to proceed on his journey under the condition that he be escorted. One of Abraham's assistants followed him closely, and it is thanks to him that we have a report on Aufschneider's last days.

After leaving East Prussia, on the way to his final destination, Vienna, the patient with three diseases had to stop off in Kraków, where the local soldiers' newspaper was edited by the fourth member of the committee who wore Freud's ring: Otto Rank. The patient didn't justify himself or make any excuses in front of Rank either, which further confirmed the subconscious basis of his self-induced illnesses. Aufschneider, who by now was exhausted, told Rank that he had come to Kraków to show him his paper 'The Psychology of the Man Sentenced to Death'. There, in the old Polish capital, he soon came down with a fourth disease: a stomach ulcer ('Rank's disease'). How he managed to stay on two legs is known only to the deep currents of the psyche, which is capable of holding us upright until our will completely fails.

The patient therefore hastened to continue his journey on from Kraków. He was obliged to move on, and the last station was known to all: Vienna, where the icy and ever gloomier Dr Freud was waiting. Still, the father of psychoanalysis cordially received his young colleague.

Why father Sigmund and daughter Anna weren't surprised at the newcomer's arrival became clear: the reason for the Freud's warm and almost fraternal reception lay in the wartime letters which had overtaken the patient. By the time he saw his 'runaway son', Freud had already received detailed reports from Ferenczi, Eitingon and Rank, as well as a complete case history on the patient written by Dr Abraham at the hospital in Olsztyn. The father of psychoanalysis naturally took an interest, which is why he immediately accepted the patient into his cold house. It bemused Aufschneider—why not use that expression—that Freud read his paper and even made suggestions in his own hand in the margins, but actually he was just observing the patient's condition. He waited maybe a week, two at the most, and then the pilgrim developed a toothache: first in one tooth, then in another, and finally the whole jaw. Before long, it was established that poor Dr Aufschneider had contracted cancer of the jaw beneath his lower right molar ('Freud's pernicious disease').

The end came swiftly and the psychoanalyst did not live to see the New Year 1916. After the Great War, his pilgrimage became the corner-stone of a study entitled 'The Psychology of the Wartime Patient', which Dr Freud only let Dr Abraham have and take credit for after much wrangling, with the former only allowing Freud to add a few words as an intimate dedication at the top. But that was not until much later, after the Great War had finally ended.

On the eve of 1916, neither Abraham nor Freud knew if they would live to see the next year, and nor did Father Donovan, who had just lost a soldier on New Year's Eve. He didn't hearten the young man this time and urge him to grab the pole. The boy arrived with an enormous, gaping hole in his stomach and it was a miracle that the chaplain managed to confess him at all. That wasn't the first time he lost a soldier, but it was New Year's Eve, for God's sake. That death at the turn of the year was a particularly hard blow for him. He came out of the wooden dugout in the trench of the Scottish 92nd Division with cap in hand and looked up into the sky. Never before had he felt he could see so much sky and so many stars with one gaze.

Hans-Dieter Huis didn't sing for the New Year 1916, but he would again soon—no doubt about it.

Guillaume Apollinaire hadn't found a new sweetheart by the time the New Year came around.

Stefan Holm didn't live to see the New Year 1916. Cholera, which he first felt as mild pain in the lower abdomen, developed so rapidly that they barely managed to lay him in bed. He died in an improvised field hospital not far from the trenches. The patients lay densely packed in that that log cabin, one beside the other, like galley slaves chained to the oars. Some men shook as they lay there wrapped in dirty blankets, others ate without appetite, others vomited. With death-like, grey faces and large, serious eyes, they just waited to die. They were no longer soldiers or men, but monstrous creatures, diseased and miserable, who were now paying the price for having survived the combat. Stefan was no different. His last words were: 'Send my cap to Warsaw.' But no one knew why he said that, so they sent it to Heidelberg instead.

Boris Dmitrievich Rizanov and two of his comrades staged a spectacular breakout from a German labour camp, which the newspaper *Russkoye Slovo* later wrote about. They cut away wooden boards to make a nutshell of a boat and rowed it with their shovels, and in this way they crossed the Little Belt into the Baltic Sea. From the island of Bågø in neutral Denmark the fugitives were sent to Assens, from where they returned via Sweden to Russia.

Field Marshal Boroevich von Boina was caressed by the southern sun for the whole of the last day of 1915, and he wore one uniform until midnight and the other after midnight. No one noticed him change identical coats or saw his left hand shake his right as he wished himself a happy new 1916.

Old Libion and Old Combes saw in the New Year 1916 in the company of prostitutes, lame artists and cocky jugglers from the provinces. The spigots of the newly arrived barrels of sour wine from Touraine were knocked out one after another amidst universal good cheer.

On that New Year's Eve, Jean Cocteau ceremoniously opened his last tin of bogus 'Madagascar' beef. It was in fact crabmeat, which melted in his mouth and mingled with the words he spoke to himself: 'I must find that seedy little Kiki de Montparnasse again. Each of her tins is well worth its money.'

Lilian Schmidt sang at another Berlin variety show to welcome in the New Year. Nothing was further from her mind now than singing 'It's a Long Way to Tipperary'; instead, her rich voice glided down to disappointed, alto depths to sing 'Die Wacht am Rhein'.

Fritz Haber didn't even notice that it was New Year's Eve. In 1915, he had lost his wife Clara Immerwahr, but much work lay ahead in the New Year: improving the cylinders for releasing the gas, better training the soldiers, and devising a totally new way of mass poisoning with the aid of the air force. No, he had no time to think that the New Year replaces the old, but he was already preparing to take stock of his life, without knowing that it would cost him dearly.

On New Year's Eve, Lucien Guirand de Scevola came up with a way of combining all his pre-war talents and became the first commander of the French camouflage company.

Submarine commander Walther Schwieger saw in the New Year 1916 as befitted him—under water, with his serpents, megalodons and giant octopuses. Singing was heard in the New Year's night; probably that of the crew. Or was it?

The soldier Giorgio de Chirico continued to paint metaphysical canvases, and during the long New Year's night he thanked God that there was no trace of his imitator, Karlo Rota.

The day 1915 was seen out and the New Year 1916 was welcomed in, Amanda Henze became the happiest and the most unhappy mother in the world. Her son Hans Henze sat down at the piano in a small auditorium and gave a perfect rendition of all the shades and nuances of Chopin's *Berceuse* (Lullaby) with his right hand, naturally without the base melody, because he couldn't play the piano with his left hand, which could only write poetry in French.

Thirteen days later, by the old calendar, the Sukhomlinovs saw in the New Year 1916. They saw out the old year under house arrest at their residence in Petrograd. As former minister of war, Sukhomlinov first tried unsuccessfully to bribe the sentries to procure him a bottle of Georgian cognac; afterwards he tried to trick his Lady Macbeth into letting him partake of the white lushness of her body, from the stern or the prow; but since he was successful at neither, he fell asleep disgruntled and saw in the New Year in his dreams.

The grand duke awaited the advent of the New Year at his headquarters in Tbilisi, with Russian Cossacks. He felt caged. The men around him were crude—real killers who had only just wiped the blood from their sabres, fists and fur hats for that one night. But this was the Caucasus, so it was with subjects such as these that the viceroy saw in the New Year.

The neurosurgeon Sergei Chestukhin was demobilized at the end of 1915 and sent back to Petrograd. Ever more soldiers were being killed by Haber's gas at the front, so the surgeon had more work back at his clinic from where he had set off for the war. Sergei and Liza Chestukhin were therefore reunited on New Year's Eve 1916. Or were they? Liza, as if abandoned, in the corner. Sergei in the doorway. Liza smiling. Sergei serious. Liza swung her copper hair and waved her hand like a child wanting to get away from the smoke of a cigar. Sergei continued smoking cigars of black tobacco. Marusya remembered that image from the previous New Year's Eve.

Mrs Lir didn't live to see 1916. She died in an artillery barrage in Nish shortly before the Bulgarians marched into the city. She lived her last moments in the street amid a hectic mass of people and animals. Men whipped oxen, while bristly Mangalitza pigs squeezed past their legs, grunting in distress. Impoverished peasants hurried past her, as well as gypsies with their tents, officers with their medals, limping soldiers wrapped in rags and wartime purveyors clenching bags under their arms. They were all leaving for somewhere. Mrs Lir was going somewhere too, but beyond the confines of this world.

Zhivka D. Spasich, the Belgrade seamstress, was glad that she had been able to move her tailor shop out of Dunavska Street. Strange things had been happening there. Everything was in good order at the new address. In fact, she liked it so much at 26 Prince Eugene Street that she hardly left the premises, even now when her clientele was limited to men in Austro-Hungarian army uniforms, and business flourished the next year and in the years that followed—and no one, no one at all, disappeared when they drew the curtain behind them in the changing room.

Dr Svetislav Simonovich saw in the New Year at the side of his king on board the torpedo boat Mameluk on the way from Brindisi to Salonika. He massaged King Peter with the old balms he knew, and then the king had him stay for the beggarly supper in the first-class cabin, which, with one of his witty remarks, he called 'dinner at the Ritz'.

Mehmed Yıldız did not mark the new-fangled, infidel New Year in any special way, except perhaps with astonishment. No, this old Turk was not disconcerted by the whiff of terror in the streets and the fact that the jails were full of prisoners who had uttered a single word of criticism against the Young Turk Committee of Union and Progress. It had risen and now ruled Turkey with terror and prisons, and that squared with the trader's expectations in the straight-and-narrow world of the righteous. But how could it be that German families were arriving at the railway station below Topkapı Palace from Bulgaria every day and then travelling on to places in Asia Minor, from where the Armenians had been expelled? Were they to settle there? To become new Anatolians? How could Germans, those Westerners with their breadth and depth, possibly help the Turks—a people without prospects?

Perhaps it was all part of that year of the trader, 1915, which he saw out with two deep scars on his soul. Why did he still believe that trade and commerce would save young lives on all sides? Had horrible 1915 not made him change his mind? Why had it not shaken his optimism? It was one thing to climb the Camondo Stairs and run a shop in swish Galata, mixing with the Jewish, Coptic and Syrian traders and lying to yourself and others that dreams and status are sold together with the goods; it was a different matter to fight so that this great war would end all future wars. But maybe he was old and gradually exiting the trading world on the downslope of life. He was seventy-six and had begun his fifty-ninth year of trading by the Bosporus. He had just one year to go before he reached the tally of three score years and fulfilled the life of a trader according to the old Turkish saying. 'You have to trade with both death and life,' the effendi muttered to himself, and with that thought he fell asleep. Thus ended the year for one trader.

His alarm clock rang in the morning of the first day of the New Year 1916. But he didn't open the shop that morning although a splendid, if scarcely warming sun rose over the Bosporus on the first day of the third year of the war.

1916
THE YEAR OF
THE KING

Grigory Rasputin, Major-General
Putyatin and Colonel Lotman, 1916

THE VALLEY OF THE DEAD

It was the morning of 1 January 1916 by the new calendar. The deep-blue dawn turned a paler shade of blue and finally went milky, like a child's undershirt, cast over the tearful Salonika sky. King Peter woke up early and stared out into the gulf. He swallowed the taste of defeat so he would not feel it in his mouth like a bad tooth. Now his gaze simply wandered. Old as he was, with muscles shrivelled and taut and with swollen veins, he had to give himself a nudge to start all over again. The Allied General Staff was in Salonika. The broad Macedonian port looked like a humming beehive. The blue gulf resembled a huge factory where the funnels of two hundred ships belched smoke. The streets were choked with soldiers of various nations: indifferent French, confused British, and Greeks, who for reasons unknown were exceedingly irritated.

Field trains and supply units followed one another in an endless line: lazily from the sea up into the hills, and then straight back down to the sea, seemingly willy-nilly, as if to just create the impression that something was happening. The surrounding heights were studded with white tents. Anxiety lingered over Salonika like a stupor, strong enough to sedate and distract from another drama—the tragic plight of the Serbian army away on the shores of the Ionian Sea. Now the king gazed down into the street. The whole Greek people seemed to be in uniform; they had taken possession of the cafés, were jostling in front of the cinemas, and bought oranges and figs from the fruit ladies. Some Frenchmen were chatting beneath his balcony, and King Peter heard and understood them. 'Do you know that the Serbs are dying behind those Albanian hills?' one of them said, and another answered: 'But we can't help them. Things here aren't going well, you know. The Greeks are against us, and we disembarked against the will of the Greek king. The Allies have been on their guard and bristling for three nights now. No, it's impossible to withdraw even just one battalion to send to the front in Macedonia. A Bartholomew's Night could be in store for us here.'

The king stopped listening. His Bartholomew's Night had already been; it had come like a frenzied, wailing banshee and was gone again, leaving him to suffer, still alive like a tragic hero. Now he was living a grotesque new life-unlife which he had blundered into like a blind man. He went to the other end of the room and closed the window, and then the noises of the street were gone. He should be king again; he should ring the bell and receive the Serbian envoy and arrange to leave the hotel. After all, he had only disembarked to stay in it for one night. He had to give himself a nudge and ring that bell. So many kings were in exile. Had he not grown up and come of age in exile himself? Had he not first been fed with the milk of foreign lands, countries safe but cold? So what was new about the situation? The new element was that an entire kingdom was in exile! Oh, it would be better not to think any more and just ring.

As he reached for the bell and his fingers clenched the handle, his hand shook by itself. The porcelain clapper rang the bell and the day began. King Peter decided not to attend the reception in Salonika prepared by representatives of the Greek and Allied authorities. Instead, he ordered that he be taken by motor launch, which now came to the quay for him, straight to the Serbian consulate further along the bay. They were to approach it as circumspectly as possible—as if the launch was carrying a conspirator or a disowned princeling rather than a king. The king had decided in advance not to remain at the hotel but to move to the consulate. He didn't want any pomp, and the guard of honour he now saw waiting in front of the consulate bothered him. 'Greece goes and rejects its 1913 agreement with us, it makes us take to the ravines of Albania where we lost so many people in that Calvary, and now it wants to show us a tad of honour and respect?' the old man muttered to himself, while at the shore in front of the consulate Colonel Todorovich tried to persuade the short, moustachioed commander of the guard of honour to move aside. 'The king is tired and doesn't want any pomp,' the colonel repeated, as the black boat of the motor-launch company glided away behind him, and a few Greek soldiers stood at attention even without being ordered to.

The king went in nevertheless, without looking at anyone. 'The Serbian monarch gives his thanks and excuses himself,' he heard behind his back, while the crowd which had gathered in front of the Serbian consulate slowly dispersed. In the days that followed, the king and his entourage returned to their pressing affairs. This afterlife showed astonishing vitality in presenting its real substance: the Belgian emissary certainly looked palpable when he came up to shake the king's hand; Edward Boyle, the philanthropist, was offering what seemed to be real assistance for the Serbs; and the Christmas greetings which King Peter received several days later from the British king, the Duke of

Orleans and the Serbian Prime Minister Nikola Pashich arrived on very convincing telegraph paper. But King Peter still didn't trust life in that abyssal year of 1916, just as one Turk didn't believe in that year either.

Let us call him Non-Bey, although he called himself Cam Zulad Bey, and his real name was Vartkes Noradungian. The tale of this harsh and relentless Turkish policeman begins with him changing his religion and extinguishing the last Armenian ember in himself. That Bey thought he was doing it solely for the sake of promotion, higher rank and stars on his lapel next to the word 'Kanun' (Law); he thought he would never have to examine what small trace of Armenianness remained in him, but things turned out differently. Cam Zulad Bey did not hesitate at all when, back in 1914 at the beginning of the Great War, ethnic Armenians were to be accused of the defeats in the Turkish army's Caucasus campaign and the subsequent disaster at the Battle of Sarikamish. He looked deep inside himself and could no longer see anything Armenian there, or in his appearance. He bought a newspaper and sat by the Bosporus like every other Turk; he read and smoked a chibouk like a Turk, and with mute movements of his lips approved of Enver Pasha's words in the paper: "The Armenians are to blame for the Turkish defeat and the sixty thousand righteous men left lying face-down in the muddy snow. The Armenian recruits must therefore be disarmed. They are a foreign body in our army." Hear, hear!, the policeman repeated inside, blew out smoke and saw that everything in his appearance, as well as inside, was in good order. And so he went on without looking back.

Non-Bey saw nothing strange in being the first Istanbul policeman entrusted with censoring Armenian mail. Not a single Bakelite button on his coat was Armenian. He didn't shrink from boycotting Armenian shops and stores, and he didn't see anything bad in the liquidation of five Armenian leaders in April 1915. He saw no justification for the Armenian rebellion in the city of Van and cursed the day the Russians aided the insurgents to withstand the siege. Pogroms spread throughout Turkey and took on a particular dread in the cobblestone streets of the capital. But Non-Bey felt quite at ease. He didn't find it strange that he, of all people, had been entrusted with shadowing Armenian intellectuals in all three parts of Istanbul and later placing them under house arrest. He peered into the black dregs of his soul and didn't see a single Armenian word warning him to stop. Therefore he didn't find it at all unusual that he sent all his previous Armenian neighbours into exile that year, in 1915. It wasn't his job to sympathise with them. He didn't shed a tear when he heard that hundreds and thousands of Armenians had died on their way to Syria and Mesopotamia.

When Talaat Pasha declared, towards the end of 1915: 'I have accomplished more towards solving the Armenian problem in three months than Sultan Abdul Hamid accomplished in thirty years,' Non-Bey felt himself to be a Turk, above all else. He was praised for his devoted service, received a promotion and was assisted in buying a splendid wooden house in the Hisar neighbourhood. He didn't find anything unusual when he entered his new home because he had thrown out everything which belonged to the old owners, down to the last towel and sheet, so nothing would smell of Christians. Then, from good Turkish homes, he had bought up divans, wicker chairs, mirrors in wooden frames and even creepers for the second-floor porch. Now he was the supervisor of the entire vilayet—him, a former Armenian policeman on the banks of the Bosporus! What had his name been back when he was Armenian? He couldn't remember. He had no time. Now he was sent to Trabzon to 'smooth things over' after the 'solution of the Armenian problem' there.

When he set off on the trip at the beginning of 1916, he thought about how he didn't trust the New Year 1916. The previous year had been the greatest for Turkdom, he felt, because they had got rid of the wretched Armenians once and for all. He entered the city of Trabzon, and before him lay a valley of the dead. He literally had to walk over bodies, there were so many of them. But Cam Zulad Bey didn't look back. Sometimes his legs would sink into pits of putrid flesh with a crunch of bones, but Non-Bey was cool and unruffled. Holes teeming with grey maggots opened up here and there beneath his feet. Most of the corpses of his fellow Armenians were covered with only a thin layer of soil, which had been washed away in places by the rain. Heaps of dead rebels lay where they had fallen in the three-day revolution in Trabzon: still half in motion, as if rising up against Turkey and the Young Turk committee again, but Cam Zulad Bey didn't feel the slightest despondency. In one place he saw the rat-gnawed skeletons of Turks and Armenians still grasping each others' throats, their arms and legs entwined in a crush they couldn't loosen even after death. Cam Zulad Bey seemed to feel nothing. But then he turned around. He, who had not hesitated at all when there was a call to accuse Armenian soldiers of the defeat at Sarikamish, who didn't shrink from boycotting Armenian shops and stores, who placed Armenian intellectuals from all three parts of Istanbul under house arrest, who sent all his neighbours into exile and who couldn't even remember his Armenian name—now stopped in his tracks.

He turned around as if he had forgotten something, just some trivial little thing like his snuffbox or the rolling paper he should have put in his pocket before leaving Istanbul. Then a single trickle of perspiration ran down his forehead as if he had broken into a sweat from walking over the corpses, although he had not hesitated when there was a call to accuse Armenian soldiers of the defeat at Sarikamish, had not shrunk from boycotting Armenian shops and stores, had placed Armenian intellectuals from all three parts of Istanbul under house arrest, had sent all his neighbours into exile, and couldn't even remember his Armenian name. Now his mouth suddenly filled with foam. He grasped for his throat, his eyes began to roll wildly as if they were about to pop out, and then he collapsed. He could bear it no longer.

Cam Zulad Bey fell: the last victim of the Armenian carnage.

The Great War ended for Non-Bey in that last hour when he remembered his Armenian name: Vartkes Noradungian. But whether he embraced it and flew up to heaven as an Armenian, or remained an Ottoman and ordinary Istanbul policeman until the end, is privy only to God, also known as Allah or Jehovah, among other names. The year 1916 remained indifferent: it neither blamed 1915 for its crimes nor thought of being any different itself.

In the French trenches on the Western Front, Guillaume Apollinaire realized what war really was. There were no more letters from the rear. Nor new girlfriends. Nor opium dens and imitation Chinese offering pipes of opium. The artilleryman was now in the grips of a 'great melancholy'. Not so much because of the weather. He got used to the awful rain. And the mud. And he got used to those trench comrades, the rats. But he couldn't get used to the stupidity of headquarters. Military councils were constantly in session. Courts martial were introduced. Every soldier who was wounded in the hand and had black marks around the wound risked being shot, because the black could be gunpowder soot, which would indicate self-mutilation.

At the beginning of 1916, near Souain, the 2nd Company of the 336th Infantry Division refused an order to attack the enemy trenches. The men were exhausted. Attack. Counter-attack. Attack. Counter-attack.

A new assault meant death. The Germans had just replaced the barbed wire in no man's land. An advance under such circumstances was nothing short of suicide. Faced with such disobedience, the French general in charge of the 336th Infantry Division thought of laying down an artillery barrage on his own trenches. At the intervention of his faithful colonel, he changed his mind. Instead, he ordered that six corporals and eighteen privates be picked from among the youngest soldiers. These 'hostages' were taken before the military council, and the court martial summarily sentenced them to death.

It transpired that the non-commissioned officers near Apollinaire didn't pick any men at all. Sometimes dice were rolled, and those with the least luck were taken and shot. Second Lieutenant Apollinaire was particularly upset by the fate of Second Lieutenant Chapelant, a twenty-year-old machine-gunner in the 98th Infantry Regiment. Second Lieutenant Chapelant was brave. He had blue eyes. And the gaze of a daydreamer. The same gaze as Apollinaire. By the time the poet met him, the dreams had already begun to fade from Chapelant's eyes. The next day, Chapelant's sector of the Front was attacked. The machine-gunner and his crew were surrounded but refused to surrender. The cut-off men would fire a burst every fifteen minutes to make the Germans think they still had enough ammunition. They were left there between dark and death, amongst all the barbed wire. When French stretcher-bearers were finally able to rescue the wounded men, Chapelant, as their officer, was taken to be court-martialled on the stretcher. They had been found behind enemy lines. The sentence was spoken: execution. The stretcher was set upright. They tied Chapelant so he wouldn't fall off and fired three bullets into his chest. 'Things like that demoralize the men,' Apollinaire wrote to his mother on an ordinary soldier's postcard. He waited for a reply from her. Nothing came, and he came to the conclusion that this was probably because the card was not one of Birot's wondrous wartime postcards.

Before the Great War, Pierre Albert-Birot had been a poet and sculptor. A self-styled poet, and unrecognized as a sculptor. But he persistently claimed that he had the face of a poet and the body of sculptor. As a matter of fact he was rickety, had a pigeon chest, and always stooped so that his shadow invariably went in front of his steps, whichever direction the sun was shining from. He launched several avant-garde magazines in the course of the Great War, but he saw they were eating away at his savings. The magazine *SIC (Son, Idées,*

Couleurs, Formes) was the one he believed in longest, but he didn't want to admit to himself that both it and *Elan*, a magazine he launched together with the Dadaists, were really just a screen for publishing his poems. Finally, he realized it was too much for him. After all, he was a man with increasing pain in his crooked frame and with the pocket of a small manufacturer.

At the beginning of the Great War, he had set up a small workshop to produce and market postcards. He printed them at his own expense and sold them to soldiers and their families to facilitate their correspondence. Outwardly, Birot's postcards looked like any others. They had an idealized French soldier on the front, with flowers in his lapel and a loving Frenchwoman by his side. They were not particularly well printed, but their value lay elsewhere—they were far more talented than other cards. While ordinary wartime correspondence took weeks to arrive, sometimes months, Birot's postcards went like express mail, evading censors and mail sorters and extracting themselves from the Red Cross depot in Geneva, where thousands of mail items from soldiers, POWs and their families lay waiting for someone to pigeon-hole, stamp and send them.

The soldiers were quick to notice this, and their families even quicker. In time, it seems the postcards themselves realized they were special. Old Birot was probably the only one who didn't notice anything. After all, he didn't trace the delivery paths of mail. He lived in the conviction that this quaint graphic of the soldier with flowers in his lapel and sweetheart by his side had been done for him by bigoted Dadaists, although they disdained figurative art. He thought it was the face of that universal soldier—that perfectly insipid, righteous man on the front of the postcard—which made his cards sell so well, but he was mistaken. When soldiers weren't busy being killed, they spent days on end sending and receiving mail. They wrote in the lulls between attacks, they wrote when they returned alive from parapet duty, and they wrote as soon as they took off their masks and the clappers gave the all-clear for gas. Since they wrote so much, they had plenty of opportunity to see that Birot's postcards reached their destinations, while others didn't. Why the otherwise diligent Guillaume Apollinaire didn't notice and, as we recall, wrote to his mother on ordinary paper, is not known. But that is not important for the story.

This is the tale of how Birot's cards began to write a parallel history of the war by continuing where the initial writers left off. The postcards were sold in many places at the front and in the rear, but a considerable number of them disappeared from the shops. Poor old Birot, he thought they were being stolen by vagabonds, but he couldn't have imagined that they left the shops all by themselves. This is what happened: while a soldier was alive and sending postcards himself, Birot's cards were compliant and just relied on their extraordinary ability to be delivered; but if the soldier was killed, they would take the initiative and continue to write his history for months to come.

'I'm well. A bit lice-ridden, but that doesn't matter,' they would begin, but the more time passed since the death of the signer, the more they became inclined to philosophise and agitate against the war. Their only limitation was space, but they were able to overcome it by using ever smaller letters and expressing their ideas more concisely. One group of Birot's postcards was particularly talented. They were used by the machine-gunner, Second Lieutenant Henri Chapelant. While he was alive, he wrote to his mother: 'Chère Maman, I think this last war has sullied even your maternal skirt.' He continued in the course of 1914: 'Don't believe the rumours, dear brother—I wasn't killed near Ypres, I pulled through with just a few scars because I bought a gas mask in good time.' There were also trivial notes like, 'I'm hungry, so wretchedly hungry. Some of my comrades have roasted rats. I watched but didn't dare to eat', and 'The snow this morning, Maman, has dusted the whole hill like icing sugar. Everything seems unreal. The fine snow just keeps falling, and when a bullet is put in the barrel it starts to turn white like when you sprinkle icing sugar over one of your cakes.'

Later Chapelant was shot—we saw it happen—but the postcards continued to send themselves. His mother in Le Havre received dozens of them, and she still thought for a long time that her son was alive. Only Chapelant's younger brother suspected something. At first, only short messages came from the machine-gunner. 'I'm alive, don't worry'; 'There was a big attack on our sector', and then 'I'm alive' and 'I'm alive' again. Later, long-expected postcards with more extensive messages began to arrive; the devoted, seventeen-year-old brother was astute enough to notice that, although the handwriting was Chapelant's, the language wasn't. There were clumsy grammatical mistakes as well as strange stray words here and there, which the pre-war daydreamer had never used. But everyone was going through the Great War, and people changed in the course of it. That's what the machine-gunner's relatives thought, and the postcards continued to send themselves. What can be said of the last cards from the workshop of Pierre Albert-Birot? They were written with strangely bulbous, distorted letters, which no longer even had accents on them. One of them said: 'The last god died on the cross and his resurrection was only to save his own skin, it seems. Yeshua Ha-Nozri took none of our sins upon himself, and if I could find those Gypsies who made the nails, I'd go into their smithy and reforge the fourth one that was lost before the crucifixion.' the last postcard to arrive in Le Havre contained a final lament, in no way worthy of a daydreamer. It read: 'Where is that inviolable God? You know, treaties are written by the great and powerful for amusement and to kill time. Paper is paper and you can write anything. God is a fictional figure invented by those with a vested interest, just as war, suffering and million-fold death are in their interest.'

Here the correspondence died. Not a single auto-written postcard more came from Chapelant from the valley of the dead. His mother and brother sent a few more of Birot's talented postcards to the Front, but there was no longer any reply. Many other French soldiers—alive or freshly dead—continued to write to their loved ones. The correspondence was only ended by those who, having departed this world, were so far away that not even magic postcards could imitate their life. But their places were taken by new soldiers who wrote and then wrote some more, so old Birot thought he had found the goose that laid the golden egg.

To be sure, there were also men who didn't write home but had so much freedom of movement that they imitated the talented postcards and extracted themselves from their units as if the war was a non-committal undertaking. One of the most talented fly-by-nights from the front to the rear was Jean Cocteau. He needed to return to civilization; he had used up his last tins of 'Madagascar' food and now had to find the girl Kiki again. He came to Paris in 1916 with sadness in his heart and nostalgia on his lips: 'This isn't the Paris of 1915, just as it wasn't at all the Paris of 1914.' And added: 'That was a good vintage, 1914...' but he didn't permit himself to wallow in melancholy. He didn't even think of looking for Picasso. Instead, he did his utmost to find his patron, the seedy little Kiki. He arrived in front of the factory in a motor taxi, once again in his dress uniform and wearing a crimson helmet, but there was a surprise in store for him.

Kiki was no longer assigned to the food factory. He asked after her: Did anyone know 'Kiki'? But no one knew her. Did she have a surname? He didn't know that Kiki's wartime record card called her by her real name of Alice Ernestine Prin, and therefore he didn't find her. A peasant woman from Provence was working in her place: simple-minded, obstinate and unyielding. He tried to curry her favour, but it was no use. He tried to bribe her, but either she didn't realize the value of wartime money or was obstinately incorruptible. In the end, he stole ten tins at the risk of being caught and court-martialled. He went to a private machinist's to have prime-quality beef sealed in them. But when he opened one to test it, his meat smelt of motor oil, so he threw away all of the tins.

Finally, while still in Paris, he heard that soldiers were fighting tooth and nail to get hold of a particular medicine for asthma. He asked around what was so special about the medicine, and they told him that Dr Wilcox's elixir consisted of glycerine, atropine sulphate (irrelevant) and cocaine hydrochloride (the important ingredient) and was used in all the Allied armies. Cocteau immediately reported to a Paris medical commission. Just like he had struggled to gain weight back in beautiful 1914 so he could join in that operatic war, now he did his best to fall ill, without it being serious. One of his last friends advised him to sleep with damp cloths on his chest—he'd get a chill and a shallow cough like an asthmatic. He did that, and for two nights he felt he had it worse than the soldiers out in the rainy trenches. On the third day, a salutary cough set in. The commission prescribed him the medicine.

How lovely the war now looked to that returnee on cocaine! He was no longer hungry. His inspiration returned. He wrote about celestial hordes, subterranean demons and the beauty of heroes' mothers in black. He didn't think of little Kiki any more. He hadn't found her because she had changed factories. She now worked on reconditioning and cobbling soldiers' boots to be sent back to the Front. The battered boots had been taken off dead soldiers. Little Kiki disinfected them, softened them with oil and touched them up with a hammer. Her new wartime job was at first no better than the old one. And she still lived in abject poverty. For fifty centimes a week she had to fix up fifty pairs: one centime per pair of boots. Kiki was lonely. She dreamed of men, and she couldn't imagine that straight after the Great War she would become the most famous model of Montparnasse and the bedmate of many celebrities. Now, in 1916, she was still no one's, and she wanted to belong to a strong man. What about that gangly fellow with beige gloves, pilot's uniform and crimson helmet? No, she no longer remembered Jean Cocteau.

When she took new a pair of boots, she imagined who had worn them. She pretended not to know they'd been taken off the legs of dead soldiers. Before she started work on the boots, she put them on her own feet, and then she saw everything: who had worn them, where he had been in them, and how he had fallen. She stood in front of the mirror and grasped the little bumps like raspberries on her rounded white chest beneath her apron, and in the reflection, behind her, she caught a glimpse of her sweetheart, perhaps one of those men, from whom Birot's illustrated postcards were still being sent. But she soon noticed that this only happened while the boots were untreated, when they came off the conveyor belt with the body odours and touch-marks of the former soldiers. Once she had worked on them—and they were washed, softened, put on a wooden last and reshaped with a heavy hammer—the boots lost all the attributes of their owners and could no longer tell her a single story. So she enjoyed them while they were shabby, but work had to go on, or else she would lose those paltry fifty sous a week, and she wasn't such a whippersnapper as not to know that she would then soon die of hunger.

Kiki therefore only chose the boots of her lovers. She liked fair-haired men the best. She didn't fall for idealists and didn't like louts. Attentive men were her favourite, ones who took care of her and her needs. Every day she had a new choice of freshly arrived boots and put aside those with the most endearing prehistory. The others were just soldiers' boots: she battered them with the hammer like she was a bad policeman; she rubbed them with oil to make them supple like a good policeman. By the end of the working day she had finished her eight to nine pairs.

Those she didn't work on she kept in the tool cupboard, and as if they were dwarves who had strayed in from the valley of the dead, she called them Jules, Jean, Jacques, Joseph, Jacob, Joël. At any given moment, our short tomboy, with the round bottom, had five or six lovers. Some had been in the cupboard for days, while others had just arrived the day before. She taught them to get along with each other: Joël should stop being jealous of Jacques, and she told off Jean for scheming against Joseph. They were all there just to please her, and when she had had enough of them she returned them to the conveyor belt and treated them like any other boots. But while they were hers, her lover-boots were not allowed to belong to anyone else. Who would think of taking them from her, those ordinary old boots of dead soldiers? But for Kiki they were real: they had faces, hands, broad shoulders, and stiff members when they became excited. At the end of the working day, she would take off her shoes and, barefooted, carefully slide her white soles into the boots. Then, in the empty workshop, where she got naked at night, their copulation took place. She had nothing on except the boots on her legs. She would sit with her bare bottom on the dirty floor and start to pant, twist, to grab her breasts with the dark nipples and moan. Kiki spread her legs and received Joseph, Jean or Joël and twitched on the floor like an epileptic. Everything simply gushed out of her: she cried, belched, farted. Then she stood up, returned to this world all sweaty, and fondled the boots as if they were lovers she had been in bed with between crisp white sheets.

New boots kept arriving, non-stop. She knew by the size of the consignments if there had been a lull at the front or if a major offensive had got under way somewhere. A hundred boots was one thing, but a thousand boots removed from the legs of soldiers in one day was something else again. The ten thousand that arrived on the last day of February 1916 shocked even Kiki, who was disinclined to sentiment and hardened to surprise. The boots smelt of a quick, common death. Not one pair attracted her enough to set it aside in her cupboard, so she began to batter them with the hammer and rub them with oil immediately. She worked during the day. She also worked at night. Where were the boots coming from? She only asked herself that a week later. She found out that they were coming from the steel-blue north, where the Germans had attacked the weakly-manned defences near the proud city of Verdun, hoping that pride would tempt the French to move up new forces to die there in droves. Nowhere did as many men ever die for just five kilometres of ground.

For Kiki, the story of this bloodiest battle in the history of warfare until 1916 would certainly have been called 'the story of a hundred pairs of boots'. We might call it 'the story of a hundred heroes', and it could go like this: shortly after seven in the morning on 21 February 1916, following the German artillery preparation which was enough to make the strongest man cringe, and after a flame-thrower onslaught fit to make him shudder with revulsion, the Battle of Verdun began. The German infantry charged, and they had a clear objective: Fort Douaumont, three kilometres away. All the attacking men thought the battle would be determined by bravery, brilliant tactics and a swift advance, but instead it was determined by the dead.

Karl Fritz (with a long face), Max Gonheim (a taciturn ferryman from the city of L.), Lieutenant Marius Burdhardt (a ferris-wheel machinist), Theodor Engelmann (with a Kaiser Wilhelm-style moustache), the cab driver Anton Kaspar Hesing (who saw horses as he lay dying), the gilder Ingelthorp F. Ruge (with gold dust under his fingernails), Felix Burkhart (a loner with no one to call his own), Sergeant Hans Mauser (a relic of better times), Theodor Val. Peter (forgetful Peter), the drunkard Johann Gruber, Otto Hoermann (with a low, creased Prussian forehead and mousey eyes), Otto Brix (a hatter who lined his standard-issue cap with red silk), Frederik Schwedler (with metal teeth, nicknamed Zigzag), Oswald Ottendorfer (a tailor with a needle and black thread in his pocket), the lace maker Jakob Uhl, the soda maker Eduard Schäffer and 12,110 other Germans from the 3rd, 7th and 18th Army Corps, were killed while attacking the French in the first kilometre.

Gaston Maréchal (with thick-lensed glasses), Hugo Léon Alphonse (who dreamed of going to Capri), the confectioner Pierre Chausson, the pastry maker Pierre Rullier, Lieutenant Marin Guillaumont (the winner of three proper duels), Henri Barbusse (who enlisted so no one would discover he had killed his neighbour), Louis Auguste Ferrier (with a neat, black-dyed moustache), Henri Alfred Lecointe (who never raised his voice at anyone), Étienne Gaston (who had himself photographed before the war in a pinstriped suit with a white rose in his lapel), Meredith Caoussinat (a little-known cubist painter), Jean Louis Marie Entéric (with a suicidal look), Pierre Jean Raymond For (also known as Bivo), the quilt maker Robert Charles Gueudet, Léon Marie Flameng (who always had a plaster on his face), the cross-eyed Léon Henri Lacroix, Alfred Mulpas (who two weeks earlier had his picture taken in his dress uniform), Henri Brune Hippolyte (a good-natured, cross-eyed fellow), the best leather craftsman in all of Champagne, Robert Bivigny, and 11,470 other soldiers of the French 30th Corps were killed in the first kilometre, defending a scrap of muddy ground around Verdun.

Night fell, and military honour prevented anyone from retreating.

The next day, it was time for the second kilometre of the Battle of Verdun.

Charles Thebault (with the face of a musketeer), the photographer Albert François Raymondi, Émile Dozol (with the look of an ordinary villager), his brother Marius Dozol (of whom only a grainy photograph remained), Jean François Antoine Escudier (perpetually smiling), Jean Baptiste Paulin Cauvin (with a balding forehead, which seemed to pull his whole face upwards), Adolphe Célestin Pégoud (with dimples around his jolly cheeks), Lucien René Louis Rain (a man with six given names, only three of which are mentioned here), Joseph Antoine Richard (as handsome as a film star), Guillaume Christophe Nedellec (a father of six children), the grouch Charles Bettend, Marcel Léon Privat (with the look of a revolutionary), Jean Georget (disappointed in this world), Julien Maximilien Papin (an arrogant ruffian), Raoul Frédéric Eugène Faurin Vassas (who fell in the second kilometre wearing a small, round lorgnette—a statement of better times), Captain Rodolphe Guépin (a poser, who had his photograph taken before the Great War in a nineteenth-century military uniform), the expressionist poet Meredith Capigny and 6,818 other Frenchmen lost their lives in the unsuccessful defence of the second kilometre.

Junior Sergeant August Willich, Joseph A. Hemann (a banker who thought he could pawn his life and pay off both the interest and the principal), Emil Klauprecht (an expert on the magic dealing of tarot cards which predicted death), pedantic Stephan Molitor, Heinrich Rödter (a pre-war manufacturer of ladies' corsets and above all a patriot), the stutterer Karl Resch, Karl Friedrich (a small manufacturer of vinegar), Heinrich Victor Blumer (the son of a strict father, a clerk in a huge insurance company), the naively ambitious Karl Bach, the disenchanted Reuben Guth, Adolph Sage (the deflowerer of several young ladies), Johann Jung (captive to the lovely nineteenth century), fat Jacob Weygandt, skinny Cornelius Schumacher, Jacob Christian (with a boyish look but the teeth of a killer), Samuel Hütter (with a little mirror in his pocket), Siegfried Hobs and 5,927 other Germans did not live to see the taking of the second kilometre.

An opaque night fell and everyone felt they had started out on a great journey, not the capturing of three kilometres of bullet-swept wasteland; but that third kilometre to Fort Douaumont took its toll of heroes nonetheless.

Marie Germain Louis Émile Cahuzac (who died worrying he would never be able to prove his aristocratic ancestry), Désiré Ildefonse Lannoye (who believed the war could be explained by logic), Georges Caron (a pre-war rodent controller, now an expert on trench rats), Irénée Antonin Contard (with the name of girl and the eyes of a dove), the pre-war actor Louis Gui, his younger brother Raymond Gui (who wrote a few words on Birot's illustrated postcards), the miller Pierre Julien Alexandre Letellier (whose last thought was a culinary dream), the brewer Élisée Félix Belle (with the look of a reveller), the match manufacturer and small-time cheat Auguste Robin, Émile Charles Tavignot (a gentleman in every respect, who died in style without a whimper), Georges Marie Ludovic Jules Guynemer (strayed into the twentieth century without any friends or family), Joseph Georges Marie Guérin (whose grandfather changed their surname to Guérrin after the French victory over the Prussians in 1871), Henri Fermin Reynaud (a South African miner who travelled half the world only to be killed in the third kilometre of the Battle of Verdun), René Hardy (who had sailed across the equator three times, but died on land), Arsène Ferrand (a pre-war café owner) and the short soda maker Pierre Germine fell in the last kilometre of that journey.

Albrecht Jacob (with a picture of his sweetheart in his inside pocket), Wilhelm Lahn (also known as 'machine-gun' because of his pervasive snoring), Junior Sergeant Richard Stiemer ('Sailor Stiemer', the darling of all of Hamburg's whores), the spiv Jacob Schnee, Jacob Stöver (a hypochondriac, whom the war cured of the fear of death), the church philanthropist Conrad Zentler, Siegfried Wollenweber, Melchior Steiner (who immediately before the war discovered the beauty of the sport of handball), the descendant of Prussian grenadiers K.J.R. Arndt, Josef Forster (a pre-war fighter against the dogmas of bourgeois society), the tailor Johannus Böhm (who supported every fad of bourgeois society), the comedian Heinrich Müller, the accountant Siegmund Jungmann, Carl Andreas (a birdwatcher and small poultry farmer), Johann Gruber, Ambrosius Henkel (a circus clown before the war, and a clown during the war), and the hundredth hero of this story, Sergeant Nepomuk Schneider, did not live to see the taking of the first fortification in the Battle of Verdun.

So fell one hundred heroes of Verdun. The fortified city of Douaumont was taken, and the German soldiers with keen eyes who hoisted the imperial German standard atop the mighty walls could make out the positions they had started from, away in the misty distance. It had been a great idea: to lure the French into a deadly trap. It was two kilometres more to Verdun, and another half a million dead.

It took the German units until the end of April 1916 to take the full five kilometres to Fort Souville. The French would win back each of those five kilometres by the end of the year. Persistent bombardment turned the battlefield into a sea of mud. Flame-throwers later scorched and burned the mud into an absurd earthenware landscape. Both armies ultimately returned to where they had started. The five thousand metres of the Verdun basin between Fort Douaumont, Vaux and Souville claimed the lives of 700,000 soldiers, including those one hundred pairs of boots, or our one hundred heroes. It had been a great idea—a grand plan meant to put an end to the Great War in the West.

But it didn't turn out that way.

At this time, Svetozar Boroevich von Boina and the pale spectre he cherished in his breast were being pampered by the southern sun. Based in Trieste, the field marshal was the same old Austro-Hungarian commander again, with his mousey eyes which demanded absolute discipline. With nine Austro-Hungarian divisions, he defeated over twenty Italian divisions in the Fifth Battle of the Isonzo. War became almost boring for him on that apathetic front, with its half-hearted attacks and lethargic defence. Dug into the snowy flanks of the Alps, with well-organized supply by cart through the hilly terrain, it seemed his troops would be able to hold on forever. Boroevich viewed every new Italian offensive as an uncured disease, which kept coming back in bouts but was soon gone again. He therefore began to look on the nicer side of things. In the late winter of 1916, Canal Rosso shone in unexpected nuances, as if it was made of oil. He opened the window and watched the curtains stir and billow in the wind like ghosts. From his apartment on the third storey of Gopchevich Palace he could see the magic colours of the canal, and his gaze began to wander rather often from the topographic maps and out through the window, on from the canal and further out to sea. A sirocco was blowing and brought the smell of summer. He breathed deeply of that breeze. He had never been a sailor; he had grown and toughened on the dry, dark soil of the borderlands between Austria-Hungary and the Ottoman Empire. He was surprised at himself that he was drawn to the aquamarine depths, and even that city in the valley of the wind-rose called him to don his dress uniform and go out.

No, he wasn't worried that Trieste could fall. There had been five offensives in 1916 and there would be a sixth, but Boroevich already considered himself a wicked puppet-master who played the Italian marionettes and he saw no chance of those harlequins and buffoons beating him. He woke up every morning and saw the Austrian ships densely dotting the Gulf of Trieste like steel sentries. Seamen called out to each other from surfaced submarines to ships and swapped descriptions of their favourite prostitutes. From the backdrop of hills, over from the direction of Gorizia, there came a constant, muffled thunder, replaced at night by the blood-curdling, wolf-like voices of unsettled animals, but the city was lively. Whenever he passed Miramare Castle in the train on the way back from the front, he hurried to see the yellow lights along the waterfront promenade, which looked as if they were filled with olive oil, and the crowds strolling in Stadion Street.

He almost fell in love but didn't know with whom. One evening he said to himself: 'Come on now, get dressed.' He washed himself with water from the white porcelain basin. It smelt of lavender, and the coat he donned suited him well. He put on the shiny metal helmet with black feathers and decked his chest with his most important medals. He chose them in the same way as a woman chooses a handbag and a fan to match her dress. First of all, he pinned on his oldest decorations: the Order of the Romanian Star, the Persian Order of the Sun and Lion, and the Order of the Iron Crown. (Medals in the lovely nineteenth century were larger than in this threadbare twentieth... he mused.) Then he attached his newer decorations: the Knight's Cross of Leopold from 1909, the Great Cross of the Iron Crown with wartime ribbons, the Great Cross of the Order of Leopold with wartime ribbons earned at the beginning of the Great War, and the Cross for Service in War 1st Class, which he was awarded after recovering at the tedious sanatorium.

Spruced up like this, Boroevich set off into town, but already in the closed coach taking him to the Piazza della Borsa something began to itch where his medals were, so he unbuttoned his tunic and scratched at the discomfort. He did up the buttons again, but then the medals began to prick him some more. He got out on Piazza della Borsa and saw many other coaches in front of him. Where was he going? Who had he fallen in love with? He stood there absent-mindedly and alone in the square as if he was someone other than the commander-in-chief of the army and as if no one knew him. Beads of sweat started to run down his forehead and onto his cheeks and chin, but he didn't dare to wipe off the sweat or scratch at the itch again.

He didn't greet anyone, and no one spoke to him. In haste, he hailed another closed coach. 'To Gopchevich Palace!' he ordered, almost shouting. Only when he reached his apartment did he settle down. He said no word to his batman and immediately got changed for bed.

He fastened his medals to the dress uniform of the other Svetozar Boroevich and swore he would never wear them again. For months afterwards he was seen in an ordinary soldier's uniform, and only the epaulettes showed that he was commander-in-chief of the Austro-Hungarian forces along the River Isonzo, which the Slovenians call the Socha. The junior commanders and troops loved him for it. It was 17 March 1916 when the field marshal thought he had worn his medals for the last time.

And it was four o'clock in the afternoon of 17 March 1916 when Apollinaire immersed himself in reading the *Mercure de France*, with salvos all around him. Bullets snarled past. He thought they sounded like the miaows of savage tomcats which had come late to February mating. He turned several pages of the magazine. Boom, dang, a rap against his helmet. A slight blow on the right, over his temple. Apollinaire ran his fingers over his head. There was a gaping hole in his helmet. Something warm ran down his cheek. Blood—his blood. He was evacuated to a collection point for the wounded. He had been hit by a piece of a 150mm shell. The chief doctor of the 246th Regiment bandaged his head. They took him to the canteen and put him to sleep. The next day, they extracted a jagged piece of shrapnel. Second Lieutenant Apollinaire spent seven hours with a foreign body in his head. Seven hours which would later cost him his life.

After the operation, he was transferred to the hospital in the Tuileries Palace. Already the next day he was awake. He wrote again. To his friends Yves Blanc and Max Jacob. He was fine, he wrote, just a little tired. Three days later they took radiographs. His head was pressed up against a large, cold photographic plate. He had an unbearable pain in his temple. They told him to keep still. He wasn't told the results, but was sent to Val-de-Grâce hospital. There his friends Blanc and Jacob visited him. He was well, he said, but his left arm felt heavy. He lost consciousness from time to time and couldn't remember the last few days. Or years. He had another operation in the annexe of Val-de-Grâce hospital, in the 'Molière' villa. They performed a trepanation and drained the swelling beneath the bone. Now he had a hole in his head and in the top of his skull as well. On 11 April 1916, he sent a telegram to his new sweetheart: Jacqueline.

The irritable artilleryman now needed a neurotic sweetheart who knew what neurosis was—her own and others'. Second Lieutenant

Apollinaire returned to Paris. He liked to say he had a 'fateful, star-shaped hole' in his right temple. He moved back into his flat in Boulevard Saint-Germain. All his pre-war friends noticed he wasn't the same any more. He had been irritable before, too, and inclined to get into fights for France, but this was altogether very different. He had been able to drink almost as much as Modigliani before, but now he drank like the parched earth. Demobilized Apollinaire was restless, moody and disenchanted, but that didn't prevent him from regularly turning up in his impeccably ironed uniform with his Cross of Honour attached. He went out dressed like that to Café de Flore and attended the banquets of cowards and the galas of traitors. He went out but did not enjoy himself. And he was like that for the next twenty-seven months.

That's how much Wilhelm Albert Wlodzimierz Apolinary de Kostrowicki, now known as Guillaume Apollinaire, had left of life: twenty-seven months.

FAR AWAY, TO THE ENDS OF THE EARTH

My name is Ferry Pisano. I am a war correspondent. I would like to inform my readers about the terrible tragedy of an entire people, a calamity which began on the River Drim and ended among the orange and fig groves of the Mediterranean, as if an army had marched all the way to paradise. The Serbian nation is the only one to have lost its homeland in this Great War and to have embarked on such a trek. Much has been written in our press about the unprecedented Calvary of this roaming people which loves France and has turned its eyes to our battlefields in the West as if it had no trials and tribulations of its own. Our inglorious role in the exodus of the Serbs, the greatest after that of the Jews, can be considered common knowledge among the French and the other guilty Allies. We hesitated and mulled over the caprices of the Greek king and his Germanophile ministers, while a whole people was starving, fighting like a ghost given a semblance of life, and waiting for the succour of their great ally, France. For thousands it arrived too late. When it seemed their Calvary was over, it continued; when it seemed they were dead, they woke up alive; when it seemed they were alive, they were found buried in the snowdrifts with a smile on their lips and a blue eye fixed on the turquoise sky above the peaks of the Prokletiye range.

The story of one ordinary Serbian artillery officer can best illustrate this extraordinary path, which is almost beyond the imagination of us civilized peoples. Half way to the village of Castrades on the outskirts of Corfu city, heading along Empress Elisabeth's cobbled boulevard, I found the camp I was looking for. There by the crystal Greek sea, in a lemon grove, the remaining Serbian Shumadiya artillerymen had pitched their tents. There was nothing there in the fragrant shade to show that they were artillerymen—neither guns nor horses. Only the cannons tattooed on the odd forearm told that these living skeletons in new British uniforms had once been gunners. Friends had advised me to seek out their officer, and he seemed to have heard I was coming. When he saw me he jumped to his feet.

'*Vive la France*!' he shouted, and then added: 'I think we met four months ago by the Danube, when there was still a Serbia. We were together that night when German shells rained down on the Serbian positions. Together, in the hour of retreat, we cast one last glance down at the city of Belgrade from Osovac Heights. Are you Ferry?'

'Yes, I am. Ferry Pisano, French newspaper reporter,' I said. 'And now I hear you have an unforgettable story for my readers.'

'Yes, unfortunately. I'd rather forget it if only I could, but I can't get it out of my mind,' the artilleryman answered and continued: 'You must be thinking of... how I got through with my men?

I nodded, and he continued:

'I'm ashamed to say it, Monsieur, but I saved all the men you see here with lies. Oh, and how I lied!'

Before us, gleaming in the lovable sun of the south, stretched a warm lagoon reaching down to the sea and girt by papyrus, olive trees and palms—the same lagoon, where the shipwrecked Ulysses once came upon Nausicaa, the Phaecian princess, bathing and washing her blond hair.

'If only you knew, Monsieur, how I lied to them. But what are lies? The truth is that I lied to deceive death. I saw it happen way back at our positions by the Danube. A wounded man with a sharp piece of shrapnel in his stomach, his mouth aflower with blood, was consigning himself to death. His gaze fixed on the heavens and death was upon him. But when the doctors moved him a little, we saw he was still alive; he just had no strength to lift his eyelids, and death had netted him and was dragging him away. I stayed beside that moribund soldier and said to him: "My son, you're not dead!" Just like that, without any charm or black magic. I spoke firmly and loudly so the wounded man would hear me. Then I saw life return to his eyes, and I took heart and immediately lied again: "You have to live because we're still going to trounce the Germans at the River Morava." They carried the wounded man away, and all that day on the sandy river banks we tried to fight back the strange, terrible attackers who emerged from the mud, firing, and we fired back at them like at a swarm of locusts. I all but forgot the wounded man I had revived by lying. Then, Monsieur, soon after you and I cast that last glance at our white city, I saw my "dead" fellow again. He was alive and I was greatly encouraged. I realized that my lies must have had some special effect, but I still had to assure myself.

'Now I began to lie to my own men. Not all were to be saved by lying, but there were some where death had only a tooth-hold on them and I was still able to outwit it. Oh, how often I would need that skill! When we withdrew further south, to the Morava, and when we also had to quit those positions after less than a week, in a terrible rainstorm, I continued to go up to many of my half-dead soldiers and say to them "Arise, ye dead, we're going to trounce the enemy in Kosovo." And they arose, Monsieur. The wounded recovered from horrific bullet wounds; our surgeons even saved those with open heads—it was miraculous. Only the completely mutilated men, those from whom I was unable to entice one last glance, were lost forever and unable to be saved with lies. All the others returned to formation and went on, and such a hard road lay ahead of us.

'On the banks of the Black Drim, the river into which we cast our cannons, strength left all of us. The hardest thing for an artilleryman is to be separated from his gun, and when the steel sank with a thud to the bed of the roaring river, my whole company cried. They all lost hope and began to lag behind. But as soon as one man fell, Monsieur, I was at his side and shouted: "On your feet, my lad! There are new guns waiting for us in Shkodër. On your feet, or the Hun will run you over for sure!" Not all of them jumped up straight away, and I fought many a tug-of-war with death, but I had become skilled and discovered many ways to deceive the grim reaper who was creeping over them. One time I countered it with an oath, another with a curse, and a third time with a rebuke. And my troops rose again. They were dead men while we were crossing through Albania, life was fast fading from them. As soon as one of them fell down from hunger, I dashed up to him and lied: "There is food for us ahead at the coast—food and drink in plenty. The Albanians are even making Serbian rakia there just for us. On your feet, laddy! Surely you want to try our good slivovitz there. Our rakiya makers have gone on ahead to set up stills."

'Why they believed me and kept on going, I don't know. It seemed as if their feet walked by themselves into the jagged Albanian mountains, crossed rickety little bridges and hid in the thickets when hostile Albanians sniped at us. When we finally arrived on the coast there was no food, of course, nor our double-distilled plum brandy, but not one of my men accused me of lying. No, Monsieur, I lied to deceive death in them, and it screamed and shrieked and did its diabolical best to rob me of at least one man at the coast. But they still trusted me and weren't angry at me. The men virtually demanded new lies because it was clear to them that a slow death was now climbing from their empty bellies to their throats.

'And so I lied. I said to them: "The ships of our great ally France are already in the Strait of Otranto. Their white decks are waiting, staffed by nurses and Sisters of Mercy ready to allay your every suffering. On your feet my lads, my brave falcons!" My wretched children from Shumadiya and Rudnik jumped up, Monsieur, and, as if they had just received sustenance, continued to endure that seven-day starvation and terrible weariness, which was enough to fell a bull, let alone a man.

'The ships finally arrived, and so it was that I got the men here, deceiving death in them all the time. Look at them: they are hardly more alive than they are dead. No one sings, and it seems they've forgotten how to laugh, but they're alive. There are hundreds of them here, but there would only be a dozen if I hadn't lied to deceive death in each of them at least several times. That is my story, Monsieur, so please convey it to our French friends.'

A bell from a Greek convent on the tiny island in the middle of the lagoon rang through the calm, fragrant air, calling to evening prayer. On the horizon, the dark blue sky fused with the violet sea. My artilleryman got up and walked away towards his soldiers. Two or three of them were waiting for him at the edge of the lemon grove; it was almost as if they had been watching over him—it seemed strangely unsoldierly. He saluted them in passing and called out these last words to me through the shade of the heavy fruit:

'Do you see that? My men are keeping tabs on me. Corfu city is only thirty minutes from here. Once I wanted to go, but my men stopped me. "I will come back," I told them, and they said: "No, we don't believe you any more." I had lied to them so much that now they were afraid of me leaving them… Farewell, Monsieur Pisano.'

And with that he went back to his camp.

But I still owe my dear French readers the end of the story. I am writing these lines two weeks later. I have to tell you that that good officer who lied to deceive death in his men is no more. That last, fateful evening, his comrades did let him go for a little recreation in Corfu city. They didn't send anyone with him. He drank just one ouzo in a tavern on the Corfu esplanade, they say, before collapsing onto the table and falling from his chair. His heart of gold couldn't hold out. I wasn't there with him. I could only find out a little about his story from a Greek in the town; they speak poor French, and I don't speak Greek at all. I know almost nothing definite about the death of the artilleryman. Therefore I think: perhaps he opened his eyes in that last moment, but there was no one at his side to lie and deceive death in him.

* * *

Dear French readers, I am writing again from Hellas, a land at once happy and unhappy. Greece is happy because of its gods, the aquamarine depths of the Aegean and Ionian Sea, the generous sun and the clear rivers which moisten the ever-thirsty, gnarled earth of the southernmost Balkans; it is also unhappy because its people, maddened by the conduct of an unaccountable, self-willed monarch and his craven retinue, see enemies in friends, and trust enemies to be saviours of the Greek cause and crown.

This atmosphere can be felt on the streets of Salonika; this thick, infected blood chugs through the Peloponnesian mainland; this by all means sickly condition can even be felt in the ordered olive groves fringing Mount Athos, which ought to be a source of clear and pious thought, like white sand silently pouring from an open hand.

In this blighted land, a refugee people has found a safe haven. Many Serbs perished on the hard road to gentle Greece. That's nothing new, some may say: the Israelites also remained in the sand of their memories when they left on their eternal exodus after the destruction of the Temple. And now an entire people leaves with its soldiers and is gone: the old and the young, barren women and mothers with babes in arms...but that's not new either, someone will say: gypsy tents—families and whole tribes—left the red earth of India like that too, never to return to their native soil. But, dear French readers, I would like to tell you something truly unprecedented: the old monarch King Peter Karadjordjevich set off on that trek with his entire people and the last kernel of the vanquished army. He did not demand a train, let alone an aeroplane; rather, he left on that journey like one of his soldiers, plodding with his elderly step from town to town, over the Prokletiye range into Albania.

That venerable old man has today found temporary and deceptive peace on the island of Euboea. He has made a small and exceedingly modest royal court for himself at the spa in Chalcis, where he received me. I almost didn't recognize him: he was visibly thinner and wore a uniform, which looked as if it had been borrowed from a happier king far fuller than him. He grew a thick beard over his parched face and told me he was not going to shave it off, out of grief for his Fatherland. We spoke courteously for thirty minutes in French as if we were two Frenchmen, and then the king handed me over to his staff, who would explain me the workings of the world's smallest court.

I spoke with many of the trusted people close to the King and learnt how hard it is for them living in this 'afterlife', as the King calls it, but what ultimately surprised me most was the story of the King's doctor. I came across this strange gentleman packing his suitcases on the sunlit veranda and preparing to leave.

'I have to go, Monsieur, because I no longer enjoy the King's grace,' he told me. 'As much as it irks me to say, I myself am probably to blame for my dismissal.'

Three Greek priests came walking past the terrace; they continued along the sinuous road up the hill, counting their rosaries and silently mouthing prayers as they went. The comforting smell of cinnamon and vanilla wafted to us from afar, as if a girl was baking a cake for her beloved, while clouds straight from the early evening were gathering on the horizon.

'Probably I wandered off into one of my dreams,' Dr Simonovich said to me.

'What happened?' I asked. 'You can trust me.'

'I know, Monsieur. You are the war correspondent Ferry Pisano. You wrote so well about our war-torn, tormented homeland.'

I nodded in confirmation, and he continued as if he was coming from far away and there would be no end to the story.

'You see, the King is an extremely light sleeper. He is lost in space, and he no longer believes in the time at his disposal. That means he can wake up in the middle of the night and shout: "Hey, is there any living soul in this house?!" All of us who happened to be nearby would reply together: "We're here, Your Majesty." Then he would strike up an insignificant night-time conversation: "What have we got on tomorrow?" he would ask. "We have to tell the royal treasurer in Athens to wire 6,000 dinars to Geneva for Dobra Ruzhich," his adjutant Djukanovich would reply. "Uh-huh. Go and get some shut-eye," the old king would say and fall asleep again.

'It was like that one night after another, and every night it got worse. At first, all of us woke up with a start and ran to our beloved king, but then the nightly commotion began to drain us so much that we agreed that the one in whom His Majesty had the most trust should sit on watch by the king's chamber. That was naturally adjutant Djukanovich to begin with, but as the nights passed, this trustworthy man could no longer make do with so little sleep, so his place was taken by the emissary Zhivoyin Balugdzhich. When diplomatic duties prevented him too from sitting on watch near the king at night, he was replaced by the orderly, Colonel Todorovich, and ultimately by me.

'As the king's doctor, I considered that I should stay at his side much longer, and since I've always been a light sleeper myself I didn't think that being on watch near His Majesty would be particularly onerous, but I was mistaken, Monsieur. The king woke up first of all twice a night, then three times, and in the end so often that I couldn't keep count. "Hey who's there?" he would yell, and I would reply: "Dr Simonovich, Your Majesty, at your service." "Uh-huh, good. Go and get some sleep." And then again: "Hey, is there anyone here near me?" and me again: "It's me—Dr Simonovich," and him, "Uh-huh, good. To bed then," and so on, without end. After seven nights, the king wanted to replace me, but I refused categorically because I saw that his condition was ever more taking on the symptoms of an illness, which his doctor should be the first to notice.

'I stayed on that dormant death-watch, but gradually I ceased to be any different to my patient. Since the king woke me up night after night, I learnt the ancient skill of the Roman patricians: I didn't wake up completely but remained in a shallow doze, like I was dreaming, and answered his questions in a routine way. "What else have we lined up for tomorrow?" the king asked, and I replied haphazardly, combining real names with fictitious tasks. "We have to write to Vesnich in Paris that he subscribe to a French war loan of 30,000 francs," I spoke as if in a delirium.'

'And what happened then?' I asked, becoming impatient now.

'Ah, I was just about to get to that, Monsieur,' this quiet and devoted man replied. 'When the king had tormented me for so long that I could no longer connect real people, imitation tasks and vain hopes, one of my obsessions, which originated on our Calvary through Albania, began to tell. I had noticed something strange about my luggage. When I closed it, it contained all the usual medicines, ointments and remedies of our age. But when I opened it again at each of our destinations there were strange new medicines inside—tiny phials of different colours, strange powders smelling of mould, and syringes of an unbreakable, transparent glass I had never seen before. Please believe me, Monsieur, and don't think I lost my mind back there in the ravines of Albania. To prove that I haven't taken leave of my senses, I should say that I never stopped examining those new medicines, but I refused to treat anyone with them on principle. I closed and opened my wondrous luggage until one day I saw that it contained only my normal medicines again; and that strange game played by my luggage ended, thank God, when we set foot on Greek soil.

'Let me briefly return to those nights, Monsieur. The king wore me out to such an extent that, like I say, I was no longer able to give him any kind of realistic reply. My technique of shallow waking made me more of a medical case than the king, and I began to reply to ordinary court questions with medical vocabulary, prescribing him medicines which I in no way wanted to use. Finally I heard myself say: "Your Majesty, your chest pains can be treated with broad-spectrum antibiotics." Even today, I don't know what "antibiotics" are and what kind of "spectrum" that is. The king kept waking up, and I kept prescribing him strange remedies. "My King," I went, "your inflammation of the costal muscles is best treated with dichlophene, but it can affect the optic nerve if it is used for too long." I didn't know what "dichlophene" was, but the king noticed I was under strain and yesterday he ordered Colonel Todorovich to relieve me of my duties. "He doesn't need a faith healer but a reliable doctor able to practice with the medicine of the day". That is what he said, word for word, and that is why I am packing and leaving.'

The Greek god Aeolus raised a wind from the west. A storm blew up suddenly and dispersed the smell of cinnamon and vanilla. Clouds of dust could be seen swirling over the land and they disturbed the small fish in the shallows, as if the doctor and I were two Prometheuses at the rock in the Caucasus and Zeus raised a tempest to frighten us.

'The worst thing of all, Monsieur, is that I think those medicines are real and could definitely have helped my beloved king. But now I have to go. And where to—I don't know. Whom should I serve, when I have no country? Whither should I wander, when my homeland is in my heart? Farewell, Mr Pisano.'

And with that, the good doctor left. The story goes that he turned to drink and spent all he had earned in the king's service on women and alcohol in Salonika, and there every trace of him vanished. Some say he risked his neck by crossing the squally Strait of Otranto, infested by German submarines, and made it to Italy on board the ship Laura; others tell of him taking refuge in the town of Aidipsos and trying to treat himself with those strange medicines, which he found again, and dying in the attempt. I'm afraid I don't know what is true; people tell all sorts of stories. Now the smallest court in the world has a new doctor: a young man with blue eyes and such a soft voice that not even those near him can hear what he says.

* * *

Le Petit Parisien (based on agency reports from the Eastern Front)

Germany has carried out poison-gas attacks from the air on the faraway Eastern Front. The invisible soldier chlorine, brainchild of Dr Fritz Haber, has shown that he loves to fly, loves to fall, and is even better at asphyxiating from the air than on the ground when he was released at our lines near Ypres from earthenware cylinders. Russian troops have perished *en masse*, and for that terrible chemist of death everything went successfully. Until one night. Soldiers from his gas unit, who were taken prisoner by the Russians, tell a strange story. Dr Haber had a dream. He saw a yellow-green cloud of chlorine which smelt like a mixture of pepper and pineapple. It separated from the big cumulus near Ypres, which had suffocated regiments of our soldiers and colonial troops in 1915. That cloud, which Dr Haber is said to have dreamed of, travelled from Ypres to Lille, from Lille to Mons, from Mons to Charleroi, from Charleroi to St Quentin, from St Quentin to Sedan, and then on towards Metz. The poisonous cumulus in the doctor's dream entered Germany at Saarbrücken and continued on through the Palatinate Forest straight towards Karlsruhe. Driven by the high air-currents along the Rhine, it sank towards the ground and flitted past Bad Bergzabern and Oberhausen. When it passed Lake Knielingen and was near Karlsruhe, it only needed a few minutes to find the house of the chemist of death, Fritz Haber, at the very moment when the doctor's wife Clara went out into the garden.

The German POWs say that the chemist of death uttered all these place names in his sleep. He started screaming when he dreamed of his beautiful wife going out into the garden with the eyes of a captured beast and a pistol in her hand. He caught a glimpse of her, they say, pointing the barrel at her heart, but she never managed to fire. The yellow cumulus dissipated above her head. And everything immediately became clear to him. The eyewitnesses say that the dry lips of the chemist of death yelled 'Clara, Clara,' when he woke up. We were unable to find out what Haber's wife really died from, but if such a death befell her then both he and she certainly deserved it because only callous beasts could come up with such a terrible killer as chlorine, known to some as bertholite.

* * *

I am Ferry Pisano, the war correspondent. I would like to describe Greece and the Greeks for you, dear French readers. This land beneath the generous sun of the Aegean is home to a strange, sullen, introverted people. The Hellenes live in back courtyards, and their children spend too long behind the skirts of matrons and grandmothers, even when they grow up, and the old folk are eternally silent and absorbed in thought with a fag of chaffy tobacco between their teeth. One is like that, thousands are like that, so it is no wonder that the Greeks are confused in times such as these, and that some will come and give you a friendly pat on the back, while others come up and punch you. King Constantine, Queen Sophia of Hohenzollern, the dismissed Prime Minister Venizelos, the Germanophile Colonel Palis and the fickle chief of staff of the Greek army, Ioannis Metaxas: those are the faces of today's Greece. The country would prefer to be on the Allied side, and to remain neutral in all matters with Turkey and Austria. That's why everything is alive in Greece in 1916, and at the same time so dead. Waking up here is more like being wrenched out of your sleep and brought to your feet than really getting up. From the very first, you are overcome by astonishment at being alive.

When you go out into the street, you find yourself in the midst of that 'treacherous bustle' again, as the Serbian king once called it in an interview for French readers: Jews rushing to open their shops, and Bulgarians and Greeks also hurrying about, because Salonika has to play the role of a city at the crossroads every day: constantly hustling and haggling, and yet on good terms with the whole world in the evening. This practical spirit rubs off on the islands, too, so the islanders are ever looking to see what is good for them, and what not.

On Corfu, that island of suffering and death, the emaciated Serbs were given shelter, although their number doubled the population of that green hill in the Ionian Sea. The locals' way of thinking was basically like this: the French and British are helping the poor wretches, supplying them with new uniforms, and they will also order that they be provided with food and other essentials, which cannot be done anywhere but here on the island. But along with this primarily practical stance, the Hellenes of Corfu also became fond of the open-hearted Serbian skeletons, bewailed their fate and even set aside one quadrant of the peaceful sea near the little island of Vido to be their watery; so many had succumbed to exhaustion and disease that their lifeless bodies had to be consigned to that silent blue tomb. It seemed to the local Greeks that none of the Serbs would survive and every last one of them would die, but then that plucky peasant people got to its feet once more because it had finally learnt how to lie in order to deceive death itself, and now a little insular government began to reconstitute itself and call itself Serbia. The units of the three armies were reinforced, the pre-war government came together again, and all the ministries moved to the island and Corfu city in order to create the illusion of a capital, an administration and the whole life they left far behind, which they sing about in one of their most beautiful songs, *Tamo Daleko*.

But strange things happened. Together with the ministers, there also came civil servants, who like all bureaucrats brought with them their stamps and seals, and they began to correspond with each other. One ministry wrote to another just two streets away, and Serbian urchins ran and carried the letters, opening them on the way and reading them aloud. Why was the Ministry of the National Economy writing to Mr Milorad Drashkovich, Minister of Public Works, when both the resources and the buildings were back in occupied Serbia, for God's sake? What were they negotiating and proposing and drafting laws about? The refugee children who were given the role of couriers knew best. But children will be children: they got carried away with the game.

Only yesterday, a Serbian Home Guard conscript, who had miraculously escaped death, otherwise a man of positive ideas and anything but an obscurantist, told me this story.

'It's a devilish business, Mr Pisano,' he said.

'In what sense, Monsieur?' I replied in French, which he understood well and spoke with some skill.

'The children really went overboard, they did.' He stopped, lit a cheap cigarette and began puffing away at it like a Greek, without taking it out of his mouth. 'They scampered around, were impudent, opened ministerial mail.'

'But those ministries, you'll agree –,' I wanted to add.

'Of course. I know what you're going to say: what is there to write about when Serbia has shrunk to the size of an atoll in the Ionian Sea?'

'But, Monsieur, what happened with the children?'

'Things went too far and we adults, occupied with our own dying, were too slow to notice. One urchin was almost killed. It all started with the children playing. First of all, they just opened the mail. Later they began to call it out in the streets to the locals and the Greek kids in their colourful pants, who didn't understand a word anyway. But then it went a step further. Down on the beach—I'm sure you know it, the lovely, sandy one a little way outside of the city—they made their own government: a children's government. There was no one to stop them playing at it. At first, it looked like an ordinary game: all children play at being kings, but these urchins of ours began taking on the roles of Crown prince Alexander, of his father, old King Peter, of Prime Minister Pashich, and finally of all the ministers of the different ministries dotted about town. It was just for fun at first, a game like chasings or team leapfrogging. But then the boys went too far, Monsieur, because after having seen death and physical decay they could never return to childhood innocence.

'Fights developed over who would play who. And just like in our cruel society where things are always put through by force alone, never with brains and ability, so our boys began to beat each other black and blue, most literally, and even to draw blood. Snotty-nosed as they were, no one paid any attention to them, so no one noticed their injuries, although we should have. The roles in that children's drama weren't shared but won with what raw muscle power those undernourished biceps could muster. The boys established in their own way that it was better to be prime minister than an ordinary minister, and Crown prince was better than prime minister. Then the strongest, I won't tell you any names for now, became Alexander; the second strongest became Pashich, the third strongest old King Peter, and the others, also after bloody fistfights, assumed the roles of Laza Pachu, Momchilo Ninchich and the other ministers.

'Afterwards the boys returned to the city, picked up the ministerial mail and immediately opened it. First they took it down to the beach and discussed every piece of mail with as much literacy and wit as they had, and only then delivered it to the ministries. The staff of the ministries which sent the letters, as well as the recipients, complained that delivery of the government mail was slow, but they knew they weren't writing anything important anyway, so they never went further than grumbling. This allowed the boys to begin running their parallel government with crooked and hot-headed decisions.'

'How did you find out about it all and prevent the children from doing the worst, Monsieur?'

'How I found out? One of my adopted sons, so to speak, a grubby, gangly boy without a family, became the "Minister of Education and Religious Affairs,

Lyubomir Davidovich", and he told me everything. Things very soon got serious, Mr Pisano. "Nikola Pashich" was a hot-tempered boy from Rudnik. He took his role very seriously, and every day he would give someone a good thrashing to serve as an example so no one would think of deposing him. But there were still pretenders. My little shrimp didn't even think of taking it any further than "Minister Davidovich", but there were petulant lads of fourteen who felt that they and no one else were born to be Crown princes and prime ministers.

'They were aided in this by the mail they opened. They understood little of the business of government, but they read the words "danger", "peril", "death" and "disease"—and ever more "death" and "dizease"—and this raised the fever in the already sickly children's bodies. In order to take on the role of Nikola Pashich, one violent brat from Prizren broke the arm and collarbone of the former "Nikola Pashich", that small boy from Rudnik, and threatened to kill him if he said a word to anyone. Like a wounded lion, the ousted boy obeyed and dutifully took on the role of the Minister of Foreign Affairs, Balugdzhich; the new "Nikola Pashich" had been in that role and now advanced to Prime Minister. But that wasn't the end of it. The "Crown prince", a boy from Barayevo, repulsed several attacks, and "old King Peter" too (played by a former shepherd boy from Homolye) was anything but meek in defending his royal dignity.

'When the dust had settled a little, as we say, and the flea-circus had stabilized, new mail began to arrive from the Serbian capital of Corfu which brought fresh turmoil and strife to the children's government. The boys saw that the real Crown prince Alexander had seriously clashed with the real Prime Minister Pashich, and they thought that if that was the way things were in the grown-up world, it had to be like that with them too. The boy from Prizren, "Nikola Pashich", started to look askance at the little Barayevo boy who was "Crown prince". If better letters had begun arriving from hotel Bella Venezia, where the seat of the Serbian government was, everything would probably have simmered down, but Alexander reprimanded Nikola Pashich in the grown-ups' mail and demanded that he give account of what he had done and whom he had met in the first months of 1916, and our Pashich replied on eleven finely typed pages.

'The boys took all that with grotesque earnest and distorted it as only children can. In the end, they decided that the dual-power situation had to end and called a fist-fight duel between "Nikola Pashich" and the "Crown prince". The other "ministers" took sides, with some helping the "premier" get ready, while others, including my "Davidovich", assisted the "future king" in this battle, which one boy was meant not to emerge from alive. They arranged the duel just like adults, stripped off their clothes and began to brawl with wild abandon, Monsieur, egged on by gruesome chants of all the other boys—it was terrible. My boy told me that they slapped, punched and scratched each other, lunged and tried to gouge out each other's eyes and tear off their testicles. They were both squeaking and shrieking like fledglings, when things started to go amiss for "Nikola Pashich". The "Crown prince" pinned him to a cliff, pushing him against the jagged rocks, which began to take the skin off his back, while from the front he stuck his thumb into his left eye and tried to gouge it out. At the last moment, some Greek shepherds arrived on the scene and separated the boys.

'The Prizren boy is now in our hospital on the other side of Corfu and the "victor" in an improvized lock-up in the city. Medics are trying to save the first boy's eye, but the authorities don't know what to do with the juvenile delinquent: the wretch weeps and says it was all just a game. Well, Monsieur, that is the story—another tale told by this war.'

My Home Guard conscript turned, spat out his cigarette butt and left. In as long as it takes to smoke a cigarette, I had heard a truly terrible children's story from the war. I looked around me: fig trees with their finger-like leaves bent down as low as my head, and their heavy, purple fruit seemed to me like children's battered faces.

Later, I asked some Greeks in Corfu city about the boys' flea-brained commune. One of them, in typical Hellenic fashion, said:

'That's Serbian business, sir. The Serbs are splendid people: we have both pleasure and benefit from them. Many have since become relatives by marriage. You are sure to have heard of Ioannis Gazis, the owner of the hotel Bella Venezia. Well, he has turned his tavern and guest house into the seat of the Serbian government, and I hear he is going to marry off a third daughter to a Serb. But in spite of the good will, sir, we Hellenes don't quite understand the Serbs. We don't know if they're alive, and if they are, how that's possible. That's the problem.'

When I finished my conversation with the Greek, who like my Serbian Home Guard conscript smoked a cheap cigarette without taking it out of his mouth, I looked up into the sky. The clouds sailed like frigates driven by the wind, and I thought about how long it will take for all the wounds and scars of this terrible war, whose end cannot be glimpsed, to be erased and undone.

* * *

Order no. 327-PR-1916

Belgrade City Council

Since Belgrade is all but deserted and the remaining population is of hostile disposition towards our army, all officers and soldiers of the Dual Monarchy are ordered to patronize the following workshops and stores in Belgrade. For small items of daily use: exclusively the Grncharevich, Krstich & Co. grocery store on Sava Quay. The proprietor is a good artisan and does not cheat at the scales. For shoe and other leather repairs, be they of harness or soldier's kit: Brothers' Markovich cobbler and saddler's shop. For sanitary and health-care products: Dushan M. Yankovich's cosmetics business. Herr Yankovich is a sympathiser of the crown and accepts both Austro-Hungarian money and impounded Serbian currency. For tobacco and rolling paper: Milisav Rakonyac's tobacconist shop on Danube Quay, and for sartorial services: exclusively the tailor shop of Zhivka D. Spasich in former Prince Eugene Street, house no. 26. The owner co-operates directly with the Miyatovich, Yovanovich & Co. fabric and accessories store, is friendly to our officers, and has even mastered German to a significant degree. All stipulations in this dispatch are to be considered orders, not mere recommendations.

Signed: Dr Schwarz

Administrator of Belgrade

Seal of the Belgrade City Council

* * *

'Monsieur, Monsieur, you must hear my story too!' said a man who grabbed my sleeve and wouldn't let go. All around me was Salonika again, that great hub of merchants, the city where Venizelos's northern-Greek revolt had led to a much better atmosphere than one month earlier. The Allies reached an agreement with the new-old Greek premier that a large part of the Central Powers' troops should be tied down on the new Salonika Front here in the south so as to give at least a short reprieve to my compatriots' unfortunate troops on the Western Front. Greek King Constantine was given the option of abdicating or of fleeing Athens with weapons in hand like the Greek kings of old. As soon as the king decided to leave the country, there was an almost universal sense of relief, and later a diffuse joy for no particular reason, and the Jews and Bulgarians called out the prices of their wares more cheerfully, passers-by strode with surer step, and the plumes of smoke from the funnels of the Allied torpedo boats rose unruffled into the sky. So I was all the more surprised when a stranger grabbed my sleeve and spoke to me in a heavy voice even before I could turn to face him.

'You are Ferry—Ferry Pisano, the war correspondent. You wrote so beautifully for *Le Parisien* about my long-suffering Serbian people. And the piece about our brats in Corfu… I hope people in France read it, even though we had to sort out the problem ourselves. But, Monsieur, would you write up what I have to tell? a very real story about the life and lovely death of one Serb in your country?'

I agreed. I was intrigued by what he called a 'lovely death'. Can death really be nice? I've heard that freezing to death is the nicest way to die and that the person even feels warm at the very end.

'I don't know about "lovely death"', I said, 'unless your compatriot perhaps froze to death. The winter of fifteen-sixteen was terrible, wasn't it?'

'No, no,' answered that unusual man, and I noticed his wrinkled forehead, sunken cheeks and the strange moustache which clung to the slopes of his rugged face. He began to flail about with his thin and pronouncedly long arms; everything about him was scraggy and loose like a riverside willow which sways in the slightest breeze. 'My bro, Monsieur, died from peace.'

'What peace?'

'He went through the Calvary of Albania; he was caught up in a bombardment by German aeroplanes in Durrës on the coast; he went to France all tense, finally came to rest there, and died.'

'And what is so interesting here for a newspaper story?'

'I'll tell you, Monsieur, just you listen.'

And so he began his tale.

'Before our troops embarked for Corfu, my poor bro Dimitriye Lekich, who was ill and particularly weak, was put straight in a sick-convoy with a dozen other men and officers and transferred to Brindisi. From there he was sent to recover in France, in the little town of Aix-le-Bains.'

'I know it. A sweet little town.'

'Sweet indeed, Monsieur, but listen to what happened to Dimitriye. He came to that little town, found out that I was on Corfu, and began to write. A first postcard came for me, an illustrated French card from the manufactory of a certain Mr Birot. On the front there was a picture of French soldier holding a bunch of flowers with a young woman by his side. My bro wrote on that first card: "Today is our second day in Aix-le-Bains. There are fifty-two of us Serbs here (soldiers, nurses and staff). In the summer, this pretty little town becomes a veritable city with up to ten tourists for every local. Now we Serbs are the tourists, who count the days and ponder the fate of our dear Fatherland, partly consoled by the hearty welcome given us by these wonderful people." Later he added on a second postcard: "We have everything we need here (accommodation and three square meals a day), and they won't let us pay for anything. Wherever we go, they won't take any money. At the beginning, we were told this was because the French Ministry of Finance hadn't issued an ordinance dealing with dinars. And until it does, our smiling hosts say, they will 'put it on the slate' or even serve us 'gratis'." After that, the postcards kept arriving but my bro felt ever more awkward.'

'Just a minute, how do you mean "bro"?'

'We say "pobratim" or "pobra". It means he's my sworn brother—a really good friend.'

'I see. Please go on.'

'And so my bro became glum. How can that be, I ask myself? He's living like Count Giesl, high on the hog, food and drink for free, and he feels awkward. And he wrote to me that the hosts were becoming ever more amiable. My bro goes out in the morning, and breakfast is for free; at noon in the searing heat there's beer for free; when he gets peckish in the afternoon, they serve him partridges, together with partridge eggs—all for free; the musicians play in the evening, and the band leader doesn't even have to be given a tip: he plays song after song for free. You see, Monsieur, he found it rather awkward. It was like that for a week, and for a second week it was still the same. Come the third week, he decided to start paying. An invalid allowance came via the Red Cross in gold, and he decided to change it into francs so he could finally start paying his costs. But not only did his hosts not want to hear of it, they also became unfriendly. At first just a little, and they nudged him away from the counter and apologized that they "didn't know the purity of the gold". Talk about a cheap excuse—every greengrocer's assistant knows the test of biting the coin!

'The first day after the invalid allowance came, Dimitriye therefore was unable to cash the gold. The gold coins remained in his pocket, and the sequence of generosity continued: another free breakfast, another cool beer at noon, quail instead of partridge in the afternoon, and in the evening there was music until after midnight, and all that without payment. Still, my bro didn't make it a late night, and in the morning he went to the bank again. Now they got really unfriendly. "You Serbs don't know what hospitality is," they yelled at him. "You insult us with your gold! If it was silver we might perhaps exchange it." He wrote to me about all this and also complained how damn much he was able to write on those postcards of Birot's, and I laughed. If only I had held my tongue, Monsieur, because shortly afterwards I received official notification from Aix-le-Bains: Junior Sergeant Dimitriye Lekich died on such and such a date from complications with jaundice. To go by the date given by the authorities, my bro could only have written me those first two cards describing the town and mentioning that the French Ministry of Finance hadn't issued an ordinance dealing with dinars. So who wrote the other postcards then, Monsieur?'

With that, the stranger whipped a wad of Birot's postcards out of his pocket and began waving them in front of my face like a ruffian who wanted to get into a fight with me right there in the street, in front of the shopkeepers and passers-by.

'Just a minute,' I said nevertheless, 'are you trying to say that Birot's postcards wrote themselves?!'

'I don't know, Monsieur, I'm just a saddler and magic is beyond me, but this should definitely be a story for the French papers. Do you want the cards, perhaps? All of them written in Dimitriye's hand after his death. Would you like someone to translate them for you?'

'No need, thank you. I believe what you say, and you have a whole dozen of Birot's postcards there—not just two.'

Having said what was pressing him, the fellow got up and took off with giant steps, swaying on his skinny, spidery legs. I was left alone, with more questions than answers. Salonika has definitely become a lively place, I thought, with fellows like that out and about.

MIRACLE CURES AND OTHER ELIXIRS

'Dear bird from Benin'. Thus begins one of the letters written at the beginning of 1916 and addressed to Picasso by Lucien Guirand de Scevola, the former stage designer in avant-garde theatres, former radio-telegrapher, former magus who saw the French soldiers choking near Ypres, and former dramaturge of the first and last theatre piece in the trenches in 1914. First of all, we have to affirm that Scevola was alive. He didn't write on Birot's postcards which wrote themselves after the death of the soldier, but used two sheets of paper and filled them with his own handwriting. In this letter, Scevola boasted a little to Pablito (he was far from the only one to do so) and flattered him in the extreme on several accounts, before getting to the main point: he asked him if the bird from faraway Benin finally wanted to join in the Great War—as a cubist in the camouflage section!

Attempts at concealing heavy guns had begun immediately after the outbreak of the Great War. A decorator, whose name has not been recorded, came up with the idea of hiding a gun and its crew beneath a canvas painted with the colours of the surrounding underbrush and leaves of French trees in the autumn. A trial was carried out at positions near Toul. Headquarters ordered a plane to fly over and reconnoitre the area where the soldiers with the large-calibre gun were camouflaged. The pilot didn't see anything except the undergrowth and lovely plane trees with their autumn leaves. But soon afterwards a storm blew up and carried the first camouflage canvas straight to the enemy trenches; fortunately for the French, no one realized what this colourfully painted covering full of holes was for.

Several months later, Scevola radioed a dispatch to the supreme command from his position in Pont-à-Mousson. On the strength of his stage-design experience and considerable imaginativeness, he proposed a revolution in camouflage: colouring the very guns and faces of the soldiers, and setting up wooden huts around them hung with colour-fully painted surfaces of firm material which would not blow away to the enemy trenches so easily. That was the reason for de Scevola writing to Picasso at the beginning of 1916. It is not known if the 'bird from Benin' replied to the letter, but Scevola did well with or without Picasso.

In the spring of 1916, he founded the first camouflage unit in the history of warfare. The thirty volunteers donned light-blue uniforms with a golden-yellow chameleon on their sleeve, embroidered on a red field. Scevola also invited the other cubists, and they responded to his call. The thirty volunteers became thirty sergeants in a company of alcoholics, who still had *klosterlikör* on their minds but weren't allowed to drink it any more because it was a nasty Boche drink. A company made up of *artists* and decorators—what a novelty for all the artistes of the Parisian bohème. These painters, who had been considered supporters of 'Boche art' and artists in the service of various Uhdes and Tannhäusers, were now all working for the good of the French Fatherland! And not only that. All of them, to a man, had sworn they were diehard cubists, and now they began to paint the first wartime surfaces in the formerly despised style of intersecting pentagons and squares. Paintings which before the Great War were most often accused of not resembling anything at all, now, in these times of immediate danger, turned out to be the only ones able to resemble everything. The camouflage started off being in motley colours. These 'harlequin disguises', as war hero Apollinaire called Scevola's work, brought the first camouflage unit initial acclaim, but our pre-war stage designer felt he had not nearly attained his goal. Now was the moment to make a name for himself after having failed in Montmartre and Montparnasse. This was the time, he thought, when he would become the first artist to paint with life itself, or rather with death.

Just where the decision to make the first French camouflage efforts more 'lively' would take him, he was soon to find out. The harlequin disguises were just the beginning, and one idea of Commander Scevola's overtook another. He called the next step 'deployed camouflage'. The intention was simple: to continue camouflaging real units of the French army with harlequin colours and wooden screens in the hues of leaves and bushes, but to additionally set up dummy emplacements with dummy soldiers, which would compel the enemy to shell an image rather than its essence. 'Original,' some tired generals said. It could almost have been called philosophical, if that were not an exaggerated term for a gruesome idea soon to be abandoned.

But for the time being, deployed camouflage was the order of the day. For weeks, Commander Scevola trod the muddy roads behind the front lines; great blue-grey clouds accompanied him when he drove up to the Headquarters of the French army in his armoured car and explained his advanced ideas to the generals, who all wore dark circles under their eyes. Deployed camouflage was finally authorized. Now two thousand more of

Old Libion's regulars received work, which he definitely did not approve of. All of them were failed sculptors, recruited at short notice from the ranks of old-fashioned eternal students and new-fashioned candidates of the Salon des Indépendants. They looked like long-bearded, untidy, somewhat uncultured and self-indulgent Home Guard conscripts, but they all became men of character, figurative sculptors who now fashioned the heads of dummy soldiers at dummy emplacements.

Several kilometres of true-to-life trenches were dug at various locations near Bois des Loges, Toul and Pont-à-Mousson in the middle of clover fields with fleet-footed hares. The German artillery proceeded to pound them with 'coal boxes' and at first hit mainly the dummy soldiers and occasionally a poor hare. The troops came through it all safe and sound. Scevola was beside himself with joy, but the German artillerymen in the third year of the war were not nearly as orderly and precise. Shells soon began raining down on the real soldiers too. It was like that for one day, and a second. Scevola's sculptors worked hard to make new dummy emplacements, but the commander of the first camouflage unit knew his superiors wouldn't be satisfied. On 21 May 1916, a ceasefire was agreed. The stretcher-bearers went out into churned-up no man's land like onto an Elizabethan stage, like Shakespearean heroes searching for their dead and dragging them back from the boards. This brief ceasefire gave Scevola the opportunity to inspect the positions and his dummy emplacements. He noticed the dead bodies and stopped.

No, death didn't shock him: he had seen it in so many stark forms that he could have compiled a whole herbarium of death. It was something else which halted his step. Not distinguishing life from death, the stretcher-bearers gathered everything they came across. Together with his dismembered dummies made of plaster, there were also real, human heads, arms and shanks in army boots. Commander Scevola immediately wrote to his superior officers and phrased his letter in Spartan spirit: 'This is the chance for our dead comrades to continue the fight against the enemy', and he came up with the idea of manning the dummy emplacements not with plaster models but with the heads and other remains of real soldiers! He would preserve them, he claimed, so they didn't smell and bother anyone. When they had fulfilled their fate and been killed a second time, he would return them to their relatives so they could be buried as heroes who gave their lives for France twice and earned two bravery medals!

That was unheard-of, but the soldiers and officers at the French positions in 1916 had had their fill of poison. If it was 1914 and the officers still had some vestige of pre-war humanity, the idea would have been rejected with disgust. Scevola would have been disciplined and the unit of good-for-nothings disbanded. But now the idea—at least initially—was authorized with praise.

The French army's new 'metaphysical positions' were gruesome indeed. Scevola calling them a 'remarkable new means of defence' didn't help. Heads and body parts from Bois des Loges were transported to positions near Toul, and those from Toul to imitation trenches near Pont-à-Mousson so that the surviving soldiers would not have to look at the leering faces, jaws full of golden teeth and the broken arms of their former comrades who now, preserved, stood like the Lacedaemonians of yore and faced a second death. But the men were still aghast, despite being protected by rows of embalmed, new comrades. Involuntarily, they imagined their own death: being torn apart by a shell near Toul and their desiccated head then being sent to the dummy emplacements near Bois des Loges, and their arms and legs to Pont-à-Mousson. As distraught and despondent as they were, the living soldiers found no consolation in such concealment, while the junior officers were quick to ingratiate themselves with senior command by praising the work of the first camouflage unit and proudly playing down their own casualties in reports. Dissatisfaction was rife, but the end of the Gothic camouflage endeavours was ultimately brought about by the German artillery. It pounded the French positions at random for three or four days, like before. Hundreds gave their lives for the Republic for the first time, and hundreds for the second time, and soon no one saw any reason to continue the horrible practice of concealing the positions. The bodies of the last Spartans were reconnected as best as could be done and returned home. The conscripted sculptors and cubists were sent back to Paris, much to the joy of Old Libion and Old Combes, and Lucien Guirand de Scevola passed into complete anonymity, as if he himself had given his life not just once but twice for *la patrie*.

On the German side, however, it was still being demanded of a particular soldier that he serve his Fatherland. It was still being expected of Hans-Dieter Huis that he sing and that he join the noble German cause in the Great War as a soldier, in typical German fashion. But the celebrated singer still had no voice at the beginning of 1916. Perhaps it was because of Elsa, who took poison because of him in the distant nineteenth century. Or perhaps it wasn't. Everything told him that he should not sing, but the maestro was a German and the Germanic in him drove him to try and not give up. He heard that his name was still being mentioned in military hospitals and that soldiers were dying to the story about the Christmas Eve singing between the trenches near Avion. Therefore he decided to find his wartime acquaintance Theodora von Stade, the great soprano from Leipzig, with whom he had sung for the Crown prince back in 1914.

Where they met is not important, how she comforted him does not concern us, and it would be best to pass over the grating screech of the maestro's frayed vocal cords when they tried to sing together. All that is relevant about maestro Huis's last attempt to sing is that Theodora recommended him a laryngologist, down south beyond Landwehr Canal, who ran a private practice and treated only a select clientele.

She had recommended him, so what was there for him to lose?

The next day, we see the great Huis on the outskirts of Berlin, taking the road which strikes out into the country behind the city's last houses. Some birds were flying high in the sky as if trying to flee the Earth, but he didn't see them. He stopped before a red-brick building and looked back as if he was the shady character, not the doctor he had come to see. He was holding a bundle under his arm, wrapped in wax paper.

Surrounded by the arms of the canal and concealed by the rustling reeds and water lilies of the marshy Berlin plain, worked Dr Straube, who charged for his services exclusively in geese and goose fat. What brought Huis to this enormous man, whose round face looked as if not even his moustache would cling to it, resembling as it did a pair of black butterflies about to take flight?

'I no longer have faith in money,' the doctor said. 'This is 1916 and, let's face it, we're losing the war. Now I only believe in good Berlin goose. What have you got for me? Aha, a good half kilo of goose fat, two drumsticks—hm, they don't smell the best—and some giblets. Heavens, that's not much, it's hardly anything, but I suppose this is 1916. Alright, I accept. Here's your potion: take it three times a day. What? Come on, surely you don't think I need to examine you. This is 1916, after all. I was told about your ailment in advance, and I've heard you singing so many times that, believe you me, I've already as good as examined you several times at the Deutsche Oper! There you go, three times a day. Mud in your eye, and good singing!'

Huis left with the potion and took it three times a day. It stank of tannis root. Nothing happened at first. The singer regretted having gone to such effort to buy the pieces of goose for the doctor, but then, one ordinary Tuesday, his voice returned all by itself. How happy Hans-Dieter Huis was, and how much he, treacherously indeed, felt himself a soldier again. Within a day, or two at the most, he was able to sing his whole repertoire once more, but then… the greatest lyric baritone of the German stage seemed to mutate. His voice became higher. Within a week or two it had risen to the next higher vocal register, that of the tenor baritones. That's it then, he thought dumbfounded: that's oblivion. What was left for him now was the opera, the unknown territory of tenor roles, and forgetting the root of his fame: *Don Giovanni*. He would never be able to sing it again with the new voice.

The soldier Huis withdrew from the street completely and shut himself away in his house. He shunned all contact, including his doctor and his superiors. He frantically began to learn new roles. How lovely it was to be a newly-fledged tenor, and he sang the role of Monteverdi's Orpheus to himself, and then Samson and Florestan too. He thought he could start a new career as a dramatic tenor, but his voice continued to rise and became even squeakier. On the tenth day after him starting to sing again, it moved to an even higher register and became buffo tenor, and he took pleasure in that, too. He began singing things he previously never could. Mozart again, and the role of Don Basilio, and then Wagner's Mime and much else besides, but not for long. Two weeks after he had begun to sing again, he arrived at the even higher register of lyric tenor, apt for the roles of André Chénier, Tamino in *the Magic Flute* and Faust. But he finally had the urge to perform and now put the music of Mozart's *Requiem* on the piano. Astonishment gripped not only Berlin but the whole of Germany all the way to the trenches on the Western Front, when the former baritone Hans-Dieter Huis intoned 'Tuba mirum' from Mozart's *Requiem* like a real German lyric tenor. The fluctuations in the maestro's voice were put down to the war and the influence of stress of some kind, and his performance at the Deutsche Oper again drew storms of ovations, just like in peacetime. Only one listener didn't clap. He was an enormous man, whose round face looked as if not even his moustache would cling to it, resembling as it did a pair of black butterflies. 'Mr Lepidoptera' only smiled and left the hall of the Deutsche Oper in Unter den Linden Street.

The same day as Huis finished his last performance before a human audience, King Peter Karadjordjevich felt the urge to write an entry in his diary. He took his pen and began, only to pause again after a few words and raise his pen from the paper. His hand hovered over the first, unfinished sentence: 'We, the kings, tsars and emperors, bear the most blame.' He thought that the monarchs ought to end the Great War and that 1916 could be the year of the kings if only rulers had the desire to look beyond their silk and ermine. In wounded Europe, almost all of them were related: uncles fought nephews, fathers warred with daughters married abroad, and grandfathers made their grandchildren mortal enemies. Where were the emissaries, those plump, suspicious fellows in thick fur coats, to deliver princely letters to the emperors of the opposite warring sides? He wanted to record all this in his diary, but he stopped. Did his heart not also harbour grave objections to one of his own relatives, Victor Emmanuel III, King of Italy; did he not consider King Nicholas of Montenegro, his father-in-law, to be a Pharisee, swindler and buffoon? Was it not rather exaggerated to believe in 1916 as the year of the kings? And what was up with the great French Republic?

In that dumbfounded Republic, civilians continued to fight recklessly against the war. In June 1916, the 'Salon d'Antin' exhibition was held in the gallery next to fashion designer Paul Poiret's atelier. It lay at the end of a beautiful avenue, which intersected gardens rather like those of Versailles. Here André Salmon brought together French and foreign artists and appealed to their sense of solidarity. This gathering represented the cream of the unrecruited and demobilized: at Picasso's side Matisse, next to them Fernand Léger and the recently demobilized Italian soldier Giorgio de Chirico, and then Gino Severini, Moïse Kisling, Kees van Dongen and Max Jacob. Guillaume Apollinaire stood in a place of honour, his head in a turban.

André Salmon spoke and tried to out-yell the clamour. When the crowd finally calmed down, words in German began to be heard from somewhere. No one knew who was speaking them; they simply sounded like an echo of the French. Salmon tried to yell, but everyone kept turning around to look. The unrest grew into chaos, and the stampede of the assembled artists almost threatened to kill the surviving cream of French modern art. The Salon d'Antin ended in fiasco, and in the confusion no one is likely to have noticed that Picasso's *Demoiselles d'Avignon* was exhibited on one of the walls for the first time. When everyone else was outside, Pablo Ruiz returned alone to the space where the German words had rung. He took his picture off the wall and carried it away without a word. He hadn't planned to put it on show anyway. As he was passing through the lovely park near Poiret's atelier with the picture, he heard a voice say: 'They've played a nasty game on us.'

The next day, the Parisian press published an erroneous piece of news by a novice journalist stating that the Salon of the famous fashion designer Poiret had been cancelled and the artists had got into a punch-up instead of affirming their solidarity! Only a few lines were written about it, nothing more. The same papers devoted far more space that day to the discovery of a miraculous elixir. The renowned French surgeon Alexis Carrel and the chemist Henry Dakin had developed a new antiseptic solution which, in spite of its rapid effectiveness as a germicide, was at the same time completely safe for living tissue. Tests had been carried out at a hospital in Compiègne and the results, the propaganda said, were quite incredible. The antiseptic solution consisted of water, a chlorine compound whose formula was kept secret, soda and boric acid. It was used on soldiers with great success. What the press didn't report remained a military secret: those tested with the solution were healed of their physical wounds, but other wounds opened in their place.

Whether it was coincidence or the fruit of espionage, the Hungarian surgeons Székely and Kis also came up with a remarkable new antiseptic for the treatment of wounds—one of very similar composition. The Hungarian press duly publicized this breakthrough, but it hushed up the fact that soldiers of the Dual Monarchy had also begun manifesting strange behaviours: the wounds of these men from the Austro-Hungarian trenches were also healed, but unexpected mental disorders developed.

The actor Béla Duránci, a native of Subotica serving with a Hungarian hussar regiment, spoke better German than he did Hungarian. He played Hamlet in 1897 in Munich and his 'To be, or not to be' soliloquy was the talk of the town. When the war came, he began to see it as a grand theatrical production, with him going from role to role. While he sat in the trench awaiting the enemy offensive, he played Macbeth expecting Birnam Wood to rise; when he killed a young Frenchman for the first time in hand-to-hand combat, he was playing Richard III;

whenever he charged out of the trenches with a bayonet on his rifle, he was playing Hamlet, as you can imagine; and when he was taken to hospital all bloody with a bad wound in his side, he played Julius Caesar.

What is significant for this story, however, is that Béla Duránci's wound was treated with Professor Székely's and Kis's wonder drug. The stab wound from a bayonet really did heal in three days, but then Duránci started to feel a mellow mood. There was no name for this condition, and at first everything was amusing, for him included. Béla felt that faces were familiar to him, but when he approached them he would see he was mistaken. At first, he thought he saw commanders out reconnoitring; later it was generals who hadn't set a foot outside their headquarters a hundred kilometres from the front. And so it went on from day to day. When he was sent to deliver a message and would be going down the trenches, he would think he could see someone from his native Subotica from ten metres away. He would shout, but when the man turned round he realized it wasn't his childhood friend and would apologize and continue on his way. But at the very next broader section of the trench, in some 'hotel', he would think he saw his long-dead brothers and playmates from the sunflower fields. He went up to them—he couldn't restrain himself from checking if it was them—but each time it would turn out he was mistaken. This too could be considered a harmless quirk, but after a while he began to have visions of well-known personalities in the Hungarian trenches and he could no longer tell he was mistaken, even from up close.

He would stop an ordinary soldier and say, 'You've just got to be Heinrich Landau, the famous Peer Gynt from the German Theatre in Hamburg,' and tell another: 'You just have to be Karl Wittek, the most noted leather craftsman in the whole of Voivodina'. The doctors who had given him the miracle cure and helped him recover therefore came to examine him. Taciturn Dr Kis arrived with his young associates. He didn't notice how beautifully the paradisiacal birds were singing that morning. He immediately went to see the smiling patient. The doctors saw that something wasn't quite right, but they found nothing in the medical records to indicate that there was anything wrong with Béla Duránci, not least because they wanted to enhance the reputation of their drug and secure the medal they thought they deserved. For that reason they kept Duránci in the trenches. 'Let him even imagine that Franz Joseph comes along—he still has two good hands to use a rifle!' they thought, and left again. But what they wished him soon actually came true.

A short while later, in the Hungarian trenches, Duránci saw the emperor himself. He remembered having seen him when he was a child, in flooded Szeged in 1879. Franz Joseph was punted past the flood victims, who sat huddled together on the roofs of their houses. The water was a muddy yellow and reeked of carcasses and contagion. The corpulent emperor sat on the prow of the fishing boat wrapped in a fur and repeated the only words of Hungarian he knew: 'Minden jó, minden szép' ('Everything is good, everything is fine'). Now every face Duránci saw struck him as being the emperor's from 1879: he halted and turned around one man after another, sergeants and full-bearded soldiers alike, and yelled 'Minden jó, minden szép'. In the end, he was relieved of his duties and sent to a sanatorium near Marburg. Béla spent the rest of the Great War here in outright opulence because he was attended to by nothing but princes and famous actors of European theatres. Even the emperor called by to pay his regards, with his face of 1879.

At the same time as this, submarine commander Walther Schwieger also mistook sunken ships for various other phenomena, although he had never been treated with Professor Kis's wonder drug. The submarine dived at daybreak, like every day off the Danish coast, and already at 10:02 hours Schwieger spotted smoke on the horizon. He sped to that point out at sea, but when the submarine drew close he saw that the thick, black smoke was not from the coal-fired boilers of a ship but was rising directly from the surface. He cursed, thinking that another German submarine had made it there before him and sunk the ship. Beneath the surface, however, he could not see the huge hull of a sinking ship. Only smoke on the surface. There were no funnels anywhere. But he didn't let that disconcert him. He continued, and at 12:49 he thought that he saw something on the North Sea horizon once more, but it wasn't a ship; maybe one of his monsters was dabbling heedlessly on the surface and admiring its reflection in the smooth surface of the sea. Later in the afternoon the same thing happened. At 17:54, he again shouted 'Ship ahoy!' but it was nothing targetable, nor were the sightings at 19:22 and 20:46. In the end, he reluctantly noted in the U-20's log for that day that there had been no combat. He ordered that the vessel submerge just a little at night so as not to disturb the sea serpents, and then went to join the crew in the galley.

So in Marburg and in the Atlantic, in spite of everything, spirits were still high; in Istanbul they weren't. Sure enough, Mehmed Yıldız's third apprentice had been killed, the brightest he had ever had—his newly-fledged bookkeeper. He had been recruited and sent to Mesopotamia, from where he wrote soldiers' cards from a certain Nurezin's stationery shop until the last day: 'Dear Master, today we reached the red city of Shaib. We besieged it, but resistance was stiff and many a righteous man perished on the iron-red earth, while others fell into captivity. My closest comrades and I remain unscathed, Allah be praised'; 'My dear Master, my good father, after the defeats near Shaib and by the River Hamisia, our commander Askerî Bey took his own life at the hospital in Baghdad, which was a terrible shock to us all'; 'Dear father, we are pulling back towards the Tigris. Our new commanding officer Nureddin—may Allah and His Prophet be praised—inspires trust in us all'; 'My loving Master, today a fresh Turkish army under Mehmed Fazil Pasha arrived to aid in the defence of Baghdad. We gave them a warm welcome and kissed like brothers'; 'Esteemed father, the fortunes of war have turned in our favour and we have driven the British into the city of Kerbala. The infidels have to make do without food and water.'

And then the cards stopped coming. If Yıldız's apprentice had used Birot's wartime cards instead of Nurezin's, he definitely would have kept writing 'I'm alive!', 'I'm alive!', even after his death, but these post-cards were not as talented. The apprentice, that bookkeeper who would never be, actually did write one more card by his own hand, but it was withheld by the censor. And then he fell, at the walls of Kerbala. No one now needed to tell Yıldız, neither a human nor a Pheme, because the apprentice had done his best to inform his master himself: if he stopped writing, that would be his end. And it was. The end. The trader extinguished one more light in the shop of his soul. Now only two of his helpers were left, whom he loved like his children: his dear bean-pole, who used to refresh them all with song and laughter, was now in Palestine; and the youngest, born in 1897 and still a boy, had been sent to Arabia. They didn't write. They weren't even literate. How would he find out about their end? Someone would tell him. His door would be open. There was no point barring it when the news could jump three walls and pass through three locks. But maybe they would pull though? Yes, he hoped now they would return and he could open the shop again, which had been closed for some time; things would be as they were before, except that the red spices, which stood for the infidels, would never again sell better than the green ones that played the role of the believers. Or was it perhaps all in vain? The year 1917 was drawing close, and he awaited it with deep anxiety: the sixtieth year of trading of that righteous man. Why did he have to be a slave of that saying? The next day, he would stop thinking about it.

The next day was 1 July 1916 by the new calendar. At exactly 07:20 hours, a mine containing eighteen thousand kilograms of trinitrotoluol detonated. That explosion was the signal for the second biggest battle on the Western Front in that year to begin: the Battle of the Somme. As with the Battle of Verdun, the generals thought that this battle, too, would bring about the end of the Great War and warfare in general, but the opposite was the case. The old Roman road from Albert to Bapaume was littered with the corpses of soldiers from both sides, and the French and British generals again underestimated the staying power of the Germans and the strength of their trenches and the new defensive constructions—bunkers. The defences were only breached along a small section of the front, on the southern part of the Roman road. The towns of Herbécourt, Buscourt and Assevillers fell, and a dozen German bunkers and their crews were stuck in no-man's-land. The French judged that capturing the bunkers would be a pointless waste of life, so they left them there, isolated amidst the quagmire, and tried instead to break through towards the cities to the north. Each bunker was surrounded by two dozen French soldiers, who dug in and provoked the defenders to use up their ammunition, while also relying on the fact that their food and water would run out, and sooner or later they would surrender.

One of the soldiers in a bunker which was still firing at the enemy happened to be Alexander Wittek, son of Karl Wittek, the most famous leather craftsman in the whole region of Voivodina. When he saw that he and the crew of the bunker were surrounded and death was inevitable, Wittek decided to make his will.

"I, Alexander Wittek from Subotica, being in full possession of my wits, hereby dispose of all my possessions, although at the moment I have none," he began. "I am the son of the renowned leather craftsman Karl Wittek, but since the old man has not yet made the shop over to me I cannot bequeath it to anyone. I have two years of architectural studies in Zürich, which I leave to my bearded professors who never took any notice of me. I have three brothers and two sisters whom

I cannot give anything but the slaps and iniquities which I, as elder brother, dealt out so liberally. On second thoughts, my only earthly possession is a dappled horse; but more about that later. Apart from that gee-gee, I only have the future. I intend to dispose of it with this last will. Today my three comrades and I ate the last of our food and we have begun to drink our own urine, so I think it is high time for me to dispose of my future.

"And now to what I bequeath: I have something of a poetic gift and intended to write poetry, but I haven't started a single poem, let alone finished it. I leave all my unwritten poems to a certain Milena from Lipica, whom I met in Zürich. I also dedicate to her the unwritten poems 'The Sentry', 'A Soldier in War Doesn't Cry' and 'At Dawn I Became Evening'. When this terrible war ends, I thought of completing my architecture studies—now, in advance, I leave them to my friend Frantishek to finish. I had even greater plans: as an architect, I imagined leaving my mark in many cities. I donate the unrealized tropical glasshouse to my native Subotica. I bequeath the Church of Francis of Assisi with the clock tower to the city of Szeged and the district administration building to Belgrade. And to Paris, where fame ought to have taken me, I leave the new hotel by the Seine, the glass pavilion for the next world exposition and the arch of the reconstructed Gare du Nord.

"Enough about buildings. Now on to youth and old age. I wanted to spend my youth in Nice, my mature years in Paris and my old age in New York, but now I see it was all a pipe dream. Therefore I leave my youth to the southern sun, my mature years to the metal latticework of the towers and Guimard's entrances to the Paris metro, and my old age to the skyscrapers of the New World, where my spirit will dwell. I also thought of getting married. I leave all my children—three lovely sons in sailor suits and two gentle, pale girls—to a woman I never met. No, no, not Milena, to whom I bequeath my poetry; this is an accommodating, intelligent, patient woman, whom I never met and so was unable to ask her hand. Fate decided that I was to have children with her, and it is to her that I now leave my unborn children.

"Now I am prepared for death. I was not fated to die in 1916 in this pillbox smelling of mould and, what is still worse, us soldiers. I ought to have lived until 1968 to see the progress of science, the application of new materials for the construction of large buildings and the prosperity of the human race, which will come when this Great War puts an end to all of humanity's wars. I give away the year when I should die of old age, surrounded by my grandchildren and admirers, to the young and the students, and I would wish for them to spend it rebelliously, as befits them.

"And now just for a few little things. I wanted to own a Louis Vuitton suitcase and I leave it now to my youngest brother to travel the world with. I had hoped to buy a pigeon-blue top hat and a walking stick at Lock & Co. in London, and now I bequeath them to my middle brother so he can become a real gentleman. I also wanted a snuffbox with Indian snuff in it; I leave it to my father. I think that is all. Oh yes—the dappled horse, my only material property. The horse bolted on me shortly before I was enlisted; if it does not turn up, I leave it to the church, and if it does, may it belong to my dear nephew Stanislav."

Perhaps that soldier of the Dual Monarchy who bequeathed his future still had other things he wanted to leave, but now it was his turn to relieve the machine-gunner. One accurate shot from outside, straight through the slit of the bunker, struck him as soon as he gripped the handle of the gun, so the will of Alexander Wittek came into force. At the sound of the shot, mocking birds took off and flew low over the ground, mimicking a child's crying with their screeches. Enormous clouds ploughed silently across the sky as if they were plodding and touching the ground. Heavy drops of rain fell. The same moment as Wittek fell, a plane flew over the bunker which would soon surrender.

The pilot, Manfred von Richthofen, did not see what had just happened below. There was nothing he could do to help the isolated German bunkers, so his orders were to watch out for enemy in the sky. This young pilot, already of somewhat conceited demeanour, had until recently been a cavalry officer in the 1st 'Kaiser Alexander III' Uhlan Regiment. He had taken part in the battles on the Eastern Front as a scout in the first years of the Great War, but cavalry lost its usefulness as early as the second year of the war. After a long spell doing mind-numbing tasks, he applied to be allowed to join the newly formed German air force. He wrote to his superior officer: 'Sir, I have not gone to war in order to collect eggs in farmyards. Please authorize my request to be transferred to aviation.' His request was granted, and towards the end of May 1915 he was transferred to a unit stationed at the airbase in Mont on the Western Front. Now he flew over the combat zone at the Somme and spotted a French plane between the clouds. He opened fire from a range of two hundred metres and shot down his first enemy over the Somme. He returned his Albatros B 2 to base, and his sweetheart was the first to be waiting for him by the grassy runway. As soon as he climbed out of the plane, she rewarded him with a kiss. When her warm mouth descended on his cold, blue lips, the superstitious pilot knew everything was alright.

DELUSIONS AS BROAD AS RUSSIA

A von B—that was his code name. He was head of the *Kundschafter-gruppe*, the chief censor of the mail of Serbian POWs. He was considered to have the best understanding of the psychology of Serbs. 'Of all South Slavs, the Serbs have the most developed cult of family life,' he said. He therefore launched a campaign called 'Good old Cyrillic' to encourage the POWs to write home in their own alphabet. Later he established: 'Serbs take captivity and separation from their families hardest, so they yearn to correspond as often as possible.'

A von B had hatched the plan as early as 1915. He presented his superior command a letter from a certain Captain Milan Stoyilkovich from the prison camp in Radafalva, in which he wrote that he had traced over the same words with his pencil for two whole weeks so as to write the letter as many times as possible before sending it. In the winter of 1915, prisoners' mail would enable a von B to work out the exact positions of the Serbian army. The operation began in January 1915 under the code name *Überläufer* (Defecter). A good organizer, a von B put together teams of translators, calligraphers and psychologists. Everything began with the 'Good old Cyrillic' leaflets handed out to the Serbs in the camps. The POWs used them to roll their cigarettes with. They were afraid of censorship and wrote with caution at first, so they tried to convey their situation in a round-about way: 'I feel like Saliya Yasharevich from Nish', one of them wrote. 'Here it's like at Uncle Bogosav's, or even worse', another told his folks. 'I'm in clover—but the paddock's tiny', a third quipped on his card. But none of that interested the censor a von B.

He and his men were interested in the mail which the soldiers and officers wrote to troops in Serbia. These cards were confiscated by the Mail Sorting Group and passed on to the Imitation Group. 'The Serbian soldier is extremely exact,' a von B claimed. 'He always writes his location.' the Imitation Group took the soldiers' postcards which interested them most. On the basis of the real cards, they wrote imitation ones with the same Cyrillic handwriting. At the end, they usually added a few lines like: 'I sent you twenty crowns in a letter, but the letter came back. Please write and tell me where you are,' or 'I've had no word from you, cuz. Where are you and your unit?' or 'Where are you? I've already sent twenty postcards, but there's never a reply'.

The fake cards were then soiled, stained and even drawn through the overcoats of Serbian soldiers to make them smell and look genuine. And then off they were sent to Serbia. The net was cast and the fish just needed to swim into it.

As early as the summer of 1915, the operation was proving to be an unexpected success. More than three hundred postcards had prompted replies from Serbia, and the soldiers there always wrote their exact position: Nikola Dragutinovich of the 1st Company, 1st Battalion, 14th Regiment, currently in reserve in Ub; Mile Milenkovich of the 1st Company, 2nd Battalion, 3rd Regiment of the 3rd Call-up, now deployed in the Rudnik mountain range; Ranko Pavlovich, searchlight squad, stationed at the old fortress of Smederevo; Miliya Peshich of the 4th Company, 1st Battalion, 20th Regiment of the Timok Division, currently based in Mladenovac; and so forth. The Serbian army censors in Nish and Belgrade worked sloppily, and by September 1915 a von B was able to trace a whole network of Serbian positions derived from the postcards. Hundreds of soldiers gave away their units' positions, so it would be wrong to just accuse Nikola, Mile, Ranko and Miliya of carelessness, especially seeing as all of them would soon be deceased defenders of their country.

And then the offensive began in the autumn of 1915.

It rained when Belgrade was evacuated on 8 October, when the 2nd Bulgarian Army reached the River Vardar and entered the strategic Kachanik Gorge on 26 October and when the last officer of the Serbian 4th Regiment, Major Radoyica Tatich, left mud-bound Knyazhevac. It rained when General Zhivkovich reported that the Germans had taken Kralyevo, when the Morava Division set off like a company of phantoms from Macedonia to defend a piece of Kosovo and when the remnants of the victorious Serbian army of 1914 huddled in the valley near Priština in the vain hope of linking up with the Allies from Salonika when they reached Kosovo Polye. It rained when the royal family dined with its generals in the Fatherland for the last time and when, from Prizren, the exodus began.

It was raining, too, when a von B arrived in Belgrade on the first train. He stepped from the platform straight into a muddy puddle. He didn't even bother to wipe his boots.

First of all, he went to the mail-sorting department of the Postal Centre by the Sava and impounded ten sacks of soldiers' letters and postcards. Black Belgrade ravens shrieked from a windowsill. The sacks stood like a last defence, turned north to face the enemy. The birds flew away. The mailbags offered no resistance. Over the following days, all three sections of the *Kundschaftergruppe* were reassembled in the former café Casino. The talented translators, psychologists and experts on Serbian Cyrillic arrived in Belgrade one after another on military trains. One operation was over, but another even larger one was about to begin. A von B had been awarded the Iron Cross, 2nd Class for Operation *Überläufer*, but he did not intend to stop there. The new operation was given the code name *Hochverräter* (Double-Crosser).

The efforts of a von B's group were now directed towards Serbian POWs in Russia—mainly Serbs from the Austro-Hungarian province of Voivodina who had fought in the Austro-Hungarian army and been taken prisoner by the Russians. A whole alternative history was created for those 'double-crossers' and written on fake Serbian-army postcards.

It began with lying. No, it wasn't raining; it was a splendid Indian summer after the battles of 1914. The Serbian defence of Belgrade had given way, admittedly after three days' heavy fighting, and the defenders had withdrawn southwards to positions near Aleksandrovac so as to reinforce the Serbian right flank, which was clashing with the Bulgarians. The forces had then dug in along the line Loznica–Valyevo–Lyig–Lapovo on the northern front and Knyazhevac–Bela Palanka–Surdulica–Kumanovo–Prilep on the Eastern Front. After three weeks of bitter fighting, the cities in eastern Serbia had to be abandoned, but it was always a strategic retreat in order to allow the rallying of troops from Macedonia and Kosovo, who had now linked up with the Allied armies near Bitola. That huge, composite army had wintered in Kosovo Polye, like the Christian host 527 years earlier, and now awaited the enemy before the decisive battle of 1916.

This entire fake history was jotted out on soldiers' cards in simple language: 'My friend, I'm retreating from Knyazhevac with my unit and our batteries', 'Uncle Svetozar, Nish now looks as big as Belgrade and is full of our troops. The enemy doesn't dare to attack us, and we are preparing for a strategic retreat to a line along the River Ibar', 'Oh Drakulich, old boy, we all cried and kissed each other like women when we linked up with the French and Greek armies from Salonika and won our first victories over the Bulgarians near Kachanik', 'Brother Stanoyko, what are you all waiting for? We're sitting out the winter here, hoping you'll come from Russia', 'Kosovo is waiting for us, Milutin—surely you fellows in Russia won't stay there high and dry like those turncoats, the Brankovichs. Come on, run away from prison camp or ask our Russian brothers to let you go!'

These cards were sent to Nizhni Novgorod, Tokorent, Odessa, Kazan and Rostov-on-Don. Any of the Serbs in Russian captivity who had studied at an academy or university in Serbia or been members of a Serbian party, had relatives south of the River Sava, a foster father in Shabac or absolutely any connection with Serbia proper, received at least a few cards from a von B's workshop. And what joy they evoked in faraway Russia. The Serbian prisoners' newspaper *Glas juga* (Voice of the South) enlisted new soldiers throughout the winter of 1916. Three battalions were formed in Odessa, and Russian counter-intelligence officers saw no reason to dishearten the men whom a von B had so successfully excited. But then the true aims of Operation *Hochverräter* came to light.

The Serbs became like a swarm of flies. Discipline in the camps deteriorated, and the prisoners demanded weapons from the amicably inclined Russians and claimed they would down tools and raise a revolution if they were not armed soon. They all wanted to go to Serbia, to Kosovo! These hot-headed, nationalist Serbs threatened those Serbs still faithful to the Austro-Hungarian crown who did not want to join the volunteer brigades, and also made the Czechs, Slovaks, Slovenians and Germans among the Austro-Hungarian POWs uneasy. Croatians converted to Orthodoxy and enlisted in the phantom new units. To top things off, there came a brief but stupefying summer, which settled on the Russian steppes like a poisonous cloud. When the capsules of red poppy drooped and the first swathes fell to the scythes, strange things started to happen to the prisoners wielding them. The harvested poppies gave off a sweet smell which caused dizziness and only amplified the yearning and nervousness of the POWs. Everyone in the Russian army knew that Serbia no longer existed, that the badly mauled Serbian army had not linked up with the Allies and that the remnants had retreated to the small Ionian island of Corfu—everyone except the POWs who kept receiving fresh word from a von B about the Serbian army rearming, restocking and expecting recruits from Russia for a new Battle of Kosovo.

How to tell them? Who could tell them? If the prisoners' heady correspondence with long-dead Serbs from the Fatherland was denied them, there would be an insurrection in the labour camps; if a whole company of well-armed soldiers went into the camps and started speaking the truth, the prisoners would hardly be likely to believe them and the troops would be lucky to get out of that seething hotbed alive. A counter-attack was therefore launched from where the attack had begun: in the realm of cards and letters. The operation was code-named *Sumashedshy* (Madman). One lie had to be displaced by another. Russian counter-intelligence officers hunted down all of a von B's postcards and formed their own counterfeiting departments. Prominent psychologists and church calligraphers from Petrograd and Yekaterinburg worked on the texts. The POWs, like real patients, could not be told the truth immediately. The new fake postcards—really copies of a von B's faked cards from Belgrade—therefore also had a bogus Battle of Kosovo as their starting point.

At that time, the conceited Serbian volunteer brigades were promised weapons which would never arrive. Russian intelligence officers disguised as railway staff were sent among the zealots; they met with the self-proclaimed commanders and discussed plans for imaginary transports through Romania along protected corridors to eastern Serbia and all the way to Kosovo. At the same time, postcards written in Odessa and Yekaterinburg progressively conveyed ever grimmer news: the battle had already joined, and the volunteers would not make it in time. Mighty army was pitted against mighty army—man against man, horse against horse, steel against steel—and it became the greatest battle the history of warfare had ever seen. Five mythical days it lasted, the August Battle of Kosovo, in the most scorching heat the year 1916 had seen. Tens of thousands laid down their lives amidst Kosovo's mythical, blood-red peonies, and all three Austro-Hungarian generals fell, as well as one German and two Bulgarian commanders, but the joint Allied army had to retreat through the valley of the Vardar towards Greece.

As the well-crafted lie gradually took on the contours of truth, the would-be Kosovo warriors lapsed into apathy and became suicidal. They traipsed through the camps in Odessa, Rostov-on-Don and Nizhni Novgorod with the eyes of ruined and broken men, but the silent discipline so desirable in prison camps was re-established and all the nationalities in Russian captivity calmed down again. The weight of the blame fell on Romania for 'refusing' the volunteer convoys passage through to Kosovo Polye, and every disenchanted Serb thought he could have changed the course of history if only he had been able to take a rifle in hand.

When several of the Russian copies of the fake postcards from Belgrade were intercepted, a von B realized that all the writing of fake letters was over. The Austro-Hungarian command assessed Operation *Hochverräter* as semi-successful; a von B was not awarded the Maria-Theresia Cross.

The Russian command considered Operation *Sumashedshy* semi-successful because the fake postcards had 'helped' the defeated Serbian army struggle through to Corfu, but the truth about the double lie would remain obscure until 1917, as would the reaction of a hundred thousand Serbs in Russian captivity who had wanted to save Serbia. Order was re-established in the camps, and that was the most important thing, but two audacious murders suggested that the fever of the POWs had not subsided. Several weeks after the modern Battle of Kosovo was 'lost', and while the heavy steppe summer still oppressed the captive souls, the body of the prisoner Marko Nikolin, who had refused to enlist in the Serbian volunteer units, was found in Odessa. A Russian by the name of Boris Dmitrievich Rizanov was also found dead there. Rizanov was a war hero who had survived the winter Battle of the Masurian Lakes and escaped from a prison camp in northern Germany in early 1916 in a hand-made boat; back in Russia, he trained the Serbian volunteers and was their liaison officer. Who killed him and why, did not come to light. For Boris Dmitrievich, the Great War ended in a side street in Odessa's port, at the back entrance of the bistro Tsaritsa. Three sailors, who were rather drunk and didn't realize he had been killed, noticed him there. They thought he was just dead-drunk like themselves.

On those summer days in 1916, the command of the POWs also had more pleasant events to report. One of the prisoners, a pre-war German pianist, was to hold a concert at the Odessa Conservatory. The name of that virtuoso was Paul Wittgenstein. His right arm had been amputated, but he did not lose heart. As soon as he recovered and learnt enough Russian to be able to find music lovers among the guards, he received better treatment and was allowed to begin practicing at the Conservatory. So maestro Wittgenstein once again rolled up his sleeve. First he played all his favourite pieces as if he was performing them with two hands, except that his left hand and fingers played real notes, while his right moved only at the shoulder and played notes audible to him alone. When he saw that his unaccompanied left was scarcely musical and realized there was no point, Wittgenstein adapted several pieces for the left hand with the help of teachers at the Conservatory, who turned their heads away and cried while they listened to him playing. He practiced with a cigarette in his mouth, smoking it like a Greek., without taking it out. He bashed away at the keys for days on end, and finally he agreed to give a concert in the Small Hall of the Conservatory on 1 August 1916.

Many tried to persuade Wittgenstein to play in the Great Hall, where there was a far better Petrof grand piano, but he declined. 'For a one-handed pianist, even the Small Hall is too big,' he said. The concert began courteously, with the music of Tchaikovsky, and continued with the German classics Brahms and Beethoven. German POWs and their Russian guards were seated in the hall, as were many citizens of Odessa, who had read the announcement for the concert in the newspaper. The teachers of the Conservatory each stood on stage for a while, turning the pages for Wittgenstein and wiping the remaining tears from the corners of their eyes with white handkerchiefs. Everyone cried 'bravo' and 'encore' at the end, but the pianist stood before the audience and silenced it with a broad swing of his left arm. As an encore, he said, he wished to play just the part for the left hand of a waltz and the *Berceuse* by Frédéric Chopin in honour of his amputated right arm. He apologized to the audience that the music would not be as beautiful as it should because they would be hearing only the harmonic accompaniment, not the melody. What Wittgenstein didn't know is that an amateur, who had achieved considerable local fame, sat down at the piano in the Alte Oper in Frankfurt at exactly the same time and announced to the audience that his right hand would be playing in honour of a left hand in Russian captivity—that of the pianist Paul Wittgenstein.

The moment the German POW Wittgenstein began to play with his left hand, Hans Henze started to play with his right: one of Chopin's waltzes and the *Berceuse*. Some pre-war critics in Frankfurt recognized the work of Wittgenstein's fingers and wanted to tell Hans's mother after the concert, but she had rushed to the backstage rooms of the Alte Oper, where she found her son dead. Beside his lifeless body lay a farewell message: 'Mother, I've decided to return God these hands, which are not mine.'

Death thus made a most terrible scene in the Alte Oper in Frankfurt, but the range of its horror was quite limited. Home Guard conscripts strolled aimlessly along the cobblestone streets around the building together with limping cripples discharged from the front, and none of them knew what had just happened inside the concert hall. If we step back a little, we encounter a different life. A little further, and the sound of laughter and the cheerful clinking of glasses can surmount any of life's tragedies.

In Geneva, Germans, Russians, British and French dined together, danced together, rubbed shoulders in spa parlours and at gambling tables, and afterwards rushed to watch the latest libertine Paris fashion review of a collection for the New Year 1916. At night, the lights shone like fireflies along the lake, humming that peace would never fail in that part of Europe. Red-jacketed musicians played the merriest of melodies for the promenaders, but the music was drowned out by the laughter and chatter of women in extravagant dresses. Tail-coated men called out to them: 'Careful where you walk, you'll muddy the stripes on my trousers.' Beneath the gas lanterns, which cast the esplanade in a yellow light, loose girls from the Parisian boulevards of love shifted from one leg to the other. They offered themselves for a handful of sous, only slightly more than a glass of absinthe, but clients were none too many. No one had much money, but the empty pockets were amply compensated for by an excess of *bonhomie* and hysterical laughter, as if every joke and jest was the last.

Here, any mention of the greatest clash in human history was considered a sign of bad upbringing and an unwarranted crudity in the presence of the fairer sex. Only a handful of sombre Ivans spoiled the atmosphere and harped on about a revolution. They were socialists, deserters and poltroons who felt at home among other cowards. They compensated for their lack of heroism with an excess of conspiratoriality. They sat at tables, ordered pastis, sambuca and klosterlikör (thus demonstrating they did not take sides in the war), gesticulated vigorously, and viewed anyone who approached them, even the waiter, as a stranger to be met with hostile looks as if to say: 'If you give away anything you've heard here, you're dead!'

The other guests did not like them until they got drunk. They thought them Russian savages and gave them a wide berth, but when they had a bit to drink a queer change came over them. Their furrowed brows relaxed, pouting mouths spread into smiles, and one cigar was lit after another. That company then became the loudest, jolliest and most frivolous. Those unpatriotic Russians cried, laughed and embraced everyone who entered the café, even those they had sent murderous looks to; they repeated 'nyet, nyet', as if they had only been joking and had never thought of harming anyone. The sober socialists spoke of doom, gloom and upheaval, while the drunken ones talked of a cheerful revolution and everything they would achieve in the new, classless society. That Janus-faced company, both joyful and grim, consisted of Vladimir Ilich Lenin, who had moved from Paris to Geneva and greatly missed his comfortable apartment in Rue Marie-Rose, Julius Martov, Ilya Ehrenburg, who worked as a translator for wealthy Russian émigrés, and Leon Trotsky, a correspondent for the newspaper *Kievskaya Mysl*.

Every evening was the same. When alcohol had well irrigated the dry human soul, Ilya Ehrenburg got up.

'Comrades, comrades,' he yelled, and stopped. He swayed and had to hold on to the table. The music played a fanfare. 'We are all socialists because we want this horrible war to end as soon as possible. ('Oho,' someone heckled over at the right.) But when it's over, what do we want? The same sort of system? To keep fattening tsars and presidents? No! We'll build a new society, where every working man will have the same rights as a ruler. (Shouts of 'Not in France!' and 'Not in Germany!') But in Russia, yes! There, comrades, the worker will wear a new pair of shoes every day. We'll have so many that we'll throw them away in the evening. A new model every day—that will be the slogan. (Shouts of 'Tell us another one!') And the old shoes? What shall we do with them? We'll send them to the poor countries of Asia, and in a year or two we'll have shod all of China and Indo-China, and Mongolia as well. That's right, comrades.'

The next evening, the same again. Comrade Ilya once more:

'Comrades, a new story. Quiet please, a new story. In Russia, comrades, everyone will first of all have a car, and when it goes out of fashion they'll have their own personal dirigible. That's right: di-ri-gi-ble! a new Zeppelin per family every five-year plan. All the balloons, of course, will belong to the State and be allotted for individual use, and they won't be given to functionaries first but to the ordinary, rank-and-file worker. There will be so many of them that highways will have to be built in the sky. After his strenuous day of labour, every working man will enter his airship and shoot up into the blue. We'll see hundreds of them on the horizon in the twilight. Those will be the most beautiful sunsets of Europe.'

Shouts from the crowd: 'Come off it!', while others yelled: 'Encore, encore!'

Ilya Ehrenburg, however, plumped back down on his chair like a sack of ship's refuse to be thrown overboard. That was the end of his stories for that evening, but more days and new evenings were to come, and each would be the same; all except one, when something quite unexpected happened, although, truth be told, it only spoiled the mood of the gathering very briefly.

As the Russian circle in the café grew ever louder that day in the late Indian summer, and as the guests asked them for more of the colourful and cheerful stories about their classless society, a vagabond came in. He looked like a drunkard, but one untypical of carefree Geneva. He wore a visor cap pulled down to his nose and had grey, sunken cheeks as if he had risen from the grave. Ilya Ehrenburg got up. He raised his finger into the air like a lightning rod and was ready to start, but the newcomer spoke in a quiet, yet sufficiently clear voice and everyone heard him:

'There will be no new shoes or Zeppelins in socialist Russia. Everyone will be poor and live in fear. They will dream of sugar but sweeten their tea with saccharin until they get sick of it and then sweeten their tea with strychnine one morning. This comrade here, Vladimir Ilich, who will be the first president of the Presidium, will be replaced by a steely comrade from Georgia, and the repression will begin. The hanging judge Andrei Vyshinsky will say: "I noticed in the records of the investigation that you went so far as to deny any subversive activity." One of the thousands of accused, Muralov, will reply: "I think there are three things which made me deny it. The first is my character. I am very excitable and easily get offended. When I was arrested, I lost my temper. The second reason is my attachment to Trotsky."

Silence reigned in the café for a moment, then one guest laughed at a table at the back, followed by another and yet one more. A moment later, the whole café resounded with laughter, and rosy pictures of a classless society were called for once more. Finally Ilya Ehrenburg spoke, and first he said with earnest:

'I will not permit anyone to insult Comrade Trotsky here. He is the first among us revolutionaries and socialists.' He paused, laughed as if nothing had happened, and began his fairy tale: 'A collision of dirigibles was only just avoided in the open sky over Russia. Congestion in the socialist heavens was the cause. That was to be the day when traffic rules were established—like those on the ground, only in the air. Afterwards, many said it would be better to return to earth and for everyone to borrow a tram from the state.'

This elated story created the noisiest atmosphere in any of Geneva's cafés. But, as with death, the range of this hubbub was limited, too. Quiet girls strolled along the cobblestone streets by café Leman, hoping for a gallant for the evening, and the wind from the lake had turned cold and announced the end of a short Swiss Indian summer. If we step back a little further from the noisy café where socialist dreams are told, the prevalent silence and mistrust are capable of killing all mirth.

One previously famous and also voluble married couple was now living out its lean days under house arrest. Governor-general Sukhomlinov, the former expert on cavalry, which irrevocably lost its importance for the Great War in 1916, was confined to his own four walls. The glory days of this red-headed and red-moustached seducer from the Solovtsov Theatre were long since past. His Katenka, the former consort of the Austrian spy Altschuler, spent these dismal days at his side.

Never again, she swore to herself, would she lead a boring, provincial life like with her first husband, the landowner Butovich, so even now she continued to play a ridiculous spy role. She looked through all the drawers, defined the value of every document which was no longer of any importance, and now began to spy on her own husband because she believed that his sequence of habits would be of great use for the Austrians when her Sukhomlinov returned to a senior position in the Russian army. But Vladimir Alexandrovich Sukhomlinov no longer had any important habits, and Katenka began to keep a truly pointless diary. The entry for 12 October 1916 read: 'Last night, he snored until half past two. Then he rolled onto his back and started to speak. I wrote down everything, word for word. Here's what he said: "Horses are racing across the steppe. They come upon a river. They go in, and they start to drown. Only their muzzles are above the water. 'Your horses have drowned,' one of the men says to me."' the next day's entry read: 'For the first time in three weeks he's finally changed his trunks, thank God. He put on socks, as well as garters to hold them up, as if he was about to go out among people. He combed his moustache—that is of great importance.' And the next: 'He snored again but didn't say anything in his sleep', and the following...etc.

But there is no point here in going through all the entries in Yekaterina Sukhomlinova's diary. What we have heard already is quite sufficient to make friends and enemies want to forget them both.

History, and this novel, only take notice of what is important. For that, we must move deeper into Asia, where another formerly great man was trying to forget his sharp-toothed dreams. Ousted and sent to distant Tbilisi with the title of viceroy, the 'Grand Duke' Nicholas Nikolaevich suddenly noticed that his fingers were becoming hard and rigid. He stared at his nails, which were going from a normal, pinkish colour to dark blue, then coppery red, and finally to a golden hue. One after another: the nails on thumb, forefinger, middle finger, ring finger and little finger of both hands. He looked like an Indian guru with those golden and now rather long nails. He raised his hands into the air and examined them as if he was in a nail studio. It all seemed not to worry him, until he noticed that this metallic hardening was spreading from his nails to the joints and knuckles and that one finger after another was also becoming metal.

Suddenly he shuddered and realized it was just a dream. He drew his fingers out from beneath the pillow and saw that the formerly metal places were dripping with blood. Was it his or someone else's? He sprang to the porcelain basin and removed the lid. Quickly he rubbed his hands with the large cake of firm, lard soap. The lather was hard to make and now mingled with the claret of the blood, which entered the basin and snaked through the water like red lampreys. Then he shuddered again and realized he had been dreaming once more, and was actually at his headquarters in Tbilisi. He looked at his hands and saw no changes. Getting up, he removed the lid of the mottled basin and slowly soaped up his hands. He wasn't worried about what he had dreamed, only the fact that he had fallen into two dreams now made him tense. Was he so tired or so dissatisfied that he had to drift off to sleep twice—and twice wake up with a shudder from a nightmare? He doubted it, but he was still worried. He called his orderly and summoned a meeting of the Eastern Army's staff, with reports from the front for that day. He was far from the capital, he thought, too far from his wife Anastasia, and worlds away from any important task. He had been sidelined with a paper crown bearing the inscription 'Viceroy of Russia'. That crown would never harden and turn golden. If he was in Petrograd or Mogilev everything would be different, he thought, but perhaps he was mistaken. In the Caucasus, the air was fresh but strangely dense, saturated with unparalleled crimes beneath the dignity of the imperial Russian army, while in the capital the air was close and heavy with insidious conspiracies and desperate decisions.

The fetid air of disaster, fateful decisions, and the hope of salvation hung over the streets and canals of Moscow, Kronstadt, and Petrograd in those last days of 1916 like the smell of decay and the taste of transience. Apparitions flitted past beneath the streetlights: half human, half idea. The collapse of the system was accompanied by the downfall of its faithful, so responsible figures discharged their duties with furrowed brows and pursed lips, praying that their labours would make the difference between triumph and disaster. Everything hung by a thread from early morning till night. It was either victory or total defeat. The light of Christian Orthodoxy on the eastern marches of Europe or the darkness of Asia and Levantine degradation. Tomorrow was another day. Demons lurked behind every corner, and the obstacles on the path ahead were so numerous that not even the staunchest defenders of the Russian monarchy could foresee its future.

The most persistent troublemaker, the most blatant menace and negator, was Rasputin, or 'Our Friend', as the tsaritsa called him. 'Our Friend', however, was only a friend of the German-born tsaritsa and perhaps the tsar. For all others he was a deathly threat and had to be eliminated. Orgies, immorality, the pretence of healing Tsarevich Alexei's haemophilia, the disgracing of the royal court and poor counsel were pushing the Empire from the Kievan gate of Europe straight towards the postern of Asia. A handful of loyalists therefore decided to kill Rasputin. The decision was taken. Their brows were furrowed. Again, the outcome would determine the difference between triumph and disaster.

The 16 December 1916, by the old calendar, was set as the decisive day. A lot of sixes in one date—three, even, if you consider the nine an upside-down six. But the job had to be done because, as with so many urgent matters, there was no one to accomplish it other than the brave conspirators. The group was headed by Prince Felix Yusupov, a strange man, who often went around his house wearing women's clothes. Yusupov was the sole surviving son of Russia's richest woman, Princess Zinaida, and he lacked for nothing. He had already tried to poison Rasputin once, but the cyanide did not affect him. It turned out that the 'man of God' had the habit of taking a little cyanide with his dinner every day. Starting in 1909, he took grain after grain of the poison and gradually became immune to the greatest murder weapon the nineteenth century had known.

Therefore, in Yusupov's second attempt, Rasputin would be killed four times over. All this was possible in Russia—and more: someone could be killed five or six times for symbolic or ritual reasons. But Yusupov received a visit from an old Oxford friend who explained that the British crown wished to participate in at least one of the four killings of Rasputin in order to strengthen the two countries' alliance in the Great War. Yusupov agreed, and his 'old Oxford friend' sent the requisite instructions to London. He asked that an accomplished assassin be sent, and everything went according to plan.

In history, this tale begins one cold night with heated carriages clattering out onto the snowy crystal of the Petrograd cobblestones to take Rasputin to Yusupov's palace by the River Neva under the pretext that Yusupov's wife Irina urgently needed the help of the seer's 'hot hands'.

But at this point we must go back; the tale actually begins much earlier with the accomplished British agent Oswald Rayner setting off with a wicker suitcase on a journey from London to Russia—a long journey even in peacetime, and now even longer, given the need to detour the theatres of war. But Rayner was not to be discouraged. This was to be his longest journey with the least luggage. He took with him a change of winter and summer clothes, a tube of toothpaste, a bar of shaving cream and a brush, a photograph of a young woman in an oval medallion and an 'envoy' of the British crown: a Webley .455 revolver, which was to leave a souvenir from the Isles in Rasputin's body.

He departed on 7 December 1916 by the old calendar, or the day before Christmas by the new, without any Yule cheer or send-off, heading from London's Victoria Station by rail to Dover. He stared through the window of the carriage at the relentless rain pouring down on the meagre British vegetation. No one was waiting for him in Dover. He changed from the train to a ship and started through the English Channel for the north of Spain by the same route which the Royal Navy under Nelson had taken on its way to defeat the Spanish fleet at Trafalgar. In Spain he spoke Spanish. He bought a ticket to Barcelona. Again he was on a train, which slowly made its way through orange-hued España. He saw trees laden with oranges and no one to pick them. In Barcelona he took another train, for the Côte d'Azur. He lied to an elderly lady and her granddaughter fluently in Spanish. In Nice he boarded a bus. He paid the driver in cash and thanked him in French, which he seemed not to speak nearly as well as Spanish. So he stayed silent in the bus. He stared into the mighty blue of the Mediterranean and felt nothing—neither satisfaction, nor sentimentality, nor sadness—when his gaze drowned in the expanses of the sea. He entered Italy at the little town of Ventimiglia. He boarded his third train on the Continent, which took him through pleasant, rust-red Tuscany and further into the gnarled south. In Brindisi he boarded another ship and travelled to Corfu, where he slept one night and didn't talk with anyone, and then on to Salonika. There, Rayner finally heard English again from British diplomats. A car was waiting for him. This inconspicuous automobile with a high windscreen and folding roof had one important feature: it was equipped with two pairs of licence plates, Greek and Bulgarian. He immediately set off on this next, far from easy leg of the journey. Near the city of Kavala the driver removed the licence plates. While he was putting on the new ones, Rayner changed from summer into winter clothing. Neither of the men spoke a word in English or any other language. The car set off again and drove another seven hours through the night. It stopped at the coast of the Black Sea. Here at the town of Tsarevo, before dawn, Rayner boarded the Russian torpedo boat Alexander III, which took him to Odessa. Then, mingling with the ordinary Russian travellers, he went by bus to Kiev. He changed there and travelled on through the western Ukraine, and then caught a third bus destined for Petrograd.

It was 16 December 1916 by the old calendar, shortly before midnight, when a heated carriage brought Rayner up to Yusupov's festively illuminated palace. Rasputin was already there. The Englishman went down the wooden stairs into the cellar. The boards creaked beneath his hurrying feet. The 'man of God' had already been killed twice: he had been poisoned with cyanide again, this time with a far larger dose, and then stabbed with various sharp objects—knives, forks, and broken glass. Now it was time for the representative of the British crown to kill him a third time. Without speaking a word, Rayner took out the Webley .455 and fired one shot into Rasputin's head. Then he returned the gun to the wicker suitcase and shook hands with the small conspiratorial committee, although he didn't know anyone. In addition to the host, those present were Grand Duke Dmitri Pavlovich for the Romanov dynasty, Lieutenant Sergei Sukhotin for the Russian armed forces, the parliamentarian Vladimir Purishkevich for the State Duma, and Dr Stanislav Lazovert, disguised as a valet, in the name of medicine.

Dr Lazovert ascertained biological death, but Rasputin still had to be killed a fourth time. The conspirators dragged Rasputin's body across the floor. His wild hair and beard snagged in the fringes of the heavy carpets. The killers tore out the snarls and continued to drag him along like a wild boar. They all left the building; the Russians made for Petrovsky Bridge to drown the 'man of God' and thus kill him a fourth time, while Rayner immediately started on his journey home.

He left without any send-off, through the enamelled Russian night which seemed it would never see the day. Prince Yusupov's heated carriage took him to the bus station. Mingling with the ordinary Russian travellers, Rayner caught the first bus to the Ukraine. He changed to a second, which made its way through sleepy Ukrainian towns, and there among the creased faces of the passengers he saw in the New Year by the Western calendar. A third bus then took him to Odessa, where he boarded the Russian torpedo boat Alexander III and was transferred over the Black Sea to Bulgaria. At the coastal town of Tsarevo he switched to a car. The inconspicuous automobile with a high windscreen and folding roof had one important feature: it was equipped with two pairs of licence plates, Bulgarian and Greek. The driver started the motor and they immediately set off on this far from easy journey. Near the city of Kavala the driver removed the licence plates. While he was putting on the new ones, Rayner changed from winter into summer clothing. Neither of the men spoke a word in English or any other language. The car set off again and drove another seven hours through the night to Salonika. There Rayner finally heard English again from British diplomats. He changed vehicles once more and was driven south to Vouliagmeni. From there he travelled on the second ship of his return journey, via Corfu where he slept one night and didn't talk with anyone, to Brindisi, the 'gate to the Adriatic'. Here, for the first time on the return journey, he boarded a train, which wound its way through the gnarled landscape of southern Italy towards pleasant, rust-red Tuscany and further north. He entered France at the little town of Ventimiglia and boarded the bus to Nice. He paid the driver in cash and thanked him in French, which he didn't speak nearly as well as Spanish. Therefore he was silent in the bus. He stared into the mighty blue of the Mediterranean and felt nothing—neither satisfaction, nor sentimentality, nor sadness—when his gaze drowned in the expanses of the sea. In Nice he bought a ticket to Barcelona. Again he was on a train slowly making its way through orange-hued España. He saw trees laden with oranges and no one to pick them. In Spain he spoke Spanish. He lied fluently to a young lady and her niece. In Barcelona he took another train to the north of Spain. There he boarded the third ship of his return journey, plied the waters which the Royal Navy under Nelson had sailed on its way to defeat the Spanish fleet at Trafalgar, and entered the English Channel. No one was waiting for him in Dover. He travelled on to London by rail. He stared through the window of the carriage at the relentless rain pouring down on the meagre British vegetation. At the end of his journey he arrived at Victoria Station. There was no welcome home or anyone waiting for him on the platform.

It was the evening of 6 January by the new calendar and Christmas Eve by the old when Rayner returned to his house in Royal Hospital Road. There he opened the wicker suitcase and took out his change of winter clothes, an empty tube of toothpaste, what was left of the bar of shaving cream, a brush, the Webley .455 revolver, and the photograph of a young woman in a small, silver oval. He kissed the photograph, prepared the winter clothes for washing, cleaned the gun and went to sleep. All was quiet in the house in Royal Hospital Road, and after his sixteen-day journey undertaken because of one single bullet, Oswald Rayner slept like a stone until morning.

Five days earlier, Rasputin's body had been found in Petrograd. Three uniformed men drew it from under the ice beneath the bridge to Petrovsky Island, and one of them asked himself as he laboured: 'Who's going to tell the tsaritsa?' No one cried or as much as sighed. The three men concentrated on the massive, bloated corpse they were dragging; they hurried to get it off the ice, which could easily break and send them all to the bottom. When they reached the embankment, some boys rushed off to fetch a doctor. It so happened that they found Sergei Vasilyevich Chestukhin, the wartime neurosurgeon. While he was examining the dead body, back at his house on Runovsky Embankment little Marusya got up and went to aunt Margarita Nikolaevna. 'Mama has fallen asleep and I can't wake her up,' she said. Aunt Margarita ran to the corner of the room and found the lifeless body of Liza Chestukhina. She screamed and then, as if she didn't already share the house with a noted surgeon, shouted: 'Get a doctor!' Sergei Chestukhin confirmed the death of the tsaritsa's once mighty friend very quickly, and then a man in a sable fur coat with a big fur hat came up and whispered in his ear: 'Doctor, you are needed in your own house. You can use my coach.' the coachman didn't need long to drive his two horses and reach Runovsky Embankment, but Lizochka was beyond all help, and

Sergei confirmed a second death that day—that of his copper-haired wife, the war hero Yelizaveta 'Liza' Chestukhina. He closed her eyes the colour of sepia for the last time. He didn't cry when he recorded the cause of death. He didn't sob when he told Marusya that Mama would be having a long sleep. And he didn't burst into tears when he said he'd go up and have a little rest in his room. Only when he had closed the door behind him did Sergei start sobbing and pounding the bed with his fists so no one would hear the blows. Then he fell to his knees by the bed and prayed for Lizochka. In the end, he also spoke the name of Grigori Rasputin in his prayers.

After all, he thought that the two of them—Rasputin and Liza—had gone before God at the same time, like one of so many chance meetings, and so it seemed appropriate that he should mention them both in his prayers.

CORPORALS, CHAPLAINS AND HELMSMEN

In the winter of 1916, Manfred von Richthofen became the Red Baron. After the death of his instructor Oswald Boelke, which was a heavy blow for him, Richthofen formed his own fighter group, an outfit known to German soldiers as the 'Flying Circus'. The discipline implemented by the Red Baron among his pilots stood in stark contrast to the vivid assortment of colours the new German single-seaters were painted with. Richthofen demanded complete devotion, intensive planning and unconditional loyalty. The pilots were known to stand over maps for hours debating the best course of action. They knew every French and British opponent by name, including their predispositions and weaknesses. Operative intelligence was taken into account, and the meteorological conditions were not left to chance, yet...

After all that, the Flying Circus went out onto the field to their planes, where their sweethearts were waiting for them, lined up like proper Prussian women. Every pilot had a wartime love, and airmen without a girl to kiss them before the flight could not belong to Manfred von Richthofen's group. It was almost a ritual. The pilots would go up to their planes like jockeys to their horses before a race, and the sweetheart of each of them would be standing by the right wing. In concert, like a real unit, the pilots embraced their girls, who kissed them long and passionately. There was loud smooching, interrupted by shrieks and laughter here and there. The kisses were known to last several minutes; then the obedient Prussian lasses stepped back from the planes, laughing to each other and starting to chatter about whose darling had the coldest lips, and only then, depending on how their sweethearts had kissed them, did the pilots make the final decision on strategy for that day.

The history of these kisses seems to have begun when the Red Baron, flying at great height, encountered Lanoe George Hawker, leader of the British 24th Squadron and one-time lover of 'Magpie' Lilian Smith. These two aces of their time fought a running battle with each other for five whole hours. Hawker fired a machine-gun and the pistol he always took with him on flights; Richthofen replied with his rapid-fire machine-gun. Brushing the tops of trees with his wheels in a low-altitude manoeuvre, the Red Baron finally managed to bring down the Briton, and after returning to base in Ostend he swore to his comrades

and brother that the whole dogfight had been prefigured by his sweetheart and her kisses.

From then on, the pilots ritually kissed their sweethearts, but no one
beyond the squadron was allowed to find out about their superstition,
not even their superior officers. How happy the German infantry were
to see them over Verdun or the Somme, flying in their bright colours
through rents in the sky and puffs of anti-aircraft fire, and no one knew
that the Prussians' loop-the-loops and evasive zigzags were determined
by their faithful Prussian girls.

One gloomy afternoon in December 1916 on the northern French
front near Fumay, Lance Corporal Adolf Hitler, one of three surviving
couriers of the 16th Bavarian Reserve Regiment (named the 'List'
Regiment after its first commander), also happened to see the Flying
Circus overhead and gave them the military salute. Then the lance
corporal immersed himself in reading the first book he had purchased
during the Great War. It was a literary guide to Berlin by Max Osborn,
a presumptuous war reporter, amateur Satanist and intellectual general
practitioner from the capital. Just before the war, with the evident
authority of the ignorant, Osborn demanded that his Berlin publisher
put out 'his' view of the German capital, where the classical Greek
austerity of the Prussians was being made to cohabit with the flagrant
decadence of the city's newcomers. Osborn's *Berlin* now occupied the
young lance corporal to such an extent that he immediately decided
to find out more about the author. That he was an intellectual who
combined the incompatible instantly attracted him; that he was
a Satanist didn't bother him; and when Hitler learnt he was a war
reporter, he promptly made efforts to get hold of the paper which
Osborn wrote for.

When Hitler procured a copy of the journal with the somewhat
pompous title *Reiter in deutscher Nacht* (Rider in German Night), he
was stuck for the first time by a wave of wartime images as real as if
they were made of trench clay and chunks of human flesh. "German
soldiers in their spiked helmets, with their bayonets turned skywards,
seem to me a latter-day incarnation of the pikemen from sixteenth-
century frescoes," wrote Osborn in one issue of *Reiter in deutscher
Nacht*, and the lance corporal simply couldn't wait for the next issue to
be delivered to him at the front in northern France. The long-expected
journal finally arrived. Osborn wrote: "The flame-throwers spouting

fire through clouds of smoke remind me of the blazes laid by our venerable seventeenth-century dukes to purge the land of heathens and savages, and the herald rushing here and there about the field through that suffocating, dim dawn on his black charger—man and proud beast both in gas masks—could be straight from a scene etched by Hieronymus Bosch."

Thanks to pieces such as these, fighting and dying became imbued with meaning, and Hitler began to think that Osborn was somewhere nearby, observing him too, and would write something equally intoxicating about him. From then on, he had a constant companion, a god watching over him, and he felt he had to be worthy of Osborn's patriotic columns for the Berlin press at all times. When he was offered a promotion, Hitler declined in the hope that Osborn would find out and report on it. One issue of the journal arrived after another, but there was no write-up on his heroic gesture. So Hitler imagined what Osborn would have written: 'The young lance corporal, who was to be promoted after heroically delivering a vital message but declined the higher rank with the words "I was only doing my duty", resembles a knight of Barbarossa's in Syria, who, entering Damascus, declines the offerings of the subject people and with his right hand blesses them as new Christians.' Oh, how dizzying this was for one ordinary *Meldegänger* (courier). The imaginary Osborn was far better than the real one. Hitler stopped subscribing to the journal and began penning a panegyric of himself in his little notebook. He wrote 'Wartime Memoirs' on the title page, and signed it 'Max Osborn'.

Everything looked finer and nobler now. Knights and their squires took to the battlefield, accompanied by armourers and swordsmiths. When he had to deliver even the least important message, marked with only one 'X', Hitler would mount his horse and search with his eyes for the omnipresent front-line reporter. Since he didn't find him, he would deliver the message and then note in his 'Wartime Memoirs': the figure of the rearing steed, its open mouth and the clenched, white teeth of horse and rider relaying the message could be from a scene in one of Wagner's operas I saw recently in Bayreuth.' But his tasks became ever more boring and absurd. When heavy rains brought everything to a halt at the front in the last weeks of 1916, Hitler and another courier were sent to search the nearby villages for new mattresses for the troops. The villages behind the front line were deserted, and the German soldiers had renamed them, giving free rein to their debased battlefield fancies: Cursed Cabin, Oven, Dead Swine. The couriers Hans Lippert and Adolf Hitler started off towards Oven. The hunt was successful: in a manor house, they found two mattresses in the cellar with hardly any traces of mould and without bedbugs.

On the way back, this scene took place: courier Hitler was carrying both mattresses because his comrade Lippert had a higher rank—exactly the one Hitler declined in the hope of being noticed by the battlefield correspondent Max Osborn. Hitler sweated beneath the mattresses, but Lippert had the leisure to stroll and talk about whatever entered his head. He spoke about a prostitute from Hamburg, who the whole port city took leave of when she died. Hitler tried to think how he would describe this undignified, humiliating work of mattress lugging in his notebook, where he recorded Osborn's words. Lippert then whistled as they went along. When the two couriers were passing through Oven and making for the trenches, Lippert said offhandedly: 'Oh Adi, you mightn't have heard: that war correspondent Max Osborn was killed. Not that he couldn't write, but it pissed me off that he was always shadowing me and comparing me with some old knights and venerable dukes.' Hitler held his tongue. Lippert kept blabbing on as they walked. Finally the mattresses were delivered. Still bathed in sweat, courier Hitler took up his notebook. Was he stunned? Did he mourn for his god Osborn? No. He wrote a splendid entry about two couriers heroically supplying the whole of the List Regiment for months.

Florid was the German which Lance Corporal Hitler set down in his album as Osborn's notes. To write and speak German like that was the dream of Zhivka the seamstress in occupied Belgrade, but she had never been good at languages. Business had now taken a definite turn for the better. Zhivka was still attractive, and as a broad-shouldered blonde she even resembled a German woman from the north. The war had left no trace on her, and she light-heartedly considered the occupation of Belgrade a stroke of luck and a chance for something positive to happen to her. Her shop in Prince Eugene Street was frequented exclusively by men in uniform, and ever since Dr Schwarz, the Administrator of Belgrade, had given it the official stamp of approval, her clientele was expanding. And every single one of them seemed to Zhivka a gentleman: more like lost, well-mannered children than soldiers prepared to kill. Many came to her shop with unrepented crimes preying on their minds, which they didn't dare to tell Zhivka about. Some even cried while she sewed their uniform or changed the lining of a winter coat. She was particularly fond of one hussar who kept coming in with a torn pocket. No sooner had she stitched up one than he would tear a hole in the other, and there he was again at the door of her shop. He rang the bell, the smile on his lips revealing his buck-teeth, and pointed to his pocket. It was for the sake of that hussar that she learnt her first German word, *Tasche* (pocket), and later her whole life would change because of him. The hussar's name was... but perhaps that's not so important here.

People remember only the names of the great—like those who are lit up by the limelight on stage. One such figure was Florrie Forde, a music-hall singer in London. She thought fate had smiled at her when her only real rival, Lilian Smith, had to leave the city in a hurry. That 'stuffed magpie' with the beady blue eyes no longer stood in the way of Florrie's success, and overnight she became the most popular singer of 'It's a Long Way to Tipperary'. It was an opportunity for her to consolidate her position in the London theatre scene of 1916 and to finally bring out all the Englishness she could muster.

That would not have been anything out of the ordinary if Mrs Forde had not been Australian. She was born Flora May Augusta Flannagan in 1875 in Fitzroy, Victoria, a place renowned for its quality horses and horse handlers. Her father and brothers knew all about horses and wanted to marry her to someone in their circle, but Florrie had higher plans for her future. When she set off for London in 1897, a little golden dust from the Australian outback travelled with her. Some would have been proud of that, but not her: when she found that dust at the bottom of her suitcase, she immediately had someone in to clean it away.

In England, Florrie Forde went to elocution lessons to change her accent, and as the twentieth century dawned, she felt she had shed her last residual Australian identity. Now she considered herself an Englishwoman above all else. During the Great War, Florrie Forde had a nice flat on the second floor of a house in Royal Hospital Road. She never met the agent Oswald Rayner, who lived in the same street, but she was acquainted with all the musical refugees in London. She was constantly inviting Eugène Ysaÿe and the young Arthur Rubinstein to tea. 'Oh, What a Lovely War' and 'Daisy Bell' were the songs she performed most often, but 'It's a Long Way to Tipperary' was the wartime hit she thought she sang the best. Only here she was up against a great rival who was evidently more successful.

When Lilian Smith was caught in 1915 and disgraced for actually being a German—a stroke of good luck for Florrie Forde—this 'real Englishwoman' started giving one charity concert after another. She seized this opportunity to distinguish herself and stated for the press like a true star that she didn't understand how anyone could bring such shame on their homeland, which she loved above all else.

So it was that she became the first among the patriotesses. 'It's a Long Way to Tipperary' was forever on her lips up until one evening, when an unknown admirer unexpectedly opened the door of her dressing room. Unusually, the door was not locked. The corridor was empty, which was also unusual. No one would later be able to say how that stranger got into the theatre. Blinded by the glare of the light bulbs around her large mirror, Florrie could see only his enormous silhouette, which took up almost the entire doorway, his black moustache and a furrowed face. The unknown man said enigmatically: 'You just sing this song tonight, madam. You just sing your "Tipperary", that will be for the best.' Then he left. He didn't speak to anyone else, and no one saw him leave. Florrie Forde became frightened. She had noticed straight away that the unknown man didn't speak English properly.

Florrie didn't realize that the intruder was actually just a drunk, and that he didn't express himself in English terribly well because his native language was Gaelic. The unmasking of Lilly Smith was still fresh in her mind, so it is not surprising that she thought someone might be trying to drag her into a spy affair too. That evening, she sang the well-known patriotic hit, but as she stood in the spotlight beams she was preoccupied with happenings in the hall. A man in the seventh row got up inexplicably and made half the row stand up so he could get out. A little girl kept crying and screaming 'Mummy', while others tried to quieten both the mother and her pampered child. A man in the gallery kept his opera glasses conspicuously trained on Florrie the whole time.

What did it all mean, and what was her role in this behind-the-scenes game? She kept hearing the words on the lips of that horribly furrowed face, 'Just you sing your "Tipperary", that will be for the best,' and in the hall where she was performing so much kept happening—all the things which she, lit up by the lights on stage, hadn't seen before. In particular, she noticed two young men (she got the impression they weren't British) who were avidly whispering in the third row as if her performance didn't interest them at all. She had a good two hours to study them, although the spotlights were focussed on her. They came the next evening, and the one after that too. They were always dressed differently, and first one sat on the left, and then the other.

After a week, she was convinced that the unknown man and those two lads were trying to drag her into a conspiracy. How could she save all her Englishness? She didn't have the strength to start unmasking the conspiracy all by herself. Perhaps she should have approached Scotland Yard that very first evening, not continued to sing. After thinking things over, she made the only real 'English' decision. It was an exceptionally cold day and London's birds were darting about the sky in the last stingy sunlight. Florrie Forde went out onto the stage on 17 December 1916 and told the audience she would no longer be singing 'It's a Long Way to Tipperary'. She didn't say why and didn't lie that she was tired, but the audience reacted loudly to her announcement. Some called out 'Just this one more evening!' and others yelled 'We've paid admission!', but Florrie was preoccupied with those two young men. Did they jeer, perhaps, or leave the hall in a hurry? Not at all. They just sat and waited blank-faced for the song she had decided she was no longer going to sing.

That's how it was that evening, and the next as well. It was another cold London day without fog, but there were no birds any more. Florrie Forde kept her promise, and the song 'It's a Long Way to Tipperary' claimed its victim in 1916 too. The first victim of that wicked song had almost been forgotten, and neither would this one be popular for much longer, to be honest. Lilian Smith, actually Lilian Schmidt, was handed over to Germany. The exchange of spies seemed a happy end to her, and the medal and her substantial fame as a spy quickly saw her back on Berlin's stages and earned her many articles in the press, including one very fiery piece in the journal *Reiter in deutscher Nacht* by the war reporter Max Osborn, written shortly before he was near killed near Dead Swine on the northern-French battlefield.

Frau Schmidt therefore found it relatively easy to rebuild a career as a variety singer. She still sang 'It's a Long Way to Tipperary' to herself for a little while, but quietly so no one would hear, while on stage she naturally shone with the 'Song of Hate against England'. It wasn't a bad song. The Germans loved it as much as the English did 'Tipperary', and Schmidt knew now to rouse the deepest Prussian patriotic emotions with her now somewhat richer, velvety voice. But she loved other wartime hits too—'Die Wacht am Rhein', 'O Strasbourg, o Strasbourg', 'Gott, Kaiser, *Vaterland*'—and sang them gladly up until one evening, when an unknown admirer unexpectedly opened the door of her dressing room. The door was not locked, as it usually was. The corridor was empty, which was also unusual. Lit up by the light bulbs around her mirror, Schmidt could only see his enormous silhouette, which almost took up the whole doorway, his black moustache and a furrowed face. The unknown man was a senior officer. Having no mind to stay, he simply said: 'You will just sing the "Song of Hate against England" from now on, madam. Do you understand? That will be for the best.' Then he left, without speaking to anyone else.

In the programme for the joint variety show with several other German singers the following evening, Frau Schmidt only saw her name next to the 'Song of Hate against England'. She had no choice in the matter. Since her return, she was gradually realizing that people didn't consider her a proper German; as if she had become infected with Englishness during the years she had spent in England—a blemish she couldn't wash off. What about the perilous work she had done? And the medal she had been given? All around her was war. Services were easily forgotten, but duties were still taken very seriously in the *Vaterland*.

'You will just sing the "Song of Hate against England" from now on, madam. Do you understand?'

She did. She almost saluted. Night after night, she sang the 'Song of Hate against England'. It began to grate on her, but she was locked into performing and the show had to go on. She wrote letters to the command and requested that she be allowed to devise a patriotic show with alternating programmes. The proposal was rejected. Then she requested permission for a small pot-pourri of the seven most popular songs, which she would sing to soldiers at the front and in hospitals where moribund cases were treated. That was not approved either. Lastly, she begged to be allowed to sing 'Die Wacht am Rhein' at least occasionally—once a month, perhaps. When that too was refused, she finally realized that she hadn't been handed over and repatriated to Germany at all; she had actually ended up in hell, where constant repetition of one and the same song was her sole punishment.

As befitted a performer, Lilian Smith died on the stage, at the end of her last show. She sang the 'Song of Hate against England', crossed her legs like a ballerina and descended in a low bow, from which she never rose. The last thing she heard was frenetic applause from the audience, who she could not see because of the spotlights shining in her face.

Many deaths concurred at that time, towards the end of 1916. It was not only Liza Chestukhina and Rasputin who went to meet their maker at the same time; thousands took flight for heaven all at once, and so it was that the music-hall singer Lilian Smith and Father Donovan of the 3rd Company, 2nd Battalion of the Scottish 92nd Division died at the same minute and the same second. But the chaplain's death was not before an audience, in the lap of glory, although the lack of interest in both bodies after death was virtually the same. Lilian Schmidt was taken to a Berlin mortuary that same evening, where she was not even properly examined. The body of Father Donovan was taken to a military hospital, where the pathologists didn't conduct a proper examination either. But it was wartime, and we can't blame them for that. The dead were dead, and they were simply struck off the list. After the death of Lilian Schmidt, no other German singer was ordered to sing just the 'Song of Hate against England'. Why that had applied to her was never explained. People spoke about her velvety voice and her heroism in London for a little longer, but then the total of 10,263 people who had seen and heard her perform after her return to Germany began to forget her. After the death of Father Donovan, a young Scottish chaplain took his place, but he sent the dead soldiers off to the other world in silence and never hauled back anyone with the six-ell pole for pulling wounded men from no-man's-land. Exactly 3,211 Scottish soldiers had recalled the Christmas Eve of 1914 when Father Donovan celebrated Mass for officers of all three armies at a farm near Avion. But it was wartime. Of those 3,211 soldiers, a total of 2,750 saw in the New Year 1915, and at New Year's Eve one year later, after the bitter Battle of the Somme, only 911 were left alive. Those nine hundred-odd wretches would occasionally remember Father Donovan, but soon after his death half of them began to get his name wrong and call him 'Father Duncan' or 'Father Donnerty'. Half of the 10,263 visitors from the variety shows in Berlin began to mix up Lilian Schmidt's name too, calling her 'Lilian Straube' and even 'Lilian Strauss'. Then time continued to flow. When the Great War ended, there would only be two Scottish soldiers left who could clearly remember Father Donovan and all he had done, and only three families who would still speak of the authoritative alto voice of the war heroine and not confuse her name with the names of others—because that's what happens to heroes in the end.

Cowards have it easier: at least they don't reckon on anyone's memory. This is the story of the biggest poltroon of the Great War. His name, Marko Murk, had a morbid ring to it. It is not easy for us to describe this young man who now, towards the end of 1916, held an Austro-Hungarian helmet on his head and counted down the last hours of his life. In the first years of the twentieth century, he was a little bit of everything, just as the time he lived in was a little bit of everything. He had a headstrong father who expected him to be an upstanding Croatian home guardsman. He also had a humming in his head, which called on him to become a revolutionary. Fear dwelt in his heart, and his inclination to bolt found its home in his flat-footedness. Between his vulnerable heels and his dreamy head, Marko Murk's body was connected by brittle bones, rubbery muscles and slender sinews.

But Marko Murk, who was rickety and built like a slightly padded skeleton from an osteology cabinet, would hardly have been an unusual phenomenon if he had not been split into two halves already as a young man: the madly brave, helmsmanly half baited the coward. It was a clear case of schizophrenia, advanced and incurable because of the malady of the entire age around him, and it was to take on tragic historical dimensions. It all began in 1897, when young Marko burned a Hungarian flag. He didn't know why he did it: he hated Hungary, but he would never have done anything of the kind if he had not heard a voice inside him ordering, 'Burn the banner'. The voice was his own, and the fear was also his. Deathly frightened, and yet as deliberate as could be, he tore down the green-and-red standard and incinerated it, for which he was sentenced to six months of harsh imprisonment at Lepoglava Prison.

He swore later that he had unsuccessfully tried to restrain himself, without success, while his influential father, a two-time candidate for deputy *Ban*, Viceroy of Croatia, treated his son's disease in the only way possible: he took him out of Lepoglava and enrolled him in Hungarian military college. The years Murk spent at the Hungarian Defence School in Pécs and the Ludoviceum Military Academy in Budapest were outwardly uninteresting for this story, but the atmosphere at the Hungarian military schools left a lasting mark and helped form the political and literary predilections of this second-rater. During that time, his helmsmanly (see note above) and his cowardly half were both far from dormant. Marko tried to get rid of one or the other: we can see this in the way he was alternately punished and praised at the Defence School; but at least no calamity occurred in those years, right up until 1912. Then the young Hungarian cadet was given leave—and promptly travelled to Serbia, whose relations with Austria-Hungary were explosive.

Marko Murk would later write: "I took that trip to Belgrade without identity papers, at a young age and without any of the normal bureaucratic formalities, with the aim of offering my services to Serbia. What services, Jesus Christ? Me, a cadet from a Hungarian military academy, the son of a two-time candidate for deputy *Ban*, and therefore with a dead-end heritage and future!" Without a doubt, his helmsmanly half had prevailed over the cowardly half again. The wretched half of Marko Murk begged his other, mighty half to leave him alone, but without success. His stay in rebellious Serbia ended up in debacle because he was treated with suspicion at every step. He was watched, shadowed, arrested, interrogated and finally deported back to Hungary. He returned to the Ludoviceum and voluntarily presented evidence of his Serbian jaunt, without hesitation or remorse. Needless to say, an internal inquiry was conducted. The result was a six-day period of strict detention and many other punishments. It was probably that very excursion which ultimately led the academy's board of directors to approve cadet Murk's application for official leave in March 1913.

In this period, Marko had his second experience with Serbia. His helmsmanly half demanded that he travel via Salonika to Skopje, recently liberated from the Ottomans, where he offered his services to the Serbian army once more. But this time, too, he was accused of spying and escorted under guard to Belgrade. For three days the cowardly half of him implored not to be released from the old Turkish jail in Topchider and to be allowed to stay in Serbia; for three days he begged and grovelled like a dog, but then they sent him by barge to the border town of Zemun and, on the basis of a wanted circular, handed him over to the Austro-Hungarian border police as a deserter.

So it was that Marko Murk's youthful idealizing of Serbia as a 'Piedmont of liberation and unification' finally collapsed after his twofold saga of adversity, and he returned to Zagreb. But now he was all alone. He no longer had a family, since his father had disowned him via the newspapers. None of the denizens of the day would accept him as one of them. None of the creatures of the night would enrol him either. Confronted with a loss of ideals, he was also overtaken by hunger. And that is how the story would have ended if the time in which he lived had not also had its helmsmanly and its cowardly half. Marko hadn't been able to put a Serbian *Shaykacha* on his head and become a private in the Morava Division, but he would have to go to war just as he was.

For Marko Murk, the Great War began in a café in Zagreb's Tushkanac neighbourhood when he saw hundreds of glasses being smashed against a wall. He fell into the embrace of the hysterical mob and passionately hated Serbia with it the whole evening. Him, of all people! On the way back, he smashed the windows of two shops, which he mistook as belonging to Serbs. The next day, he bitterly regretted it all and swore to himself that he would become as silent as a thief and tread in his own footsteps, trying to leave as little trace as possible in 1914 which could reveal him and commend him to the sirens of war. But Murk, with the morbid ring to his name, was mistaken.

This former Hungarian cadet was not mobilized immediately at the beginning of the war, and he managed to stay in civvies for all of 1915. Only in July 1916 was he drafted into the Reserve Officers School in Zagreb, so as to be transferred to a Croatian Home Guard regiment as of 1 August; military education ran its course here, and he was allocated to one of the lower command positions and tasked with training the recruits who would soon be 'taking their final test' before the enemy. Him, the former pyromaniac, Lepoglava inmate, 'Serbian spy' and POW! But the cowardly wartime half was satisfied that Marko saw neither gas, bayonet nor bullet and thus won a short-lived victory over the helmsmanly half. Was this other force in the body and mind of Marko Murk dormant? Not at all, it was just biding its time. The coward Murk was able to avoid being sent to the battlefield almost until the end of 1916 thanks to being diagnosed with tuberculosis (whether real or fictitious is secondary at this point). He was hospitalized in the picturesque town of Lovran on the Adriatic, and as soon as the doctors noticed his fever subside a little he was sent to the Eastern Front, to Galicia. Brusilov's Russian offensive was under way and the Dual Monarchy needed every pair of hands it could muster, even Murk's.

He travelled by overloaded troop train. The soldiers around him stood, smoked, took turns sitting on one another's laps, bumped each other at the slightest attempt to move and apologized to one another like old-fashioned greenhorns. Murk already felt strange in the compartment. The dark half of him was rising from the bitter dregs and Marko slowly entered the phase of heroism. Whatever he had thought or been waiting for before—he heard himself say, and it sounded foreign—this now was his hour for fame! Leaving the train, he was almost carried on the hands of the new recruits he had prepared for their 'final test' before the enemy. He had changed beyond recognition. He had his own 'class' of cadets who looked up to him like a god. Did he tell them anything about his sprees to Serbia? No, he dared not. He pretended to be a leader and reassured himself he was. He was waiting and just itching for the first day of combat, but the bothersome rains of Galicia would prolong his life for twenty more unnecessary days. During that time, he strove unsuccessfully to calm his helmsmanly half.

He prayed. Whined. Pined. Begged.

No one noticed. In the severe cold at Christmas 1916, an attack was ordered. 'Class leader' Murk was the first to leap out of the trench. He screamed, as if at a loss what to do with himself. Several black birds descended towards him as if they were coming to perch on his head. He traversed some ten metres of no-man's-land, flailing with his arms like a mad thing. Then he suddenly stopped. He was hit by a single bullet, which put an end to everything. He crossed his legs like a ballerina and fell in a low bow, from which he would never rise. He died in a sitting position, not lying like most others. The last thing he saw around him were the ravens; wheeling above the frozen Galician earth and cawing, as if to sing the praises of a hero.

One thousand five hundred kilometres to the south-west, the deceased Emperor Franz Joseph was now succeeded by the last Austro-Hungarian monarch: Charles I. The new helmsman of the dynasty destined to rule for a thousand years was handed all the insignia of the crown... and a war. One he was expected to win.

Nothing terrible. Just a war.

Each new ruler always inherits a war. But Charles was frightened. He too had his helmsmanly and his cowardly half. And his people, he suspected, were the same. He smiled. He made an effort to appear composed at the emperor's funeral and later at his own coronation. He stepped through the streets of Vienna with Empress Zita and little Archduke Otto, but he didn't look into the crowd. His gaze wandered across the grey Vienna facades. He saw the faces of his subjects pressed up against the windows, and he felt their heads resembled pale pumpkins. His thoughts were blank. The horses with black tassels, black coaches and escorts with black-plumed helmets all resembled rain-soaked ravens to him, just like the ones from Galicia. Afterwards he stood in front of the chapel at the foot of an enormous hill of wreaths and flowers brought by the populace. He left the funeral escorted by men who smelt of the damp. He received the crown and the sceptre, but he refused to use the old emperor's chambers in the Hofburg and Belvedere palaces. Instead, he moved into the apartments once used by the first secretaries of the court. There was certainly no lack of luxury here either, but he was sleepy. He felt terribly tired and had to lie down.

Had he fallen asleep or not? He couldn't remember. He got up as if he was strong and well rested. He sat on the edge of the bed in his nightshirt and didn't reach for the bell or get out the chamber pot from under the bed. He looked and saw that someone was coming to visit. At first, he recognized Crown prince Rudolf, who had killed himself back in the nineteenth century, even though it had been a nicer century than this. After him came the late Empress Elisabeth of Austria, also known as Sisi; and behind her the heir presumptive Franz Ferdinand and the Duchess of Hohenberg with their bullet wounds. Were the visitors crying? Moaning? No, it was more of a rustling like the sound of sheets in the wind. They wanted to tell him something, but their voices failed them. They moved in circles around his bed, deathly white, naked, wretchedly built, with coats of fat which looked as if they had been pinned onto the bone like formless sacks—but he was not afraid. He tried to read from their lips what they wanted to say to him. But what was it? Empress Elisabeth of Austria had the smallest mouth but spoke the most clearly. He tried to halt her, but she tore herself from his grasp and continued to circle his bed with the others. He would have to wait for her to pass and catch the movements of her lips in flight as they now danced in a bacchanalian frenzy, flinging their heads back and turning them so he couldn't read their lips at all. Now they were tirelessly repeating one and the same refrain like satyrs. Empress Elisabeth turned, and her mouth was pointing right towards him. She said… what did she say? It was a date she spoke: '11 November 1918!' Now he saw the other mouths too. Yes, Franz Ferdinand was saying the same, and the Duchess of Hohenberg and Crown prince Rudolf too. Charles thought that was the day when an attempt would be made on his life. Nothing else. All the deceased aristocrats were warning him about the same thing.

He woke up, or perhaps he hadn't been asleep at all. There was no one near him now. Without thinking, he grabbed the bell. He asked for a stargazer to be brought to him. The best were in Bavaria, where there seemed to be thousands of them. They could almost have set up shop in the high streets and predicted the future for soldiers and their mothers: the date of the young man's death or his happy homecoming. Charles asked for the best, while the staff of the late Emperor Franz Joseph looked at each other in astonishment. Nevertheless, two of them travelled all the way to the dubious quarters of Munich and came back with a magus who had been recommended to them by several knowledgeable people. His name was Franz Hartmann and he had a far better opinion of himself than the people around him, who called him 'Dirty Franz'. Hartmann claimed to have learnt the ropes of the occult in Madras and to have returned to Germany in 1907, after which he ensured himself a place in theosophist societies through his skill and powers alone, whatever evil tongues might say. He called himself Franz of Bavaria, as if he was a duke. Now he was brought before the emperor and listened carefully to what the emperor told him in confidence. Afterwards the stargazer withdrew into a chamber with his astral maps and other aids. Seven hours later he emerged triumphantly. 'Your Majesty,' he exclaimed, 'that is the day when an attempt will be made on your life, but you will survive that attack on 11 November 1918. Nothing else need worry you. By then, our countries will already have won the Great War. There is no reason to be concerned, I assure you.'

Several days later it was the New Year. Charles I waited in white Belvedere palace. His gaze wandered off down the green avenue and further, into the city. He was surrounded by subjects who drank and ate at his table as if it was their last meal. Even the generals were wolfing down mouthfuls of cold turkey before they had finished the previous ones. But Charles wasn't concerned. He didn't realize that even the most senior government officials and army commanders were hungry. Shortly before the New Year 1917 he was even a little cheerful, groundlessly so. That is how the last Austrian emperor saw in the New Year 1917.

Old Libion and Old Combes saw in the New Year 1917 with raids. Dozens of uniformed gendarmes on bicycles arrived in front of their respective cafés and started arresting the tipsy artists, who had just been drinking to the freedom of the French people and were now mortally insulted. Neither Old Libion nor Old Combes felt sorry for those freakish, so-called artists. Those who were released from custody first would be back the very next day, and the others would come as soon as they got a first whiff of freedom themselves. Both publicans wondered if the raid had been only on their own café. Each of them immediately sent their errand boy, and the two almost collided in the middle on the way to check whether the rival had also been blitzed. The café owners breathed a sigh of relief when they heard that the gendarmes on wheels had 'visited' both places simultaneously. Everything was alright then. It was just part and parcel of seeing in the New Year 1917, they said to themselves, and about three hours after midnight each of them closed his café for the evening.

For the actor Béla Duránci, the Great War ended at New Year's Eve 1917 when Emperor Franz Joseph visited him for the last time. The emperor had his familiar face from 1879, with a combed, silky moustache, and called from the door of the room loudly enough for him to hear but quietly enough so as not to wake the other patients: 'Minden jó'. To which Duránci replied 'Minden szép', and then fell into a sleep, from which he would never wake up.

To usher in the New Year 1917, Guillaume Apollinaire threw one of his legendary parties in his flat in Boulevard Saint-Germain. He sat in the middle of the merry gathering, with a turban on his head like a sultan and telling anecdotes. In keeping with the fashion of the third year of the war, everyone present was smoking a clay pipe. He was surrounded by folk less significant than him who he called 'young' and 'intelligent'. Among them was Giorgio de Chirico. He laughed at Apollinaire's jokes and worried when the 'sultan' retired before midnight due to feeling so run-down.

Jean Cocteau, the former member of an aviation unit near Bussigny, and then of the Paris army-supply office and medical corps under Étienne de Beaumont, saw in the New Year 1917 in groundless good cheer. He swore to make it a custom for the years to come that he would welcome each New Year with merrymaking, even if the Great War lasted a decade. A promise he went on to fulfil.

The girl of a woman Kiki was promiscuous on New Year's Eve. She made love on the workshop floor with three pairs of boots. In the end she was left simply exhausted and drained.

Fritz Haber slept through New Year's Eve 1917. He thought of nothing and dreamed of nothing.

Svetozar Boroevich von Boina also spent New Year's Eve sleeping. He was in pyjamas. Both uniforms stayed in the wardrobe and had a whale of a time seeing in the New Year 1917 without their wearer.

After the fiasco of his gruesome camouflage positions, Lucien Guirand de Scevola ceased to be real, so how he saw in 1917 was utterly unimportant.

Hans-Dieter Huis saw in the New Year 1917 alone. He didn't speak with anyone because he had lost his voice. To be precise, he hadn't quite lost his voice, but his throat continued to sound squeaky and ever squeakier, and soon it went beyond the range of human hearing. That was the end of his career. Or maybe it wasn't.

Walther Schwieger was quite the opposite: he didn't lose his voice. And the fact that he had lost a second submarine didn't worry him. His U-20, the shark which had sunk the Lusitania, ran aground on 4 November 1916 just off the Danish coast. Commander Schwieger disembarked the crew, mined the vessel, surveyed the sea and blew up the U-20. In the port of L. he was immediately given a new submarine, the U-88, which would later become his tomb, and he continued his previous mission. For the New Year 1917, too, he locked himself into his cabin and bellowed at the top of his voice. He had quite a bit to drink, contrary to the rules of the naval service and the dignity of a decorated officer, and wouldn't let anyone in to see him. He yelled and shouted with the shadowy sea floor through until morning, when he nodded off and saw in 1917—his last year—in his sleep.

A von B welcomed in the New Year in Vienna. As a senior official of the 'k and k' monarchy, he also took part in the funeral procession of beloved Emperor Franz Joseph. He saw the new Emperor Charles I somewhere at the side and thought him unworthy of the imperial crown.

The Red Baron saw in 1917 with his sweetheart in his embrace. From Christmas Eve 1916 until the first days of the New Year 1917 there were no sorties on either side, so on New Year's Eve he was finally able to kiss his sweetheart in many different ways, without it having any bearing on operational plans.

The courier of the 16th Bavarian Reserve Regiment, Adolf Hitler, saw in the New Year wounded in Beelitz Hospital near Berlin. He was indebted to a dog for being alive at all. The dog was a mongrel, disobedient and stupid; the soldiers laughed at courier Hitler, and he in turn beat the dog. At the very moment when a trench-howitzer shell was whistling in an arc towards the German trenches, courier Hitler ran out to grab that disobedient whelp. The shell exploded with a mighty blast, killing all of Hitler's comrades. The stupid mutt was dead too. Now Hitler lied to the other patients and told them tales about a dog which dashed out in front of him, shielding him with its body and thus saving him from certain death. The men laughed at him and jeered: 'Be that as it may, Adi, your hero-dog will still have ended up in the stew!' Hitler didn't want to listen. Instead of quarrelling, he turned to Max Osborn's notebook and wrote: 'The German soldiers in the trenches, who saw in the New Year 1917 wet to the skin in their hooded raincoats, with faithful Alsatians at their side, seem to me like Flying Dutchmen singing "Through storm and gale we sail the open sea".'

The singer Florrie Forde did not sing 'It's a Long Way to Tipperary' for the New Year 1917, although many begged her to. For a moment she was tempted to sing that ominous song, but then a stranger, one of the many guests gathered at the Scott's Arms for the New Year's Eve party, gave her a wink, and that completely threw her off balance. She left the party before midnight and was thus one of those who saw in the New Year 1917 in bed.

Thirteen days later, Vladimir Alexandrovich Sukhomlinov saw in the New Year 1917 by the Julian calendar in his sleep, but Yekaterina Sukhomlinova was awake. She made a list of all the socks owned by her husband, the former governor-general of Kiev. She wrote: 'Twelve pairs of black socks, only twelve pairs! Of those, four of silk and five pairs of worn-out ones. I stress: twelve pairs!'

Zhivka the seamstress celebrated her first 'Kraut New Year', and the later Serbian New Year, in her shop in 26 Prince Eugene Street. There is nothing to say about her 'Kraut New Year'. There is almost nothing to tell about how she spent the Serbian New Year either. And on 1 January by the Julian calendar she was alone. She was violently sick. In the morning, she thought for the first time that she might be pregnant. Only one person could be the father: the officer with the hole in his pocket.

On New Year's Eve, Sergei Chestukhin showered his small daughter Marusya with kisses. He hugged her so long and warmly that she soon fell asleep in his arms.

Grand Duke Nicholas received a visit on New Year's Eve from his wife Anastasia, who had had to travel for seven whole days to see the 'Viceroy of Russia' in the Caucasus. Anastasia was accompanied by her sister Milica, as if she had come not to see in the New Year but to fight a duel. But she was unable to start a family feud because Nicholas silenced her each time with an abrupt movement of his hand and the words: 'Milica, it's New Year's Eve. We're celebrating!'

At some time around the infidel New Year, Mehmed Yıldız resolved to leave the silence of his dimly lit shop, which now was almost always closed and had begun to resemble some kind of hideout with the spices of different colours strewn like treasures in the dust. Coming out of the woodwork like this seemed to him a bit like jumping over his own shadow. He was entering his last year of trading, his sixtieth, so he could afford to lean back. He decided to go out into the world and become a good, sociable Turk. He began his search for new friends in a café, over a cup of jasmine tea. Here he met two other old men much like himself. The one was invariably silent, the other spoke incessantly. The talker called himself Hayyim the Merry. He had an incredibly sonorous voice and a loud, clucking tongue, and the words left his mouth with a twang like bolts from a crossbow. He told Yıldız that he could hardly wait for victory or defeat in the Great War. Victory, because Istanbul would greet it with an incredible celebration in all three parts of the city, with flags, horses, silken sheets to be lowered from the minarets like giant pantaloons, and lotus flowers to be strewn over the waters of the Golden Horn. But why defeat? Because then it would all be put on for the occupation troops, Hayyim replied elatedly, so the pomp and Oriental feeling would be even more pronounced. 'And a celebration is a celebration,' Hayyim added, 'no matter whether victory or defeat'. 'Hm,' the spice trader replied to these words of his new friend and went out into the street again. There he was met by a rain which seemed to beat down wrathfully from the heavens. He pulled up the collar of his woollen coat and pushed his fez down further over his forehead. Now he had two friends from the tearoom: the silent one, whose name he didn't know, and Hayyim the Merry. In the street he collected two more chance companions, so now his tally had reached four. He aligned them in his straight-and-narrow consciousness so they would stand one behind the other like profiles cut out of cardboard. Four new friends, but he was unhappy nonetheless.

King Peter saw in the New Year 1917 by the Julian calendar in Salonika once again. He had returned, fearing that southern Greece could be cut off in what was looking like civil war. The night in the rebellious city was calm. When he summed up the year 1916, he could only recall ordinary things: he had dismissed his doctor, quarrelled with the cook, been unable to get a good chauffeur, and he hadn't seen his son Alexander for almost a whole year. In the end he had become a refugee again, this time within Greece, and had had to be evacuated on board a French torpedo boat. Was that worthy of a king who had thought that 1916 could be the year of the kings, and that they might use their consanguine connections to end the Great War? Before retiring for the night, he still had to look at the replies to the New Year telegrams. The next day, 14 January by the new calendar, emissary Balugdzhich was to despatch telegrams to the British king George V, the Dutch queen Wilhelmina, the Belgian king Albert and the Italian sovereign Victor Emmanuel III, all of whom had sent New Year's greetings for 1917 to the Serbian king. He would open the telegrams and write the messages himself. Perhaps one single word: 'Enough'. No, he couldn't do that. The replies had to be courteous. After all, kings were just crowned marionettes on the strings of an evil puppeteer, he thought, put on his nightshirt and went to bed. The telegrams remained on the table without being looked at: So ended the year of one king without a kingdom.

The first day of the New Year dawned in Salonika with the murmur of palm trees. Someone had opened the venetian blinds while the king slept. The sun shone forth, and the sea in the bay seemed as transparent and crystalline as ice. But King Peter was not in the mood. His beard was ever longer and his eyes ever more sunken, like embers burning deeper and deeper into his face, so his new doctor tried to find his predecessor in order to seek his advice. His search was unsuccessful, and that further concerned him.

1917
THE YEAR OF THE TSAR

The dancer Mata Hari in costume for a performance, 1917

BETRAYAL, COWARDICE AND LIES

That night, the hoar frost came down on the capped and bare heads of people like harsh sugar crystals, and a cold crust also formed on people's souls. The detectives of the Petrograd Okhrana saw in the New Year of 1917 with big pots of black tea. The malcontents they kept tabs on and arrested were firing salvos of tense joy that night and swearing to one another that they were prepared to believe any slander and insults in the New Year 1917. The temperature fell to minus twenty degrees everywhere. Dirty little mongrels moseyed around in the streets like foxes, weasels or badgers looking for a warren. People seeking shelter hurried by between the dogs: walking, falling and then crawling on all fours as if they were foxes, weasels or badgers.

Grand Duke Alexander was writing to the tsar, stringing together awkward, tortured letters. 'The masses are not revolutionary,' he wrote, weighing every word, 'but every ill-considered edict and ban pushes them towards the leftist camp. In circumstances such as this, why is it so hard to imagine that a few words from the tsar could change everything?' Then he folded the letter twice, screwed it up and threw it in the bin.

Why was it so hard to imagine that a word from the tsar could change everything? On the first day of the New Year 1917, Tsar Nicholas woke up in his bed in Tsarskoye Selo alone. The hoar frost had ornamented the window overnight as it used to do when he was child. A stony sun began to shine on the snow-covered hills, a harsh light without warmth, but it also put some life into people. It was very loud at court in the first days of the New Year, with a flux of delegations, people loyal to the cause, as well as brothers and uncles of the tsar. And all of them demanded that Nicholas address the masses with just a few words which might change the situation. And yet how hard it was to imagine Nicholas saying them.

After Rasputin's death, from the day that holy man was drawn dishevelled, blue and bloated from the Malaya Nevka, the tsar fell into a strange and worrying state of lethargy. Life had left him behind and was heading off, like a long train he had just missed, and now he watched the days glide past like windows and compartments: each of them lit up and with unknown travellers inside. One word would change everything; but he was not on board, the windows of the moving train were closed, and if the tsar had called from the platform he would just have strained his voice in vain and no one would have heard him. That is what made it so hard to conceive of Nicholas speaking to the masses. And on top of that, there were so many strange things which took away his thoughts. Early 1917 in Tsarskoye Selo was marked by the visits of peace brokers. They came before the tsar like wind-up toys, or evil warlocks from Russian fairy tales. January of the fourth year of the war marked the beginning of the peace-agreement season. Each side had a knife at its throat in this war and everyone was offering everyone else special conditions so as to end the Great War on their fronts. Germany then made four attempts. Four human toys were sent to the tsar to offer him a separate peace agreement and the salvation of the empire. They came before him like heroes in a play, who introduce themselves to the audience and proceed to talk with them.

Enter a certain Joseph Kolishko. His tweed suit fastened with the slender belt of his jacket, his nervous shifting from one leg to the other and his vagabond appearance made him the very caricature of a Russian abroad. Kolishko's hair was as yellow as straw, his lips raspberry red, pouted and much too full for a man, and his eyes moved erratically as if the optic nerve was not completely in control. When he faced the tsar, his eyes widened, his gaze fled, and he minced and mumbled his words. This exhausted neurotic introduced himself to the tsar as a journalist, a correspondent of the Russian émigré papers *Grazhdanin* and *Russkoye Slovo*. He claimed to maintain close ties with Swedish bankers. And, not to be forgotten, there were also his special contacts with German industrial magnates. He had come in the name of Hugo Stinnes, the most powerful of them all, to offer peace and a German renewal of Russia. The tsar replied, or he didn't; that wasn't important because the magnate Stinnes, all the Swedish bankers and the peace offer itself were made of paper and hemp, glued together with a paste of foreign desires.

He sent Kolishko away without even having him stay for lunch, but several days later another intermediary came before the tsar. This time it was a lady by the name of Maria Vasilchikova. She was built like a pear: the pointy crown of her head spread down into full, chubby cheeks; her thick neck continued into huge, flabby breasts, which drooped down to her belly; and this was connected to her sagging behind. She turned around in front of the tsar so he would see she was dressed in skirts and wrapped in scarves like a traditional Russian woman, and her fat buttocks stood out from under her skirt just like the bulging bottom of an enormous red pear. Vasilchikova then took the scarf off her head and, yes, burst into tears. She reminded Nicholas that she had been a maid-of-honour to both the tsaritsa and Duchess Yelizaveta before the Great War, before departing for her estate in Klein Wartenstein. She begged the tsar, despite his countless laurels, to add the wreath of immortality to them, and then came out with the proposition: she was offering him the Dardanelles in the name of the German crown, and she opened up the vision of Russia acquiring them without the aid of Britain and France.

Nicholas, however, didn't have time to think about her because a new character had taken the stage in that theatre of intermediaries: the Dane, Hans Nils Andersen. He stood there before the tsar proudly, as straight as a ramrod, with blue eyes and the look of a stuffed bird. He was a man who possessed reading glasses, glasses for special occasions, glasses for the winter, and he now came before the emperor, wiping those specially reserved for his journey through the Russian provinces. 'This winter is terrible,' he said, 'my glasses have completely fogged up.' He put away the travelling glasses and placed the round spectacles reserved for special occasions on his nose, only to take them off again as soon as he wanted to read something to the tsar. He wore that third pair for as long as he was reading but changed to a fourth as soon as the servants brought tea. Four pairs of spectacles, the tsar thought: one for the train and the muzhiks, one for the audience, one for reading and one for drinking black tea! Was there a fifth and a sixth pair hiding in his inside pocket? Hans Nils Andersen was the director of the East Asia Company, a privy counsellor and, in his own assessment, a prudent politician of the neutral Kingdom of Denmark. He claimed to be a trusted old acquaintance of Nicholas's mother, the dowager tsaritsa, who was Danish by extraction, and therefore he was bearing a fraternal letter from the Danish king Christian X to the Russian tsar. Andersen proudly produced the letter, broke the seals, and changed his glasses for drinking tea for his reading glasses. The letter was cordial, and Nicholas replied warmly, knowing this wasn't the end.

The fourth intermediary was the Hamburg banker Mark Wartburg. This German of Swedish ancestry had cheeks like inflated silk balloons covered with tiny red veins. He breathed with difficulty and had high blood pressure. It seemed winter didn't agree with him: the Russian winter in particular. He came before the tsar wearing a leather coat, on top of which he had donned two long fur coats reaching down to the soles of his boots. These pelts of polar fox and sable on top of his portly body made him look like some kind of strange bear. He shed his layers before the tsar: first the sable, then the fox, and finally, with a little hesitation, his leather coat. 'It is warm in the palace, Your Majesty,' he said in German, which the tsar understood well, and proceeded to present the situation like a minister rather than a banker: 'The Great War was provoked by Britain, and it alone is to blame. In the same way, the Russian victories of 1878 came to nought when the British fleet turned up in the Sea of Marmara. Territorial issues will easily be resolved between the German and Russian empires. Poland will remain a distinct country, Russia will control the south and east all the way to the Serbian border, and Germany will have Baltic Courland.' 'What about the Latvians?' the tsar asked, and Wartburg replied: 'The Latvians are not worth talking about—a mere trifle!' 'The Latvians are not worth worrying about,' the tsar repeated to himself in Russian and sent away the fourth peace broker, but he lived in fear that things were far from over and that 1917 was fated to be the year of the tsar and his emissaries.

He was mistaken, as were many others involved in the Great War. Any illusions of the might of the Danube empire were shattered in that fourth year of the war. The bread ration dwindled every month, and only a lucky few had sugar. In these conditions, the monarchy became a paradise for theosophists and charlatans of every ilk. Even the court was occupied by them since the reading of the new emperor's dream in November of the previous year, when a dubious fortune-teller from Bavaria prophesied that the new emperor of millions would survive an assassination attempt on 11 November 1918. Yes, that's what he foretold, and it was impossible that the theosophist could be wrong.

Now he and his unkempt comrades were needed once more. A crucial dispatch was penned in the capital of the Dual Empire, and it had to be protected by all means canny and uncanny. The dispatch was an ordinary piece of correspondence, in no way different to any other, yet it was to decide the fate of millions. Empress Zita was far more energetic than her drowsy husband Charles I and drafted the dispatch to her brother, Prince Sixt of Bourbon-Parma, a Belgian officer serving in the French army. The dispatch would propose an end to the Great War, even if it be under circumstances shameful for the 'k and k' monarchy, because that was the only way to save the court and the crown. Absent-minded Charles, with the ardent intercession of his wife, even offered Alsace-Lorraine and various other lands, like a reckless medieval lord. The dispatch was to be conveyed by Maria Antonia, the empress's trustworthy mother; but what if the letter with the humiliating peace offer fell into enemy hands? What if Sixt, whom Zita had not seen for more than a decade, passed it on to the French premier, as every loyal officer should?

The dispatch therefore had to be protected, but how could it be written in code if that meant that the coder had to go on the mission together with the empress's mother—she in one coach, he in another? They would surely be intercepted. So the dispatch had to be secured by different means. The solution was typically German, and two loyal men of the crown were again sent to the north in search of occultists: to masked Munich and obscure Prince Regent Street, where fortune-tellers and soothsayers had shops and put up signs advertising their mystical 'services'. Motley folk with dark rings under their eyes and a stone in their stomachs loitered in those streets, searching for their destiny like a lost coin. Among them were two envoys of the Austro-Hungarian court. They immediately set about finding an old acquaintance from 1916, Franz Hartmann, 'Duke Franz of Bavaria', but they soon learnt that he had been killed in mysterious circumstances. After his illustrious auguring in Vienna, things seemed to have gone amiss for the duke. Unfortunately, he hadn't managed to foresee his own demise. He was found dead in a dilapidated, grey building and his corpse was so filthy that he posthumously confirmed his nickname of 'Dirty Franz'.

So the court envoys had to find someone else. 'Dirty Franz' was said to have had an apprentice. After some effort, they found a cross-eyed young man by the name of Hugo Vollrath. He was a proud member of the theosophist sects, the Universal Brotherhood, Brothers of Light and the Mazdaznan Movement. He had even founded the *Astrologische Rundschau* magazine, whose first issue was number twelve, thereby skipping the first eleven issues! Vollrath claimed to be a trained occultist and said his teacher had been about to issue him his certificate of apprenticeship when he was killed. He immediately accepted the assignment.

Vollrath was silent during the journey to Vienna and did not reveal his intentions to anyone. Only at the court did he come out with his brilliant plan. He offered the empress a special kind of 'invisible ink', whose writing would be erased if touched by French hands.

What the dickens? How could ink recognize the skin of Frenchmen? Quite easily, replied this introverted, strangely occluded man: the palm of every hand sweats in a different way. Magic writing was able to recognize the sweat of French hands and immediately erase itself as soon as it was touched. But what about Sixt: what if his hands were sweaty? Sixt was different. Vollrath would take a sample of the sweat of Empress Zita and use it to take account of the sweat of her brother, the Belgian officer in the French army. It was simple: the letters would not erase themselves if they came in contact with his sweat!

An offer like this was too good to refuse. The trained theosophist, who had been just a few days short of receiving his 'certificate of apprenticeship', withdrew into a special chamber with the ready-written dispatch. For three days he took neither food nor water, which they left for him at the door like for a leper. Howls and moans were periodically heard from the room, and occasionally a tremendous racket. On the second day, a strange yellow wisp of smoke crept through the slit under the door, like the poison gas bertholite, but it wasn't lethal, because Vollrath came out several hours later and asked Empress Zita to hold out her right hand. He took a sample of sweat from her palm, and a little later he emerged triumphantly with the dispatch. It was safe, he said. Having accomplished the task, he collected the agreed payment and immediately set off back north, to dark Bavaria, but the empress was not convinced. She demanded another protective spell.

So a second theosophist came, this time from the fiendish city of Leipzig in crazy Saxony. He claimed to have learned the arts at Faust's tavern. His name was Karl Brandler-Pracht and his only condition for helping was that the court never approach the charlatan Hugo Vollrath, who had stolen from him the publishing rights to most of the books of the famous Alan Leo. Although no one knew who Leo was and why the rights to his works were so important, the people loyal to the throne immediately agreed that the dispatch had nothing to do with Vollrath and naturally remained calm when Brandler-Pracht said: 'I'll be able to tell straight away if you're lying, and then the deal will be off.' He didn't notice that the dispatch had been in Vollrath's hands, of course, so the touchy autodidact from the inn recommended his good services: after he had applied his magic, all the letters would turn into unintelligible squiggles if anyone with evil thoughts as much as came near the dispatch. No one asked how letters written on paper could sense such thoughts. The empress was in a bad mood, and the spineless court attendants knew it was a time when they had best show unconditional obedience. Like his predecessor, this theosophist stewed and screamed over the dispatch for two days. Unlike his arch-enemy Vollrath, this one ate everything they left for him at the door and often greedily asked for more. He finished the work, visibly fattened, one week later. He too said at the end that the dispatch was now safe. Taking an immodest sum of money, he immediately headed back to obscure Saxony and the diabolical cellars of Leipzig.

Were the two protective spells enough? No, the dispatch was also presented to sober-headed subjects of the empire, and they realized it had to be upgraded in some way; it didn't matter how, just so that the hysterical empress would be satisfied. The dispatch therefore lay around at the supreme headquarters of the army for another week. Since no one there was superstitiously inclined, it was simply left lying on the desk of a general with a silver moustache. After a considerable number of days, the army confirmed that the dispatch was safe from a military point of view.

Immediately afterwards it was taken to a von B, who had to add a little counter-espionage magic. What could this diligent subject of the empire do, after having played to a draw in a major contest with Russian counter-intelligence the previous year? As with the silver-moustached general, the dispatch was left to lie on his desk for several days and then returned to the empress with a note: 'Approved by the *Kundschaftergruppe*'.

After all this to-do, the dispatch so crucial for the Danube Empire was ready to be sent, and at first everything went smoothly. On 24 March 1917, the empress embraced her mother and whispered something to her; she got straight into the coach without a word in reply. Two days later, she saw Sixt. The dispatch was delivered and read. Lieutenant Sixt shed a single tear. Or he didn't. But then the dispatch fell into the wrong hands. When Sixt, as a loyal soldier, passed it on to the French, not a single letter erased itself as it was touched by evil French hands. When the dispatch finally reached Georges Clemenceau, not a single word turned into unintelligible squiggles, even though you can be sure that this influential Frenchman had evil thoughts when wondering what to do with this absolute proof of high treason. Imagine urging France to secretly seek an armistice! The new French premier's response to the Viennese court's diplomatic offensive was to publish the dispatch, and the Ministry of War's protective measure proved ineffective. When *Le Figaro* came out with Emperor Charles's dispatch on the front page, the protection from the *Kundschaftergruppe* also failed. Germany accused the Viennese court of undermining their alliance, and the emperor had to make many concessions to assuage his pugnacious northern neighbours. In the end, it was all quite an embarrassment, although for some more than others.

Several days after it became known that the French press had printed the emperor's dispatch, a von B went to work as usual. He didn't confide in anyone. It looked like it would be just another day for him and his spy ring. But a von B decided to spoil his subordinates' calm. He took out his pistol and placed it next to a sheet of white paper. For the Austrian spymaster, the Great War ended when he began his farewell letter: 'Given my responsibility towards myself and the monarchy...', he wrote, and then stopped. He quickly raised his gun and, without hesitation, fired a single round into his heart. The drops of his blood provided the last argument for the suicide of this loyal servant of the Empire. Three deep-red drops fell right beside the words 'myself and the monarchy'.

All the plans for an armistice therefore failed. Nothing on earth or anything supernatural could bring about peace; with people wavering, war now took the initiative and raged like a sudden storm out of the clear, western sky. A merciless submarine war began in the Atlantic. Britain ordered that all her ships sail in convoys, and new underwater mines were laid to sink shallow-diving German submarines: shredded metal and dismembered crewmen were blown sky-high. On several occasions early in that year, mines exploded close to the U-88 of highly decorated submarine commander Walther Schwieger, but his vessel was saved once again by the huge serpents, megalodons with huge maws, and legendary giant octopuses. None of the crew saw the monsters this time either, but Schwieger manoeuvred like mad, and many times the submarine truly seemed have been seized by a huge paw and briskly moved sideways or into the deep seconds before a depth charge blasted an air pocket the size of a whale. 'What did I tell you–', roared the captain, now almost constantly drunk, 'we have the aid of all the serpents!' To which the crew replied in a rather bewildered chorus: 'Yes sir, we have the aid of all the sea serpents.'

It was magic—magic which produced good results under water rather than on dry land. But on the Western Front in the spring of 1918, the Germans unexpectedly withdrew to the long-prepared Hindenburg

Line without a fight. There was nothing magic in that, but what was about to happen in deserted Bapaume would call for the aid of the supernatural once more. That retreat was probably the cause of it all. 'Old Fritz', as the British called the Germans, moved back quite abruptly, and, like receding water, left behind a lot of human sludge. It was a strange feeling for the Englishmen and Scotsmen to walk through those devastated cities. They read the German names of the towns Gommecourt and Miraumont: Cursed Cabin, Oven and Dead Swine. The enemy was holding out near Achiet-le-Petit and Bucquoy. The trenches ran between the towns Pys and Petit-Miraumont, and everything else was left to the Allies. The soldiers saw all manner of things in those dead towns: discarded mattresses, emptied bottles of French red wine, and even doggerels daubed with oil paint by slovenly soldiers: 'Schnell und gut ist unser Schuss, deutscher Artilleristen Gruss' (You'll soon be six feet under from the German gunners' thunder!). But nothing could compare with what the Scotsmen came across in a house in Bapaume.

The town had been almost totally destroyed by French and British shells and the road the soldiers were walking along had craters two metres deep. A dirty rain was falling and got under the men's collars and into their boots. The Scotsmen who had once been blessed by Father Donovan did not meet a living soul, not even a cat, and when they thought the town was completely deserted they noticed a woman with three small children through a window. The woman was staring away into the distance, with the children snuggled up to her, making it hard to tell whether they were dead or alive. The young Scotsmen approached the woman with caution. They looked at her, touched her and sniffed at her as if they were hungry dogs and she their prey. She smelt of sandalwood, and her children of mother's milk. Finally they noticed that she was breathing faintly. Both she and the children took one breath every few minutes; they seemed more dead than alive, but breathing was breathing, and that meant life.

That woman with a face like a mask was neither happy nor sad. She gazed straight ahead with eyes unblinking, and everyone who stood in front of her open window felt she was looking at him and wanted to say something to him. This made quite an impression on the Highland Boys of the Scottish 92nd Division. They had seen death in a hundred ways and renounced all their pre-war errors, but this was something new for them. Some soon confessed their sins to the dead-living woman and her children, others cried before her, others again spoke to her children with different names to see if one of them at least would make an optic nerve flicker. Then, madly in love with her, they tried to feed her because they were frightened she would become malnourished and die of hunger, but they were unable to make her mouth accept a single morsel of food or sip of drink. Her lips were firmly shut, she held her children tight, and they seemed to need no sustenance. The Scotsmen stayed at her side for a whole week and saw that she wasn't wasting away. She remained alive—if that was the right word—even without food.

That encouraged them. They set off for the devastated nearby towns, which until recently had struck fear into them, and began to ask around among subjects of the British Empire for faith healers who could perhaps help the mother with her children, whom they had become so fond of. They searched for shamans among the soldiers from the Orient. These men possessed all manner of proficiencies and abilities; alive, in distant India, they resembled the dead, yet they resurrected many dead before the eyes of the living. Several of the Scotsmen therefore called on their comrades from the 2nd Indian Cavalry Division, whose gaze was ever downcast. They saw the silent men with their heads in dusty, blood-stained turbans. Among them, they found several soldiers from the area of Bombay beyond the seven seas, from the red Indian earth alive with poisonous snakes, who were medicine men and faith healers at home.

One was most warmly recommended to them, and they took him to see the family in Bapaume. Other Indians, weighing only forty-five kilo consisting of loose skin and bent bone, with British uniforms hanging from their haggard frames, visited the frozen family. They sniffed at them too and said they smelled of sandalwood. That was a good sign. They sang special songs around them and then smelled them again. They still smelled of sandalwood, they said—that was a bad sign. In the end, they gave up.

Soon afterwards the troops were given the signal to move out. They had to go. A hundred soldiers, one after another, took leave of the mother with her three children, but she just stared at them and didn't shed a single tear when they kissed her, put flowers in her hand, implored her or cried with their heads on her lap. The mask-woman didn't object when the Indians placed a garland of flowers over her shoulders and painted a red dot on her face and those of her children.

Now the soldiers really had to go. They left the mother and her children still alive. Or not. She was waiting for liberation or ultimate death. The British and their obedient Indians, wandering shamans in a war which was not their own, had to attack 'Old Fritz' again. Magic wouldn't work in the West. In Central Europe it was the same. But could magic be effective in Russia, a country still awash with wicked emotions, surrounded by savage nations who dreamed solely of destroying it?

After those many audiences, Tsar Nicholas left Tsarskoye Selo and departed for the Stavka. Was it a strange coincidence that he set off on that last journey so shortly before being deposed? Not at all. The tsar left for the front on 22 February, almost fleeing from the various emissaries and the madness of his wife, who continued to invoke Rasputin even though he was dead. On the Romanian Front he inspected a starving but seemingly still loyal army. Times were hard but he was satisfied. He left for home again and got into his special train as tsar for the last time.

In the night between 27 and 28 February, two armoured trains set off from Mogilev heading for Tsarskoye Selo and Petrograd. The one with the tsar's entourage went first, and the tsar's train followed five kilometres behind. That last evening, too, the last Russian tsar went to sleep in his coach surrounded by his adjutants and ministers of the court. The disturbing message from General Dubensky about unrest in the capital reached the tsar's train in the course of the night. But it continued on its way, passing the stations of Likhoslav and Bologoyev, and travelling ever deeper into the Russian night and the frozen land controlled by the revolutionaries. No one dared to wake the tsar; His Majesty was not yet to be told. The very next day he would become a prisoner.

But in that decisive night he was still the tsar. He woke up and remembered his imaginings of not so long ago: of standing on a platform, and a strange train gliding past and taking with it the lights of its compartments. He didn't manage to speak because everything that was his flashed past in that train. Now the tsar felt as if everything that had once been his had been left behind: he looked through the window, hidden in the dark like a thief, and wiped the fogged-up pane with his sleeve: here was the sleepy station of Malaya Vishera, then the station of Staraya Rus, and finally the provincial capital, Pskov. As he stared sleepily through the glass into that crystal night, which gleamed in heaven and earth as if illuminated, there came a knock at the door and the news: 'Your Majesty, a message has come from the advance train. No trains can go any further than Tosnoye, they say. Lyuban is already under the control of revolutionary forces. General Dubensky suggests stopping in the old city of Pskov and joining up with the forces of General Ruzsky, with which you could then head to the capital.'

Then everything began to unfold very quickly. Two nights and one day passed in the tsar's train like a dream, like a leaden nightmare, in which one piece of bad news outstripped another. On the evening of the next day, the tsar abdicated in favour of his brother, Mikhail Alexandrovich, and became a prisoner. He recorded in his diary: 'I leave Pskov tonight despondent because of what I have experienced. All around are betrayal, cowardice and lies.'

And then he left. First of all by train, moving from one station to another, and it seemed as if he was not moving forwards but perpetually going in circles, to finally be lost and not know which part of Russia he was in. The fate of a deposed ruler, perhaps. In the end, he arrived in Tsarskoye Selo, where he encountered a striking example of human wretchedness: when he got out at the station, his courtiers and officers fled before him without a second's hesitation. Having heard that the tsar had abdicated, they were afraid he might recognize them and expect them to stay on in his company. Instead of being received with warm words and trusted handshakes, the prisoner was met by three strangers: one stocky, and the other two both tall. They took the tsar to an armoured car. The fat man drove, while one tall fellow sat on either side of him on the back seat. Only a little light came in through a slit from the driver's window. Nicholas caught a glimpse of empty streets, pebbles flung up by the wheels and occasional groups of people who cut across the path of the car, scampering like foxes, weasels or badgers.

He entered the palace and found the tsaritsa dressed in a black habit with a white collar. He said to her: 'Alix, you are no longer empress.' And she said to him: 'Our time is yet to come. Sit down, and let us call our friend from the heavens. Our good chief of police, Protopopov, who was able to *make the table move*, is no more; but we are still here.' Before the tsar could say a word, the tsaritsa silenced him. 'I know you wanted to send me away to the French Riviera, my Nicholas,' she said, 'and you even negotiated with that fat French ambassador Paléologue, but I forgive you, my dear. I forgive you.'

At that instant, as if by command, the lady-in-waiting, Anna Vyrubova, and the great court lady Naryshkina entered the room together with some maids they had taken by surprise. Vyrubova had pronounced dark circles under her eyes, wrinkled like brocade curtains; Madam Naryshkina with the double chin beneath her fat face was virtually blind because of the cataracts on both her eyes; while the maids seemed scared to death. Alexandra stood in the middle and no one dared to refuse. Without a word, she extended her hand to Nicholas, too. He simply replied and took her icy hand. He wanted to decline, but now he no longer saw any reason to avoid that 'occult ministry', as all of the tsaritsa's circle called it. The invokers joined hands. Nicholas's were taken by the tsaritsa on one side and Naryshkina on the other. All the women closed their eyes. The curtain over the window moved and a ray of light entered the room. Nicholas could hear nothing from the world of ghosts, but the women moaned and called out 'yes, yes' and 'we are here, we are here'. The other-worldly silence was now filled by the tsaritsa, and she spoke in a husky, almost hoarse voice: 'You will come back. Yes, you will come back. The Russian throne forever belongs to the Romanovs. The Vladimirovichs will accept the throne, those sordid weasels, but they will fast give it back to the Nikolaevichs.

'What do you still have to say, friend?' the tsaritsa yelled with all her might as if calling into the wind. 'What do you still have to tell us? Bring us light, bring us more light, friend...' and there was light, caused not by the occult but the movement of a man, whom the circle could hardly recognize at first because their eyes were now used to the dark. 'You wanted more light,' spoke a haughty voice not at all like the sound of a phantasm, and its owner walked the length of the room and closed the doors behind him. The heavy curtain was drawn aside to reveal Alexander Kerensky, the new Russian Minister of Justice. He curtly signalled for the maids and court ladies to leave. The tsar and tsaritsa remained with him. As soon as they were alone, the newcomer kissed the tsaritsa's hand and offered her to be seated. 'You don't need to offer me a chair in my own palace,' she hissed in that husky, occult voice. The tsar looked at Kerensky, pushed the tsaritsa into an armchair and made an effort to smooth out the situation. 'You are a fine young man,' he said, although he wasn't sure if *young man* would be an affront to Kerensky, whose age he was unable to judge. 'I'm sorry I didn't rely on your services earlier. You're not going to harm us, I trust?' Kerensky smiled. The grin clung to his cheekbones just a little too long. All at once, he became serious and the smile dissolved from his face like a spectre. He announced loudly: 'The former tsar and tsaritsa are to be separated and only to see each other at mealtimes.'

Thus began the tsar's captivity—inescapable, undisputed and inevitable—because the revolution continued to seethe beneath the windows of his palace. And just a stone's throw from there, Russia bloomed in a hundred colours. All those who had been sidelined or repressed, with no choice but to stew and scheme, now flocked to the streets to declare at the top of their voices that they were alive, had a voice, and could glimpse the future of Russia. And all those of the old order, loyal to the tsar, did not flee to the cellars or drown themselves in the Neva, but drew and swung their ornamented Caucasian sabres.

Tauride Palace, the hub of the new political developments in the capital, was teeming like an anthill with everyone from shabbily dressed folk to those with starched collars. Bosses and heads of staff still acted as such, and counsellors did not consider being anything other than counsellors—none of them could imagine forfeiting their civil-service grade of Peter the Great's provenance, although a tectonic shift had taken grip of all the known world and a sea change was casting it into desperate, swirling disorder.

Speeches were held everywhere: in factories, circuses and streets. The theatres were still open and the public gathered there every evening as if they had no work to do the following day. The tsarist eagles were removed from the royal boxes, but young cadets of the tsar's Corps of Pages, lost in the new times, kept rising and saluting the tsar's empty box before each performance as if he was still there. Yet the days were utterly different to the cultivated theatrical nights. The streets were patrolled by stern policemen who loved to read; they killed enemies of tsarism who loved to read. The soldiers of the 12th Army, bogged down at the muddy front near Riga, desperately sought for books so they would have something to read.

Kill and then read—after a massacre you simply had to read something. *Nula dies sine linea...* In these circumstances, everyone's attention waned. Barriers disappeared, as did old merits, old sins and old debts. After two years of overseeing the Sukhomlinovs' house arrest, the sentries were suddenly gone from outside the lovely house near the Church of the Saviour. Had they run away? Probably they thought they ought to join the revolution or perish at its hands like happy wretches in a great moment of history. In any case, as of 1 March the ex-minister of war's front door was no longer guarded. There was theatre outside and a kind of drama inside as well. Sukhomlinov and his wife hadn't heard that the revolution had begun in Petrograd; or rather, to tell the truth, they didn't understand its momentousness because their world within the walls of house arrest had strangely warped the outside world and adapted it to the inner realm of silk socks and unwashed pants.

When the guards fled from the front of their once lovely house and chaos arrived at their doorstep—freedom was there for the taking. The door opened all by itself. After two years of house arrest and with the sentries gone, Yekaterina Sukhomlinova went to the front door. The once stunningly beautiful solicitor's assistant now had scruffy hair, bulging eyes and breasts bigger than ever before, with two large nipples standing forth. The days of Parisian emollients for her breasts and a uniform for her as general's wife had long passed. Sukhomlinova walked out of the house just when a group of people were running past like bolting dogs. Two men crashed into her from behind and knocked her to the pavement. She got to her feet and looked at the canal, which shone in the morning sun as if it was flowing or awash with molten metal rather than water. In the distance she caught a glimpse of the Church of the Saviour, wrapped in mist like in the fur of an arctic fox. Then she watched as passers-by frantically attacked one of the shops which still had flour—and closed the door again.

Her world was different. The greatest lady spy could be a spy queen even in a matchbox, but not with bad dreams like that. As she locked the door behind her, she saw her dishevelled, red-headed, red-moustached Zeus of a husband drowsily descending the stairs into the entrance hall. 'What's all that racket, Katenka?' he asked. 'Nothing,' she said, 'just some panicky people running to and fro. Heaven knows what they want in this wide world. But nothing can harm us here. Let's just stay at home, darling. My head hurts terribly and I've been having bad dreams. Could you perhaps give me a foot rub?'

However, not everyone thought that one's home was still one's castle, behind the bulwark of the threshold. Dr Chestukhin felt unsafe in his house on Runovsky Embankment. He too had considered staying there in the familiarity of home, but the house faced onto the canal and the street, and when a burst of gunfire broke all the windows, he decided to move. But where to? Like every old Russian, he thought of going to a hotel, as if he was on Capri or visiting Paris. When your wife throws you out of the flat, you go to a hotel with your mistress. In 1917, the revolution was that wife, but there was no mistress waiting for him at the hotel. War hero Dr Chestukhin took little Marusya by the hand and pulled along terrified aunt Margarita and the maid Nastia, who had just managed to pack a few things for each of them in a wicker suitcase. They ran, evading the bullets and trying to mind their own business in the middle of a revolution, and finally made it to the Hotel Astoria on St Isaac's Square, opposite St Isaac's Cathedral.

The Hotel Astoria, with all its staff, was one of the institutions which underwent a peculiar three-day metamorphosis during the February Revolution, and the doctor and his family would get to know it first hand. The whole building became like a five-storey ship. None of the hotel workers went home any more; rather, the hotel became the home of all its transformed and enlightened employees. How they reached an agreement, organized, and were able to function as one big, self-managed trap for guests in those few days, is hard to say. The revolution was to blame, for sure—such upheavals extract the best from every person and mix it with the worst; just as blood, in septicaemia, becomes mixed with putrescence.

Such was the Hotel Astoria which Dr Chestukhin entered. Fleeing from the street, he blundered into the hotel and stumbled. He stopped by the revolving doors, regained his posture and smoothed down his hair with what remained of his former dignity; he soothed crying Marusya and stepped up to the reception desk just as if he was on Capri, or in Venice. He rang the bell and then filled in the registration form in front of the amiable hotel clerk. He said he would be staying for several days and waved aside the somewhat undiscerning question: 'Do you have sufficient money, sir?' Strangely enough, this convinced the receptionist that the doctor had plenty of money.

Which was actually true, but Dr Chestukhin would need all the money he had with him in the days ahead because the Astoria functioned as one big collective for catching and wringing out fallen souls. Every little service in the hotel had to be paid for, and the guests were obliged to play the part of big-spender tourists whether they liked it or not.

You want to go down for breakfast? No, that's not possible because the banquet hall where breakfast used to be served is on the ground floor facing onto the street, and therefore it's not safe. You have to order breakfast in your room, and that costs six roubles. It's the same with the midday meal and supper. If you want to clean your shoes before going to bed, you can't do it yourself because there are only three bellboys in the hotel who clean shoes—they alone have shoe brushes. Whether you like it or not, you have to call one of them up to your room to clean your footwear and pay three roubles per pair. Four people in the doctor's room means twelve roubles. And if you don't want to clean your shoes, a bellboy will still amiably ring at the door and shout: 'Shoe-cleaning time, sir; open up, it's time to have your shoes cleaned.' And when you open the door they will ask you, of course, how many of you there are in the room. Everyone's shoes have to be cleaned at the Astoria, even Marusya's bootlets. That is the custom of the house, and its standards of hygiene are strictly observed.

It was the same with all other things: the weak, red-hibiscus tea, which cost one rouble per person and had to be drunk at least once a day, as if it was medicine; new bedlinen, which had to be changed every day and cost two roubles; even every question asked of the receptionist cost twenty kopeks, whether he knew the answer or not. Whoever was able to stand it stayed on. Hotel bills were paid at noon and at eight in the evening. 'There you are, sir. It was a pleasure, madam. Goodbye, and thank you for staying at the Astoria,' was the last Dr Chestukhin heard when he had used up all his money after three days at that bloodsucking hotel and decided to return to his house on Runovsky Embankment.

Three days had passed and the revolution had flared up like a fire with no one to fight it, so returning home turned into a whole day of stumbling about, running and ducking into side streets, which sometimes headed towards Runovsky Embankment but just as often led our fugitives away from it. Immediately after exiting the hotel, Dr Chestukhin, as a devout Christian, had wanted to go into St Isaac's Cathedral for a moment with the others, but an old sexton at the entrance said: 'You shouldn't all go in—it's not a sight for children's eyes.' Then the old man whispered to him, as if the doctor was his only friend, that Cossacks had come out of it with bloody hands and sabres not ten minutes earlier. They had caught twenty policemen loyal to the revolution and the Republic sleeping in the cathedral beneath the great dome, dead tired after three full days on patrol. The Cossacks crept in, and the policemen were so exhausted that they didn't notice; so they went among them and twisted each one's neck, or cut his throat with their sabres. Many of the policemen didn't even realize they were killed. They breathed their last and just gave a little squeal like a pig slaughtered for Christmas. None of the sleeping men could get up and try to defend themselves.

'You shouldn't go in yourself, sir,' the good man repeated, but Chestukhin replied: 'I am a doctor. There may be survivors.' He left Marusya with Margarita and entered St Isaac's Cathedral. The sight he saw resembled an oil painting: waxen bodies and coagulated blood which looked like paint thickly applied to the corpses. At first he walked among the bodies, but then he ran and turned them over as if in a delirium. A bluish light made its way in through the cathedral's high windows and mixed with the dark red of the blood and the white collars of the policemen. Their bodies lay there heavy and stiff, but still warm as if their life and dreams had not yet left them. He examined one of them—he was dead, and a second, and a third, and a tenth, and each and every one of them in turn. It was all like in a grisly painting: signet rings shone on stiff fingers, gold teeth gleamed in gaping mouths. The Cossacks had done their bloody work quickly and efficiently, making sure no one was alive when they left. The smell of coagulating blood rose to the dome of the cathedral and was so heavy that not even a surgeon could stand it. He ran, staggered, and came out onto St Isaac's Square again. 'There's nothing I can do here. Let's go,' he said taciturnly. He left a few coins with the sexton while the smell of the dead was still fresh in his nose.

But he knew he mustn't give up and be weak. He grabbed Marusya and turned sharply from the square into Little Konyushennaya Street, where he saw a strange sight. A devoted officer was being buried in the small lawn by the entrance of a house. The mourners were few in number, but they blocked the street. 'Just a minute please, just a minute,' they repeated to Dr Chestukhin and his company, as if the funeral would only be holding up the traffic for a little while. Not just one, but two Orthodox priests were reading prayers for that two-day hero of the Petrograd streets. The doctor stopped and took off his hat. He listened to the priests, who seemed to box his ears with their 'Glory to you, O Lord', 'Pure and immaculate' and 'Forgive him his transgressions', and he felt like bursting into tears and laughing hysterically at the same time. But he didn't dare to do one or the other, because the surviving comrades of the unknown hero now already considered him one of their own and even called out to him: 'He was a great man and a brave soldier.' 'Yes, he was a soldier,' the doctor replied. He and his company now managed to squeeze through the knot of people and hurry on. They spent the whole afternoon avoiding volleys of gunfire and individual bullets. He, aunt Margarita and the maid now no longer lugged the wicker suitcase; they had abandoned it when its handle broke in Liteyny Avenue.

By early evening, all of them were so tired that they would have lain down in the street and surrendered to the tide of chaos, but they saw that just a little more exertion was needed to make it back to the house. After that long day of wandering, they finally reached Runovsky Embankment and home. The doors of the house were broken open, and the apartment was ransacked and everything turned upside down. They entered. They wanted to cry but didn't have the strength. Inevitably, they regretted having gone off into the revolutionary city at all. Margarita and Nastia immediately began clearing away all that was broken, and the doctor embraced his child again and for the first time sank into a deep sleep. He was home again, and that was the most important thing.

The grand duke now also had to finally head home. He had never felt comfortable as Russian viceroy in the Caucasus. In the first months of the New Year 1917, however, he was still a loyal soldier of the Empire. So it was that he was preparing an offensive in the Caucasus and dreaming of the construction of a railway line from Russia to Georgia when he received word of his brother's abdication and his reappointment as commander-in-chief of the Russian forces in the Great War.

Whether or not he made any comment was known only to his closest associates. Whether or not he felt sorry for his brother was known to him alone. His staff officers saw him preparing calmly and without a single twitch on his wrinkled, iron face. He was to leave for Mogilev and take command. It was a long journey even in peacetime—from Asia to Europe. He packed only a few essentials. He was a soldier, after all. He didn't yet know that he would be commanding the ill-equipped Russian forces for less than ten days, so he wouldn't need much gear on that trip anyway.

THEIR TIME HAS PASSED

'Father, my Father,' the trader in oriental and European spices Mehmed Yıldız muttered to himself. 'Father, my unjust Father, my prophetic Father, my lonely Father, my faithless Father, my Father who wrenched himself out of our culture—sixty years have passed since I too became a trader in Istanbul's cobblestone streets. 1917 has come, and I must leave on a journey. Remember how the saying goes: a trader needs to spend six decades in Istanbul if he wants to stay and consolidate his business.'

'Six centuries—why shouldn't six centuries be the measure for us Yıldızes?' Mehmed felt he heard his father Şefket say. 'According to the old adage, a good, devout Turk and his descendants need to stay in Istanbul for six centuries if they want their generations to merge with the wood, waters and lifeblood of this city on the water.'

'Father, my Father, you are to blame,' the spice trader replied. 'You broke the matrix that was meant for us. Do you remember the fur? You offered your wares like a prophet, not like a trader; like an infidel, not like a Turk. You were more like the Syrians, the people from the stone; the Iraqis, the people from between the two rivers; the Jews, the people from the desert. And you were left all alone, belonging to no one. Alien. The Jews didn't want you among them, the Syrians turned their heads away from you in the street, and the Mesopotamians pretended they didn't know you. The Turks threw you out of their guild.'

'But you have set everything right, my son,' he felt he heard old Şefket Yıldız speak again. 'You sold the fur business, left the Jewish quarter and descended the icy Camondo Stairs for the last time. Away from the infidels, you became a Turk down to the last grey hair on your head. You took on five apprentices like a proper Turk. And you loved them as your own sons like a proper Turk. You sent them to the Great War like every Turk should. And you prayed and cherished hope like a proper Turk. And you viewed every depth two-dimensionally like a proper Turk. And you read the untruthful *Tanin* every morning with your tea, like a good Turk. And you still think the righteous Padishah dwells by the Golden Horn and comes out every morning to pat his tame nightingales startled by the harsh, early snow! In all these years, have you not sold your six decades of trading ten times over and made them into six centuries? Was that not the sense of my end, when you left me to waste away and die like a sick dog?'

'No, my Father,' Yıldız the younger would reply, 'your fate and your foreign, Western habits wormed their way under my skin, into my bloodstream and to my very grain. I have failed. I sold and vended, diddled and cheated at the scales—but it was no good. We Yıldızes will never make the mark of six centuries in Istanbul, only six decades. Yesterday I turned seventy-six and reached the tally of sixty years of trading. Now I am waiting, waiting for the final news, and I am ever more cheerful. That is a sure sign that the worst is to come.'

Thus spoke the trader with words reminiscent of his father, and indeed, the worst now came to pass. Some people's end, mainly that of infidels, comes with bad news; but for the righteous, who wager all they have, their time is up when the portents are good. The end of our trader in European and oriental spices came with favourable rumours from the battlefield. The Turkish fronts were advancing in the only two regions where the Great War still interested him. He was indifferent now to the Caucasian theatre of war where his first apprentice—his father's namesake Şefket—had been cut down by Cossacks in the Battle of Ostip; he no longer wanted to know about the movements of the army at Gallipoli because his second apprentice, Şefket's brother Orhan, had fallen there; and he had no more interest in Mesopotamia because there, at the walls of the red city of Kerbala, he had lost his third young apprentice, the bookkeeper who would never be.

Reading his newspaper *Tanin*, he now skipped the news from these fronts and cared only about two particular lines of battle between the righteous and the infidels. In the first months of 1917 it was exclusively good news, that came from those far-flung lands! The German commander Count Kaunitz had killed himself in Persia at the end of 1916, and the Russians were melting away from Palestine after news of the unrest back home. Yıldız was glad when he read these reports, but the smile on his lips was little more than an outward grin, the polite patriotism desired by the Young Turk dictators whom Yıldız called righteous. That's why he was of no interest to the spies who, like shadows, always drank one tea too many at the next table in the smoky tearoom. The old man from the Golden Horn fraternized with others like himself, but he only had a handful of friends, who mostly dozed as he told them edifying stories from the history of the great Padishah. Those were the 'new friends' he had enlisted at the end of 1916. And so 1917 arrived, and Yıldız was still wearing his put-on smile. He glanced to the side, looked emptily at his new acquaintances and grinned.

He didn't want to think of the end, he didn't dare to, because the end would definitely be thinking of him.

Thus it was. In the wake of the First Battle of Gaza on 26 March 1917, he heard rumour that his fourth apprentice had been killed. Was the old trader able to cry? Did he need to grieve? No, the smile did not leave his face because his apprentice Nagin, his dear beanpole with the infectious smile which dispersed all their worries, had died defending Jerusalem, the navel of the earth. Why should he not laugh? Why should the death his fourth apprentice not inspire him? After all, Nagin had died barring the approach to the city with its rich Christian, Jewish and Muslim fabric. He had refused to allow passage to the British infidels, and all the colours and smells of the city came to the defenders like oriental dancers. Only the defence of Istanbul could compare with the defence of Jerusalem, because only beneath a city like Istanbul did there flow such mighty, infidel nether rivers; only at that curve of the earth's crust were they were so close to the surface that they could inundate the city with a different faith, a different colour and different smells at any moment. Was it not a beautiful thing to give one's life so that the Turkish colour would prevail in Jerusalem? Perhaps only the manner of Nagin's death embittered him: for he was crushed by a metal monster which the British infidels called a 'tank'. It reduced him to a bloody pulp, and there was no telling which part was his head and which part were his white heels. No, no, Yıldız refused to believe it—he was simply killed, one way or another, at the walls of the city above wild waters. Nagin fell at the approaches to the city, which thanks to his sacrifice would remain Turkish, if only for a little longer.

Such were the thoughts of Mehmed Yıldız, who deceived himself that a smile and a game of dominoes with his sleepy new two-dimensional friends, or babbling with Hayyim the Merry, could delay the inevitable end. But 1917 exacted its merciless due. It was his sixtieth year of trading, as we recall, and it turned out very, very differently from how things had been in the first century, at the start of the Yıldızes' time in Istanbul. Just one day later, they told Mehmed Yıldız that his fifth and last apprentice was dead. He had been killed by the last loyal Kuban Cossacks on the front where the Russians, paralysed by the revolution, were in full retreat and would soon exit the Great War for good. There fell his youngest apprentice, still a child, born in 1897. He was the last victim to be cut down by those same Russian Cossacks—grim, ferocious horsemen who went on killing for a day more because they had been sent to distant Arabia and could not bring their sabres to the aid of the tsar in the capital.

That was the end. The smile vanished from the trader's face. He repeated aloud the names of his apprentices: red-headed Şefket Fişkeçi was killed near Ostip in the Caucasus, cut in half by a Cossack's sabre out in some God-forsaken steppe; Orhan Fişkeçi, his black-haired brother, died at Gallipoli, killed by an accurate shot from the Australian lines, just when he was dreaming the most beautiful of dreams; Omer Kutluer died of scurvy on the iron-red earth beneath the fortifications of Kerbala; Nagin Türkoğlu fell on the outskirts of Jerusalem; and his youngest assistant, the illiterate Omer Aktan, was cut down by the last loyal Kuban Cossacks.

Rain began falling again in Istanbul; that intricate, embellished, fortified city of the righteous above the wild, infidel nether rivers—a city which only had to sleep too long and deep one night to wake up as Christian and Byzantine in the morning. Drop by drop, life by life... the rain seemed to be saying again that there was nothing more to be traded here. Should he give up? Should he sell off his shop and everything in it for a pittance? Was it worth haggling and short-weighting? Or should he try and run away?

No, all the lights in his aged body had gone out. Now we see Mehmed Yıldız, the trader in oriental spices, preparing for a journey. In his thoughts, he wraps each of his apprentices in pale-green cloth and lowers him into the pit of his memory. He packs five suitcases. Soon he repacks the most essential things in three suitcases. He stops and thinks, and reduces his luggage to one suitcase. He throws it aside, too, and takes only one small, motley, camel-hide bag and puts almost nothing in it. He leaves the key in the lock, without turning it: a small trove of spices for bums or burglars to find. He looks one last time at the bridge over the Bosporus and up to the Galata Tower. Somewhere there are the Camondo Stairs which he descended when he broke off all ties with the Jewish traders. Now he goes down along the Golden Horn. He departs into the unknown. His time is over. Six decades of trading will end in six deaths. Was there ever a trader less successful than him? He stops and looks back.

The Great War ended for Mehmed Yıldız when he vanished from life and entered the realm of tales. Some say Yıldız Effendi's heart broke at the coach station by the Bosporus: he collapsed like a sack, they say, like a sad body whose cheerful soul has finally flown. Others tell of him setting off into the unknown, far away, to live out his seventy-sixth year in that non-life, or afterlife, following sixty impressive years of trading in Istanbul. Others again claim he wandered as a carefree hermit far away from the Great War, happy among the infidels, and still clutching the camel-hide bag he had taken with him.

But all of them agree on one thing: no one ever again heard of Mehmed Yıldız, the trader in oriental and European spices.

The Great War thus ended for one successful Istanbul trader even before it was over; and even before it began, it was a more or less an ongoing affair in New York. The first morning ring of the reception bell at the Hotel Astor in New York marked the beginning of another great day for the many Germans gathered there. The Astor was the meeting place of many 'little fish' as well as big shots with German surnames, of all those who spared no effort to help the *Vaterland* and persuade America not to enter the Great War. It was 5 April 1917, and that morning, like every day, ten million German Americans asked what they could do for the Fatherland, not what the Fatherland could do for them. The cartographer Dr Willi Bertling arrived at the hotel in the early hours of the morning. He and Adolf Pavenstedt, the founder of the New York *Staats-Zeitung* newspaper, reviewed the maps of Belgium they intended to publish in the paper. According to those carefully falsified maps, Belgium had not been captured but 'divided equitably' between the great powers, making King Albert irrelevant. The two men glanced over the material again and agreed that it would dissuade America from entering the war.

Just one and a quarter hours later, Dr Hugo Munsterberg entered the elegant smoker's lounge of the Hotel Astor and took a seat beneath a large stuffed barracuda. He stroked his black-dyed moustache and looked around like a man satisfied with himself. Munsterberg was a lobotomist born in Massachusetts, a brilliant student of the University of California but also a person steeped in the chauvinism of the early twentieth century. His acquaintance with Dr Lombrozo's theories that certain skull shapes made people criminals or revolutionaries changed Dr Munsterberg's professional life. Beginning in 1907, he searched for 'typical skull forms' and put his knowledge at the service of Germany even before 1914. Now he had arrived at the ultimate discovery that the head shapes of 'the typical American' corresponded completely to the cranium parameters of 'the typical German' and wanted to share his findings with the German Ambassador in Washington, Count von Bernstorff. The two men met at around ten in the morning. They shook hands and then looked for a long time at drawings of dead men's heads. Ultimately they agreed that it was a good thing and would convince the Americans not to enter the war.

Around noon, the reception bell at the Hotel Astor rang once again. Walter Dresler arrived in New York. He was an American, head of a Berlin news agency, and travelled freely despite being under surveillance. He had graduated from the Juilliard School with flying colours, and before the Great War he had been headmaster of a selective school for German boys in Virginia. Now he felt his place was in Europe, at the side of the kaiser. His assignment at the Astor was to meet an unfortunate man, Robert Fay. This rebel was not German and did not have a German name, but his desire to destroy the British put him on a par with the most zealous of Teutonic chauvinists. Fay would show Dresler a blueprint of 'the most destructive bomb the human mind has devized'. When Dresler rang the reception bell and asked in German for a single room for one night, Fay was already shifting from one leg to the other in the ballroom, where a small brass band was playing German wartime hits. Their meeting began as soon as the important visitor from Berlin had freshened up a little in his room.

Dresler recognized Fay immediately from the photograph. A thin face with a toothbrush moustache, a pronounced nose shadowing half his jaw, and eyes which cast glances full of hate and envy at everything around him. Fay removed his grey gloves and imitating a gentleman, put aside his stick.. He said he had finished a sketch of the bomb at his hidden laboratory in the Bronx; it was to be smuggled on board a merchant ship and declared as something else. The composition of the bomb was: 25 pounds of TNT, 25 sticks of dynamite, 150 pounds of saltpetre, 200 bomb shells and 400 pieces of scrap metal. A certain Paul König was to help them put this sizeable charge on board one of the ships, and he too came to the hotel that day bearing some important information from the New York docks. The three men continued to talk and the band played the 'Gott, Kaiser, *Vaterland*' march ever louder. In the end, they agreed that the sinking of ships with Fay's bombs would exasperate the Americans but wouldn't make them decide to enter the war. 'They didn't go to war after the Lusitania, so why should they now?' Dresler said and laughed like a jokester. The other two joined in the laughter and each of them ordered a cigar from the waiter. Then each of the men, satisfied with himself, smoked in silence.

One o'clock in the afternoon was time for the Europeans' midday meal. At the Astor, no one respected the American custom of having the main meal later in the day, so there was much clattering of cutlery on plates as the guests ate the Bavarian soup followed by stuffed Alpine-roast-hare washed down with Rhine Riesling. Shortly after the meal, at half past two, another unusual man arrived at the hotel: Richard Stegler, an expert on invisible ink. Having experimented with lemon juice and heard the rumour that the British wrote letters with semen, he combined all of this in a new formula using secret additives known to him alone. Now he wished to hand the formula to the first attaché of the German embassy, who arrived at the meeting with a staff member from the coding section. All three of them watched the demonstration of Stegler's invisible ink and were satisfied with the results. Afterwards, as colleagues who had no secrets from each other, they spoke about the network of wireless telegraph stations on both American continents and also about the famous English-German dictionary (a rare edition from 1826) which served as the code book for the wireless telegraph messages. Although Stegler was an America born in Oregon, he and the two Germans laughed sweetly at American stupidity in being unable to break the codes. All three of them were convinced that the golden age of espionage would last until ultimate German victory, with America remaining neutral throughout the war.

It was late in the afternoon by the time their meeting ended. At six o'clock, the translator Karl A. Führ had an assignment at the Hotel Astor. He didn't meet anyone. He went to room 212, which was kept permanently for use by the German embassy, to do a translation. He finished the task at around seven and stayed on in the room a little longer. Afterwards he went downstairs, and in the foyer he passed Hans von Wedel and his wife going in the opposite direction. It was almost eight o'clock when these two counterfeiters met with a man whose name they didn't know. The stranger spoke German with an American accent; they handed him twenty-two forged passports, and he immediately disappeared, taking the shortest route across the hotel foyer. The couple then ordered absinthe. For a little while longer they looked like ordinary Americans who had come to refresh themselves after a successful working day: he with a Borsalino hat, which he fanned himself with; she like a plump American lady in a floral dress emphasizing her hips. After nine in the evening, the woman asked her husband: 'Hansi, do you think there'll be war?' 'No,' her husband replied without hesitation and continued to sip his absinthe like a man whose conscience was completely clear.

The last business meeting of that day took place shortly before midnight. Representatives of the American Correspondent Film Company, an American-German production firm, reported on the numerous newsreel propaganda films from the *Vaterland* which they screened in their cinemas in Massachusetts. The sizeable audience filled them with pride, and everyone in that cheerful midnight crowd was confident that America would never go to war. The reception bell at the Hotel Astor rang for the last time at one o'clock in the morning, ending another successful day for the Germans in America. The bell would sound again in the morning and a colourful collection of people with a restless past and a clear conscience would begin to stroll the halls of the hotel again, or they wouldn't. At dawn on 6 April 1917, the President of the United States of America announced that the country had declared war on Germany. That was the end.

All the Germans in America knew in their hearts that the *Vaterland* would be unable to withstand a war against America. The age of German espionage and propaganda came to an abrupt end. Up until that fateful date, all the Germans had made a great effort to prevent that from happening, and no one felt it was their fault that America had entered the Great War; therefore, on 6 April 1917, the film-makers, counterfeiters, bombers, coders, cartographers, lobotomists, translators, newspaper editors and saboteurs from the New York docks still had a clear conscience.

'I have a clear conscience preparing this play at old Birot's expense,' Guillaume Apollinaire said and added: 'Birot is an absolute fool. He made a packet selling his wartime postcards, so why shouldn't I accept his money?'

This was a wonderful period for Apollinaire again. And a terrible one at the same time. His latest girlfriend, Ruby, told him she was pregnant. But the child would not be born, Ruby was adamant. The unhappy father therefore turned to theatre. He wanted to put on his *Breasts of Tiresias* at the René Mobel Theatre in Montmartre. The idea of staging a play came from Pierre Albert-Birot, the small manufacturer of the wondrous wartime postcards which wrote themselves even after the death of the soldier. The two men had sat together at the end of 1916. The poet and lover had recommended Birot his play about Thérèse, who changes her sex and becomes Tiresias, and then obtains power over men like the Theban soothsayer Teiresias. A stupid plot—Apollinaire even thought so himself—but old Birot was enthusiastic. The stupider the better, Apollinaire mused, and rolled up his sleeves.

The theatre was leased and the actors paid in advance. The writer adapted the play. Old Birot was still enthusiastic. The women on stage had to be naked: Birot applauded. A sex scene at the end would attract a young audience: Birot lewdly approved. All the affectation and playing around with music and shooting would attract Paris's artistic rabble and extract the last centime from their pockets to pay for a ticket: the manufacturer in the role of producer gave a knowing nod. The worse the better. Avant-garde. Rehearsals began.

The director and writer invariably spoke about pacifism at the rehearsals, but inside he was thinking of defeatism. He knew it—he knew his time had passed. He no longer believed in war. Where were the times when the urge had taken him down to the recruitment office twice? Now his head hurt terribly and he was living his last year. The worse the better. His rehearsals boiled down to tirades of swearing. Whoever didn't want to undress was literally chucked out. Whoever agreed to undress had to sing from the proscenium immediately so that the pretty pianist, who Apollinaire had his eye on and imagined as his next sweetheart, had something to do.

When the play was finally being rehearsed, old Birot came onto the stage.

'What should I put on the poster?'

'Just the title: *the Breasts of Tiresias*,' replied the poet and aspiring director.

'That's too short. People will think it's some kind of cubist drama, and that's not patriotic.'

'Piss off!'

'Guillaume, Guillaume, you're as a son to me. Don't talk like that with your foster father. Come on, what should we write?'

'Let's write: a crude play... No, wait: a supernaturalist drama, or a surrealist drama.'

And so a movement was born. A drama with nudity, shooting, singing and a sex scene at the end turned out to be a flop in 1917. But the play caused quite an outcry. All the surviving artists were at the première. André Breton came together with the returnee Cocteau. Breton was dissatisfied with the play's lyricism, or paucity thereof, but how irritated Jean Cocteau was! At the end of the second act, he got up with his revolver in hand and headed towards the conductor. He cocked the gun and demanded that the he stop the performance. The music paused for a moment, but then the audience thought *the Breasts of Tiresias* must really have something going for it if a little guy in an ironed French army uniform with a gun in hand wanted to stop it, so they managed to push Cocteau aside and told the deathly-pale conductor to continue the performance. Breton took the tidy soldier outside, and Cocteau grinned.

'Why didn't you fire, you idiot?' Breton yelled at him.

'What, kill that weakling with the white baton? Never! The gun isn't loaded, see?'

'But killing him would have got the best reviews and everyone would have taken notice of you.'

'In jail perhaps. This way, I'll become more famous than *the Breasts of Tiresias*.'

'Jean, you're a fool,' Breton shouted.

'No, I'm a lie that speaks the truth!' Cocteau replied and set off by the shortest route to the Seine.

The others, of course, rushed to Old Combes's Closerie des Lilas and Old Libion's Rotonde after this successfully unsuccessful play. That was one of the few evenings which resembled the way things used to be. Most others were quite unlike those of the golden days of 1914 and 1915. In the idle nights when there were no smutty premières, the two old publicans sat at their respective bars feeling bored. Just the day before, Old Libion had stroked his thick grey moustache and pondered how long it had been since someone last got up on a table and made a speech; how long it had been since someone had pissed down their leg (oh, those were the days!) or taken out a revolver and shouted, 'I'll kill you all!', and everyone in the café had ducked under the tables; how many years had it been since he heard the hate-filled cry, 'Damn Boches!'? No, he thought, his time had passed. Old Combes reflected on things similarly. Just the other day he had watched a sticky fly, from the toilet, with little legs bound not to be particularly clean. It slowly climbed up the clean champagne glasses in the bar, but Old Combes didn't think of swatting it. So what if it soiled the glasses? Who was going to order any 1909 *Dom Pérignon* now, thinking it a good vintage? No, Old Combes thought too that his time had passed.

But that is not what that girl of a woman, Kiki de Montparnasse thought. She quit her job at the canning factory and would not go to the boot workshop any more because all the dead who had loved her in their cobwebby arms became a weight on her mind. She heard that America had entered the war, and she saw the whole of Paris celebrating and waving little French and American flags. The war was as good as over, she thought. But she didn't think her time had passed; on the contrary, it seemed just about to come. As if she was acting out *the Breasts of Tiresias* in real life, she realized she had gone around for long enough in a man's hat and overcoat. She had to bare herself, take off her clothes and set off through life naked. She wanted to earn her living with her body, but not in a million years would she prostitute herself. Yes, she may have been an illegitimate child, but she had a mother who taught her morals! She would go naked and be a model, but she would always remain true to herself: she would work in one place and take her money in another. That would stop her from resembling a courtesan, to herself or others.

This new flirt entered the Rotonde. She looked gorgeous: a mixture of a Greek caryatid and a child's toy. She sat down at a table by herself (how ribald!), lit up a cigarette (unheard-of for a lady!), crossed her legs, raised her pert dress so everyone could see her thighs going up to her bottom and, to jeers from café visitors, ordered an absinthe (a German drink!). 'There is no absinthe, we only serve French drinks,' Old Libion said, and behind the bar he asked the painter Kisling who the new floozie was. Kisling replied in mock confidence. He cupped his hand over his mouth and turned towards the proprietor, but he spoke so loudly that even passers-by on street could hear: 'Oh, that's just a little slut, an easy lay.' Everyone laughed, but Kiki knew she had bagged her first painter. She stayed till late in the evening, and Kisling came ever closer to her. First he had been sitting at the bar. Later he was at the neighbouring table. And finally he asked Kiki the smoker for a light and joined her at her table. They left for his house. The painter sang in the street, and people pelted him with empty tins from their windows. He groaned above Kiki all that night, but for her it was something new. She hadn't made love with a man of flesh and blood in two years. She no longer had Jean, Jacques and Jules, the spirits from the boots—now she had a real painter instead. He wasn't exactly a great lover, but she climaxed all the same. Or simulated it.

From the next day on, the two of them were inseparable. Kiki became Kisling's model, but she wouldn't accept any remuneration for posing. She made love but didn't charge for it either. She was managing to nicely implement her plan, when she met her next protector. He was the most famous Japanese man in Paris, the painter Tsuguharu Foujita. Fate brought them together via a raid at Old Libion's. Gendarmes on bicycles made a swoop on the café searching for Bolsheviks who drank there. Libion crossed himself. He knew nothing about Bolsheviks or Mensheviks; they were all good-for-nothings to him. Kiki and Foujita were the last to leave. He was wearing a white silk kimono, which disconcerted the police so much that they didn't put him in the Black Maria. And when he, in his strange 'dress', claimed Kiki was his companion, they didn't arrest her either. She stood there on the Paris sidewalk: the rain had rather soaked her hair and thighs. Her dress clung to her chest. She looked passionate. Foujita couldn't take his eyes off her. Kisling wailed in vain from the Black Maria, as desperate as a dog being dragged off to the pound: 'Kiki, you're mine! Kikiii!' But she became Foujita's.

Two days later, Kisling was released from custody and Kiki met up with him. She didn't tell him straight away that they were no longer a couple. She could pretend to be a model for two painters at the same time. But now she needed money, she said in a pleading sort of tone, times were hard. And so Kisling offered her money. Day after day she made him pay for everything they did together, but she didn't go back to him. Kisling's time was up. Now she was with Foujita, and she didn't demand anything from him. She posed for him naked. The Japanese explained poses 26 and 37 of traditional Japanese lovemaking to her. He showed her a book with lascivious Japanese watercolours, in which the men had enormous members and the women incredibly shaggy crotches. Without taking their eyes off the book, the two of them made love, sometimes several times a day. Kiki no longer knew where her legs were: she spread them upwards, stretched them to the side, and did the splits. The Japanese was a great lover in a small body, but he would still have to pay one day when she decided to leave him. But for now everything was alright. They made love in the morning, at noon, in the afternoon, and also late in the evening when nothing else was happening. When the setting sun shone low into the painter's atelier, it seemed to Kiki that their long shadows on the wall were frantically making love in time with their frenzied bodies. She wasn't afraid of the shadows or the passing thought that she could get syphilis, that tragic seal of all libertines.

But another footloose figure—a real refugee, in fact—was afraid even of his own shadow. He wasn't a rake and didn't have a lover. He was quiet. His wife, son and daughter had remained behind in Serbia. In Paris in 1917, Vladislav Petkovich Dis was only a shadow of his former self. He walked along Rue Monge, where he had a cramped little flat, and his shadow, which reached all the way up to the first-storey balconies, was significantly longer than those of other passers-by. Why didn't anyone notice? He himself watched the dark, freakish shape plodding along with him like some giant, articulated insect and rushed from narrow Rue Monge to Boulevard du Montparnasse, where there was more light and the sidewalk was wider. That made him feel a little more at peace, but he didn't stay there among the nervous cars which seemed to be blowing their horns just at him. Instead, he hurried to the Luxembourg Gardens and a metal sculpture of a mother clasping her two children in her arms; to him, they looked like his own Mutimir and Gordana.

This poet with the tousled, curly hair hurried to see the metal mother and her children that day, too, because a stranger—he couldn't remember who—had told him that the metal family would soon be melted down. The French Republic needed as much metal as it could get for the production of munitions. 'Hard times have come, my good sir, and I too am sad about this mother and her children,' the stranger said. 'You mean you have a son and daughter back in Serbia? Sorry to hear it.' the poet didn't reply and didn't think of saving this copper family if he couldn't save his own. Every day he hurried to the gardens and was glad to see the family still together. 'Just this one day more,' he repeated inside, 'and when they remove you I'm going home to my own family.'

All through the spring, the family in the Luxembourg Gardens remained together, and then they vanished overnight, just as the warden of the gardens had predicted. Only a mark remained in the grass where they had stood. Nothing was left behind: not even the pedestal the mother and her children had stood on. Everything was taken to be melted down in the foundries of war, and that was the sign for Vladislav Petkovich Dis to head home. He returned to the flat in Rue Monge and started putting his things in a small wicker suitcase. As a refugee he didn't have much to take with him. He decided to pack everything which was still in good nick—several shirts, long underwear, a few pairs of socks and a straw hat—and then something happened which he didn't find unusual at first. He packed the things in the evening, paid the landlady for the flat with the last of his money and was even a few sous short, and then went to bed, ready to leave Rue Monge the next day. When he looked at his suitcase in the morning, he saw that all his things were wet, as if a washbasin of water had been spilt over them during the night. That was not such a surprise in itself, as his small room contained a bath and, with plenty of leaks, it seemed possible that water had come in from somewhere. He leaned outside, held out the palms of his hands and looked into the low, grey Paris sky. There was no sun, but no rain either. The landlady had no explanation; she told him she had slept soundly all night and hadn't heard a thing. So he asked if he could stay a day or two longer so as to dry his things, and she kindly obliged although he had been several coins short with the rent.

After craning his neck and looking up to find the faithless sun, the poet decided to hang up his shirts, trousers and long underwear with pegs on the small French balcony and leave them there. He spent the day at the editorial office of *La patrie Serbe* and took part in erudite discussions. A certain Dr Alexander Purkovich was visiting and defended his opinions in a thunderous voice. 'They're all crooks, my dear Dragomir,' the moustachioed stranger emphasized, 'victims of their own ambitions and inner urges they're unable to curb. They strive for power and care little for the misfortunes of the people.' And Dragomir Ikonich, the editor of the magazine, replied in much the same vein. Dis added a word or two, but all his thoughts were with his coarse linen shirts and long winter-underwear which he hoped had dried.

In the late afternoon, he went back to Rue Monge and was satisfied that his clothes were now dry. He folded them once again, put them in the suitcase... and then slapped himself on the forehead. How could he decide to return home to Serbia without having told anyone in France? He couldn't steal away and leave just like that, even if he was a refugee. Was that why his clothes had got wet? He had to get over being such a loner, he resolved, so he wrote two farewell letters to his fellow refugees in Les Petites Dalles. He would tell his Paris friends about his decision the next day. And so he went to bed, but in the morning another unpleasant surprise was in store for him: his clothes were wet yet again. Once more, he hung them up on the little terrace and thought he could write a poem about the strange occurrence; it had to be connected to his plans to journey home to his family. He sent the two letters to Les Petites Dalles, and later he told the editor of *La patrie Serbe* that he wanted to go back. Ikonich replied laconically and was then surprised when the poet requested if he could come to sleep a few nights at the editorial office; Dis confided in him that his clothes were wet every morning although they had been dry when he put them in the suitcase the previous evening. 'That must be the damp, my dear Dis. All the little Parisian flats are damp these days. We've just got used to it and don't notice it any more. If your lease has expired and you haven't renewed it, of course you can move here and dry your pants.'

And that is what Dis did, except that his clothes were wet again in the morning even after having dried in the editorial office. Now Ikonich, too, called it a 'mystery', but the poet would wait no longer. 'I'm leaving now, dear fellow. The money I send isn't reaching my family, and I can't bear being out of the country any more.' And he left. Via Marseilles, Rome and Naples, straight to his death. He embarked on the ship *Italy*, which sailed for Corfu at nine in the evening on 15 May 1917 by the Julian calendar. On board the ship, he no longer took his things out of the suitcase. Nor did he even try to hang them up on the lower, third-class deck. He hoped that the kind sun of the south on Corfu would dry him, as well as his shirts and long underpants, but he was mistaken. On the morning of 17 May by the old calendar, the *Italy* was torpedoed out at sea. The passengers screamed, and shortly before the ship went under the priests prayed with their small flock. The ship's bell tolled, and the passengers who could swim were the first to rush and grab the safety rings. Our poet fell into the cold water and didn't even try to swim because he had never learnt. His suitcase was with him and now finally revealed to him why the clothes inside it were always wet. He thrashed about like a hooked fish for a little longer and then went under. He sank slowly, like a sack of salt, and circled with his right arm as if writing fluid blank verse on invisible paper. The poet's last thought was that nothing could compare with the silence of the sea.

The next day, his body was washed ashore close to Corfu city. For Vladislav Petkovich Dis, the Great War ended when his body was found by a group of local boys. He had one and a half drachmas and a broken pair of spare glasses in his pocket. No one found the suitcase with the wet clothes, because war devours people and everything human, along with all that is inanimate and inhuman. No one knows or can keep track of all that is discarded and expended, to be lost to memory.

In Russia there was a great attrition of good and bad alike, of the human and the brutish. The Republic was foundering in a ferment of blood, sweat, hopes, words and disappointments. The government and its ministries issued *ukases*, one more ridiculous and monstrous than the other. The country was grumpy, bumpy and disorganized, with the government's authority scarcely felt more than ten kilometres beyond the capital. Wild Cossacks, angry at having been unable to preserve tsarism, now brandished their sabres at the talkative and the taciturn alike. A Cossack Republic was founded on the River Don with its own laws, different to those of Petrograd: laws written in blood. The Cossacks broke up the soviets in Rostov-on-Don, and in Kharkiv they attacked and killed the striking coal miners as if they were Turks, cleaving many of the fleeing men from shoulder to groin with their sabres. Terror reigned on the roads, robbery in the side streets, and rhetoric in the squares. Soldiers' delegates came from the front, desperate to get their arguments across. Tauride Palace, the seat of the new government, was full to bursting with words: some tender, others harsh. Words marched in columns down Nevsky Prospekt, along the promenades by the Church of the Saviour and down the promenade by the Malaya Nevka; despite their utter devaluation, everyone thought that one single word—just the right one—would be able to save the whole situation.

The prisoner Nicholas Romanov knew virtually nothing about what was going on. Occasionally one of the guards would say a thing or two, and sometimes his infrequent visitors would bring news, but Nicholas felt like a ship which had sailed out to sea and ever more rarely received word from land. So he worked more and more in the garden, spoke little and tried to get as much sleep as possible. Something strange started happening in his dreams: he dreamed of himself, but not as if he was alive, but rather as if he was in the dreams of others. He couldn't say how it happened, but clearly they were people in the future who were dreaming of him. To begin with, one night he dreamed he was being dreamed of by a nun, Maria Ivanovna. In his dream, that is in Maria Ivanovna's, he saw a house in the provinces and brutish guards like wild animals who drank vodka by the tumblerful all night. He heard that they were preparing to kill the imprisoned tsar and his family, and he saw himself in Maria's dream silently eating fish at the dinner table and hoping he would choke on a bone and die like an ordinary coward. Then one night in Maria's dream they were abruptly fetched and taken down to the cellar. It was for safety reasons, they were told. The tsar saw himself going down and carrying Tsarevich Alexei, who was too weak to walk. Later in that dream, which was not his own, he saw those savage men from the ground floor, their faces red from vodka, coming in and pointing their rifles and pistols at them. He couldn't believe it: Maria seemed unable to accept the death of the tsar's family in her dream. The pistols just clicked as if they were empty, the rifles jammed, and, as things go in dreams, they were saved at the last minute by Polish forces loyal to General Denikin. Where was that place? What was that house? He couldn't find that out from Maria Ivanovna's dream because she always woke up at the same time. But the dream also revealed a little from Maria's real life: it seemed she lived in the future, perhaps in the year 1928 or 1933, and she was a nun at the Russian monastery in Belgrade, who every night persistently dreamed of the tsar.

Nikolai Romanov did not just seize on her dream as a way of interpreting his own. He was also dreamed of by a Russian porter at the railway station in Vienna. Then there was a former Russian soldier from the Eastern Front, as well as a rakish Russian son who never ceased to pine for his parents' endless fields in his dear old motherland and spent his time in Venice with a terminally ill Italian woman. There was also a former landowner who danced the kazachok between the tables of smoky Parisian cafés as a refugee in the distant future, and there were various cripples and otherwise impaired men who published émigré newspapers, moved in dubious circles and loved dangerous women. And all of them lived in the future and dreamed of the tsar. There was another strange thing too: all of them seemed to dream one and the same dream with only slight variations. It was one and the same house. He soon became familiar with its appearance and the layout of the rooms, and with his family in it. Withdrawn into himself, the tsar worked the small estate. He ate in silence, and his fork clanked against the mismatched plates. The fish tasted mouldy. The bunch of barbaric men guarding them got ferociously drunk and said through the dreams of those visionaries in the future that they were going to kill the tsar, but that they wouldn't harm the grand duchesses. Then there was a moonless night. Animals howled in the wolfish forests above the house. Soldiers took the tsar's family away in silence, or they burst into their rooms, stabbed the eiderdown quilts (feathers flew everywhere like fine snow), smashed the wooden icons and read Nilov's *Antichrist*—the tsaritsa's favourite book—and grinned like hyenas. Then the cellar. Always that cellar! They were taken there under the pretext that it was safer. A moment later, in the dreams of the editors, rakes, kazachok dancers and nuns, the pistols and rifles were unable to fire. They broke, seized up or clicked empty. The officers yelled at the executors. The killers cried. Or they didn't. He and his family were saved by loyal White Guard forces. The dreamers in the future awoke with a scream. The imprisoned tsar deceived himself and thought: if these people, like holy fools, are really dreaming of us in the future, that means we won't be killed and our time won't be over. That encouraged him a little in his confinement; but how wrong the last Russian monarch was.

His killers set off from Zürich in a sealed wagon of the German railways. Over a decade had passed since these diurnally sombre but nocturnally ebullient Bolsheviks had fled from Russia. Now, in March 1917, they felt the time had come to return to their frayed and troubled country. But how were they to get to Russia? The whole of warring Germany lay in their path. England and France were of no mind to help the deserters and send them back to Russia via orange-hued España, the route by which, in 1916, they had sent the assassin Oswald Rayner, who had killed in the name of the British crown,. The small Bolshevik committee from Lake Geneva and Zürich therefore asked Germany for assistance. Seeking passage from Russia's enemy did not disturb those cheerful revolutionaries who dreamed of change and a new pair of shoes each day. Besides, they were against the war and, at the same time, above it. They wanted to halt the war, so they were good human cargo on the German railways. Their request, lodged by the Swiss socialist Fritz Platten, was duly approved. Forty comrades with families and luggage would set off in two sealed wagons which would be joined to the trains of the state railways of Baden, Württemberg and Hessen following exact German timetables. The passengers travelled incognito. They weren't allowed to leave the wagons or receive any visitors during the journey. The Bolsheviks accepted these conditions and began packing their suitcases. None of them found damp clothes in their suitcases in the morning and only one of the travellers would have any doubts as to whether returning to Russia was a good idea.

This momentous journey by train began at ten past five on the morning of 24 March 1917. All of Lenin's companions, like Ulysses's sailors, turned up to their appointment with destiny. Russian, Swiss and Austrian Bolsheviks started out on the journey from Zürich that day; among them was the Austrian Karl Radek, the only one who would not be the same after the ten-day journey. It was all because of a boy—one such as Radek would have liked to have as a son. As soon as the train with its happily singing passengers in twenty compartments (first-, second- and third-class) crossed the Swiss-German border, these *personae non grata* realized for themselves what war meant. They had spent five years as cultured refugees, poor but with neatly-mended clothes, drinking coffee with whipped cream in cheap, dusty Swiss cafés. Now the time had come to see the face of the Great War through the windows of their compartments. Dead horses and donkeys with wide-open, foaming mouths lay on both sides of the railway line, and they didn't see a single man on the platforms of the small stations where they stopped. At one station, a crowd pushed up to the window of the compartment where comrades Zina Zinovieva and Nadya Krupskaya were sitting because they had spotted half a loaf of crumbling white bread behind the glass of the window. The German nights they made their way through shone with thousands of stars, but there was ever a dull flickering and a hint of thunder in the distance.

No one seemed to want to attach any importance to that, however. A tense vivacity prevailed in the sealed wagons. Nadya made tea on an old Swedish alcohol stove, while Lenin read, or briskly debated with comrades in German, Russian and French. The travellers admired the beauty and majesty of the black German forests and the crystal green of the winding River Neckar as if they were a group biologists or art historians on an excursion. They were inspired when they passed through medieval German cities, dark and seared, which bowed their reactionary facades to greet the travellers.

All of them were in high spirits; all of them, like the mariners of Antiquity, were sure of the journey, although no one knew how the opposite shore would look. Only Comrade Radek was despondent. He tried to relax with the others at first, and joined in when they played the guitar and sang, but he was forever peering through the window. And all because of a boy. He first noticed him at the station in Rottweil pushing a large luggage cart overloaded with the bags of late travellers, as an adult porter might. You might ask what was so special about that boy, whom the Austrian Bolshevik watched through the bluish window pane of the sealed wagon that night, far after midnight. He was delicate, skinny to the extreme, with a freckled nose and a look both sad and ruffianly, as of a child grown up prematurely. Did he feel he'd like his son to look like that, if he had one, or was he touched by the sight of the boy pulling a load which dwarfed his tiny figure? He couldn't say.

The train stood at the station for a whole half hour, and he watched the boy pushing the luggage cart up and down the platform, hardly getting it to move, and throwing on suitcases which fell off along the way. Who was that boy, and what was it that moved him that night? He didn't know; the train moved off again and he was sure that this sight would mingle with the mosaic of other unpleasantries in warring Germany. But already at the following station, in Oberndorf, he could have sworn that he saw the same boy again. Now he was standing on the platform all alone, as if he was waiting for someone. How had he managed to get there at the same speed at which the State Railways of Baden travelled? Or perhaps he had a twin brother. Radek wanted to open the window and call out to him, but the train started off again, and he waited for the next stop in the old town of Stuttgart, where he saw the same boy again. He wailed and covered his mouth with his hand so the others wouldn't hear. The boy was wounded and leaning on a crutch. It was the same face and the same freckled nose, but his face had the look of an abandoned puppy. The boy was standing alone, about to renounce his hastily acquired earnestness and flee beneath his mother's skirts, but there was no one who would come to his aid from the group of Bolsheviks or the nearby carriages of the German and Swiss railways. Were there no other travellers? And where was the boy's mother, Comrade Radek asked himself when the train with the two sealed wagons continued its journey.

It was always the same boy at the stations in Karlsruhe, Mannheim, Frankfurt and Berlin-Friedrichstrasse, only in a different role each time. He watched idly like a pickpocket, cried as if lost, pulled a luggage cart again, or was all black and blue. Radek was relieved when the train finally reached the north German coast and the revolutionaries left the country. He didn't see any boys in Sweden or snowy Finland, but a boy with the same face was waiting for him at the station in Petrograd. That German boy again! With freckles, that same look in his blue eyes, and his premature earnest. This new-old boy now introduced himself as a Russian.

'Hello, Comrade Radek, I recognize you,' he said and held out his hand seriously like an adult.

'Where do you know me from?' the Austrian Bolshevik replied in broken Russian and shook the boy's small hand like he would a grown man's.

'They told me to meet you at the station and see to your needs until you settle in.'

'So you have nothing to do with the German boys in Rottweil, Karlsruhe, Stuttgart and all the other cities in Germany?'

'I don't understand, Comrade Radek. I hate the Germans. What did you see there in Germany?'

'Nothing, nothing,' Karl Radek replied, thinking that his time may well have passed. He embraced this Russian boy like he was hugging all those German ones and realized that nothing would be the same any more. Three years after the World War, Karl Radek would be a refugee once again. He would thunder against Lenin and the Party, calling them "the Bolshevist bacillus of Russia" in an American newspaper, and he wouldn't tell anyone that the first crack in his revolutionary views appeared when he felt that every city in Germany and Russia had one identical, fair-haired boy who was visible only to him.

At least Radek had someone waiting for him. When the train with the two sealed wagons passed through Karlsruhe, the chemist Fritz Haber, the father of all Gothic doctors, was sitting in his house alone. He was a widower, and he had sent his son to military school. He had been given several days of leave so he could sell the old family house, which still smelled of his Clara Immerwahr. The chemist of death, too, now felt the time of his successes had passed. He was still the same, and he still thought that a scientist belonged to the whole world in peacetime, but in wartime only to his nation. Yet he had already considered himself a dead man for some time. He reflected like a scientist: what percentage of him was already dead?

When his wife died, part of him also died—thirty-two per cent, to be precise. When he saw how devastating the effects of chlorine were, he was not greatly shocked, but another six percent of him died all the same. When they didn't promote him from captain to the rank of medical corps major, this terrible insult caused another two percent of him to die; all together, in 1917, that made a total of forty percent of Haber dead!

And the prospects? The savage, poorly armed enemy on the Russian Front, who was beneath the dignity of the German soldier, was melting away. The sixty-per cent part of him perked up at that news, but then things were not going well in the west, as Captain Haber knew too well. The retreat to the Hindenburg Line, along with the abandonment of the towns of Bapaume, Ypres and Péronne, was leading to Germany's defeat in the Great War, as inevitable as it was incomprehensible. That blow killed at least another seven per cent of the life in him. The misfortune and apathy of people behind the lines also did their bit. Wounded soldiers who were happy to lounge in hospital for six months or more also exasperated him. Those unworthy, unpatriotic Germans together killed another five per cent of him, so Fritz Haber, the chemist of his body, could only say that forty-eight per cent of him was still alive in 1917. That's right, less than half of him. His time was up, he thought, but he was wrong... significant parts of the living Fritz Haber were still to die in 1918!

DEATH WEARS NO WATCH

Bare earth all around. The coppery, dusty Greek earth once trod by the sandalled feet of ancient Greek heroes, now plodded on by the boots of Greek conscripts almost treading on each other's toes. The occasional gnarled tree behind the lines, and wind raising clouds of dust. No people anywhere—those merry, carousing ones. In 1917, King Peter felt he had ultimately been left alone. Abandoned and at the mercy of his ailments, he had a vivid image of life entering a train and of him standing alone on the platform, trying to make out the silhouettes in the moving carriages, just as the last Russian tsar felt. The old king had not made war in 1914 either; he had trusted people loyal to the throne in 1915; in 1916, he had left the war completely to his son; and still he could not have believed that people would turn their backs on him, here and now in 1917. Yes, now even the king thought his time was up. Who could he tell, who could he confide in? He fled and changed his abode: Euboea, Salonika, Edessa, and back to Athens again. Now they told him that Greece had finally and wholeheartedly come down on the side of the Allies, and King Constantine was far away in some pleasant but obtuse foreign land.

What had become of 1916, the year of the kings? The outcome was more than disappointing. Constantine was a case in point. Nicholas II, too. Who would be next? Surely it would be him. 'I am entering my last year,' King Peter noted in his diary. The old king was no longer waiting for anyone human, but only for sickness and death. He looked on illness and decay as malicious enemies, and death for him was the great bell in the dome of his church on Oplenac Hill. If only he could live to see Serbia again; but even if he didn't, it was all over anyway. How strange to be putting an end to everything, willy-nilly, before his life was over, and finishing things he had only just begun. Things he hadn't even begun were well and truly over. He felt interrupted and his life cut short half way through. Death, it seemed, wore no watch. The king spoke like this to his new doctor, who listened to him and, like others, tried not to get into an argument. This caused nothing but rage in the fiery, youthful ember buried deep in the soul of the old king— a fury he couldn't find the strength to express.

So no one asked him about anything any more. He watched his infrequent guests listening to him and glancing furtively at their watches.

Prime Minister Nikola Pashich and the President of the Yugoslav Committee, Dragoslav Yankovich, were visiting. Pashich informed King Peter about the Allies' attitude towards Serbia, and Yankovich spoke about the idea of unifying the South Slavs, and his cheeks flushed as he pronounced 'Yugoslavia, Yugoslavia': It all looked like a visit with meaning and substance. But then the king saw off his guests and, for no particular reason, went out for a walk around Athens. He thought the visitors would already have left and would be getting on with their business, when he saw them both down at the port. They were waiting for their boat and moving around with nervous steps, each by himself. The king walked past just one step away from one of them and then almost brushed the back of the other, and neither of them noticed him. They were so close that they could have reached out and touched him, but now he was out of sight and out of mind for them. Yankovich was staring into the distance as if he wanted to spot the boat first, and Pashich was muttering to himself. Soon the boat arrived and they left, but the impression steadily grew on the king that he only existed for visitors when he was standing right in front of them.

A week later, the Minister of War, General Bozhidar Terzich, came to see him. He looked at the king with his warm but shifty eyes and evidently lied to him about something. At the end of the visit, he took leave of the king in the upper chambers of the house in Athens and went down to the ground floor. There he waited for his coach, twirled his black moustache and cursed under his breath. The king went down the same stairs and walked up to Terzich from behind, but the minister neither heard nor sensed him and just kept on muttering to himself. The king therefore turned, went out the back door and walked round past the bougainvillea, by the house to the gravel path at the front so the nefarious visitor would easily see him. Terzich's coach arrived and he got in; the king waved to him from the side, but the general no longer noticed him.

Yes, the king thought after that: they only see me when I'm in front of their very noses. Then they hurry off, stare at their pocket watches and debate with invisible others before finally leaving. He tested it once or twice more with new visitors, and it was always the same.

'They ought to just write me postcards—that's how much I mean to them,' the king wrote in his diary, without realizing that hard times had come, there in the foreign country: the time of the first victories in the Battle of Kaymakchalan, but also of the first suspicions and conspiracies.

The spectres who had once slogged through Albania now regained strength, and the fresh blood flowing through their veins now began to become tainted with self-interest, revanchism and vengefulness. It was the same with junior and senior officers, members of the government, and the Regent himself. Many old wounds were reopened in Salonika in 1917, a host of old disputes from the nineteenth century simmered up again, and many ideas were left unfinished; so the ambitious and the frustrated now conspired to implement them then and there, on the dry earth of Greece.

One who had long been a nuisance, wielded greater influence over the army than the officer corps, and had founded the secret society, *Black Hand*, was Colonel Dragutin Dimitriyevich, code-named Apis. Regent Alexander had long considered removing him. He mentioned Apis in a conversation with Prime Minister Pashich, and he almost gave him a dressing-down in front of the supreme command when discussing future plans. After surviving an assassination attempt near Salonika, Alexander returned to the city in anger, and spoke out in his own characteristic way, as if breaking a branch: 'Let's get rid of this nuisance!'

Apis and one hundred and twenty-four other officers were charged in connection with the shots fired at the regent. The trial took place in restless Salonika accompanied by protests from the commanders of all the other foreign armies, and it raised the temperature of the city, whose fever had only just subsided. The proceedings were opened on 28 May 1917 at the barracks of the Serbian 3rd Army and presided over by General Mirko Milosavlyevich, but this is not the story of that harsh, loyalist officer. Many non-commissioned officers and their superiors were summoned before the tribunal, and all of them corroborated the charges which had been laid, but nor is this the tale of those frightened witnesses with only their own careers in mind. Initially nine men were sentenced to death, some of them officers and others civilians; by the end, it was only three. The story which follows is about just one of those men, Major of the Artillery Lyubomir 'Lyuba' Vulovich. It is similar to a Hungarian story from the nineteenth century which has come down to us by strange paths: the tale of a mother who wished to strengthen her son's courage before his execution. She told him she would wear a sumptuous dress with white flounces on the day of the execution if a pardon came and was read out before the executioner at the last minute. A pardon did not come, the mother was wearing those immaculate white satin lilies, and her son died hoping until the last, courageous like a heroic Hungarian nobleman.

In this new tale, which was passed from mouth to mouth among soldiers in a faithless and seditious century, in Salonika in 1917, the role of the mother in white was played by another artillery major by the name of Radoyica Tatich, a hero of the engagements at Tekerish, Begluk, Beli Kamen and the Battle of Kaymakchalan. He didn't wear white and was dressed no differently to the condemned man. He felt it was his soldierly duty ('It was his moral duty, mate,' the troops used to say) to prevent his bosom friend from cadet school from losing his soldierly dignity in front of the firing squad. Therefore he went to Vulovich's cell and spoke to his friend in French so the rather rustic guard wouldn't understand.

'I'm prepared to die,' Vulovich in turn replied in French, which both of them had learnt well at military school in Paris.

'Mon ami, reprenez courage!' Tatich reprimanded him sternly. Then he led him to the far part of the cell and switched to a more friendly tone, and to Serbian. He then spoke to his friend in confidence:

'Tomorrow I'm taking the overnight express train to Athens. I'll throw myself at old King Peter's feet and beg him to pardon you, but if I don't succeed I have something else to protect you when you're in front of the firing squad. Don't laugh, Vulovich, when I'm pledging my honour as an officer and risking my career because of you! You know I was the greatest hero at the Battle of Cer, and in all the battles since. Why should I adorn myself with false modesty? You've heard what the army says about me: "He's reckless, as if nothing can harm him: There's no man faster in a charge". The reason for my mad bravery was a little mirror. A strange little mirror. I discovered its special powers back during the Balkan wars, and I continued to rely on it right up to the Battle of Kaymakchalan, and even today. I have that little mirror with me now. What kind of contrivance it is, you ask? The mirror contains an aged and ugly me. Once we were the same: me and the face in that mirror, but then I realized that my reflection behind the line of the mirror was abruptly beginning to change, age, and become worn out. Whenever I looked at myself in fear, my astonished reflection seemed to age a year or two. I was often frightened and looked in the mirror rather often, before each battle: in Macedonia and Kosovo, in Bulgaria, and now in the Great War. Don't smirk, Vulovich, you know old Tatich doesn't lie and isn't a poetic daydreamer like some officers! I carried the little mirror with me all the time. Looking at my ever more haggard image made me realize that I was transferring my fears to it, ever more and more; soon I also realized that neither bullet nor bayonet nor bomb could harm me if I was freed of shame in this way. And I'm alive, as you can see, without a single scratch. Was that possible for anyone else but me, Vulovich? No, because only I had the little mirror with me, and now I want to give it to you. Look at yourself in it ("That was the hardest part of the lie, my good fellow"). Can't you see your aged and frightened self? Careful now, don't turn around. Don't let the guard see I'm giving you this miraculous little thing. Hide it now, quickly, so they don't take it off you. Now I'm going. Remember, my friend: you can't die with that little mirror in your pocket. The rifles will jam, the commanding officer of the firing squad will get a lump in his throat when he's about to shout 'Fire!', or a pardon will arrive from Athens at the last moment. Just you look in it, and whenever you look you will pass one more fear to your image. It can't fail. Goodbye now, farewell. Let us embrace like brothers, my dear Vulovich.'

Thus Major Radoyica Tatich left his friend. Evening came, and still he did not go to Salonika railway station. One train after another left for Athens. ('He didn't even think of going, cuz; it was all a lie, but the mirror began to do its work.') Major Lyuba Vulovich looked at himself in the little mirror every morning and there, behind the reflection, just as his friend Tatich had said, he saw his frightened and aged self. He maintained that countenance for several days, and then his mouth twisted into a sad grimace. He thought that was his reflection suffering after being given all his fears, but he was wrong. Vulovich didn't see that the same thing was happening to his own face, since he had none other than Tatich's 'miraculous' little mirror. And he began to hope, madly expecting that the firing squad's bullet would miss him too. ('Tatich, who owned the miraculous little mirror until just before, never had as much as a scratch, I can vouch for that.')

Day after day passed, then week after week; for there was reluctance to carry out the three officers' sentence. This only strengthened Vulovich's certainty that there was nothing to fear. But then 26 June 1917 by the new calendar arrived, and the condemned men were driven to the Salonika military cemetery, where graves had already been dug for them. No one, not even Apis, chatted on the way with the officers who escorted them; they were calm and apologized for what they must do in the line of duty. No one looked at the Salonika landscape, its harsh rocks jarring with the aquamarine coast with such serenity, for the last time. No one inhaled the Mediterranean air with its soothing aromas of almond, laurel and pine with so much confidence. Even the stern soldier Apis started to tremble when they were taken out of the truck like tied sacks, but not Vulovich. ('He smiled—I swear he did—because I was in the firing squad. He smiled like a girl.')

The rolling of the drums scarcely moved the bravest of the three condemned men. That sound brought home an image which stood like stone in his hopes like the jagged Salonika rockscape they were leaving behind and which now, strangely animated, came up to within a metre or two of where they stood. Vulovich saw rifles with bayonets on, soldiers who didn't want to kill them, and a small, very nervous commander of the firing squad, who was shifting from one leg to the other. But it couldn't be, he thought, they couldn't all be here because of him; he had Tatich's mirror on him, after all. Look, a senior officer was racing along the path to the cemetery. With a pardon, surely, or maybe not... This officer now stood in front of the three condemned men and, as if to torment them, read out the full text of the indictment and sentence; it lasted two hours. There was no pardon, but Vulovich was still hoping. ('You know, even a small animal in a trap hopes it will be able to pull and tug its way out.') the other men asked for a last cigarette before death, and Vulovich wanted to look in his mirror. In it, he saw a frightened, deathly pale and broken man. It was he himself whom he saw, but once again he thought he had given all his fear to the image in Tatich's miraculous little mirror. Now he stood in front of the squad, the drums rolled, the rifles were raised. Where was that pardon? a month earlier Tatich had gone to kneel before old King Peter - the shots echoed in the quarry like a monstrous profanity to the wrongfully condemned men, in a strange metallic language. The men fell straight into their graves: all three of them, including the bravest, artillery Major Lyuba Vulovich.

For the conspirator Lyuba Vulovich, the Great War ended when he looked for the last time at his astonished countenance in the magic mirror of his friend from cadet school. No medals are given for that sort of bravery, except in the thoughts of friends. Major Radoyica Tatich asked his acquaintances how Lyuba Vulovich had behaved that day. When he heard that the executioners praised him ('You have our word as officers that he died like a Herculean hero. We bound his eyes as if we were putting a satin scarf on him.'), he left satisfied. Without a word, he lit up a cigarette and blew out thick puffs of smoke; he no longer expected anything of his return to the Fatherland, nor of his military career. He bent down, picked up a small handful of bronze, Greek dust and felt as if he was in no-man's-land.

Manfred von Richthofen also found himself in no-man's-land. In June 1917, the kaiser finally awarded him the highest German medal, *Pour le Mérite*. He had had to bring down sixteen enemy planes to receive the 'Blue Max', but finally the telegram arrived with this most joyful piece of news. Soon the slender cross with the sky-blue points came, which the Red Baron always wore on his coat. But this decoration seemed not to bring him luck. He shot down seven more French planes, but after twenty-three kills his red triplane was shot down for the first time. A machine-gun burst from a British plane hit the motor of Richthofen's plane and gasoline gushed into the cockpit up to his ankles. The aircraft could have caught fire at any moment, but the Red Baron managed to land it, and then destroy it. His heavy pilot's coat was singed and blackened all over with oil, so he did not give the impression of a great ace. Worse still, he found himself far behind British lines, some thirty kilometres from the Hindenburg Line. The first thing he encountered were the rifles of frightened Scottish soldiers. One of them knew some German and struck up a gentlemanly conversation as they were escorting him to the Royal Flying Corps command.

'What's your name, sir?'

'Manfred von Richthofen.'

'I didn't quite catch that, but never mind. How many of our planes have you shot down? Two or three?'

'Twenty-three!'

'You must be joking,' the guard said in his cumbersome German. 'Is that the truth?'

'Yes, it is.'

'I don't believe it. No one has downed as many of our planes as the Red Baron. Do you know him?'

'Quite well, in fact. I'd say we're on first-name terms.'

'What sort of fellow is he?' the inquisitive Scotsman asked again. 'A brutal cad, I bet.'

'He's actually a tender-hearted fellow and loves to kiss his sweetheart. By the way she kisses him, he knows how you Tommies are going to attack.'

'So he's that kind of ace. Superstitious. He might be your comrade but, believe me, I'd bash in his noggin if I met him!'

'Why not straight away?' Richthofen challenged him and took off his grimy leather coat. Beneath it, the Scotsman saw an immaculately ironed, light-blue jacket with the 'Blue Max', which gleamed with every movement. 'I am Manfred von Richthofen. Do you get my name now?'

The Scotsman was dumbfounded. Still, he clenched his fists, and Richthofen raised his guard in response. They exchanged several classy hooks and uppercuts before being separated by the other men. Later, in the British pilots' canteen, Richthofen was treated to coffee and cigarettes. He even began to sing a few songs with the Scotsman, who now apologized for his quick temper and the exchange of blows. Two days later, Richthofen was taken to the Hindenburg Line and exchanged for a British pilot. That was a sign that chivalry still existed in the air and on the ground. And the Red Baron thought that the 'Blue Max' maybe did bring him good luck after all.

Whether this medal, coveted by every German officer, would have brought good luck to the submarine commander Walther Schwieger, is hard to say. A telegramme arrived for Schwieger, too, at his base in L., with notification that the kaiser had awarded him the 'Blue Max'. It was 30 July 1917, but Captain-Lieutenant Schwieger—a mariner born inland—was not on shore. His medal came by mail two weeks later, but he was not at base in August either. The valuable medal was safe in a glass-case, and everyone thought submarine U-88 and its crew would soon return to its home port, but things turned out differently. All of August passed, the beginning of September came, and Schwieger still wasn't back in L. Then 5 September came, the last day of Schwieger's life. His submarine was on a routine patrol, had rounded the northern coast of Scotland and was not far from the Old Head of Kinsale where it had sunk the RMS Lusitania in 1915, when there was a mighty explosion. The submarine had entered an underwater minefield, for the officer on watch hadn't noticed the balls floating like lanterns at a depth of twenty metres. The blast practically tore the U-88 in half. Water began to rush in, and the crew members who had survived the explosion soon drowned in their cabins, unable to get out. Strangely thrown free, as if by some great force, Schwieger's body began to sink. For a brief moment, it seemed there was still life in him. But then he stopped moving. He didn't struggle for air. His loose blond hair waved in a gentle undersea breeze. When he had sunk to the border between light and the dark depths of the sea, large shadows began to glide close by his body, as if to sniff at him. These were most probably the sea monsters, and they took him in and sheltered him like a baby. For Schwieger, the Great War ended when the megalodons carried him away forever in a strange funeral procession, accompanied by sea serpents, to their kingdom on the sea floor.

Thus ended the life of the highly decorated officer, Walther Schwieger. For Zhivka D. Spasich, the seamstress who moved her tailor shop from strange Dunavska Street to safe and tranquil Prince Eugene Street, an unexpected new life began. The same day as the death of submarine commander Schwieger, whom she had never heard of, the seamstress gave birth in her shop. She confided in no one that she was carrying the baby. Corpulent as she was, she claimed to the last day not to be pregnant. It was a warm day on 5 September in Belgrade, with the shadows of officers chasing each other on the sidewalks and someone wailing in the distance like an abandoned cat, when Zhivka lay down on the floor and, with the help of her two assistants, gave birth to a healthy son. Only one person could have been the father: the Austrian officer with the perpetual hole in his pocket. She swaddled her son and named him Eugene. She was neither ashamed nor proud. The boy realized that he had to be very quiet in this world, and within just a few days Zhivka was back at the sewing machine. Quiet gentlemen came to her shop once again and left their uniforms to be mended. She met many new officers—tall, with large moustaches, heavy-set, red-faced, bloated or rickety—but never again did she see the officer with the hole in his pocket.

There was a professional spy who thought in those days that he too had a hole in his pocket. One thread came loose and he pulled at it, and as soon as he tore it off it seemed that a new one appeared, which he could pull at without end. The owner of that recalcitrant pocket was Frederick 'Fritz' Joubert Duquesne. This writer, soldier and adventurer had a narrow face, a pronounced nose, and the boyish smirk of a man who didn't know the meaning of fear. They called him 'the Cat', and he himself was convinced that he had at least seven lives. In his first, as a young man in South Africa, Duquesne fought against the British Empire in the First Boer War. He was on the verge of being captured several times, but he always saved himself by fleeing unexpectedly at the last minute. Before the Second Boer War, there in distant diamond Africa, he decided to start a second life. He audaciously enlisted to serve in the British Army—him, Duquesne, a Boer soldier and commando! How could they not have remembered him from the beginning of the century, when he wore a farmer's hat and two cartridge belts over his shoulders, and sowed fear like a guerrilla hero? Had he changed, maybe? Not at all. Duquesne, now a British officer, continued to work against the Empire. He planned acts of sabotage in Cape Town, that city which smelt of goat fat, with twenty fellow traitors in the army. They almost succeeded in blowing up several strategic British installations, but someone blew a whistle. In just a few more minutes Duquesne would have been caught, but that afternoon, while the bells of the distant Catholic mission rang and reverberated unusually long, he Houdini'ed out of that second life, too.

Before the Great War, he took up residence in New York. Now he was a news correspondent. He had reported faithfully on the Russian-Japanese War. Later he sent brilliant dispatches from blue Morocco, which brought him into the circles of US President, Theodore Roosevelt. He gained American citizenship in 1913. His diplomatic passport would take him to South America, but before leaving he had to drop in at the New York hotel Astor. As an old enemy of the British crown, he now began his third life as a German spy. All the doors in east and west were open to him. Under personal protection of the US president, Duquesne passed himself off as an engineer and spied in the rubber plantations of Brazil. Later, under the name Frederick Frederickson, he became involved in the 'gold affair' in Bolivia and emerged from it with a personal fortune. In the second year of the Great War, he took back his name Duquesne again, and President Roosevelt posted him as second attaché to the American embassy in Managua, Nicaragua.

His spying career was at its height. Just when he felt he was living perhaps the fourth of his seven lives, his pockets began to tear. First one, then the other. Thread after thread came loose and he didn't understand how his expensive suits could be so badly made. He blamed the humidity of the Central American torrid belt, where Nicaragua is nestled, and then a warrant for his arrest suddenly arrived in November 1917. It appeared that the president could no longer save this former brave boy who went around during the First Boer War with two cartridge belts over his shoulders like an insurrectionary leader. He was reaching the twilight of his career in the Great War, and it all seems to have happened because of a loose thread which he pulled and pulled at, and which must have unravelled his destiny.

The twilight of another spy, too, began in 1917 with the pulling of a thread. Sidney Reilly's pockets also began to tear without reason. One loose thread, then another. Was it best to pull them out or tear them off? At the end of the nineteenth century, Sidney Reilly realized that his manifold spying activities were an opportunity to make his mark. By the beginning of the twentieth century—as soon as he entered that blasphemous era—he was working for so many intelligence services that he often had trouble seeing through the thick web of double-agentry. But he was a master of disguise and the owner of the largest number of forged passports as soon as they were introduced in the distrustful twentieth-century.

Many a lady got to know that mousy face with its seductive, dark, button eyes, its long aristocratic nose, and fine lips, which invariably held cigars of vanilla-flavoured black tobacco. Reilly was known for his cheerful character and short-lived romances which usually ended in the betrayal of a state secret through tears of joy or guilt. In the Great War, he was the key agent of the British secret service, the SIS. That did not prevent him, however, from having a firm in New York which sold munitions to both the Russians and the Germans on the Eastern Front. A man had to live from something, after all, and life as a spy was only good for costly wardrobe and hotels at the expense of the British crown.

When business died down in October 1917 due to Russian's withdrawal from the Great War, he returned to Britain. Once or twice he met the assassin Oswald Rayner and, as a handler, gave him assignments which had to be accomplished with just one bullet. He was able to give orders—and more than that: to blackmail and be blackmailed. He thus acquired the reputation in upper circles of a man who could be relied upon. He was therefore sent to Petrograd towards the end of October 1917, shortly before the Bolshevik Revolution. Coming from a Russian-speaking background, Reilly had connections with the tsarist secret service, the Okhrana. His group had the task of killing several corrupt ministers of the transitional government so as to boost Lenin's coup, as strange as that seemed, for reasons known only to the SIS. Once again, everything looked simple for our 'Mr Rybenko' (the name he went under in Russia). Russian women had always appealed to him more than British or American ones, and his nervous, mousey eyes very soon made him the darling of Petrograd's spinsters. They smiled at him, flirted, and confided in him: 'You speak Russian like a Tatar, but your English is very professional.' Everything therefore went smoothly until his pockets began to tear. First one, then the other. He too pulled on thread after thread, and he too was baffled as to how such expensive suits could be so poorly made. He blamed the Russian October, the worst month in Petrograd, when the rain changes to sharp needles of frost and snow. In that hoary month, he was unmasked. He too seems to have unravelled his destiny by pulling at threads. His associates were arrested and summarily shot, but Reilly managed to escape by assuming the identity of a German and fleeing to Finland via Petrograd's Warsaw Railway Station, where Lenin had arrived several months earlier. He saved his skin, but the Great War was over for this master spy.

Career threads were also becoming entangled for a third spy that winter. Known commonly as Mata Hari, she was an unparalleled oriental dancer. She even had her own show, in which she played a devotee of the Javanese gods. She had round cheeks, a marble face and the look of a cold and ruthless seductress. The skimpy skirts she wore on stage emphasized her thighs and calf muscles. This winsome exterior concealed a ruthlessly ambitious and fame-hungry manipulator. Everyone had to see Mata Hari's show—it was a must—and everyone believed that the Javanese gods spoke in the same way that Mata Hari danced to their music.

The stage lights, make-up and powder concealed the sorry life of the Dutchwoman, Margaretha Geertruida Zelle. When she was eight, her father went bankrupt, by the age of fifteen she was supporting herself, and at nineteen she entered a marriage of convenience with a Dutch colonial official and went with him to Java. At twenty-four she lost her son to scurvy. At twenty-six she returned to Paris to try her luck as a dancer. Plagued by money troubles in the 'City of Light', she scraped by as a stripper, circus assistant and occasionally as a photographer's model. In desperation, and used to taking revenge and suffering the vengeance of others, she decided to reinvent her past: as of early 1910, she presented herself as a Javanese princess who had been given to a temple at a tender age to become a vestal virgin devoted to divinity and dance.

That was a biography repugnant and touching at the same time; one of those popular myths which everyone believes because they're so clearly a lie. But when the lights went up on stage and Mata Hari appeared with her ivory skin, and when she began to snake to the sounds of oriental music, as skinny as a rake and as supple as an eel, male eyes forgot all propriety, and almost every story became credible.

Mata Hari was a libertine. Inclined to dubious affairs, she, like Kiki, was not at all frightened by the spectre of syphilis haunting Europe, and she was given to using her fatal charm. A host of lovers would consolidate her fame. One of them would bring about the end of her life. Immediately before the Great War, she got to know Friedrich Wilhelm of Hohenzollern, the Crown prince of the German Empire, who showered her with affection and gifts, as well as visiting her performances throughout Europe indecently often. Everything else is legend. With her Dutch passport, Mata Hari travelled widely during the Great War. She was shadowed as a suspected German spy, while she herself claimed to be working for the French intelligence service. In February 1916, the skimpy dresses she performed in began to tear. Before performances, she would notice a loose silken thread which she tried in vain to pluck off or wrap into the lining. She would change her dress before the next performance, but then the new one would begin to tear too.

She was arrested on 13 February 1917 at the Hotel Plaza Athénée and accused of betrayal by passing British tank designs to the Germans. As evidence, they showed her intercepted messages of a German military attaché code-named H21. She said she had never heard of him and repeated that she was a spy for the French. Afterwards, some rough-hewn men with black moustaches down to their shoulders, hideous scars and sunken red-eyes came in. Her admirers certainly didn't look like that… they interrogated her for several days, and she fluttered around the indictment like a moth trying not to plunge and become entrapped. In the end, her strength gave way. The men with raw skin on their cheeks and foreheads explained to her that she had never worked for the French intelligence service but only for the Germans. She was sentenced to death.

It was 15 October 1917 when she walked her last path, accompanied by the sighs of all of Paris. She, the Javanese princess, was wearing a long fur-coat and high-heeled shoes. A cold wind whistled through the branches as they took her to the Bois de Vincennes. The firing squad consisted of twelve young recruits, just boys, who had never seen her dance; the officers were afraid that older men could take leave of their senses and try to help her at the last moment, instead of shooting her. And so they chose smooth-faced striplings from other parts of France to be her executors. A doctor also stood near the condemned woman—he was to confirm her death—and Mata Hari's solicitor was present too.

When they arrived at the place where the dancer was to be shot, Geertruida said goodbye to the solicitor and gave the doctor some money because he was to examine her after the execution. When asked what her last wish was, she unbuttoned her fur coat and let it fall to the ground. The firing squad saw her naked body, which shone in the morning sun like mother-of-pearl: rounded girlish shoulders, small breasts like silver fleece fastened to her ribs and a crotch freshly shaved and perfumed that morning. The soldier boys froze and could barely raise their rifles. The salvo rang out like a stammering atonement for the guilt of those who cast the Javanese princess to her death. Covered with blood, Mata Hari collapsed like Ingres's *Odalisque*. She crossed her legs, threw her left arm out over her plaited hair, and grasped convulsively for the grass with her right. Very soon, the doctor confirmed her death—a death which was the talk of all Paris.

'Beware of loose threads,' Guillaume Apollinaire often spoke in those days, acting the sage, while Paris was mourning for Mata Hari and every man felt at least a little guilty for not having tried to save her. However, a city like Paris could not have heroes for long or mourn for fallen souls for more than a month. That perfumed cloaca simply had to amuse itself, just as a clown has to perform and paint a smile on his face before the show, even if it be swollen from crying. Within a week, the sun shone and every arrondissement of the city threw off the mask of guilt and began to enjoy the last of the sun in the dying autumn, which covered the Avenue de la Republique with red leaves, sent strange rays into the Tuileries Gardens, saw unusual folk out strolling by the Grand Palais, and witnessed a strange wedding in the world of licentious artists.

The protagonists of that wedding were a painter and a married woman. How could a married woman remarry? It was 1917 and young women became free-minded. Morning affairs alternated with evening flings. The men were away on the battlefield, and every summer beneath the hot, bright star of Sirius the starved women sought someone to substitute their husbands in bed. The most ragged-skirted wenches claimed they hadn't heard from their husbands for weeks, or even months. It was easy enough to establish if they were dead, at least, but who was going to look into their whereabouts if even their wives had forgotten them? a few francs at the city mortuary and a few more at the army administration office sufficed for the issuing of a certificate confirming the 'temporary disappearance' of a husband, and in Paris this was sufficient for a married woman to remarry.

The painter Kisling fell in love with Renée Jeannou, a twenty-year-old blonde with a bob fringe down to her eyebrows, who wore shorts and mismatched socks. She looked a bit like Kiki but was far more classy and, as the painter said, 'never farted outside the toilet'. Kisling needed Renée Jeannou to heal his wounds from Kiki (the source of her income dried up overnight), and Jeannou needed Kisling so she could remarry. She didn't think Kisling was a paragon of virtue. She knew he was a rake and that his manners were no better than a bandit's, but she reasoned that if only she could remarry and cast off her 'temporarily disappeared' Breton sculptor, everything else would be a piece of cake. Her second husband would be replaced by a third, and where there was a third he could easily be replaced in bed by a fourth.

Fiancé Kisling knew Renée Jeannou's first husband. He had even gone out boozing and philandering with him in 1914, and now he turned up to console his 'widow' and 'cherish the memory of the great artist'. He arranged a grandiose wedding, where the wedding guests would parade through the streets like a religious procession. The day came round and all of Paris gathered for that dubious celebration with wedding rings and vows. The procession left from Kisling's flat in Rue Joseph Bara. Everyone was in that crowd: Kiki and Foujita, Old Combes and Old Libion, André Breton, Jean Cocteau (without the pistol at his belt), Apollinaire and the flirt who played the piano at his première of *the Breasts of Tiresias*. The merry company rolled along the street. Some played the mouth organ, others beat drums without any rhythm, while others blew whistles. When the procession was passing the Rotonde, Old Libion stepped aside for a minute and came back to salute all the wedding guests with his sourest wine, which he claimed had been maturing in the cellar for ten years. (Ten years? Tell us another one!)

Once the mob had inundated the Hotel Villa, the bride and groom were determined to say their fateful-fickle 'yes' at the district office.

The mayor's assistant was in attendance. All at once, the bride uttered a scream: she was looking at Kisling, but in his face she had suddenly seen her former husband, who undoubtedly was still alive. Had there been a mix-up? Had the Breton sculptor managed to ensconce himself in the building and surprise his faithless wife? Nothing of the sort. The bride had just temporarily lost her wits. Kisling, disconcerted, felt he had lost his respectable fiancée there in front of the altar. But then the best man and the witnesses dashed out of the crowd. They tried to reassure Jeannou that her former husband was 'temporarily disappeared', but she wouldn't listen to them. She yelled and screamed, pounding her fists on Kisling's shoulders: 'Get out of my sight, you Breton shit, and let me live!'

Of course she should have a life, but why did Kisling have to have bruises? Now Cocteau stepped forth from the crowd. Calmly, he took out his razor (he always carried one with him) and said: 'Dear Renée, look, this is not your husband. This is the failed painter Kisling', and as he spoke he started to dry-shave the painter's moustache, then his sideburns and finally Kisling's eyebrows. Before Renée Jeannou there now stood a freak with a face like a doll from a Boulevard Haussmann toyshop; but the bride was cured. A normal look returned to her eyes, and a smile to her lips. The district mayor's assistant was finally able to read out the wedding vows, and he proceeded as fast as possible because he wanted to get this gaggle of tipplers and ex-soldiers out of his building.

The marriage ceremony was carried out in complete silence. Finally it was done. The bridegroom looked as if he had just survived a fire, and the bride as if she had just finished a good round of vomiting after a night out drinking. Both of them were pale, but the procession went on. The music was becoming ever more distant and the merrymaking moved to other streets and squares.

Songs of travelling musicians were still heard towards the end of October in Venice, too, although no one was in the mood for music in those days. The Austro-Hungarian 5th Army, under the command of Svetozar Boroevich von Boina, was joined by nine Austrian and six German divisions under Otto von Below, which had been withdrawn from the Eastern Front. The offensive southwards into Italy, towards the River Tagliamento and the town of Caporetto, began two hours after midnight on 24 October and completely surprised the Italians.

Soon Venice was under siege. The front line was just ten kilometres from Mestre and the isthmus leading to the city on the water. Thick fog flourished, descending on the canals, alleyways and streets like a nocturnal decoration.

Many musicians were trapped in the fog, but still they played their slightly lascivious southern melodies, even if no one put a lousy lira their way. Their desire was to entertain people, not make a killing in those hard times, when the old families were beginning to pack their silverware and the gondoliers ferried those latter-day patricians for free; these fallen gentry, ashamed by their circumstances, entered the gondolas directly from their damp lower rooms. Everyone hoped the sun would shine or rain would fall the very next day, but the fog did not lift, and fear moved into the city. People moved through the streets like apparitions and living masks, and they spoke to each other only in Venetian dialect. When they noticed someone who looked like a stranger approaching in the fog, they were to say in Venetian: 'Be vigilant, a German spy is on the lurk', and the other was to reply: 'Vigilant, for king and Fatherland!' That meant that two good Venetians had passed each other. Unfortunately, German spies still walked the streets despite these precautions. To make matters worse, these spies were not Germans or other foreigners who could easily be recognized by their speech; they were Venetians too, who knew the dialect well and merrily greeted each other with 'Be vigilant, a German spy is on the lurk'. Everyone was out and about; the musicians still played and sang, and their tiny monkeys beat unceasingly on little cymbals.

Singing was the easiest. Or was it? There were two singers who would no longer sing in 1917, although it could be said that one of them did sing after all, albeit in a strange way. Florrie Forde, the plump, Australian music-hall singer who had replaced the runaway German, Lilian Schmidt, in London didn't sing a single song in 1917. She continued to hold tea parties and soirées in her sunny flat in Royal Hospital Road all year, but she refused to sing with piano accompaniment again. She pretended to have been indisposed, to have had a few problems with her vocal cords, and said she would be making arrangements for another concert the very next day—she so looked forward to inspiring her devotees from the West End to Edith Grove again. But it was a lie. She was lying to herself and others, and she knew it best when she sang 'Oh, what a Lovely War' or 'Daisy Bell' to herself in the evenings, quietly so that not even the mice in the walls would hear her. After her involvement in what she still called the 'spy affair', this plump Australian thus began to pale in people's memories. The young musicians she so loved now came to visit her ever less; audiences no longer remembered her; and in the end Florrie Forde became a lonely has-been. She lived on a small pension and had to scrimp and save, although she still had a golden voice in her throat.

No one will probably know what Hans-Dieter Huis had in his throat, except the mysterious laryngologist Dr Straube, who worked in a house surrounded by water lilies, canals and reeds, and had prescribed the soldier Huis a strange potion which smelled of tannis root. It made the former baritone mutate, causing his voice to climb to ever higher registers. In 1916, he first became a dramatic tenor, then a buffo tenor and finally a lyric tenor. The whole of Germany, all the way to the trenches on the Western Front, was enthusiastic when the former baritone Hans-Dieter Huis intoned 'Tuba mirum' from Mozart's *Requiem* like a real German lyric tenor. People put the fluctuations in his voice down to stress, and the soldier Huis was happy for just one evening, and perhaps the two following ones, when the same musicians repeated the *Requiem* as an encore. Already by the third concert, Huis had problems finishing the 'Tuba mirum' because his voice became squeakier and squeakier. It was unstoppable.

Just one week later, he was no longer able to sing the pieces written for lyric tenors, only remnant pages from the baroque period, intended for the historical castrati voice. But now Huis took no pleasure in anything any more. He felt like a man in no-man's-land, because he knew he would only stay in the register of counter-tenor for a day or two. He spoke in a very high-pitched, wheezy voice when people were still able to hear him. Then Huis became speechless to everyone around him. He didn't lose his voice, strictly speaking, but it went beyond the range of human hearing. No one could now hear what the once great-est baritone of the German stage was saying. However, Berlin's dogs could still hear him! The former Don Giovanni soon learnt that those four-legged friends were his sole audience, so he walked the streets and sang with all his might, intoning everything he could remember and everything he could in any way adapt to his unnaturally, inaudible voice. And the Berlin dogs stopped and pricked their ears. Mozart's arias sounded like divine howling to the canines. Poodles and boxers listened to him, dachshunds and bird dogs, Russian wolfhounds and St Bernards; strays and pampered pet dogs alike soon began to follow Huis as if he were a pied piper enthralling them with his song. All the Berliners thought this was the end—the famous Huis had obviously gone crazy. Inaudible to humans, he paced the streets bareheaded and with his mouth open as if singing, while the dogs followed him in packs and howled as his choristers.

THE REVOLUTION TRAVELS BY TRAIN

It was the beginning of November by the new calendar. Old Europe was dying inch by inch in the fading West - in the frivolities of Paris, the uncertainty of London, the one-sidedness of Berlin, the twilight of Rome and the fires of Vienna. The East, at that time, was also breaking and crumbling like a dilapidated facade, under which the walls of the old Duma and the rotten beams of landowners' estates were giving way. The masses were arming themselves and preparing for insurrection everywhere from Trieste to Königsberg and from Pécs to Berlin, but the fever was running highest in Petrograd. The first snow fell in early November 1917, when the licentious Russian capital lived out its last Babylonian days.

The gambling clubs where champagne flowed and stakes were raised as high as 25,000 roubles operated feverishly from dusk till dawn. Bejewelled prostitutes draped in precious fur coats walked up and down in the city centre and populated the cafés. Monarchist conspirators and German spies were their clients, as were bold smugglers and worried landowners selling off their properties for a handful of roubles. Many still wanted to halt the mad merry-go-round, to stop and reflect, but feverish Petrograd raced on and on beneath the grey clouds and the first severe frost. Where was it heading?

At the corner of Morskaya Street and Nevsky Prospekt, detachments of soldiers with bayonetted rifles were stopping all private automobiles. They threw out the passengers and ordered the drivers to head for the Winter Palace. A little further along, in front of Kazan Cathedral, it was the same sight: the automobiles were ordered to drive back to Nevsky Prospekt. Just then, five or six sailors appeared with the ribbons of the ships Aurora and Zarya Svobody on their caps. They whispered to the arbitrary traffic policemen: 'Kronstadt has rebelled, the sailors are coming.'

The Bolshevik Petrograd Soviet was in constant session at the Smolny Institute. Delegates fell to the floor from fatigue and lack of sleep, and then got up again to continue taking part in the debates. On 19 October by the old calendar, or 4 November by the new, the most important revolutionary meeting was held. Comrade Trotsky spoke: 'The Mensheviks, SRs, Kadets, Kerenskyists, various Danites, buglers of General Kornilov and those who attended ambassador Buchanan's East-West Divan are of no interest to us.' Then a delegate of the 3rd Bicycle Battalion stood up: 'Three days ago, the bicycle corps on the South-Western Front were ordered to move on Petrograd. The order seemed suspicious to us, and at the station in Peredolsk we met the delegates of the 5th Tsarskoye Selo Battalion. We held a joint meeting and established that not one cyclist was willing to give his blood to support the government of the landowners and the bourgeoisie.' Cries of approval; the enthusiasm crescendoed into the smashing of tables and chairs. Comrade Mikhail Liber tried to calm the atmosphere: 'Engels and Marx say the proletariat has no right to seize power until it is prepared, and we aren't prepared yet.' Cries of protest, and a beer bottle came flying from somewhere near the door. Comrade Maratov, constantly interrupted and shouted down, could hardly hear his own voice: 'The Internationalists do not oppose the transfer of power to democracy, but they do not agree with the methods of the Bolsheviks.' Then a tall, bony soldier, whose eyes flashed at the assembled delegates, got up. They called him Lazarus because they had thought for two months that he was dead. 'The soldier masses no longer trust their officers,' he said. 'What are you waiting for?'

What conclusions were reached is not well known. At four in the morning, bands of revolutionaries were seen with rifles in their hands. 'Let's go,' said citizen Zorin. 'We've caught the deputy minister of justice and the minister of religious affairs. The sailors from Kronstadt will be here any time now. The Red Guards are on the streets and intercepting all automobiles with their lights on. There will be no bed for us tonight. Our task is to take over the post and telegraph office, and also the State bank.'

It was Monday, 5 November, and the trams still scudded along Nevsky Prospekt, with men, women and children hanging on to them on all sides. The Hotel Astoria opposite St Isaac's Cathedral had been requisitioned, and all the proponents of self-management who had made the guests pay for every trifle back in February were dispersed. The only two newspapers on sale were Rabochy Put and Dyen, printed in the occupied editorial office of Russkaya Volya. People resold the papers after reading them, and a small group of confused citizens ran into Captain Gomberg, a Menshevik and the secretary of the military wing of the party. 'Has there really been an insurrection?' they asked him, to which he answered: 'Who the hell knows! The Bolsheviks may be able to seize power, but they won't hold it for more than three days. How are they going to rule Russia?!'

Everyone wanted to travel again in those days. The trains carried people, but also apparitions. People went out onto the platforms of Petrograd's Warsaw Railway Station with clothing tied up into round bales, which they rolled in front of them like big balls. There were also elegant passengers, their faces somewhat Turkish-looking, travelling with just one motley camel-hide bag each. In those days, there was a gypsy woman travelling on the trains. She was dressed like a fairground fortune-teller: scarves the colour of borsch were draped across her enormous chest and three layers of colourful skirts covered her haunches. Her black hair was tied up into a bun and her eyes moved restlessly as she studied the disoriented travellers, but she didn't tell anyone's future there in the train compartment. She was starting out from the capital on what seemed a long-planned trip to Tallinn. It took a whole day because some passenger or other was always being thrown out of the train between stations and someone else thrown in. In the afternoon, the train also stopped so that certain officials could be decorated right there in the carriage, and the passengers had no choice but to be the audience at that 'ceremony'. The gypsy woman endured all this in silence. She didn't complain or protest like so many others. Late in the afternoon, she finally arrived at her destination: Tallinn railway station. It was the day before the revolution and she had come to see Jaan Anvelt, the president of the Tallinn soviet. Comrade Anvelt had circles under his eyes which came down to his upper lip. He had not slept more than a few hours in all of the previous week. He had completely lost his voice; it had changed to a shrill whisper and seemed it would soon shift to a register so high that only Tallinn's dogs could hear it.

The fortune-teller found Comrade Anvelt at the core of the Bolshevik committee, in a requisitioned wooden building near Tallinn's castle. She said she wanted to convey him an important message. While she was waiting for him men wearing braided northern caps bustled in and out and pushed her aside time after time, and the fortune-teller's thoughts hovered precariously over the world of the dead, which Gypsies may have insight into but are never allowed to mention or meddle in. Once again, 'yesterday' seemed to her the same as 'tomorrow', and almost ritually she spoke to herself the word 'taysa', which means both 'yesterday' and 'tomorrow'—a blended 'yesterday-tomorrow'. Then she laughed as if to cast off those concerns, as if she was not in Tallinn to enter the dangerous nether world by barque on a river of leering skeletons, but just to deceive someone. At that moment, Comrade Anvelt came up to her. He looked at her, and she saw death in his eyes. Dead Gypsies called out to her: 'Anvelt, Anvelt… he will be Secretary of the International Control Commission of the Comintern: In 1937 he will be arrested… arrested and shot like a dog.' Thus the chorus of forlorn Gypsies cried out to her, but she just smiled. She had come to lie to Jaan Anvelt, not to tell him the truth. She offered him her hand, and when he accepted it she shook hands with him politely, then bent at the waist into a bow and kissed his hand. 'I know you don't believe in prophesies, but I foresee a great future for you. I've come to greet Comrade Jaan Anvelt, the first president of Soviet Russia.'

Then she quickly turned and dashed straight back to Tallinn's yellow, railway station. There she boarded a compartment once again. She pretended to be asleep, and with her eyes open just a slit she contemplated the coming and going of travellers, mothers quietening their children and handsome officers casting sullen looks all around them. She returned to the capital on Tuesday, 6 November by the new calendar. Just an hour or two before the storming of the Winter Palace, the gypsy woman managed to find Comrade Vladimir Alexandrovich Antonov-Ovseyenko. A few hours earlier he had taken command of the Red Guards, who were to seize that vile nest of tsarism. Comrade Antonov-Ovseyenko was ruffled when he came up to the fortune-teller. He brushed his rebellious hair from his forehead and looked more like a scrawny bourgeois than a revolutionary. His mouth, however, spoke a different language as he pedantically issued the final commands. He didn't know why he had even took notice of the gypsy woman when the Winter Palace was about to be stormed. She stood there in silence, and he screamed: 'What damn Junkers? Kill them! What, women soldiers in the palace? They need a good raping!' Then she offered him her hand, and he accepted it with reluctance. She saw that Antonov-Ovseyenko was a dead man too. Death had already begun to take control of his bones and his limbs; only his eyes didn't know it yet. The gypsy woman knew that this revolutionary would also become just unsavoury food for the revolution. She saw that he would be arrested in 1938 and that his position as people's commissar for justice wouldn't save him, but she had come to delude him too. She quickly bowed and kissed his hand, as if he was a king, but he snatched it back in revulsion. 'Don't believe a fortune-teller,' she said to him, 'but I've come here, near the Winter Palace, to presage the great future which awaits you. I greet Comrade Antonov-Ovseyenko, the first president of Soviet Russia.'

Before the Bolshevik commander could say a single word, the gypsy woman turned and, plump though she was, vanished into the crowd of nervous Red Guards. That night, in the express train for Kronstadt which had been decorated with little red flags out on the track, she heard that the Winter Palace had fallen. The air in the compartment was full of coal dust. A grumpy conductor wanted to check people's tickets, but none of the passengers had one. The whole night passed in quarrels and bitter political debates. The gypsy woman reached Kronstadt in the early morning of Wednesday, 7 November. The oily November sun shed its feeble rays, too faint to warm the revolutionary earth, but the fortune-teller was not cold. She made straight for the Kronstadt Sailors Soviet and promptly found the sailors' leader, Stepan Maximovich Petrichenko. She went up to him just as he had unfurled a black banner which had a crossed rifle and scythe and was embroidered with the words: 'Death to the bourgeoisie'. His large mouth, which always looked like it was smiling, opened wide as he shouted orders to the sailors. His voice was hoarse and rough, but it seemed he could shout forever. The gypsy woman saw that this leader of sailors would be in exile as of 1921, but she repeated her choreography with a kiss on the hand and told the same future again for the revolutionary: 'I see you as the first president of Soviet Russia.' And with that she was gone.

Who knows how many ebullient souls she visited in those five revolutionary days and why she prophesied to those who would be devoured by the revolution that they would become the first president of Soviet Russia. Did she want to strengthen the volition of those cogs in the machinery of insurrection? Was she sent by comrades Kamenev and Zinoviev? Could she have been a messenger from the world of dead Gypsies? The answer is known only to the trains of the revolution.

The actor Yuri Yuriev also decided to take a train-trip, but not until the week of 11 November by the Gregorian calendar. During the first five days of the revolution, while the gypsy fortune-teller was travelling by train, he simply couldn't make up his mind. Besides, there were performances on Monday 5 November and all that week: the Krivoye Zerkalo (Distorting Mirror) Theatre was staging a lavish production of Arthur Schnitzler's play *La Ronde*, his Alexandrinsky Theatre was putting on repeat performances of *the Death of Ivan the Terrible*, directed by Vsevolod Meyerhold, and one in his honour was to be given on Friday, 9 November 1917 on the main stage of the theatre. He was also performing in Lermontov's *Masquerade* and couldn't go anywhere before that important event. Besides, he didn't think there was really a revolution going on—he felt that the difficulties would pass, and that the unrest was abating day by day. But he was wrong. The revolution marched on with hobnail boots, and by the next week the actor Yuri Yuriev was no longer able to think all difficulties would pass.

He felt miserable. He was hungry, first and foremost: And thirsty: And dirty: And desperate. He found an old pistol, pointed it at his chest and anticipated a theatrical death. He got what he wanted: the bullet corroded in the barrel, the operating rod jammed, and no theatrical blood was shed. Then he arrived at a salutary idea: a great performance was being acted out in Petrograd, in the streets and palaces. He simply needed to 'drop out of the play', just as he changed roles freely and went from one script to another. In the week of 11 November, he too made up his mind and set off for the railway station to leave Petrograd. Most people were heading to other cities, but Yuriev was travelling to another play—one in peaceful settings with white snow, a wooden dacha with a Russian bathhouse attached, and a beautiful woman making a homely fire in the hearth. Yes, he decided to find himself just such a play when he arrived at southbound Nikolaevsky station with its impressive, tall, glass dome; but when he arrived he saw its panes were dirty and a litter of fallen branches prevented much light from getting through.

Yuri Yuriev's intentions were not much different to those of the other travellers at the railway station that day, although he was an actor and a bard. The waiting rooms were hopelessly overcrowded. People had to jump over other exhausted travellers who had lain down on the floor; they coughed desperately and loudly, only opening their eyes occasionally as if they had been pushed into the nether world, where sooner or later they would start to decay and make human humus. Those who were still on their feet had to jump over them carefully because there were some among those Hadean people who still had enough strength to shout at anyone who bumped them or woke them from their comatose sleep.

The actor hopped over two or three bodies in the second-class waiting room and sat down at the only vacant spot on a wooden bench, between a corpulent woman and a completely emaciated one. The fat woman spoke to the other, who was young and had a pock-marked face: 'I'm telling you, pet, the most important thing today is to pack properly. It's best to take as much as you can in terms of textiles: different kinds, multiple changes of clothes, for Novosibirsk and for Sochi! And travel in a worn-out old jacket, certainly not a fur coat. Divide up your things so there are little bundles for the children and larger ones for the adults. And forget about baskets and big suitcases—who's going to haul them? Roll things up in bales instead. You should always hide something embroidered with silver or colourful thread in the middle of the bundle in case you need to barter for food on the trip. Don't forget salt and tobacco, but that's always at your own risk.'

How had Yuri Yuriev set off on his journey in search of the new play? With two bulging suitcases and wearing his best Prince Albert coat! Now he slapped himself on the forehead and went back to his flat in Liteyny Avenue. With the help of his neighbour Mrs Zavrotkina, a good soul and future head of the tenants' collective who always had her fellow residents' welfare in mind, he took his things out of the suitcases and wrapped them into bales. He hid his best piece of clothing in the middle, as he had learnt. Zavrotkina told him that he shouldn't go on his journey unarmed; he had to have some kind of weapon, even if it be the rusty old theatre pistol he had been unable to kill himself with. So he put a revolver in his luggage, took off his Prince Albert coat and put on an old one he had bought back in 1882. Once a handsome black piece of clothing with showy silk lapels, which were now worn to such a shine that he could see his reflection in them. Before he left, Zavrotkina tore this museum piece a little at the back and said: 'Now you can go on your trip! Farewell, Mr Yuriev, and may God be with you.'

Yuri was now properly ready and started on his journey with a bundle on his shoulders like a cheerful actor going off into a comedy to flee from a tragedy. He arrived at Nikolaevsky railway station again, jumped over those human dregs which lay heaped on the marble slabs of the waiting rooms, and went out to the platforms. He was surprised to see that not a single train stood beneath the station clocks, which were still keeping time. A passer-by told him that the trains were not being boarded from the platforms but a good half a verst down the line, near the departure signal. Since there was no one to clean the stations and approaches, the engines came up to the edge of the rubbish and stopped there, as ordered by Vikzhel, the swaggering railway workers' committee. The actor therefore had to hurry, and he felt the advantage of the new clothing and his re-formed luggage for the first time as he slung the bale up onto on his shoulders and headed off with rapid steps.

But he was still out of breath, his embarrassment causing beads of sweat to form on his forehead when he arrived at the trains.

Several trains were waiting for their passengers. The engines lazily churned out puffs of grey smoke, which rose phlegmatically, and it seemed as if the fugitives would have to beg them to set off. Only two or three carriages were attached to every engine, like to a stubborn old nag, and there were at least three times as many passengers as the carriages could hold. Yuriev had decided on this journey into the very heart of Russia, to the southern Urals. There he hoped to find his play with the wooden dacha, the bathhouse, some virgin snow, a beautiful woman and a traditional Russian stove. He managed to get into an overcrowded carriage and almost sat on a gypsy woman's lap. 'Sorry, sorry,' he apologized, and made space for himself by squeezing in between the passengers as if they were a pliable human mass. They had to wait at least three quarters of an hour more before the train departed, and in the meantime Yuri listened to the talk of the travellers. 'Kerensky is within reach of the city, here in Gatchina. The smell of his soldiers was on the south-west wind.' 'Cruel General Kornilov already tried to attack Petrograd once this year. He escaped from jail after killing his guards with his own hands, they say, and his savage Turkmen cavalry division is now threatening everyone.' 'The junkers' counter-revolution will begin at midnight. They signed their proclamation: Gotz and Polkovnikov'. 'Is it true that the Bolsheviks have fled to the Aurora and are ready to leave port at any minute?'

The play being staged in Petrograd would undoubtedly be a tragedy, so the fearful actor was glad to be on the train. If only it would leave. Finally it set in motion and started off down the soot-blackened track, past water towers and walls on which the morning's slogans were daubed over with the evening ones. Yuri directed a last glance at Petrograd without curiosity and sentiment. Frozen fields began to alternate with the low scrub of the Russian steppe, and small black birds with yellow breaks flew alongside merrily just a few metres away. This train, too, often stopped. Once it was almost requisitioned for the use of the People's Committee of Ufa and Zlatoust. The passengers were part arrested, part molested and part conscripted out on the track in the middle of nowhere, but later the train was allowed to continue its journey nonetheless. When they had passed Zlatoust, Yuri decided he would find his play in Churilov. That was real provincial Russia. He recalled once having passed through Churilov on the way to the neighbouring city of Chelyabinsk where he acted in Turgenev's *a Month in the Country*.

Yuri could hardly wait to get there and find his peace. After what seemed like an eternity, the train arrived at the small wooden station building in Churilov, and the actor almost leapt onto the platform with his bale. He looked for a cab but couldn't find one. He asked about a bus but was told they all had been requisitioned for use by the soviet of Chelyabinsk oblast. Then he shuddered and told himself he had ended up in the wrong play, again. He had to wait three days in that disaster of a play for the next train. He went to the local market and sold pieces of his expensive clothing 'from the middle of the bale' for a mouldy-smelling chunk of bacon. Finally, dirty and hungry, he just sat and waited for the train to take him away. The next lovely Russian town was Medvedka, but the picture was much the same again, only worse. What looked like a dead man lay beside the platform, and no one thought of removing him; the actor Yuri Yuriev felt he was in one of Shakespeare's tragedies. It seemed nothing but tragedies were played on the Russian stage, but this star of the Alexandrinsky Theatre, in whose honour Lermontov's *Masquerade* had been performed a week earlier, did not think of giving up. He was a celebrated, old thespian and had the right to choose his repertoire.

Back on the train again, leaving Chelyabinsk. Three days and three nights were needed for the next leg of the journey—three terrible, neb-ulous days and three even more terrible, opaque nights—before he made it to Yaroslavl oblast. There he wanted to search for one more ideal little provincial town, Lesnaya Polyana, but when he saw that the revolution had also reached this part of Russia and his longed-for snow, enamelled like a mirror, was no longer to be found anywhere, he took out his theatrical pistol again. The bullet failed this time too. No one knows where the actor stopped on his round trip of Russia, but his neighbour, Mrs Zavrotkina, swore that he never returned to his comfortable flat in Liteyny Avenue.

At Dr Chestukhin's house on Runovsky Embankment everyone was in a hurry again. Bales of clothing were being readied: one for the doctor to carry, one for aunt Margarita, one for Nastia and a small one for Marusya. The Chestukhins had also heard how best to prepare for a journey, except that instead of a gun the doctor put the most essential medical supplies and instruments in his bale. The others rebuked him for taking them, but he was adamant: a doctor does not go travelling without his instruments. So they let him have his way. After rushing about for a while and almost running into each other in comedic fashion as they tried to add valuable oddments to their luggage, they held a family meeting. Each of them put on the table what they thought needed to be taken, and it was quite a display of wealth: a silver-plated samovar, two small icons, an imitation Fabergé egg, two large goblins with bucolic motifs, Liza's two rings of twelve-carat gold with little rubies, the beautiful piece of amber with a bee in the centre, which Sergei had given her for the New Year 1915, the Cross of St George she was awarded on the Eastern Front, and finally Marusya's two favourite dolls. Now the family meeting had to decide what to take. The doctor's instruments remained in their bale, despite the 'auction'. They decided to take the goblins, Liza's rings, the amber, the medal and Marusya's two dolls. They had already gone out the door and, like all fugitives, were asking themselves whether to lock it or not, when Dr Chestukhin suddenly slapped himself on the forehead as if he had forgotten something. He stood there and unexpectedly announced that he had changed his mind: this time they were not going to run away. None of the others protested. They all seemed relieved. By evening, they had unpacked all their things again and hidden the valuables as best they could in holes in the stove pipe and under loose floorboards.

The Chestukhins may have been able to give up the idea of leaving Petrograd, but the Romanovs could not. Their first set of guards was replaced by another; more brutal and less cultured. Someone mentioned to them in passing that the new, Bolshevik revolution had come. Then the tsar's family left on their journey—the complete family, together with the royal physician, Dr Botkin, one maid, and the tsarevich's faithful personal attendant, a former sailor. To begin with, they set off in a special armoured bus adapted 'for purposes of the revolution'. That first stage of the journey didn't last long, ending on the outskirts of the city. They had been allowed to take all the essentials with them: icons, a little of the family jewellery, a silver urn, a small turquoise bird from the Fabergé workshop, one arctic-fox collar each for the tsaritsa and the princesses, a few books from the tsaritsa's library, in which Nilov's *Antichrist* had pride of place, and a change of clothes. No one forced them to make bales of their clothing. At first, the revolutionaries even tried to be, if not friendly, then at least practical and obliging. They told the family they were taking them to safety.

At the second stop, in Tobolsk in Siberia, they claimed the family would be staying for at least several months, but the tsar, going by the dreams in which he had seen others dreaming of him, realized this wasn't the spacious house he had seen. Therefore he told the others: 'Don't unpack, we're leaving again'. Several days later, they were put on board a train. The special carriage, similar to the one in which Nicholas had signed the fateful act of abdication, was sealed and joined to an ordinary train. All the blinds were lowered, and anyone who yelled or tried to come up to the window risked being shot. Their escorts were now not nearly as friendly as in the armoured bus. After three days on the rails with virtually no food, tiding over their hunger with crusts of black bread and weak tea from the samovar, the family reached a small town near the Urals.

When they finally arrived, the tsar didn't recognize this house from his dreams either and again ordered that the family not unpack. They set off on the third leg of their journey separately: first of all the tsar and tsaritsa, then the children. This last journey by ox-cart to Yekaterinburg took almost a week, but when they all finally arrived at Ipatiev Palace, which looked just like the dreamers had seen it, the tsar finally allowed the family to unpack. It was to be their home—their last home—but still a home.

Grand duke Nicholas also found a new home, in the Crimea. He was still considered the generalissimo, and many continued to see him as commander, but he felt like a broken man. So much had come to pass: the abdication of his brother, ten days commanding the Russian forces, being relieved of his duties again, and then his deportation to the Crimea where he was to be kept in complete isolation. He remembered the six-day odyssey by train from Mogilev to Kiev, from Kiev to Petrograd, and from Petrograd all the way to the small station of Simferopol. There he was met by men in an armoured car. 'It's for your safety, Majesty –,' they told him, 'the streets are crawling with bandits these days.' the grand duke was able to see a small excerpt of the surroundings through the driver's window-slit in the metal plate. He caught a glimpse of palms, orange trees, oleander and bougainvillea, and thought a revolution would be impossible in a natural paradise like the Crimea, but he was mistaken.

He was confined to a large colonial house on the outskirts of Sevastopol. Once it had probably been a beautiful house in Moorish style, coated with vines and nestled in a birch grove, but after the death of its last owner it had rapidly begun to deteriorate. The garden around the house was overgrown with weeds and had merged with the surrounding forest. The huge rooms were dark and damp, the wallpaper was torn; dirty, yellowish water dripped from the taps, and large black beetles teemed by the neglected, half-ruined pool. Soon after taking him there, they placed sentries around the house and gave him an old Tatar man and a lady as servants. Those two quiet and industrious people soon put the house in some semblance of order, and the grand duke was able to feel like a nobleman again, albeit one under house arrest.

He couldn't go outside and wasn't allowed to go for strolls along the riviera, and to begin with he wasn't allowed to receive visitors, but none of the restrictions were of great duration. Sevastopol was far from the October unrest, and the soldiers on sentry duty were lazy and easily bribed. The city was under the nominal control of the Bolsheviks, but every little while Cossacks would come on a plundering spree and no one dared to lay a finger on them. The grand duke's sentries therefore saw no reason not to turn a blind eye or two. Soon they let him do everything he wanted as long as their superiors who were far away didn't notice.. Later they pretended to be gentlemen and admirers of the royal family, and in the end they almost became batmen and porters for Nicholas. They ushered in delegations and announced them with an air of importance: 'Admiral Kolchak, Commander-in-Chief of the Black Sea Fleet', 'the Cossack gentleman from Kuban oblast', 'the esteemed representatives of the city of Yalta', 'His Reverend Bishop Vasily of Crimea,' and so forth.

But what audiences they were with such savages! Disorderly, dissolute and disturbing men came to see the duke, proposing that he take command of this and that. On Monday, it was Admiral Kolchak. He came up to Nicholas in dirty trousers and muddy boots, repeating 'Forgive me, forgive me, My Tsar'. As he spoke, he shot arrows from his dark eyes on bloodshot whites, and proposed that Nicholas take charge of the Crimean fleet, making it sound like a threat and leaving him no choice. On Tuesday, the Cossacks who had recently plundered parts of the city came to see him. They had curly, unkempt beards like satyrs and had sabres poorly cleansed of blood... and called on him to revive the Russian Empire! On Wednesday, it was a delegation from the city of Yalta. Three leading female citizens in patched, pre-war redingotes sat opposite the duke, and when they were brought the weak tea and a few insipid buckwheat cakes made by his industrious Tatar housekeeper, they tucked in as if they hadn't eaten for days. Only after the third cup of tea did they tell him that Yalta was an old and rich city, that everything was alright there despite it being in the hands of the Bolsheviks, and that they would like the grand duke to become their fellow citizen and leave that measly house so close to Sevastopol! On Thursday, he again received some careworn soul who had turned grey overnight, on Friday once again someone with traces of blood on their clothes, and on Saturday the Bishop of Crimea, immersed in disappointment and clad in fanaticism.

There had been no end of audiences and receptions for Nicholas in Tsarskoye Selo at the beginning of 1917, and now, towards the end of that unhappy year, it was the same for the grand duke. Things were no better on the opposite, Bolshevik side. Every Ivan was receiving every Vladimir or going by train to rounds of negotiations in those days. People who would never have slept, eaten or even drunk tea together now negotiated with each other daily. Hyenas negotiated with lions, but the hyenas donned lion skins, and lions grinned like hyenas. Leon Trotsky, the one for whom the unknown drunk in Geneva had predicted persecution and death in indifferent foreign climes, was at the peak of his power in 1917. As people's commissar for foreign affairs, he set off for Brest-Litovsk to conduct talks with the Germans and Turks on ending the Great War on the Eastern Front.

He too travelled by rail. One month after the revolution, his train was no longer running several days late, nor did anyone hold it up bandit-like in the middle of nowhere.. In a comfortably furnished coach of the former tsarist government, Comrade Trotsky sat alone at a large desk lit by a lamp with a green glass-shade. It was 22 December 1917; Soviet Russia had concluded an armistice with the Central Powers, and the commissar thought the peace negotiations with them would now be just a formality. He too looked out through the window at the frozen Russian earth, and it seemed to him that even the meagre winter green he saw grew differently under the new system. He had completely forgotten the drunk in Geneva. In his leather suit, with his knobbly face, short goatee beard and moustache, he was now completely in step with his time and felt that nothing could throw him off balance; but he was mistaken.

Only a few people were waiting for him when he arrived at the station in Brest-Litovsk. There were German and Turkish soldiers, and among the small group of travellers who seemed to be stranded there on the Belorussian-Polish border he noticed four strange figures.

The first was a scrawny little gentleman. His tweed suit fastened with the slender belt of his jacket, his nervous shifting from one leg to the other and his vagabond appearance made him the very caricature of a Russian abroad. This traveller's hair was as yellow as straw, his lips raspberry red, pouted and much too full for a man, and his eyes moved erratically as if the optic nerves were not completely in control.

Immediately next to him stood a corpulent woman. She was built like a pear: the pointy crown of her head spread down into full, chubby cheeks; her thick neck continued into huge, flabby breasts, which drooped down to her belly; and this was connected to her sagging behind. She was dressed in skirts and wrapped in scarves like a traditional Russian woman, and her fat buttocks stood out from under her skirt just like the bulging bottom of an enormous red pear.

Next to her there stood a man who could not possibly be Russian. He was a proud foreigner, as straight as a ramrod, with blue eyes and the look of a stuffed bird. He had reading glasses, glasses for special occasions, glasses for the winter. One pair popped into his pocket and another was put on his nose—all the better to see Comrade Trotsky with.

The last stranger in the group struck people's commissar Trotsky as being a German. He had cheeks like inflated silk balloons covered with tiny red veins. He breathed with difficulty, had high blood pressure, and it looked as if winter didn't agree with him. The Russian winter in particular. He seemed to have been waiting for Trotsky too, for quite some time. He was wearing a leather coat, on top of which he had donned two long fur coats reaching down to the soles of his boots. These pelts of polar fox and sable on top of his portly body made him look like some kind of strange bear.

This fourth figure, of such strange appearance, immediately headed towards people's commissar Trotsky, and the others followed suit. It seemed they wanted to speak to him before the Germans did. Trotsky wanted to hide from them, but where? Now they surrounded him on all sides, and he was at their mercy. They touched him and prodded him and whispered in his ear: 'It will be far from straightforward, Comrade Trotsky, it won't be easy at all.' He wanted to run away from them, but fortunately they moved away themselves and proceeded to watch him from a respectful distance with expressions of parental fondness. When the representatives of the German Supreme Command finally came up to Trotsky, the fourth figure was still watching him from a safe distance. They had smiles on their lips and tears in their eyes as if they were seeing him off on a long and uncertain journey.

After several days of talks, people's commissar Trotsky realized that it wouldn't be easy and that the path of negotiations would be full of pitfalls. He had come to demand the restoration of the pre-war situation, but the Germans wouldn't hear of it because they considered themselves the victors. After seven days, the negotiations were suspended so the Germans could return to their families and see in the New Year. 1918. Trotsky decided to take the opportunity to return to Moscow and give Lenin the first report from the negotiations. He went to the Brest-Litovsk railway station and saw that accursed group-of-four there again. They didn't want to surround him now, nor did they think of coming up to him; he just had the impression that their faces were sadder this time.

Back in Moscow, Trotsky naturally forgot about the Western New Year's Eve, and also about those four figures. There had been so much work that he had only slept a few hours a day, sitting at his desk.

Adolf Hitler, the courier of the List Regiment, saw in the New Year 1918 in good cheer. He had been on leave in Berlin and returned to the Front with a jotter full of drawings and plans. In that notebook he 'reorganized' the National Gallery. Hitler did not see why the work of the Bavarian painter Peter von Cornelius was given prominence of place at the expense of artists he considered much greater, such as Adolph von Menzel and the Austrian Moritz von Schwind. He therefore took his notepad and drew up a new plan for the National Gallery; he, the great rearranger, now moved Menzel and Schwind to the central hall, while Cornelius was shifted to a side room. He told his comrades this was just the beginning and that he intended to do over the whole of Berlin, to which they roared with drunken laughter again and showered him with mouthfuls of beer.

The last Austrian emperor decided to spend New Year's Eve with his victorious units at the Italian Front. He made the decision on the spur of the moment and arrived at the banks of the River Piava virtually unannounced, so that his subordinates were unable to clear all the dead from his path. The emperor was a little surprised and felt awkward—they were dead people, after all—but he found the strength to greet the bravest offensive unit of Captain Erwin Rommel as befitted heroes.

New Year's Eve in Paris was cheerful. Old Libion from the Rotonde, Old Combes from the Closerie des Lilas and Old Cambon from the Dôme agreed to share the welcoming in of what they hoped would be the last year of the war: from seven till nine at Libion's, from nine till midnight at Combes's, and the New Year 1918 at Cambon's. When the merry procession of all the artists who had also been at Kisling's wedding set off at nine, they could still walk in a straight line; when they left the Closerie des Lilas for the once despised Dôme at midnight, they were already staggering and tottering. When they came out of the Dôme before daybreak, most of them were vomiting. Apollinaire had drunk and eaten a lot. He started to vomit and eject whole chunks of country-style sausage he hadn't digested. A skinny dog came running up and started greedily eating the meat, to which the drunkard wisely said: 'I knew I'd eaten sausage, but I had no idea I'd eaten a whole dog.'

At midnight, Kiki de Montparnasse passionately kissed the painter Foujita. She closed her eyes and ran her little tongue over his lips, but in her thoughts she already imagined she'd met someone new. As she was kissing him she thought: a fog has fallen on Paris and everyone thinks they can have whoever they find in the street. She sauntered over the Pont Royal, and her new gallant was coming right towards her. Let it be a photographer this time. That's modern now!

At the New Year 1918, the living forty-eight per cent of the still-breathing Fritz Haber envied the dead fifty-two per cent.

How Florrie Forde and Hans-Dieter Huis saw in the New Year 1918 is not worth mentioning. The silence surrounding them was heavier than death.

Boina saw in the New Year 1918 quietly and far from danger, he thought, but he was mistaken. On New Year's Eve, his medals resolved to kill him. How those pieces of sapphire, topaz and gilded nickel came up with the idea is hard to say. It's easier to describe how they intended to do it. They hoped the field marshal would receive an invitation to a celebration from a chief of staff or a young officer he was fond of; as commanding officer, he would then be sure to don his dress uniform. They—the medals he hadn't worn for a long time—expected that he would pin them to it, and then they would have the chance to stab him to death with their needles and the sharp points of their crosses, thus taking revenge for his inexcusable disregard of them. Boina had received a whole cupboard full of decorations but many of them had never been worn in public. It was quite unforgiveable. It therefore had to be a New Year's Eve celebration, perhaps a ball in Trieste, and he should receive an invitation and say to himself: 'Now we're going to get dressed up.' But had he not sworn the previous year of the war, when he went to the Piazza della Borsa all dressed up and felt that his faithful medals were pricking him, that he would never wear his dress uniform again? That's right, and that made the task difficult. The medals couldn't attach themselves to the uniform without help. Fortunately there were a number of junior officers who had dealings with Boina and were on the side of the neglected decorations' in the sense that, from Christmas onwards, they encouraged their commander to dress up for the senior officers' New Year's Eve ball as befitted a commander-in-chief, which would mean putting on all the medals he never wore. The medals counted on that. The ringleaders among the disappointed decorations were St Mary's Cross of the Order of Teutonic Knights, the Austro-Hungarian Silver Bar with Swords, the Golden Medal of the Ottoman Empire, the Mecklenburg-Schwerin Service Cross, the Star of Merit of the Red Cross Society and the Prussian Medal for Service. At first, everything went as the medals had hoped. The invitation came. Boina took out both his uniforms, both helmets of black Bakelite with plumes and both pairs of boots which shone like black gypsy eyes. He began to get dressed... and then suddenly stopped. He decided to go to the party in his uniform without epaulettes, without a helmet and without a single medal, almost like an ordinary soldier. That evening he was the star of Below's table, and the decorations he left to pine in the dark had to wait for another opportunity—one which would never eventuate.

The Red Baron celebrated his last New Year's Eve in the pilots' canteen. The kisses of his sweetheart were as intoxicating as death. Her lips clung to his and it seemed they were fused together forever. The girl's lips tasted of overripe cherries and, although he saw no good in that, they allured him to kiss them more.

Zhivka the seamstress saw in the New Year 1918 with her son in her arms. She had begun to teach Eugene some first words, but instead of 'Mama' or 'aunty' (there was no mention of a father) the very first thing he said was something like: 'ta-ta-tasche'

Sergei Chestukhin spent New Year's Eve by the Julian calendar at home in his house. He read in a magazine that shoes would be changed once a month in Soviet Russia, and a few minutes before midnight he woke Marusya with the words: 'Marusya, dear Marusya, happy new 1918 to you. And for the New Year 1919, you and I will have ten pairs of shoes each!' Marusya asked him if that meant that everyone in the new Russia would have twenty feet, to which Sergei only laughed and let her go back to sleep.

The grand duke saw in the New Year in Sevastopol. He was not looking forward to it, and not a single smile flitted across his stony face. As if the New Year 1918 was yet another onerous audience he had to give. What had he achieved in the year that was ending? He hadn't moved to Yalta, hadn't accepted a single phantom appointment, and had declined all honours as if he was brushing away cobwebs or dispelling apparitions. He saw that his departure from Russia was drawing near and he felt that the only things he would miss in the obtuse world abroad were his unique borzoi hunting dogs, which he would certainly not be able to take with him.

The Sukhomlinovs were... but they are no longer worth mentioning in these chronicles.

Shortly before the New Year 1918, King Peter received an unusual visitor. This stranger in the uniform of a Serbian major did not come before the king like the others: with a mixture of annoyance and indignity at having to bring a matter before the old ruler which he was in no position to act on. Now it was exactly the opposite. Major Radoyica Tatich, a hero of many battles, had to wait in Athens for three days for the old man to give him an audience. First the king's staff had neglected to inform him that the major was coming, and then Peter had to see off several top-level delegations, whose members nodded with such nonchalance that the flies on their foreheads and cheeks saw no reason to fly away. As it turned out, the king received Major Tatich on the last day of 1917 by the Julian calendar.

'What can I do for you, major?' the king asked.

'Nothing, Your Majesty,' Tatich answered to the king's surprise, 'I've come to tell you a story.'

'A story?'

'Yes, a soldier's tale. You may have heard my name, Your Majesty— I am a hero from the Drina and Kaymakchalan. You've awarded me three medals: one for the battle on accursed Mount Kaymakchalan in the terrible, biting cold when we charged the Bulgarians with bayonets on St Elijah's Peak, as I'm sure you know. What you perhaps do not know is that I was at the fore of that assault, as well as every engagement before that, without being scratched by a knife or grazed by a bullet in any of the battles.'

'Was it luck or something else?' the king asked.

'Something else, My King. I had a truly remarkable little mirror. I entrusted all my fears to it, and it saved me from danger, madly brave as I was.'

'A strange little mirror indeed,' the king said, 'and how did you give your fears to it?'

'There was a frightened me there in the reflection, who consumed all my trembles and shakes, and grew older and older, and left me invulnerable on this side of the glass.'

Then the king inquired in confidence: 'Would you lend me your little mirror, major? I am afraid of so many things, believe it or not, the chief of which is death.'

'I can't, Your Majesty, because I've already given the mirror away.'

'To whom?'

'To a hero, Major Lyuba Vulovich.'

'Vulovich… that name rings a bell… so he is now a hero with your mirror, and you are vulnerable like Achilles with his heel? Anyway, what has become of Vulovich?'

'He died, Your Majesty.'

'How? Did the mirror break, or did its effect wear off?' the king wondered.

'It seems so, My King. Vulovich's death was probably inevitable, so not even the mirror could save him.'

'We'll raise a monument to him when we return home.'

'Yes, Your Majesty.'

Then the king got up and asked the hero Tatich: 'Will you not stay for supper? It's late, and soon the New Year 1918 will be with us.'

'I can't, Your Majesty,' Major Tatich declined, 'I promised my friend that I would inform you of his end, which I have duly done. Now I need to hurry: the overnight express train to Salonika leaves in less than an hour, and I have leave only until morning. Farewell.'

And with that, Tatich left. He saw in the New Year 1918 by himself on a platform of Athens railway station. The train arrived one hour after midnight. Tatich got up. 'There, my friend. I've kept my promise.

I even knelt before the king, but he too had forgotten you,' he muttered to himself, and entered the train.

1917, the year of the tsar, came to an end in Ipatiev Palace in Yekaterinburg. Tsar Nicholas and his family saw in the New Year eating from an odd assortment of plates. His fork clanked against the side of the china—like in the visions of his dreamers in the future—and he prepared to act like a coward in asphyxiating himself by intentionally swallowing a fishbone.. He chose a suitable one, looked down the table and was silently taking his leave of each of the children, when he stopped. He recalled the words of the philosopher Nikolai Fyodorov: "The spirit of brotherhood should not be limited to the people living here and now. Humankind is a whole, and the spirit of fraternization must be extended to the dead—'our fathers'." Nicholas spat out the suicide fishbone and smiled at Anastasia, who looked at him as if she understood everything immediately. He kept eating and remembered the thinker, Vladimir Solovyov, who had foreseen that the followers of Christ would be reduced to an oppressed minority without the power to impose their will on others. All earthly power would thus pass into the hands of the Antichrist. What did that mean to him on the last day of 1917, imprisoned in Yekaterinburg and surrounded by guards who were celebrating New Year's Eve in the next room and bellowing like wild beasts? What did it mean to him that Solovyov also foresaw the unification of all Christians before the end of the twentieth century and their ultimate triumph on earth? He decided he would kill himself and wait with Fyodorov in the galley of the dead for those new Christians in the two thousandth year. The dead tsar and the dead philosopher would join them there. Again he readied the white, thorn-like suicide bone, pushed it to the back of his palate… and then gave up like a coward once more. The whole of 1917, the year of the deposed tsar, had been like this, he thought: like a fish which offered its bones and rubbery back to everyone who wanted to choke themselves. He would kill himself the following year as soon as Tsarevich Alexei had regained a little strength, he thought, but he was deluding himself. And in that illusion ended the year of that tsar without a tsardom.

1918

THE YEAR OF
THE CRIMINOLOGIST

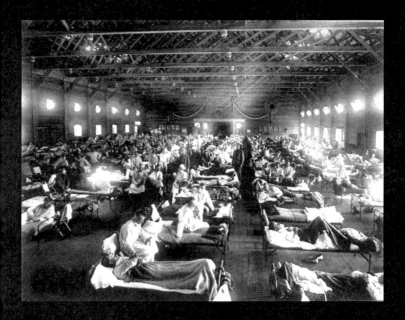

Military hospital in Britain, and rows of H1N1 flew patients, 1918

THE END – KAPUT

'What has this war done to people? As a criminologist, I had expected that it would turn people into animals and even reconciled myself to the fact at the bottom of my justice-loving heart. Nor was it necessary to be a psychologist or clairvoyant to tell that it would turn people into cowards. But the realization that it can turn a person into a poisonous and cynical intellectual gave me quite a fright recently. I came back from Corfu after three weeks of watching Serbian politicians savagely fight for power and provoke one ministerial crisis after another. Disgusted that the Serbian name, unblemished on the battlefield, was being sullied in this way, I myself was ashamed, although I am a native of Switzerland. I walked the streets of Salonika, fed the pigeons and thought I would never speak a word to anyone again.

'Quite unexpectedly, however, an outwardly amiable and genteel Serb came into my life. We soon became friends, but I have to admit I was careless. When I think back to the first few hours of our friendship, I realize that I only asked questions, like every foreigner, and he, like a real Balkan gentleman, never tired of replying. I thought I had finally found a proper intellectual: we spoke long and passionately about ancient Greece and her bronze heroes, with much old stone verse, especially Homer, which that amiable officer surprisingly knew by heart. Perhaps it was his reciting of that archaic Hellenic language which captivated me. Admittedly I've also read Homer in Greek, but I've never been gifted with an encyclopaedic memory for verse, even entire poems, in my own or any other language. My new friend was evidently quite unlike me. The first verse of the *Iliad* rang in my ears: "Menin aeide, Thea, Peleiadeo Akhileos oulomenen, e muri Akhaiois alge etheke", and in Greece it resonated with greater force and solemnity than it would have anywhere else.

'After a few days had passed, this newcomer began to reveal himself and increasingly brag about his speculative knowledge. Ever more often I caught him in superficialities, flimsy contradictions and insidious conclusions, be it about Nietzsche and other modern philosophers or Beethoven and his successors. But there was nothing I could do to get rid of him, and a good part of the blame certainly lies with me. He came to my little flat every day determined to spend time with me, as if he didn't notice my growing sense of discomfort. Once we went for a little excursion to the south, to the pretty Peloponnesian beaches and the glittering Aegean which hugs them, and there he told me all sorts of things. A second time we went for a walk in an olive grove on the northern outskirts of Salonika, where he told me enthusiastically that every wood he enters reminds him of Beethoven's forest from the *Pastoral Symphony*, which beautifully imitates the chirping of birds. What birds, what symphony?! We were just one month away from the great offensive on the Salonika Front, intended to obliterate everything which still had a toehold on life. Perhaps it was that proximity of death, and nothing else, which prompted young Kapetanovich to enlist me as one of his confidants and tell me his life history. It strangely resembled his glib, self-satisfied opinions.

'He started back in the last century, but I'll spare you the petty-bourgeois flights of fancy from his heroic childhood. When his tale and that of his family reached 1914, I got quite a fright because young Kapetanovich didn't think of omitting any of his depravities. He only sanitized things to the extent of covering them with a layer of moral make-up and trying to present them in the best light. Like so many from the Balkans, he probably considered that I was a naive foreigner and would accept everything at face value. He told me most openly: "The truth is, my good Mr Reiss, that I never intended to die in this war. But is that a shortcoming? You'll say it's cowardice, but I would reply that it's a heroism which will be celebrated. Look at it this way: millions have been killed, and tens of thousands more will join them this year. Whoever went out to challenge death at the wild River Drina and on the slopes of Mount Suvobor in 1914 can no longer be alive today, you'll agree. And the dead, my good sir, are remembered by no one. The best way is to hide away, like I did, and then to join in the final battle—looking after number one, of course—and march in with the victors. You're talking to a future Serbian hero here, let that be clear. But since you and I are friends, I can tell you: I've never really been a hero."

'After that prelude, I had to admit that all the arguments were on his side. The capricious fellow seemed to know that and went on to tell me how his illustrious contribution to the war effort began. He arrived in Shabac the day before the Great War started, on 29 July 1914 by the Serbian calendar, driving his father's automobile. A child of rich parents. He was wearing an ironed, grey-blue reserve officer's uniform. One glance beyond the limousine's footboard was enough to seduce the major's virtuous wife, Ruzha. He invited her to get in and took her for a drive around Shabac, then they went into a wood by the River Sava. He repeated to her, too, that every forest always reminded him of Beethoven's *Pastoral Symphony*, and then they made promises to each other and came up with a plan. That ruined the life of a major and took the major's wife off into the unknown. And listen how the culprit lamented about it four years down the track: "You mustn't overlook, sir, that I also did Ruzha a favour. What would she have had if she didn't meet me? She would have become a widow in the first week of the war one way or another. This way she was at least free, and eloping gave her a fresh lease of womanhood. Like in the picaresque novels which libertine ladies have devoured since time immemorial. I mean, who would dare say that I used her? I took her with me to Bitola, where my father had arranged me a posting as far away as possible from the Front. Oh, how I enjoyed my time with her. She was all mine: like a moth which flies around a flame. She cast away her old life—lock, stock and barrel—and no longer had anyone to call her own. But, as you can imagine, it soon began to bore me. I left Bitola very quickly, towards the end of September. Without her, of course. Later I was told that she was looking for me, and that she quickly declined and ended up outside the church as a beggar woman, lying to naive people about having been ruined through no fault of her own. But what did that have to do with me? I never promised her a secure old age, only another fling of youth, and that's what she got: my youth, Mr Archibald, for three weeks. She has to make good by herself for the rest, isn't that right?"

'This really has gone too far, I thought, but instead of protesting I kept quiet, and Kapetanovich continued his tale. He told me he had been a member of the Serbian parliament since 1914 and adduced this as another reason why he would eventually end up as a hero. It was he, together with Velizar Vulovich, who proposed the disgraceful law allowing members of parliament to be called up but not sent to the front line, which he justified with the logic of the probable and the necessary. Then there was the story about the parliament being transferred from sunny Corfu to even sunnier Nice. That was the shameful episode where those shirkers, who were meant to be representing a heroic, warrior nation, thought the island of Corfu wasn't comfortable enough, and perhaps not safe enough, so they decided to shift their seat to the Côte d'Azur. My friend Kapetanovich had a fine excuse for this too: "What would have happened if we'd have stayed on Corfu? The government would have dragged us into its whirlpool of factional squabbling and we wouldn't have been able to make sober decisions for the good of our displaced nation. No, Dr Reiss, we had to move further away from Serbia in order to regard it properly, as a whole, to love it even more and decide what was best for it."

'After two winters of parliamentary contentment on the Côte d'Azur, my young friend returned to Salonika after all. He came right on the eve of the decisive offensive, probably in order to prepare for heroic deeds in the Great War, as planned. And that brings us up to the present day. Young Mr Kapetanovich is ready to return to freshly liberated Belgrade, which he described to me as a city of doom and gloom ("Imagine who has survived there: human abominations and moral degenerates"), but he also seems to be itching to go. I didn't believe my friends and didn't have confidence in the military might of the enemy, but I still thought: he can't go riding into Belgrade just like that. He'll be met by a stray bullet with his name on it, even if he's surrounded by a hundred staff members and officers. So I said to him: "Goodbye, Mr Kapetanovich. I hope Belgrade will be at least a little nicer than you expect."'

'I bid my mother goodbye. She had snarled at me: I hope they catch you today. I'm not taking you down to the Baudeocque for an illicit abortion, and I'm not coming to look after you. She called me a "slattern" and a "strumpet" and threw me out into the street. Take me back, Foujita, please. I get wet thinking of you. Your sweetheart, Kiki.' Alice Ernestine Prin, alias Kiki, wrote this on the back of a greasy calling card with two or three spots of red wine, and tried to have it passed via ten hands to Foujita the painter, who was sitting in a happy circle of drinkers at the other end of the Café de la Rotonde. Kiki's name wasn't on it, of course—she never had a calling card of her own; it belonged to a stained-glass artist, who wrote his important name with a flourish: Pierre-Henri-Michel Orlan. The first pair of hands accepted the card and understood where it had to go, but the second and third pair of hands diverted it a little from Foujita's direction, and the fifth and sixth pair sent it straight to the bar; where, like a stray lamb, it was seized by Old Libion. He took the card in his meaty hands, read the message and began to snigger. Then he read it aloud: 'I bid my mother goodbye… I get wet thinking of you. Your sweetheart, Kiki.' Then he turned over the card and, as if he didn't realize that Kiki had written it to Foujita, yelled out: 'Is there anyone here by the name of

Pierre-Henri… just a minute, Pierre-Henri-Michel Orlan? Where are you Orlan? Pipe up, you lucky dick, this girl is creaming herself at the thought of you!'

The whole café burst out laughing, Kiki sank deeper into the man's coat she was cloaked in, and Foujita didn't as much as cast a glance towards the bar. So ended another of Kiki's romances. She was homeless again. She would have to sleep at her friend Eva's. Eva had a little room in Plaisance with a metal bedside table and a double bed of brass rods, which was big enough to sleep three. Eva was not a prostitute, or at least she claimed not to be. She didn't make love for money; in the last year of the war she made do with food, tins of 'Madagascar', and even the odd, not exactly aromatic sausage she had been given by a cavalier. Kiki was still young, and yet she felt her life had reached a dead end; she had arrived at a wall with dishevelled trees jutting up from behind it and there was no way through—but then the last German offensive began. It was 21 March 1918. The dull rumble of long-range artillery could be heard even in the centre of Paris. After the defeat of the French Northern Army Group at Chemin des Dames, the Germans were once more only twenty kilometres from the capital. Georges Clemenceau decided to replace General Guillaume, Commander of the Eastern Army Group, and General d'Espèrey, Commander of the Northern Army Group. Paris was under siege again. The Germans had a fine view of the city from the hill of Montparnasse until, after a morning drizzle, it became enveloped in thick fog.

The Parisians seemed to go mad with fear and uncertainty in that spring haze. Their strange behaviour was not so visible on the first day, but when the wisps of mist hadn't lifted by noon on the second it became clear that people had turned wild and voracious. It was first noticed on the Pont d'Austerlitz: strangers out walking went up to each other. He would say: 'I am Jean Fabro, a picture-framer, and from now on your husband.' She would answer: 'I am Hana Mendiczka, a linotypist, a Polish refugee, and glad to be your wife,' and they would take each other by the hand as if they were a couple that had been seeing each other for a long time. On the other side of the bridge it was the same sight. He said: 'I am Roger Rubod, a variety-show actor, a clown to be precise, and I'm your husband'. She replied: 'I am Bernarda Lulo, a cab driver and I'm all yours.' One couple was just like another. As soon as someone went onto the Pont d'Austerlitz and met a stranger coming from the opposite direction, they had a new partner. All of a sudden no one was alone; husbands cheated on their wives there on the bridge, and wives left their husbands in the blink of an eye.

People who were not yet love-struck heard about this affliction and hurried to the Pont d'Austerlitz, but there was no need to jostle there because a similar phenomenon was soon to be observed on the Pont National, Pont du Alexandre III and finally on one of the oldest bridges over the Seine, the Pont Royal. Soon everyone became everyone else's companion in Paris. In the four days the fog oppressed the city, everyone found alternative partners, but they never went all the way in their adultery. They petted and passionately embraced, hidden in the fog; women wantonly raised a leg and wrapped it around the men while they were kissing, but the couples from under the bridges split up after a few blocks or neighbourhoods, as if their parading was only for the benefit of that pervasive fog. Even so, for many it was beautiful because men who were far from handsome hugged belles just because they met them in the middle of a bridge, and pale wormettes from the suburbs walked with cavaliers two heads taller than themselves all the way along Boulevard Haussmann. Everyone wanted to find a 'partner in the mist'.

Kiki too plunged into that love haze, but how different everything was now: in a world of the abnormal, she became normal. In the middle of the Pont Royal she met a young man with an elderly forehead and sideburns, but with lively boyish eyes. He said to her with a strong American accent: 'I am Emmanuel Radnitzky, a photographer, and this is my first time in Paris. I've just been here for a few days, but I'd like to be your admirer'. She answered: 'I am Alice Prin, but everyone knows me as Kiki de Montparnasse; I want you to be my protector'. And so the only real love of those four days was born; a passion which was not merely posing for the fog. Kiki became the lover of a photographer, the future surrealist Man Ray. Later he would return to America and did not move back to Paris until after the Great War, but that is a story from a different time.

Manfred von Richthofen also saw a story from a different time on his last sortie on 21 April 1918, a tale told in vivid and unforgettable closing images. That day, the Red Baron was shot down by ground fire from Australian troops—by complete chance, for no reason, and not determined in any way by freak of circumstance or whim of history. He, who was unequalled in the air, who decimated the Royal Flying Corps and was infamous in Britain for having killed the greatest British pilot, Lanoe George Hawker, was brought down by a small-calibre round fired by an almost illiterate infantryman.

Could that whimsical knot of circumstance have been foreseen? The lips of Richthofen's sweetheart didn't tell him anything that last day: they were dry, crisp like autumn leaves and kissed him gently, but they didn't afford him the slightest protection. He spent the last night in his room at the base in Ostend. He looked at the walls where he had scribbled the markings of the British and French planes he had shot down; above him hung a gas lamp hidden behind the propeller and part of the motor of Major Hawker's plane, casting him in a sallow light. He couldn't sleep even that last night of his life. How many pilots had he turned into minced meat? He liked to think he couldn't remember their faces and that only the number of planes he shot down was important to him, but his insomnia, trembling and hallucinations brought it home to him that this wasn't true.

He was almost relieved when he was brought down by erratic fire from the Australian lines the next day. This must be the end, he thought; he was certain of it. The propeller stopped and the rudder no longer responded. He looked in the direction in which he was starting to plunge and saw the slanting line leading to the ground; he realized he would be leaving this world in a number of seconds, a minute at the most, and thought he could finally relax; but then something happened which the mortally-wounded pilot could in no way have expected. On that nose-dive into nothingness, strange aircraft began to close in on the Red Baron's triplane and zoom past.

First of all, he saw a biplane quite like the planes from the Great War, but of infinitely more modern design: with a broad fuselage, larger engine and a metallic front. The plane had German markings, so the dying pilot thought it was a new model made for use late in the war. But why then had they not let him use it first? He almost felt offended as the new aircraft began coming up to him. The next one had a revolutionary new design: the swept upper wings and very short lower ones told him that biplanes would very soon turn into monoplanes; the heart-shaped tail bore a strange symbol unfamiliar to him, like a crooked or folded cross. Only now did he realize what was happening in the last few seconds of his life: he was plummeting to his death but passing forwards through time and seeing the new flying machines of the future. Could there be a nicer end for a fighter ace of the Great War?

The god of the air, the demiurge, the greatest aviator of them all, sent him a procession of planes from the future as a last salute. Richthofen sank back in his seat and watched those airborne wonders approaching him from the horizon. Here were some small, rounded planes made completely of metal. They had one wing bent back like a swallow's and moved through the sky with such incredible ease. Now another strange craft was coming towards him. It had an unusual antenna in the centre of its wing, and a little to the left of it was a long fuselage like a metal cigar ending in a powerful propeller engine. But where did the pilot sit? He was in a capsule positioned a little to the right of the central aerial. What a strange flying machine, but weirder things were still to come: planes without propellers and powered by jet engines completely unknown to him. One strange model with the German coat of arms and that strange crooked cross on the tail looked like a large, elongated egg. The pilot sat at the front in the fully-glazed capsule, with five jet engines arranged around and above him, and three below. That plane looked more like a time machine than an aircraft, he thought—it was so fast.

Richthofen looked around in confusion. The ground was ever closer now. He only managed to cross paths with one more German plane. But was it a plane? The central part of the fuselage had a rotating hub with three wings, at the ends of which were those remarkable jet engines set at an angle of ninety degrees in relation to the fuselage. Their propulsion made the hub turn with incredible speed and it looked to him like a huge, rotating wheel encircling the fuselage. There were no longer wings or a tail on that aircraft, but he didn't have time to gaze into that astonishing future any more. His plane thudded into the parapet of an Australian trench. He felt a second of unbearable pain, which quickly passed. Now he was ashamed that he seemed all sticky and bloody beneath his leather coat. Some soldiers came running, not knowing whom they had brought down, and the swollen mouth of Manfred von Richthofen, full of blood and broken teeth, only managed to say: 'Kaput.'

THE PANDEMIC

The smallest hero of this novel is undoubtedly a virus. This hero is unable to speak, does not have the faculty to love and hate, and therefore cannot be a proper protagonist. But it does not distinguish good from evil, attacks its host with abandon, and as such can be considered a sinister anti-hero. Moreover, the virus is also able to travel, which is undeniably a good basis for a story—the story of the path of a mutated H1N1 virus. This tale, told largely by cold graphs with the numbers of infections and deaths, probably begins in China. Reliable witnesses would not stake their reputation on it, but with a mug of good black beer in hand they would loudly dispute the thesis that the virus mutated and become deadly in Kansas, at the local army bases for training young American soldiers for the Great War. There was evidence enough that the virus had started out from China. That's right, in the forests of China, or on the islands of Fiji, or somewhere else in Asia, which for centuries had been a source of caravan contagions and sailors' diseases. The Pacific Ocean was the cradle of this killer, and only later—the reliable eyewitnesses would agree—did it arrive in America.

The virus scaled sunny Vallejo Street in old San Francisco, which has no shadow at any time of the day, and infected twelve families there. The Jews among them coughed in Yiddish, the Italians seemed to sing 'Caruso' through their tears, and the Poles suffered in a strange mixture of a dry northern European cough and a migrant's expulsion of phlegm. Then the virus moved into Russian Hill and there infected the whole Russian population. Good, taciturn people who didn't know a word of English came down with a high temperature and a chill. They stoked their tin stoves with the crooked chimneys, wrapped themselves up in whatever they had—old rags or colourful scarves—and the women put on a dozen skirts even though it was midsummer. These hard-working people didn't speak with anyone, in Russian or English, but the disease still spread to the artists' ateliers on top of the hills with lovely views down over the gleaming San Francisco Bay. The virus also made a showing in the piano-equipped atelier of the sculptor César Santini, who would take it further into the Continent.

Now not even those reliable witnesses would dispute that the disease had emerged at the army training bases in Kansas, however many mugs of strong black beer they drank. The soldiers who were being prepared for the Great War were young and strong, however, so the pale hue of their faces and their slight coughing was not seen as an obstacle for them to be sent to the Western Front to be killed there. They all started together, the healthy and the sick, by ship across the Atlantic, and soon after the first combat they infected French soldiers near Brest.

At that time, London was still in good cheer. Everyone found a reason to dance, sing or have some fun in the last year of the war. Young musicians came and went at Sylvia Sparrow's house, many satisfied faces dined at the Savoy and the Scott's Arms as if there wasn't a war going on, and the only person who did not partake of that feverish merrymaking in blithe ignorance of Spanish Influenza was Florrie Forde. This once fiery Australian sat silently in her flat in Royal Hospital Road. In the evenings, she would wind up the old gramophone in her room illuminated by a red lamp and listen to the only two records she had managed to record before the Great War. Nothing seemed likely to change in the life of this singer whom all had forgotten, but then Florrie got it into her head that her punishment should end.

She set off for her encounter with fate the same day as Captain Joseph Sylers felt the first symptoms of Spanish Influenza coming on. He had returned home to London from Brest, and Florrie was asked by some old friends to sing 'It's a Long Way to Tipperary' again, for a decorated war veteran. She thought of declining, but unfortunately she agreed. A small performance, her first in almost two years, was arranged to take place at Sylvia Sparrow's. The captain arrived in London and spent the night at his bachelor flat. It was his second night with the virus in his lungs, which had come from the forests of China, or from Fiji. He slept and didn't think he was sick. Only that afternoon, when he put on his dress uniform and set off to the reception to be held in his honour, did he have a slight cough. The captain registered that his sweat-beaded forehead was a little hot, but he put it down to the excitement of being about to hear Florrie Forde for the first time.

So he left from his flat at the edge of Belsize Park, and she from Royal Hospital Road. The performance took place… but why waste words on it. The captain was rapt, and more…but why go into that? At the end of her little performance he jumped to his feet, with the virus inside him. He kissed both the prima donna's hands, and she incautiously fell into his embrace, tear-stained and delighted that her voluntary incarceration was finally over. A week later she fell ill. Her condition worsened by the day. The last thing she remembered was singing a silly little ditty: I had a little bird, / Its name was Enza. / I opened the window, / And in-flu-enza/.

Florrie Forde was the first victim of Spanish Influenza in Britain. The Great War ended for her when her dry mouth hummed that last little song of her repertoire. Florrie Forde was buried the following week in London, along with Captain Joseph Sylers and a good many others, as the virus continued its journey east.

Although he was a doctor, it took Sergei Chestukhin a long time to realize that Petersburg had been hit by the second wave of Spanish Influenza. He can hardly be blamed—it was a time of rapture and haste, when everyone was hurrying somewhere, and the disease was hard to notice at first. The Red Guards marched to the north and the south, rushing to oppose military interventions on the distant borders of the country, in Arkhangelsk and Odessa. Ordinary people hurried about because of ration cards, remittances, errands or the lack of them, or simply because they were hungry. Everyone had some kind of money: Don roubles, Duma roubles, Kerensky roubles. Their hope-filled pockets also contained shares, title deeds for estates, and nineteenth-century tsarist promissory notes for purchased grain; all this had to remain in circulation, to be changed and rearranged following the dictate of rumours and each person's level of nervousness.

Sergei, too, had to go out every day. He put on his woollen, doctor's cloak and rushed to one of the formerly large Petersburg banks; he didn't go in the front door, which was now boarded up, but round the back. There he cashed the cheques he had received instead of ration cards. From the street, the bank looked like a haunted institution where only phantasms and human abominations still stamped forms and counted money, but the door at the back opened at eight every morning. There was a strange counter area looking out onto a side alley. It looked more like a slovenly mail-sorting depot with overtired staff, all of whom had dark circles under their eyes. But this didn't bother Sergei because he, like everyone else, was in a hurry. One day he received money, the next it was strange vouchers. The money could be cashed at the counters immediately at the bank's exit, and the dubious-looking vouchers were accepted at an abattoir in the north of the city which reeked of mould. Both the money and the vouchers needed to be used quickly. That's why the doctor was always in a hurry, and he told his daughter: 'That's the way things are today, dear Marusya—people live fast lives.'

That is how he survived from day to day; he felt he didn't get around to thinking about Liza and had even begun to forget her. But then Spanish Influenza arrived in Petrograd too. It came on tiptoe. Slowly. From northern Silesia. It spoke German, the language of the occupiers, and a little Russian from the White Guards' positions. At first it was in no hurry, but then it saw the bewildered people running to and fro, and it started to rush itself as if it also had to cash an uncovered promissory note. Sergei Chestukhin couldn't explain to himself why he didn't notice the second wave of the contagion immediately. It's true that no one in their building on Runovsky Embankment was affected at first. The stench of decay and disease could not be smelled by the canal and in the riverside puddles in September. Only towards the end of autumn did the city administration instruct each tenant's council to provide one person each day to work as a grave-digger at the municipal cemeteries. Did all that prevent him from noticing the disease until the end of September? Or was he rushing about so much that he had begun to forget his calling?

Only when it was his turn to be grave-digger did he snap awake. He called Margarita Nikolaevna and said he would be leaving the next day and going away for a while; he wasn't being of much use as a father anyway. He told her he would be teaming up with other doctors; he waved dismissively when Margarita warned him it was dangerous; he didn't reply when she asked him what she and Marusya would do alone, now that Nastia had left them, and he pretended not to hear when the good woman burst into tears. He stole out at dawn without casting a glance at Marusya, because he knew he wouldn't be able to leave her if he saw a lock of her hair which was slowly changing from blond to coppery red.

That's why he stole away like a thief and began to mix with the smell of carbolic acid and the taste of death. At first he wore a mask, washed his hands as a surgeon should, and was careful not to have a hangnail or any little cuts on his fingers, but then his vigilance gave way to distress. There were so many patients now that they had to be laid out in tight rows in large tents like human cargo. Each tent had two hundred beds and one duty-doctor. The surgeon and war hero Chestukhin was on duty every second night. Whom could he help of those who coughed so violently, as if they were about to cough up their insides?

Whose temperature could he bring down when the stocks of Bayer's new aspirin from Germany were already running out? He was still able to help and comfort the occasional person in those sleepless nights. Or was he just there because he wanted to ease his own burden? Yes, he was, he thought, and resolved to go all the way.

Every night he was on duty, Dr Chestukhin walked along the rows of patients and looked for the infected woman who most closely resembled his Lizochka. When he found such a patient, with copper hair, pale skin and eyes the colour of sepia, he would devote himself to her and commune with her face to face, heedless of the danger. Instead of doing the rounds of the patients, he would lie beside the moribund woman long after midnight as she spoke confusedly, in a trance, and hugged her tight, wishing for only one thing: to die together with her. He also spoke chaotically, raving as if feverish. He proposed to the dying woman, knowing no one could hear him and no one would stop him. But then his chosen one died, and the doctor passionately hoped she had passed the deadly virus on to him. But his temperature remained normal and he didn't have any stabbing pains in the chest, although every part of him was a living scream. On his next duty he was already sharing the bed with his new fiancée, the sufferer who now struck him as most closely resembling Liza with her flowing red hair. He kissed her and hugged her fragile frame, but she vanished in his arms and melted away like snow in the spring sun. Afterwards another and yet another. He stole up at night and passionately hugged the dying women—but he remained healthy nonetheless.

For Sergei Vasilyevich Chestukhin, the wartime surgeon and hero, the Great War ended when the contagion passed and he was miraculously still alive, although he had cheated on his wife with eyes the colour of sepia so many times. Two months after he had up and left, Sergei returned home to Runovsky Embankment. So shamefully alive, exactly the opposite of a tragic hero, he now continued to rush to the back premises of that once large bank to change doubtlessly valuable gold for dubious money. He told his red-haired daughter again: 'That's how things are, Marusya dear—life goes faster and faster', and she looked at him with eyes the colour of sepia. But he was not the same man any more.

This other man, a certain Sergei Chestukhin, who began to live a life not worthy of being chronicled, hurriedly departs this novel and merges with the dust and smoke of everyday life. He does not stand out from all the others. Even if someone stopped one passer-by after another in the street and peered into their faces, they wouldn't think this pale, drawn fellow was the former wartime hero and truly remarkable neurosurgeon, Chestukhin. Now the doctor did everything as others did. Like everyone else, he didn't hear of the death of the tsar's family until long afterwards; like everyone else, he didn't believe it at first, and later he found no emotion inside of him; and like everyone else in Russia, he never dreamed of the tsar.

It was 17 July 1918 when the last Russian Tsar, Nicholas II, and his family were killed in Yekaterinburg. They were woken in the middle of the night by their drunk, slurring guards, who mumbled that they were being taken to the lower rooms of Ipatiev Palace for their safety, whereas in fact they were to be executed. And the tsar knew it, but he went to the cellar calmly, convinced there was no need to worry. He knew the guards were trigger-happy, but everything told him that the visions of his dreamers in the future were now coming true: he would go down, stop in the middle of the brightly illuminated empty space, and red-nosed and ruddy-cheeked guards would burst in and try to shoot them; but their rifles would jam, and the commander would curse at the firing squad and try to cock his pistol, also in vain.

So the disinherited sovereign descended into the cellar with a sure step, without hesitation. He carried Tsarevich Alexei, since his son was too weak to walk to the execution by himself. He entered the illuminated space and pretended to believe they had been woken up for their safety. Then the wild guards burst into the cellar. 'Death to the Tsar!' they shouted and started firing. Not one bullet got stuck in the barrel, and within just a few minutes all of the family was dead. As soon as the tsar had breathed his last, the years began to race through a time warp and dreamers in future decades began to dream of the tsar. It was 1919, 1921, 1922, 1927, and people kept seeing one and the same dream.

The chef Nikolai Kornilov, since 1921 proprietor of the luxury restaurant La Cantine Russe in Paris, saw the tsar's family in his dreams as vividly as if they were still alive. In that dream, Polish units loyal to General Denikin marched into Yekaterinburg and rushed to the Ipatiev House to liberate the Romanov family. The killers were unable to unjam their guns, so the tsar was saved at the last minute. Thousands had that same dream. Count Razumov also woke up with a start in 1922 and remembered the scene from his dream as if it was real; there, in the slums near the Pont de Grenelle, he looked up at the blue bruises of the morning Paris sky, with a few wet dawn birds cutting across it. The Russian engineer Andrei Vasilyevich Papkov, a constructor of steel bridges in Belgrade, dreamed an identical dream about the tsar in 1927. When he woke up in lower Dorchol, in a courtyard house rented from a Sephardic Jew, little black moths flitted from one downtown garden to another. Eight years earlier, in 1919, Dr Pyotr Vladimirovich Ritikh dreamed of the tsar in Istanbul; when he woke up with a start, petals of apricot blossom filled the air like eiderdown from a torn pillow. And many, many others also dreamed of the tsar.

But the Great War really did end for Nicholas Romanov, the last Russian tsar, and his family when that ominous volley rang out—the salvo so many dreamers were unable to imagine. With his last strength, the tsar looked up at the bare light bulb and its glowing filament. He felt it was blinding him and that a moment later he would lose his eye-sight, but then he truly went blind when the final dark of the shroud fell over him.

The fast rise and hard fall of most tragic heroes is delineated by death; the most unfortunate, however, are punished with life. Roughly in the middle of the pandemic, not knowing that it was wreaking havoc in the Crimea as well, newly arrived, harsh Red Guards placed the Grand Duke and his 'family' under house arrest. There were no longer any sentries who could readily be bribed and turned into orderlies and doormen. The advantage was that, being isolated in this way, the Grand Duke could hardly contract the disease; the disadvantage was that he was just one night away from being taken down to the cellar there at the Dilber estate—allegedly for his safety—and shot together with his Crimean 'family'. But this drama in the Crimea was not a tragedy like in Yekaterinburg, but rather a comedy. Immediately after the grand duke's arrest, a war of sorts began between the Sevastopol and Yalta soviets. The Sevastopol soviet was hesitant, while the Yalta soviet wanted the duke and his family to be executed immediately. In Sevastopol, the soviet consisted of plump, middle-aged men with balding heads, whose eyes still had a glint of old-fashioned dignity. The members of the Yalta soviet were totally the opposite: tall, thin and gnarled. Their eyes flashed fiercely beneath raised eyebrows, and they reinforced every resolution they passed by shouting 'Hurraaah!' or pounding their fists on the table. How many times was the order sent from Yalta, 'Citizen Grand Duke

Nicholas is to be shot', only to change on its way through Sevastopol and the mouth-to-mouth conveying by reliable couriers into 'Citizen Grand Duke Nicholas is to be spared again today'. And it was like that every single day: he was just one night away from being killed.

Three weeks saw three acts of this tasteless comedy full of yelling and screaming, order-sending and chest-beating, seasoned with litres of vodka. The final curtain on that crude Crimean stage, where frogs acted as hyenas, was then lowered by the Germans. Under the Brest-Litovsk Agreement, which people's commissar Leon Trotsky was finally able to sign thanks to no longer being haunted and hounded by those four smiling freaks, the Germans received control of the entire Black Sea coast. Their advance guard, in grey summer uniforms, entered Yalta and Sevastopol in the last year of the war. The revolutionaries changed masks and fled for their lives, no one knows where to. On the way, the good men of the Sevastopol soviet dwelt on those remnants of old-fashioned manners they could dredge up from their memories, while those from the Yalta soviet fled north and further north in compartments of local trains, making lonely resolutions and dreaming of reaching snow and a proper Russian winter, as if it would turn them from frogs into hyenas just like that.

So it was that the Germans came at the last minute and Nicholas Nikolaevich became free again; he was a 'free' man, at least in theory. Half his associates immediately fell victim to Spanish Influenza in freedom, but the Grand Duke was still 'alive', at least in theory. By the end of the year he realized he would have to go into exile himself. Permanently - for life. He couldn't take his borzoi dogs along with him, or his estates and his Russia, a country which resembled a myth, whose grandeur could compare only with the unattainable loftiness of Hellenic kings. Where to go? To the south, where shallow rivers murmured between the roots of orange trees? Or to the north, where the snow would be the only thing which resembled Russia in that baleful, democratic century?

Like so many others, he went to Sevastopol harbour. He was neither tense nor angry. Only his gaze, condescending as once before, looked down on that reality. And that day, his last day in his homeland, was striving to break away from him and bolt as if thousands of zephyr horses were snapping at each other in the air with wide-open mouths, rending the ether like lily-white lace. As he arrived, the cove and the access roads from Cape Kherson and Balaclava Bay were shaken by mighty detonations. White Guard soldiers stood somewhere behind the hills, on the Crimean isthmus. They were dead, like the Peloponnesians of yore, and awaited further orders. And below, by the sea, the docks were brimming over. A very strange procession of refugees came rolling towards the port: magnificent, petrol-less automobiles drawn by six horses, complete home furnishings, ladies with yapping doglets, officers on peasant carts with a suicidal look. You name it, it was there in that procession.

For Grand Duke Nicholas Nikolaevich, alias the Iron Duke, twice appointed commander-in-chief of all Russian forces, the Great War ended as he boarded the steamer Konstantin and grabbed for the railing of the gangway as if he was about to collapse. He didn't feel anything at that moment—a north wind was blowing through his heart—but he had a vague notion that 'history was watching him', so he felt he ought to show at least a little ordinary emotion although there was none inside him. But he was mistaken in his notion, like so many others, because in exile he would join the same anaemic blood group and become just another 'man of the twenty-fifth hour'. History turned its back on him right there on the gangway of the steamer Konstantin when he so theatrically grasped for the railing as if he was about to fall into the Black Sea and drown there in the silence of the water, dragged under by the hull of the ship.

The same day that the Grand Duke exited this war novel and became an ordinary citizen, Lance Corporal Adolf Hitler of the List Regiment was blinded by British gas in one of the last offensive actions on the Western Front. It was 14 September 1918 when he was taken to the front-line hospital and given first aid. Later he was transferred to a reserve hospital in Pasewalk. The doctor in charge concluded that the lance corporal had not sustained any lasting injury to his eyes or respiratory tract, and that his temporary loss of vision had resulted from 'hysterical blindness', while his momentary loss of speech was the effect of 'hysterical muteness'.

That hysterical patient roamed the corridors of the hospital in Pasewalk at the very end of the Great War. He walked through those corridors upright and with a proud step like a real wounded hero, even though he was reduced to touching blunt objects and other patients to do so. He couldn't set down his thoughts in 'Max Osborn's notebook' by himself any more, so he found a young, freckled nurse to do it for him.

His sibilant voice could hardly speak the grand words he wanted to record. Although a different name was on his medical card, he introduced himself to her as Max Osborn, *the* Max Osborn—explorer of the underbelly of Berlin and voice of the heroic Prussian past. He lied that the sketches about German soldiers were drafts of articles he was sending to a tourism journal in Berlin. Directing the hand of that good-natured nurse, he wrote: 'The German soldiers at the Hindenburg Line resemble…', but then he heard that the last line of defence had been breached. He tried to burst into tears, but the gauze over his face impeded him. He thrust away the nurse, who had already fallen in love with him, and sat down on the bed. He tore off his bandages, looked around as best he could, and in the pale gleam he saw the patients' room with its ten beds. Then he spoke to himself in his former, full voice: 'Treachery! Betrayal!'

For Lance Corporal Adolf Hitler of the List Regiment, the Great War ended when he absconded from the hospital in Pasewalk. His medical documentation disappeared that night, too, because he stole it at the last moment and took it with him.

The Great War was over. Or was it?

SILENT LIBERATION

The Great War was decided, but at the very end it had to be sealed with still more dead. General Franchet d'Espèrey, Commander-in-Chief of the Balkan Allied armies in Salonika, visited Serbian Regent Alexander in his log cabin at the front, near Yelak. They spoke about the breakthrough at the front and about recent victories, but their thoughts dwelt on death. Wholesale death. And when such a calamity is in the offing, who notices a little love affair? It was so ephemeral that it was almost overlooked in the small Salonika street where people quarrel every day at four in the afternoon. No. 24 noticed that love affair. For the second floor of that red, three-storey building it amounted to a scandal, but it was still a small romance in the shadow of wholesale death. Major Radoyica Tatich himself was unable to say how it came about. He only remembered that he was given one day and night of leave immediately before the offensive on the Balkan Front so he could return to Salonika and collect his winter clothing from his small rented flat in 24 Ermou Street. It took him half a day to travel from the Front to the Rear. He didn't see anything special on the way, and nothing from that day need be recorded. It was the night which the major would never forget.

Later he was unable to explain to any of his lieutenants how he met the British nurse on the evening of 12 September. Her name was Annabel. Annabel Walden. She came up to him like a shadow, a pale-faced woman who looked exhausted. He stopped in his tracks in the dusty street. She stood facing him. Neighbours from both sides of Ermou Street were bickering in spiteful Greek, although it was long past four and now growing dark. Annabel had short fair hair, a round English face, and eyes like two big buttons sewn on with blue thread. The major turned towards her and stood there enthralled, leaning on his left leg which had been numb since crossing through Albania with what remained of the Serbian army. He looked at her, and she at him. He knew he would be going off to his death the very next day and desperately needed a woman. 'Major Tatich,' he introduced himself, touching the braid of his sheepskin hat. 'Annabel Walden,' she said, as if she had wandered straight out of an English novel from that better, nineteenth century. He offered her his hand. She took it.

He knew only two things: that he had to touch her and that his insides would bloom like an ugly flower on the battlefield if he didn't spend that last night with a woman. But he was a Serb, and she was English. She spoke English and a little Greek. He spoke Serbian and 'trench French'. They climbed the stairs to the second floor of that ordinary, red three-storey building. The major opened the door. They sat down together on the bed in his Spartan room. Nothing there bothered them: neither the odour of dankness and coal dust, nor the broken venetian blinds letting in the last rays of sun from the broad bay. There were no romantic props: neither the aroma of almonds nor the distant song of barefooted women. Nothing, yet they fell in love.

He wanted to say something to Annabel but only had his *Soldier's Phrase Book in Five Languages*. How could he express his love for her? How could he tell her everything he wanted to say? He began to flip through the pages of the little phrase book, but found nothing of any help in the section entitled 'Laundry'. Nor did the 'Post Office' section provide anything which would explain how to say 'love'. He remembered how to say he was sick, and he certainly was lovesick if he desired Annabel so much on that last evening before the offensive. He flipped furiously through the pages up to the section called 'Seeing the Doctor', and he began in Greek: 'Den ime kala', and continued in French 'Je ne suis pas bien', and ultimately in English 'I am not well'. Finally, he added a few desperate words in his own Serbian: 'Ja nisam dobro'. Then he stopped. He turned the pages again. He didn't have diarrhoea or stomach pains, and his tooth, which certainly had caries, was not aching; no, everything hurt. Finally he found the doctor's expression: 'Donnez moi votre main'!

Annabel seemed to understand and to want to give herself to him. 'Give me your hand,' he said and took her by both her cold hands, but she pulled away. He was disappointed. He turned aside a little; she caressed his hair. Finally, he turned his gaze to Annabel again. His shirt was open at the chest now, his penis erect. He no longer knew who he was; he only knew what he wanted. He pushed the Englishwoman down onto the bed, but she slapped him, got up and left the little room. The major was angry now. She had left the room and was standing out in the hallway on the other side of the door. There was now no sound either in the room or in the hallway, and the squabble in the street also seemed to have passed. He listened from the inside, his ear up against the wooden door. She stood just ten centimetres, or four British inches, away from him and clenched her small fists as if she was about to pummel on the door with them. Then she broke the silence. She yelled something in

English, and the ever-ready Greek neighbours gathered. Now Annabel slumped to the foot of the door like an abandoned little animal and burst into tears, and the neighbours began to yell and threaten that they would call the authorities. The major heard that, opened the door and let his Englishwoman in again. He closed the door behind them. Finally he shifted to Serbian. He spoke, and she listened to him as if she understood.

'I once had a mirror, a miraculous little mirror,' he told her. 'I entrusted all my fears to it and was madly brave. You should have seen me at the Battles of Cer, Kolubara and Kaymakchalan, how I rushed and charged. I was the last to leave mud-bound Knyazhevac in 1915, firing behind me with my pistol. I was decorated for bravery three times... but this isn't about me. I had a good friend, Major Lyuba Vulovich. He went too far and got involved in a conspiracy, I don't dispute it. And those who tried him also went too far. He was sentenced to death. I went to his cell on death row, took him the little mirror and told a lie. I told him it would save him, and I did it just so he would be brave and not blench before the firing squad. My friend was a hero and put up a brave face at his execution in that damned quarry. He died a martyr's death, and then I took a trip. Why am I telling you this, Annabel? I took a trip by express train overnight to see our king in Athens. "My King," I said to him, "I had a good friend—a wonderful man, a major like me... He fell, he was killed." And the king? He didn't remember. Like an absent-minded god with a white beard he said to me: "If he died bravely we'll raise a monument to him." Therefore I left King Peter and saw in the New Year 1918 by myself on a platform of Athens railway station. The train arrived one hour after midnight. I got up and muttered to myself: "There, my friend. I've kept my promise. I even knelt before the king, but he too had forgotten you," and got into the train. But who cares about that now? Does it mean anything to you, Annabel? All that matters now is for me to touch your white skin, because I'll die before the bullet hits me if I don't touch you. I have to love you tonight, Annabel. I have a wife back in Serbia. I don't know if she's still alive. I'm cheating on her tonight, but I know it has to be this way.'

He stroked her straw-coloured hair and encircled her two blue 'buttons' with gentle caresses. Annabel switched to English. She spoke, and he listened to her as if he understood.

'I had a husband back in Scotland,' she told him. 'He died in my arms. That's why I came to Serbia at the beginning of 1915. I was alone and wanted to help. I came down with typhus but was cured. Surprisingly, it left no trace on my sensitive skin. I took a liking to you Serbs, although God is my witness how many of your bad traits I've seen. However brave you were in 1914, you became cowards the following year. Weakness, disease, loss of confidence—whatever. You were so frightened and small in the autumn of 1915 when the enemy invasion began. And with it came the rain. It rained when I left Kraguyevac with Hannah Hardy and headed south. It rained when we arrived in Kosovska Mitrovica with dishevelled hair, like Hecuba and her daughters. As we trudged along the potholed roads we saw bristly pigs fleeing with us, and the columns of refugees were looking not ahead but backwards, at their homeland. Somewhere in the middle of that trek, automobiles blew their horns at the refugees and what luxurious limousines they were. In them sat capricious majors and colonels who had crammed in everything they could: their wives and children, mistresses and family riches, and ridiculous home furnishings: a Turkish narghile, icons, a wall clock with broken glass and family portraits from happier times. Now I'm here, and I desperately need a man in this Greek night because I'll die if I don't touch a man again. But I'm English and ashamed to show my feelings. I'm also afraid because so many men have died beneath my hand already—first my husband, then all those other poor wretches. I fear that anyone who touches me dies. Do you want to be an exception?'

Now everything had been said. Or nothing at all. Now everything was understood, although nothing had been understood. She said nothing more. He caressed her again. He ran his heavy soldier's fingers through her velvety hair. He touched her slowly, slowly, like when the wind plucks the last autumn leaf from a tree. She closed her eyes: gently, gently, like when a little, nameless star goes out in a distant part of the universe. What happened afterwards was privy to the night. The stars in the black Salonika firmament whispered to each other about the love of Major Radoyica Tatich and the English nurse Annabel Walden. But for the streets of Salonika it remained a secret. Nor did the hallway on the second floor find out about their love. In fact, no one from no. 24 suspected anything, and Ermou Street could have sworn that nothing dishonourable happened there that night. Salonika would join the surrounding hills in hiding that forbidden love. Only the Front, which the artillery would shower with a rain of shells the very next day, had no sense of humour and no time for pretexts.

The morning of 13 September 1918 came; the major had to return to the Front and he never saw his Annabel Walden again. But perhaps he didn't need to because her short, fair hair, round English face and big blue eyes settled deep into the most intimate part of his memory, never to re-emerge and never to reveal themselves to anyone.

In the evening of that day he was a soldier again. He joined his unit on the slopes of Mount Floka. He ate little and smoked a lot, fitting cheap cigarettes into his cigarette holder like a Greek. The night was no good for sleeping, nor did the day bring peace. An ominous silence crept under the soldiers' helmets and into their uniforms, and some were already starting to say that the whole army on the Salonika Front was cursed. But then the silence broke into a roar from an armada of artillery pieces. At five o'clock on the morning of 14 September, Regent Alexander came out of his log cabin on Mount Yelak. Thick fog lay all around, but as the day progressed the fog lifted in the Dobro Selo area. At eight in the morning, the order was given to the Serbian artillery, and two thousand heavy guns opened fire at the Bulgarian positions opposite. The wailing of missiles, crying of guns and the shrieks of migratory birds went on for two whole days, and then the infantry went over the top.

One of the Serbian units which brought about the breakthrough on the Salonika Front near Vetrenik was the 2nd Battalion of the Combined Drina Reserve Division led by Major Radoyica Tatich. He had a thousand soldiers and four young lieutenants under his command. The thousand soldiers were barely literate and saw themselves as blades of grass for the grim reaper; no one cared about them and no one would raise a monument to them when they died. They relied on spells and charms, oaths and curses, amulets and a rustic keeping of time. Only the four lieutenants of the 2nd Battalion and their commander had pocket watches. Those lieutenants were young and educated; it was their destiny to live until 1964 or even longer. Or was it?

To begin with, none of the four thought they needed to keep the time. When the order to attack was given, the allied Serbian and French soldiers soon intermingled; split into groups of ten or twelve, they started to scale the rocky slope. Their uniforms were soon ragged, and almost every man was losing blood from cuts and wounds. In this way, they took metre after metre of ground. The air was full of machine-gun fire at first; then there were short bursts of rifle fire; in the end, everything died down and bayonets began to do their work, punctuating the silence with futile screams. Who would think of his watch amidst such confusion?

One of the major's lieutenants was Ivan Filipovich from Ub. His watch stopped on the very first day of the breakthrough on the Salonika Front. The mechanism simply failed. There had been no blow to the watch and there was not even a scratch on the glass. The hands came to rest on the morning of 16 September in cheery alignment at ten-past-ten, but the lieutenant didn't consider it a bad omen. He hadn't looked at his watch for half a day, and when he saw it had stopped he didn't have time to take it off its chain. 'Forward boys, war isn't a picnic!' he called out to his men that day and plunged ahead. Twice Lieutenant Filipovich was in a strangling, stabbing melee with the Bulgarians and twice he saw his own and others' blood on him and didn't have time to wipe it off. It seemed he was a darling of fortune whom death couldn't touch, like the major when he had had the magic little mirror with him. But in the evening, when the fighting ebbed away and the men settled down on the rocky slopes of Sivo Brdo Hill and gave themselves up to counting stars and killing snakes, Ivan Filipovich was found dead. No one heard a shot, not even those close at hand heard him moan, and there was no sign of a snake bite on his skin, so something supernatural had to be blamed for the lieutenant's death. Then they found the 'culprit'—an ordinary pocket watch, with its hands halted in that optimistic symmetry of ten-past-ten.

Major Tatich was told about the death of his lieutenant straight away. He sprang to his feet and ran to the lad, who was scarcely more than a boy. He grabbed him by the collar of his coat and started to shake him.

'On your feet, lad,' the soldiers heard him yell. 'Get up. You mustn't die. You don't have a single wound that could have killed you!'

'The dickory, major,' one man called to him.

'What "dickory", damn it?' Major Tatich screamed.

'It was the dickory that killed 'im, major sir. It stopped and didn't tick. We think the lieutenant's life stopped with it. 'E was still alive until this evening and throttled them two Bulgarians, and then he simply stopped, like this 'ere dickory. See, he died at ten-past-ten in the evening.'

'But that's... that's just fantasy. Miliya, come over here,' the major called out to his second lieutenant. 'Men, you're to bury our hero even if it takes all night in this rocky ground. And you, Miliya my lad, take the watch off Lieutenant Filipovich and give it to me for safe keeping.'

'Let me take it, major sir,' the lieutenant said. 'I've got my good one and Ivan's dud one. Please let me have it as a keepsake to remember him by.'

'You wear it then, blast it. But look after your own.'

'I will, major sir.'

So the second lieutenant, Miliya Yovovich from Oplenac, looked after the watch. He yelled at his soldiers at times like men, at times like livestock, and the men still had their amulets and kept time by the sun and the stars. They said the death of an artilleryman went down in the annals of a regiment, and the death of a horseman was reason enough for a monument, but the death of a footslogger only sufficed for a shallow grave. The 2nd Battalion of the Combined Drina Reserve Division set off in victorious pursuit of the enemy. French planes showered the Bulgarians now with bombs, now with leaflets calling on them to surrender. The Bulgarians fled, but their Austrian and German allies regrouped. Major Tatich's men ran into the Austro-Hungarian army near Preshevo. The city fell after three days of fighting, and on the third day, just before the city was taken, Lieutenant Yovovich was killed. Again, a watch seemed to be the cause of death. The glass of Miliya's watch was smashed; the watch stopped on 29 September at five-past-six in the morning, and early in the evening he was dead. Unlike the first lieutenant, the second one noticed immediately that his watch had stopped, but he didn't want to tell anyone so his men wouldn't take it as cowardice. He charged out in front the others, rushing into mortal combat, and when the enemy started to surrender he thought he had come through it alive. He died at exactly five-past-six in the evening. It was clear that Tatich's second young lieutenant had been cut down by a stray bullet; the shot was fired in desperation just at the moment when a ceasefire agreement for the Preshevo area was reached. Lieutenant Yovovich was giving some last orders when he was hit. He stopped in mid-movement, turned on one leg as if dancing with death, shrieked like a girl, and crashed to the ground. There were no traces of blood on his coat, as if he had been hit by a needle rather than a bullet.

Again, Major Tatich came running as if his very own son—the son he never had—had fallen there on the outskirts of Preshevo.

'Miliya, lad,' he yelled with a rough voice, as if he was speaking in the name of the whole army, 'I told you, but you didn't listen: guard that watch like the apple of your eye. I warned you, Miliya, but you didn't look after it.'

'Major sir,' the third lieutenant offered. Please let me take the two broken watches. Two bad ones is like one good one. I'll guard my own like the eyes of my fiancée, and I'll put these two in the left inside pocket of my coat.'

And so Milentiye Djorich from Loznica put the watches deep inside his pocket, right at the bottom. He cherished his own watch like the eyes of his beloved, but alas, the glass of this watch also broke, and that inevitably meant the end of the war for this third lieutenant. On 12 October, the Serbian forces halted near Nish, but the third lieutenant never saw that city. The major ordered that Lieutenant Djorich be buried at the Nish cemetery with full military honours, as befitted a hero, and took all three killer-watches. He wanted to take the good one off his fourth lieutenant, he insisted, but then he relented. As much as he regretted not having taken the broken watches off his three dead lieutenants straight away, and as much as he would regret not taking the good watch off his last lieutenant, it had to be said that Lieutenant Ranko Boyovich from Smederevo looked after his watch as diligently as humanly possible. He cleaned it, guarded it and wound it. In fact, he was so frightened it could stop that he overwound it during the final battle for Belgrade and broke the spring. The watch stopped, the back lid burst open, and cogs, spindles and tiny wheels spilt out like entrails in front of the petrified lieutenant. Lieutenant Boyovich therefore did not live to see the capital.

Major Radoyica Tatich marched into Belgrade as a victor. His watch, which never failed him, was in the left-hand outer pocket of his uniform, and in his right-hand pocket there lay four broken ones: one which had stopped at ten-past-ten and looked as if it was still good; a second, with a broken glass, which had frozen at five-past-six; a third, completely smashed, with hands showing exactly three o'clock; and a fourth, with its entrails protruding, which had stopped at one minute to twelve.

The Great War ended for Major Radoyica Tatich on 1 November 1918 on Slaviya Square; to the surprise of onlookers, he took out the four watches on their chains and said, as if addressing those timepieces: 'My lieutenants, we liberated Belgrade together.'

Regent Alexander entered the city that same day, but how very different his arrival was to that of the Drina Division's advance guard. He came in through the outlying Zvezdara neighbourhood. It was early evening and the autumn sky over the capital was the colour of rust. The Mayor of Belgrade, Kosta Glavinich, wanted to welcome there him in Zvezdara by the observatory. He stood on the gravel path beneath the dome, where people gazed into the sky, and spread his arms as if to embrace Alexander. But then he stopped, moved a little to the side, bowed, and decided to make a speech. Lots of big words came to Glavinich's mouth, but each and every one of them stuck to his tongue or the back of his mouth and couldn't get out. The future king was patient as the speaker struggled. Finally, the mayor managed to force a loud wheeze out of his throat: 'Long live the young king! Long live our free Fatherland!' Alexander found all of this rather strange, but he didn't have time to think about it. A car was now waiting to take him to Slaviya Square, he was told, and they requested that he then walk along King Milan Street, Teraziye Boulevard and Knez Mihailova Street to St Michael's Cathedral on foot, so that the people would be able to see and touch him.

Alexander agreed, but when he finally got out of the car on Slaviya Square he saw a strange sight. No, the people who thronged and reached out like crazy to touch him were not weird, and it was not unusual that they were ragged, with yellow skin and bulging eyes, with pupils that looked like they were floating in oil. What surprised him was that no sound rose up to meet him and his escorts, not even the most restrained of cries. The people rustled around him like spectres, touching him, smiling strange smiles and showing dark teeth. The regent raised his head and looked into the crowd, into those tight rows of little heads which seemed to rest on bodies of straw wrapped in dirty rags and tatters. The people were cheerful; children gave Alexander bunches of autumn flowers, which brought tears to his eyes, but there was no end to his astonishment. No one was yelling and there was none of the usual hubbub produced by crowds, even when everyone in the throng thinks they are being quiet. The king and liberator went on, and this hushed procession followed after him like an army of ghosts. At the beginning of King Milan Street the crowd numbered thousands, and when he entered the broad square of Teraziye Boulevard it seemed the entire city was flocking after the future king—and everyone was silent.

Here on Teraziye Boulevard was finally someone who still had a voice. A mischievous fellow, a Belgrade noise-maker swept along by the crowd like a piece of flotsam, suddenly appeared before the regent. The man turned around in panic, drove away invisible enemies with his arms and stopped. Alexander saw that he was a wretched fellow, his face devoured by deep folds, while his bony arms hung from his pigeon-chest like two broken poles. Still, this ugly drunkard had what the multitude behind him did not. He yelled at the top of his voice, as if he was the only person who had one: 'Long live the king and liberator! Long live our Fatherland, much tormented but now free!' the people closest wanted to silence him and sluice him back into the liquid mass of the crowd like a foreign body, but Alexander ordered them to stop. He spoke out clearly, which showed him he still had vocal chords, and said that everyone had a right to make merry and celebrate in honour of the Fatherland, even if they shouted drunken slogans. The crowd mutely agreed, nodding like wind-up dolls, but the regent couldn't find the strength to ask why everyone was so quiet. He had to go on. Knez Mihailova Street was too narrow to receive all those silent spectres, like a procession of the living and the dead, who were now joined by all the mothers with sons who perished back in 1914.

There, in front of the *Russian Tsar* coffee house, Alexander gave a speech. He alone had a voice. He yelled so that as many as possible would hear him, but only the first few rows could make out his words: 'Today you have welcomed my army, which has come from the distant mountains and brings you freedom. This great joy is the reward for your great suffering.' What joy? What reward? Who was rejoicing? And where was that noise-maker—the only one to have met him with some semblance of joy on his disfigured face? Alexander now felt ill at ease. What was waiting for him around the next corner? What would happen when he arrived at St Michael's?

The Cathedral looked as if the building was gone and only its essence remained. Alexander saw there was no light, and candles alone illuminated the nave, and silence was all around that deep, divine, cathedral once more. Not even the Serbian archbishops who kissed his hand in front if the church could speak a word. They opened their mouths, but instead of words he heard only a murmur like the rustle of flower petals or the dying breath of an infirm patient. Where was Patriarch Dimitriye? And where were the army chaplains with whom he had returned to Serbia? He entered the churchyard, which was strewn with straw, and then St Michael's itself. He was ushered—almost pushed—with theatrical movements to a special line of wooden chairs for deserving citizens, and then a truly mute and solemn service began. The provost of the cathedral and his servers opened their mouths, and the three candles in one hand and two in the other crossed. The procession of ecclesiastics moved through the congregation, waving the censer of frankincense, but there was not a word of prayer, and not a single sound came from the gallery where a choir of weary citizens opened their mouths as if to accompany the priests with a pastoral song. The church was filled with people to the end of the nave and the doors could no longer be closed. The young king turned his head and looked at all those tired, glazed eyes in the candlelight and was still astonished by the deathly silence. Everyone seemed to have merged into the unlikely silhouette of a single organism unable to express its joy at liberation.

The end of the service also meant the end of his strange march to the capital. Only in the house of the merchant Krsmanovich, where it was decided to spend that first night in Belgrade, did Alexander repeatedly hear voices, as well as clamour in other rooms which long kept him awake. Try as he might, he simply could not get to sleep, and he sat at the edge of the bed barefooted and in his nightshirt. He bared his chest and looked at the embarrassing tattoo of the Austro-Hungarian two-headed eagle, which even his father didn't know about. He had had that heraldic beast etched into his skin as a young man. Back then, he had carelessly thought the Dual Monarchy would be Serbia's eternal ally. He looked now at that tattoo and said softly to himself: 'The war is over.' Peace would follow, and the unification of three neighbouring Slavic peoples, and then possibly the renewal of Serbia. But what kind of Serbia would it be if the first day of freedom was like this? For a long while still, he asked himself where all the voices and sounds of the liberated city had fled to, and, sure enough, they had run down to Sava Quay.

Not everyone had been a hero. Not everyone kept quiet.

Many silhouettes with a guilty conscience were fleeing Belgrade. Among them was the seamstress Zhivka. She realized she had to leave her cosy tailor shop. None of her assistants urged her to stay, nor did she try to persuade any of them to go with her. She knew everyone would look at her askance after the fall of the capital, so she decided to leave the city shortly before the end. She led her blond son Eugene by the hand down to Sava Quay, where a deafening clamour reigned. People were cursing and swearing, shouting to each other and bandying ugly names. Smoke from fires mingled with the throng of people pushing and shoving and treading on each other. A boat capsized in the middle of the river. The horses it had been carrying were drowning in the swollen waters; their muzzles desperately broke the dark surface and their nostrils inflated. Zhivka got into a fishing boat in Bara Venecia. The cantankerous owner agreed to take her for an immodest sum of money; he realized it was daylight robbery and almost felt guilty. He pushed out through the middle of the marsh and entered the current of the river. The horses had disappeared. Had they drowned or perhaps struggled to the bank? It didn't matter. A low fog descended on the Sava. Eugene slept, and Zhivka got up and stood straight like a little heroine—her, the seamstress who had once owned a shop with a change room where people vanished into the distant future. She cast a last glance back. Belgrade rose up out of the fog like a jewel, the pride of a prematurely frozen land. But it was no longer her city, no longer her 1 November, and certainly not her 1918. Nor was she any longer herself. Only Eugene still had a future. Only Eugene. For Zhivka the seamstress, the Great War ended when she turned her head towards Zemun and the Austro-Hungarian border and there saw the roads, whose illusorily straightness would only lead her in circles from then on.

The next day, everything was back to normal in Belgrade. The clamour of guilty consciences at the quay climbed the steep streets of Savamala to the inner city during the night, and on 2 November the capital celebrated victory loudly and boisterously; it was hard to believe that people had been so hushed and silent the previous day.

Then 11 November 1918 came. The Great War was over.

Many Belgraders reflected on what peace would look like. No one believed that the war had ended that day and everyone was waiting to see that peace, as if it was a mighty demiurge or simply a rainbow which would reward the one who ran under it first. A certain criminologist was destined to be the first person to see a sign of peace, but for him it did not resemble a rainbow stretched across the sky. No, he sighted that 'Beethoven's forest' intellectual again. He had been flown in, probably without touching one clod of Serbian soil. Not even a stray bullet would have had him. Dr Reiss saw young Mr Kapetanovich on the other side of Teraziye Boulevard. There he was: hurrying along, no longer dressed in a bluish-grey army coat on that muddy day, beneath thick clouds which dropped a dirty rain mixed with sleet. No, he was now clad in a white civilian suit. He went along the streets of the capital with a white handkerchief over his nose and beckoned freakishly from the opposite pavement, like a creature dead inside but outwardly alive, as if to say: you must come over, my good sir—step in the mud, tread in the puddles gaping like seas of quicksand, because I am peace. What was the criminologist waiting for? He just had to stride over towards that man in white on the other side of the road; that figure, his face powdered and creamed, with dyed hair and a grin which horribly creased and contorted his features, who was calling him to come over. Archibald Reiss was thus the first to see peace—peace dressed all in white—but it didn't bring him anything resembling happiness. He just turned away, disgusted, and made his way down to Savamala, where he leaned up against a grey building, breathing heavily and fighting for air.

Maybe that Swiss criminologist was up too close. Peace can look quite different in foreign climes to how it looks at home. As soon as King Peter heard at his residence in Greece that Serbian troops had entered Serbia, he ordered that all his things be packed into five large suitcases. Soon he repacked the most essential things in three suitcases. He stopped and thought for a moment, and then reduced his luggage to one suitcase. He threw that aside, too, and took only one small bag, which he had recently acquired. Where did he get it from? Not long ago, someone had given him this rather ordinary camel-hair bag as a gift, saying it had belonged to an oriental trader and travelled half the world. Who was it who had brought him this little caravan bag? And why had it been given to him, of all people? The king couldn't remember, but he recalled that he had taken it with reluctance at first.

Now he decided to repack only the most essential things in that camel-hair bag. He ended up hardly putting anything in it, but that isn't important. Gradually, like a desperate geriatric, he became ever more attached to that only piece of luggage he cared for. He even called it 'my camellia'. The hide was dark red on the back, orange at its curves, and bristly on the front. This strange piece of baggage started to shape strange thoughts. King Peter began to believe that the little travelling bag would help him return to the Fatherland too.

Several days later, King Peter started to feel unwell, and on 19 October 1918 he suffered a stroke. Although his subsequent recovery was slow and difficult, he didn't let the 'camellia' out of his sight. As soon as he was able to stand again, he examined its contents once more and telegraphed his son that he wanted to return to the liberated town of Belgrade straight away, even if he had to travel via Dubrovnik and Sarajevo. He looked at the motley camel-hide bag and was convinced it was calling on him to take that journey, but he was mistaken. The plans for the trip were deferred. The regent was against his father returning before the formal act of unification of the Kingdom of Serbs, Croats and Slovenes. Days passed, and the old king didn't realize that the 'camellia' was actually his anchor, pulling him down and holding him in that pleasant but foreign suburb of Athens. So it was that the Great War ended for the old man in contemplating that cursed camel-hair bag, which after ending the life of a trader in oriental spices now entangled the life-threads of a king.

Much later, King Peter would return to his Fatherland. But that would be in a new life, and he would be a man marked and marred by his stroke, unable to even sign a legible signature on his Act of Abdication. When it was finally time to leave on that journey, old King Peter would be unable to find that little camel-hair bag which he should have thrown away without thinking, back in 1918.

I AM NOW DEAD

'I am Wilhelm Albert Wlodzimierz Apolinary de Kostrowicki. I am now dead. The shrapnel from March 1916 finally caught up with me, a good two years after it came whistling up and hit me in the head, hissing like a savage cat which has come late to February mating. It is 9 November 1918 at three o'clock in the afternoon, or a few minutes thereafter. Every comma of my eyelashes has died, and my huge pear-shaped head is beginning to dry from the stalk down. It's strange that I can describe my path after death, but this is how it happened: I died and suddenly had two bodies. The one lying motionless in bed sank deeper into the linen and the pillow beneath my head. Two men grabbed the second body, this new one, and took me away like gendarmes. First of all, they dragged me off to the police station. They accused me of having stolen all my life and summarily took me to a lock-up quite like La Santé prison, where I had spent the three most dishonourable weeks of my life. They told me I was dead. I just leered at them and made all the commas of my eyelashes bristle. But they seemed not to care. I heard one of them say: "He has no right to any visits. Even the advocate of the dead isn't to be allowed to see him for three days!" In the registry I was given a shirt, towel, sheet and blanket. That further convinced me that I wasn't dead, because what does a person need all that for if they're dead? But I was mistaken. Still smiling from ear to ear, I pulled the shirt over my strange, translucent body, but since it too was transparent it looked as if I hadn't put anything on over bare chest; I wrapped the towel around my transparent neck, and it too ceased being visible. Only then did I realize that I was probably dead.

'They took me away to my cell. It was exactly one hundred and eleven steps straight on, then seventy-six down the right-hand corridor, and twenty-two more straight on, and then ten quite strange steps backwards—and there I was at my cell. The door slammed shut behind me by itself. Then I heard the latch. I was locked up. I longed to sing and write beautiful poems, but even my verse was empty and everything I put on paper left no trace. All I could hear was the melody of quatrains. I didn't understand what was going on. It was maddening in the extreme. I spent one, two, three sleepless nights in the cell and kept asking myself one and the same thing: why is it not transparent too? As if in answer to my question, on the fourth day the rear wall of my isolation cell began to pale and grow thin.. Finally I touched it and it tore like the cobweb of some evil spider I had written about. I passed through that hole in the cobweb into a wide field, and there I saw many, many people; it was as if a whole town was there in front of me, all the people of a city, like Paris with all its inhabitants standing and waiting. Some were in large groups, others stood alone. One of them told me these were all the French victims of the Great War. Oh my God.

'The victims started coming up to me, and each of them asked for a piece of bread and a drop of water. First of all, there were fifty French heroes of Verdun, all of them wearing new boots: Marin Guillaumont (the victor of three proper duels), Jean Louis Marie Enteric (with a suicidal look), Pierre Jean Raymond Faure (nicknamed Biveau), Lucien René Louis Renn (a man with six names, of which I cite only three), Joseph Antoine Richard (as handsome as a film star), Eugene Fauren Vasin (who fell in the second kilometre of the Battle of Verdun wearing a small, round lorgnette—a statement of better times) and forty-four other heroes covered me from head to foot with their begging hands, and my transparent body was clad in their five hundred fingers!

'I pushed them away with effort because I wanted to see more of that field-of-the-dead. A lieutenant came up to me and said his name was Germain D'Esparbès. He told me he had played cards with the dead near Lunéville in 1914. He wasn't able to finish the tale and I didn't manage to ask who won that ghostly game because the next fellow now barged up, pushing D'Esparbès aside. It was Lucien Guirand de Scevola, and he said he had organized the first wartime drama in a broad section of trench dubbed "Hotel Ritz", but he couldn't finish his story either because I was now approached by Stanislaw Witkiewicz. He was looking for his wife, who had died of tuberculosis in heart-rending agony in the first year of the war, and asked me if I had seen her. "No, I haven't," I told him, and then I saw my machine-gunner Chapelant. He was still sitting and writing home on Old Birot's postcards, which folk told me were magic and really did keep writing themselves after the soldier had died. "That's enough," a voice boomed, "stop all going up to him like Ulysses. He has no right to that."

'"Wait," I yelled: "I don't want to die before I've found love here— I almost said the love of my life—because I have to love when I'm dead too, you know!" Someone seemed to call out to me from afar. There she was: a tiny girl, but a real beauty. She was wearing a long white-fur coat down to her ankles. She was looking at me and came up close.

Mata Hari! How lucky I am. She pressed her body against mine. She unbuttoned the fur coat and hugged me, and I felt her bare breasts, hips and thighs. Then she lifted her deathly pale, emerald leg and wrapped it around my waist. My male member was still alive, but my sense of smell too, it seemed. I smelt blood. "O Mata Hari, the silver fleece of your breasts is red and glistening. Look, a trickle of your blood has soiled my uniform. I still love you, but now I am dead."

'What a vast sea of the dead, and I was one of them. I saw so many there whom I knew and recognized. But I had to check who wasn't here, so I called out: "Has anyone heard if Picasso is here? The painter. The Spaniard. No? Good then. André Salmon! Saaalmon, old chum, what about you? He's not here either, thank God—therefore he's alive. Old Birot, is he here somewhere? No? Great. And Old Combes? Him neither. Very good, Paris will be able to go on after this massacre."'

'My name is Yuri Yuriev and I am now dead. Whether it's for real now or just another farce, God only knows. I was an actor—the leading player of the Alexandrinsky Theatre. I returned home to the house in Liteyny Avenue in 1917 half dead, and I think I have reason to say: Russia was the end of me! You know, I toured my country in the hope of finding a province without revolution: an untainted district with its governor, postmaster, charity lady and local landowner with three hills of cherry orchards… but it wasn't like that anywhere. My tour of Russia brought me back to Petrograd a broken man, and then the unthinkable happened.

'No one recognized me any more. I realized straight away that I was unwanted. I had left, fled, and my theatre continued to put on new plays without me. So I tried to remind the older actors of my existence, but no one could remember me. I was so amazed. I flew into a rage. It all dented my self-esteem, but then I realized the advantages of my new role as an invisible man. No one in the theatre knew me any more, but the theatre itself still remembered me: I entered the building and strolled along the rows of empty seats, went through the galleries and visited the former tsar's box; I sank into chairs re-upholstered with red plush, slept, and when I woke up people were walking about all around me, moving faster and faster.

'New managers went up onto the stage and swung their arms as if in bad plays. I didn't hear what they said, but the tails of their leather coats waved as they shook their fists. I didn't interfere in the new set-up because I realized I had found my role: I became the only actor of the theatre. I never returned home. People at the former Alexandrinsky Theatre greeted each other, calling out over my shoulders, and some would brush me in passing as if I was a length of drapery that falls to the floor in a sea of folds.I am now a dead actor, but, to tell the truth, I didn't think of continuing life after this terrible Great War and the even more terrible revolution. If you remember me, you'll find me in row twelve, seat seven. It's never sold—it's always mine. Goodbye, I wish you all the best. And good luck—you'll need it.'

'I am Fritz Haber, and I think I must be dead after all that has happened, although I haven't really died or changed worlds, have just received the Nobel Prize for Chemistry. But it's clear to me now, at the awards ceremony, how alone I am. Germany lost the war, although I had poisoned thousands with bertholite. I've just been awarded the prize for discovering the synthesis of ammonia, and now I see that I'm dead. Back in 1917, I already calculated how much of me had died. As a chemist, I had to establish the formula of my life. I have that modicum of personal integrity. Then I wrote it down on a piece of paper, which I still carry in my pocket today: "Fifty-two per cent of me has died—only forty-eight per cent is left". Therefore I am chemically dead. And now? I'm up on the stage in the Swedish Academy of Sciences, dressed in a tailcoat and with impeccably white gaiters atop my patent leather shoes. Everything has to be in keeping with the protocol of the awards ceremony. But look there, a boat is making its way up the aisle between the rows of invited guests. It glides calmly, as if the Styx is flowing there. I see a galley with two rows of oars: the barque of the dead. The ferryman Charon, with a pole in hand, is calling to me: "What is it? Have you changed your mind? We've been waiting for you for so long."

'And I go. I separate myself from my body, leaving my smiling face behind to crease my cheeks and jowls with its artificial grin. The ferryman beckons to me, and here I am at the boat. The others in the vessel see me and wave as if I know them and they just need to remind me of who they are. "Fritz Krupp, Zeppelin bombardier and five-time killer of Ruiz Picasso. The fellow with the flappy ears here is my faithful machine-gunner," one of them calls out. "Stefan Holm, German and Polish hero," another says. The others introduce themselves too: "Walther Schwieger, the butcher of Kinsale, commanding officer of the submarine U-20 which sank the Lusitania"; "Alexander Wittek, student. I ended up in this mess although I was meant to live until 1968"; "Lilian Smith, music-hall singer—I died on the stage singing the 'Song of Hate against England'". Hold on, the fighter ace Manfred von Richthofen is also in the boat! He says nothing and just greets me the Prussian way, as a nobleman, by gently lowering his head to his chest. And there is that poor boy with the withered arms. "I am Hans Henze," he called. "I play piano with the right hand of Paul Wittgenstein and write poems in French with the left hand of Blaise Cendrars." Finally, oh dear, my wife Clara Immerwahr is in the galley of the dead too. Before she manages to speak, I say: "Stop, this is too much," and don't get into the boat after all, and everyone in it looks at me with incomparable sadness. I withdraw step-by-step, until finally, moving backwards with the gait of a crab, I drown completely in my body, which still stands on the stage about to address the Nobel Committee. A figure on the stage finally announces: "Fritz Haber, recipient of the Nobel Prize for Chemistry", and I see myself going up to the stage again. I, the dead chemist, Fritz Haber, am now going to make a speech to all the living in the rows of chairs and all the dead in Charon's barque. "Ladies and gentlemen," I begin, but inside I say: "My dear wife Clara..."'

'I am Hans-Dieter Huis: I scream, but you can't hear me. I am now dead. Once I was Don Giovanni, the greatest in all of Germany, but then my voice ceased to obey me. I wanted to get better. God is my witness that I desperately sought a cure. I paid Dr Straube in good Berlin goose, and he prescribed me a potion. It was a strange concoction. It made my voice squeaky and ever more higher-pitched until it went beyond the range of human hearing. Now not even the Berlin dogs can hear me. Is there an upper limit for tone? For me, the upper notes are like a crumb seen from an aeroplane. My voice is now so high that I can only hear it with my own inner ear. For everyone else I am mute. Even the Berlin dogs who once followed me in packs, barking and howling, have now left me, deaf to my troubles. With them, my last audience is gone. That's why I left for the north. Beside a mill, near the free city of L., I sang to the water and its wheel turning, aware that my road is one without end. The world is boundless, and the tones of my throat can rise higher and infinitely higher. My voice can now hardly shake the thread of a spider's web, although the tremor of that silken thread was once the consummation of all my roles. I am now dead for everyone and everything, except for the music of gossamer, heavenly spheres.'

'I am Dr Baltazar Straube and I have just died. In case you don't know, I am the laryngologist who prescribed the potion for the renowned baritone Hans-Dieter Huis, which subsequently ruined his voice. The maestro paid for his death as a singer with half a kilo of goose tallow, two drumsticks which didn't smell the best, and some giblets. He's lying when he says he brought me a whole goose as a gift, but one way or another it was a cheaply bought elixir for such a magnificent death on stage. If you ask me why I ruined his voice, first you should know that I truly loved Germany and her master- singers once. But when I began to hate my homeland for having drawn a whole young generation into the meat-grinder of the Great War, nothing remained of my love for the singers. I felt they were a vanguard who had led us into a swamp—errant knights whom I had to consign to hell, and that's just what I did. After Huis, I ruined the voice of Theodora von Stade and many others. Now, at the door to hell, I just hope the devil will show more understanding for me than I had for Germany and her master-singers.'

'I am now dead. I have finally become one. Ordinary. A vanquished general of the Austro-Hungarian army. How we have all gone to the dogs in the last few months, how everything rotten in us has come out and now reeks of neglect and infirmity! We fought bravely, like true soldiers. We thought we were winning the war on the Eastern Front in 1914; we thought we would liberate Przemysl in 1915; I was convinced I could repulse ten more offensives by those Italian yokels at the Isonzo Front—and then we foundered. One torpedo fired from the Rear, away from the Front, holed our proud ship. Hunger, despair and communist agitation made penniless commoners in mouldy coats take to the streets and squares. The crowd's clamour and hubbub made our brave weapons fall silent; and then I myself, I'm ashamed to say, showed my worst face.

'Once I was a soldier. Strict, equitable and orderly. For the last few months I've felt like a wandering Vlach salesman, forever holding the scales of his life in his hands. I'm brawling over a title with a failed country, in which I invested all my skill and made my career. The Military Order of Maria-Theresia from 1917 entitled me to be raised to the gentry with a barony. But I wanted more. The ship was sinking, so I didn't see why I should be prudent. I was negotiating with Vienna to gain a higher title than baron, nothing less than count. But nothing came of it because the Great War ended and I was left without a country, court, countship or emperor.

'Now I'm writing a sycophantic letter to the National Council of Serbs, Croats and Slovenes. I warn them that reopening the railways in these poisonous post-war times would be disastrous. I pretend to be concerned, but I'm thinking only of how to save my skin when I write: "The consequences would be catastrophic for the whole South Slavic region because hordes of undisciplined troops and Italians, who at the moment cannot be halted, would rampage through Carniola and then Croatia. Therefore I beg you, not as a general or the last son of the Fatherland but as an ordinary patriot who loves his country, to prevent this misfortune."

'I stop and don't send the letter. Suddenly it's as clear as day to me: I am now dead. Throughout the war, I had everything in duplicate: two sets of staff officers, two horses, two pairs of boots, two metal helmets with black plumes, and two coats. That's enough of lies: it's time for me to decide. This separation has to end once and for all. I get out all my things: the coats of both field marshals. Finally, I choose the one I had long put aside. That is the uniform for the Svetozar who languished for so long in the dregs of my bitter soul: who couldn't die, and therefore had to live. I look at myself: from my fingers to my hands and arms and slightly pigeon-chested torso, and I see myself becoming that old Svetozar again.

'All through the years, this Orthodox heart has beat in time with that of the Austro-Hungarian soldier, which was devoted to the imperial crown, but that Austro-Hungarian heart now beats ever more faintly and finally stops. A heart attack and—death. I'm no longer Field Marshal Boina. Now I'm just an ordinary Serb, Svetozar Boroevich, son of First Lieutenant Adam Boroevich of the border regiment, and Stana Boroevich, née Kovarbashich. I was baptized in the Orthodox church in Umetich in 1857. I have a brother, Nikola, and a sister, Lyubica. There are four hundred and forty-two of us Boroevichs, and one of them has just died. Me.'

'Today is 12 November 1918 and I have finally realized the significance of the dream in which Empress Elisabeth, Archduke Franz Ferdinand, the Duchess of Hohenberg and Crown prince Rudolf all shouted the same date to me: "11 November 1918". I am now a dead emperor, the last ruler of the Danube monarchy, and that bacchanalian dance of dead relatives was not telling me the day I would survive an assassination attempt, but the day our whole world would collapse.

'Farewell, everyone. This is the end of me: quiet and absent-minded Charles I, the last Emperor of the Dual Monarchy. This is the end of you, too. What remains of you will become someone else.'

WISHES FOR THE NEW WORLD

'After this endlessly long war, I hope people will drink and carouse even more merrily than they did before. That's what I would say—me, Old Libion, proprietor of the famous Café de la Rotonde. I'd also say this: I don't approve of those devilish chibouks with opium, which I'm seeing ever more often in my café. They only harm young people. Alcohol? Well, alcohol is different, especially if it's champagne. There was so much bad blood during the Great War. If I just think back to the two weeks in April 1915 when those two witches from Touraine really had us on the go. I'm ashamed now that Old Combes and I almost went to war because of those two snobbish tarts, but what could I do? It all began with bad wine, and luckily everything was drowned in bad wine in the end.'

'I always thought Old Libion was a bit loopy, starting with the wine affair with those female pirates from Touraine. A new world built on champagne, my foot! The world will be based on lies, extortion and corruption. The young generation has become perverted, that's just the way things are. How can someone who comes back from the war and remembers the dozens of men he's bayonetted refrain from stealing from my café? I'm going to keep an eye on every glass and every bottle of bubbly in the Closerie des Lilas, even if they say behind my back: "Old Combes is heartless—he must have eaten his heart for dinner." I'll sack the lads behind the bar on the third of every month and find new ones on the fifth. Just think: there will be so many unemployed that I'll be able to change them like underpants: on Tuesdays and Thursdays. Now let someone try and swipe something! And the guests? Huh. Once they used to piss down their legs, get up on tables and hold drunken speeches, and draw their Brownings and fire into the air. Now they'll shoot to kill from point-blank range.'

'Old Combes has always been a miser, I guess, but his stingy ways only go as far as the bar and no further. Let him prattle on about a crisis. People will become better after this war because they'll learn to appreciate life, beauty, comfort and good company. Gentlemen will become more refined, ladies more elegant, and even our loose women will cast off their crudity and ply their trade for shares in the great factories to be built—not like today for dubious money and the crude pictures of untalented daubers.'

'I'm telling you, Libion, there's a big crisis looming, and money won't be worth the paper it's printed on. You'll reach down to your duds and find there's nothing in them. You'll slam the door of your "artists' haunt" and lock it so the debt collectors don't whisk away the whole inventory with your guests still on the chairs. But I'm not going to be as mad as you and pour away my common sense with the champagne. No way! I'll pay the waiters thousands and millions of francs, and I'll laugh when I see them running to buy half a loaf of bread for what I've given them, but my "artists' pub" will survive while yours fails!

'Your pipe dreams about the vagabonds all shifting to your place will come to nothing. We'll see who comes out on top, Combes!'

'The world is like a postcard: the sender's address may get soiled or stained, but the addressee's never does, I'm telling you. I know because I made a fortune during the Great War with the famous postcards from my manufactory, the Printer Pierre Albert Birot. They have a secret feature which prevents writing from smudging on the right-hand side where the address is, because they know they have to arrive at their destination. A heap of cards have come over the last few days, strangely enough, written by soldiers I've never heard of. At first, I got angry at the postmen and the Red Cross for not sorting the postcards from the Front properly, but when I tried to find out who the senders were I realized they're all dead. Now I'm trying to work out how that many dead men were able to write so many postcards.

'And if you're asking me about the new world: it won't be like Old Libion sees it, and not like grouchy Old Combes expects either. You just need to look at the two of them and everything becomes clear. Old Libion is well-fed but not so well-bred, while Old Combes is all skinny and bent, with his ugly nut hanging like a gas lantern over the Paris boulevard of his shoulders. Naturally the former thinks everything will go swimmingly, like champagne, and the latter fears that even a hitch will have a hitch.'

'I am Hayyim-the-Merry. Yes, I remember Mehmed Yıldız, the trader in oriental and European spices. I don't know why you're asking about him. I only saw him a few times. Ah, I understand... You've heard from him that I said I could hardly wait for victory or defeat. True enough, I went out to see the British in the streets when they entered Istanbul on 13 November 1918 by your calendar, but still more to admire the pride and oriental pomp we received them with. Come and watch it with me, come on a stroll through my memory: the horses rearing, jubilation in all three parts of the city. Look, there are flags, columns of black horses, and silken sheets lowered from the minarets like giant pantaloons, and someone has strewn lotus flowers on the humiliated waters of the Golden Horn. But I don't mind. Perhaps I even prefer defeat to victory because we showed so much to the infidels.

'If you ask me what I think is going to happen, I hope the new world will steer well clear of Turkey. The Young Turks overdid it. That's right, they went way too far with the Armenians, although I don't like them either. That's the truth, effendi, I don't like them and I guess I'm even proud of it, but it would have been enough to just to drive them away to another city. Asia is big, as we Turks know better than anyone. The torrid belt of the Mediterranean is broad indeed. Maybe the Copts in Alexandria or the Syrians in Damascus would have accepted them, and if they wouldn't have, we could have forced them on someone else, and they could have killed them rather than us having to. They shouldn't have been driven into the desert like that, like wild animals. Somebody or other would have taken them in. They still would have been good for someone. But now we've got rid of them, in any case, and are left alone with ourselves. I'm telling you, we Turks should shut ourselves away again. We don't need anyone else.

'I'm going to begin with myself. This is what I've decided: I'll leave a smile on my face for a long time to come, like washing swaying in the wind, to remind those around me that I am still Hayyim-the-Merry. I'll go to the tearooms, tell funny stories and grin. I'll entertain the coach drivers and ferrymen by the Galata Bridge, but before the laughter leaves my face I'll steal out of myself and, like a sprit, begin to search for Turks similar to myself. Do you think I'll be alone, effendi? Oh no, you'll see a whole new Istanbul of people who have come out of themselves and walk the city like spirits. All of us will be as white as paper; we'll have breadth and width, but not depth; two dimensions will be enough for us to get into boats and tell the two-dimensional boatmen: "To Emirgân, where the paint factory burned down and Yıldız Effendi heard of the death of his first apprentice." And the boats will cast off. Everything will be like in the old miniatures: us, the water, diligent vessels plying it, the Emirgân neighbourhood, wooden houses, mosques with minarets, and the whole of Turkey. And everyone will finally be happy.'

'I swear to you, invalids will be better lovers than men with arms, as long as the tool in their grungy pants has come through it all unscathed. I know what I'm talking about, I've known many dead men. That's right, and I'm not ashamed to admit it: I put on the boots of dead soldiers. I called them Jules, Jean, Jacques, Joseph, Jacob, Joël: Then I rolled on the floor and imagined them embracing me in their invisible, cobwebbed arms. Later I decided to replace the dead with the living: I bared myself and set off through life naked. First of all, I found the painter Kisling. I hadn't made love with a man's body for two years and it was wonderful. Afterwards I found Foujita, a Japanese artist. He sure gave me a workout. Bed was like gymnastics, but when I think about it now, both of them were cowards. Where were they in the trenches? Where were they when the gas was sent towards our positions? They were giving Kiki de Montparnasse a workout! I've had enough of painters who preferred 'fat cowardice' to 'lean heroism'. I'll also leave Man Ray like he left me and went back to New York. I'll find myself a war invalid! The new age will be a time of the pre-eminent wounded because we'll all devote ourselves to love, and whoever is best will be elected president of France, whether he has both legs and both arms or not. Now the president is... um... that Poincaré guy, who looks like a brewer from Alsace. I think he looks more like a German than a Frenchman. 'I will give him another year—let's see—two years at most as president, and then he'll be replaced by the best lover in Paris: a man without arms, the real symbol of the Great War and everything that's coming after.'

'I think the same as others, to put it simply, and I'm not ashamed to say it. I went to war as the real Cocteau: in style, and also managed to come through it all alive. Quite an achievement, don't you think? It's true that the war also reduced my standard of living, so to speak. The year 1914 was better than 1915, but 1915 was gold compared to 1916. Every day of 1916 was like a rose petal compared to any day in 1917, and 1918 was one big cock-up. Just to think back to my first leave in Paris in 1914. I arrived home like a real wartime popinjay: in an ironed and scented uniform with a crimson helmet. Everyone at the Rotonde and the Dôme was to see how I had 'gone to war in style' in 1914. I didn't find Picasso then. But may he go with God. We all loved him so much, although he trod all over us. Oh yes, and you asked me about the new world after the Great War. The new world will be toilet paper for the old: Anyone who was anything before the Great War will end up wiping the arse of the new world. Brother will trample brother into the mud in a mad rush to 'make it'. Slutty little Kiki must be crazy if she thinks Poincaré would be replaced by an invalid-president with a huge phallus. Only a nymphomaniac like her could come up with nonsense like that. The new world will be... Oh, who cares about new world. I went to war in style, and it's luxury for me in peacetime, too. I'll charge everyone for everything and won't even tip-my-hat for free. I'm not so stupid as to daydream about a better world while others are just getting rich and living off the fat of the land. I may not be able to gain a simple gram, whatever I eat, but instead I'll find a wallet which can get nice and fat.'

'I don't know why anyone expects me to say what the new world will be like. I am Oswald Rayner. I killed Rasputin a third time, in the name of the British crown, and you'll probably see that I speak much better with a gun than with words. Therefore I'll load my revolver and put a bullet in the chamber. That, gentlemen, is what the new world will look like after this Great War.'

'Don't expect me to say much about the new world, either. I'm just a gypsy woman, a fortune-teller from Russia. I changed trains during the Bolshevik Revolution in 1917 and lied to a few misguided revolutionaries a great future was ahead of them. Why did I do that, I hear you ask? I'm not going to tell you. There have to be a few secrets left for the caravans to take with them.'

'I am Dr Sándor Ferenczi, and I hope this worst and best time for a psychoanalyst ends as soon as possible. I don't know what my colleague Aufschneider would say about it all. I still remember him: he set off on a round trip to see each of us, and at each station he developed a totemic disease. Now everyone around me is in the terminal phase of one or several such diseases, and probably I am myself. The world has become one big hospital—the whole world is a madhouse. Just as a bee doesn't like every flower to have pollen, I don't think I'd like it if all of my patients were walking the street together.

'It's difficult for me to describe Hungary for you, I must admit— defeated, humbled Hungary. Here is just one little excerpt from Pécs, the city of my happy, untroubled childhood. The main role in the story is played by a boy pianist. As you know, Béla Kun founded the Kommunisták Magyarországi Pártja, the Hungarian Communist Party. In our small town with its clay-rich soil, it was joined by serious men with large moustaches. The Jewish community in particular was torn between the different camps: one half was for Kun, the other for the Republic and its first president Mihály Károlyi. The young pianist from Pécs, Andor "Andi" Prager, always listened to his elders. To get to music school, he had to take the clay-red road past the workers' shed of the Zsolnay Ceramics Factory. Things were tense at the enterprise, and the workers were rostered on to control production. One day, young Andi was on his way to his piano lesson and saw the revolutionary socialists on guard at the factory gate, and among them he recognized Old Isaak, Old Haim and Old David, whom he used to see at the synagogue. They shouted to him: "Andi, we're all counting on you. On the way back we want to see what your teacher has written." Andi went to his lesson and told his piano teacher about the very serious socialists, all of whom had massive moustaches like drooping whips, and after the lesson the teacher wrote in his journal: "Comrade Andor has progressed exceptionally well. He shows great technical and musical maturity." On the way home, Andi came past Isaak, Haim and David again, but they had just read the "Comrade Andor" introduction and gave a deferential nod. The next day, the young pianist passed the ceramics factory again, but the tables had turned and the republicans had taken control. He saw new faces at the gate. Among them, Andi recognized Old Jákob, Old Miska and Old Noel, neighbours whom he also used to see at the synagogue. They shouted to him: "Andi, we all believe in you, and on the way back we want to see what your piano teacher has written." This time Andi told his teacher about the strict republicans, whose hair fell down to their shoulders like snakes, and after the lesson the teacher automatically entered in the journal: "Master Andor has progressed extremely well since yesterday. His skilful, rhythmic keywork seems set to gain a dimension of earnest." That's my Hungary for you, a republic resembling a roast chicken: people are still tightly holding the bones, but they've been gnawed clean.'

'We consider that this world has come off the rails and that, with the end of the Great War, reality has lost its shameful equilibrium. Parapsychology will replace psychology in the new world; occultism will take the place of physics; paranoia will eclipse common sense, and the family will be replaced by hordes and sects. But this does not worry us at all. There will be more than enough work for us. Some Munich theosophists will still quarrel with their Leipzig brothers, and we will be conceited like the deceased pre-war German opera singers, but all of us will work together on distorting the globe and driving out what little sense remains in people's heads after this war. Cheers! Hell is our certainty, and we accept our future in it with complete indifference. Yours sincerely and satanically, Franz Hartmann ("Dirty Franz", falsely declared to be dead), his graduate apprentice Hugo Vollrath from Munich, and Karl Brandler Pracht, c/o Faust's diabolical tavern in Leipzig.'

'I am Archibald Reiss and I still hope that the new world will be more equitable than the old, though I don't know what keeps this conviction alive in me after seeing, as a criminologist, that nothing has changed in the human soul or in the body, whatever strain or distress you expose it to.'

EPILOGUE: DREAMS MADE OF DREAMS

A new and very important patient arrived at a sanatorium near the German-Dutch border, which was a home for the deranged and mentally ill. Black automobiles with high windscreens had driven up the gravel path in strange silence several days earlier. They stopped right in front of the entrance, and that suggested something unusual was afoot. A handful of uniformed men got out in front of the large, dark, two-winged house overgrown with bougainvillea and ivy. It was a strange company, more like a troupe of buffoons than bodyguards; without exchanging a single word, they began to bend at the waist, stand on their tiptoes and cover their eyes with their hands so they could stare into the distance towards the low sun.

Those nervous soldiers were also seen by the deranged and mentally ill. The patients were unable to explain their presence at the comfortable sanatorium which had hardly felt the war, because it was a home for rich patients. If someone did stray in from the Great War, he was by no means an ordinary, rank-and-file soldier from the front who had copped a dose of bertholite or suffered unbearable headaches from recently having a piece of shrapnel removed from his crazy head. No, that sanatorium treated serious patients along with conceited ones, and the small staff of doctors, all of whom lived on site, took both categories seriously, because all the residents of that convalescent home on the green hill were important in some way, and every neurosis and psychosis they had was special in some way or another.

Each patient had a medical card, a personal doctor, their own room and a nurse who seemed to look after them alone. Even so, that exclusive society of the deranged and mentally ill immediately realized that someone special was coming to their sanatorium, special even compared to them. That unusual guest became the topic of conversation for all: for those who rarely spoke, those who only muttered to themselves on occasion, and those who held fiery speeches every afternoon. And then the patient arrived. It had been three days since those secretive soldiers had come to view the building and its surroundings and to stretch as if doing their morning exercises, and now—everyone claimed—Kaiser Wilhelm in person was arriving at the sanatorium. Only one or two residents doubted it for a short time longer, although no one had actually seen the newcomer and his arrival could therefore be neither confirmed nor denied.

There was only one patient who refused to believe in the kaiser's arrival. Raising his right forefinger in the air theatrically, he claimed that the kaiser ruled Germany and half the world and was therefore on his throne in Berlin. 'Come on,' he repeated, 'is there any good reason why Kaiser Wilhelm would come to our dark house on the green hill?' Everyone calmed down in the end and agreed that the patient spoke rationally, but he was still mistaken. After embittered unrest on the Home Front, Germany capitulated in the Great War. Her army—undefeated militarily—was withdrawn to the borders of the Prussian Empire, and Kaiser Wilhelm was forced to relinquish his throne to the last German Emperor, Adolf II, Prince of Schaumburg-Lippe. Weak and inept at ruling in those bitter, bitter times, Wilhelm's successor only held on to power for a week before handing the republican reins to the leaders of the German revolution on 15 November, 1918.

Consequently it was not correct that the kaiser 'was on his throne in Berlin', nor that he 'ruled' or had half the world under his control. The only thing that was correct was that the important guest who arrived at the sanatorium right on the German-Dutch border was indeed the Kaiser, Friedrich Wilhelm Viktor Albert of Prussia. Crushed by his defeat, a nervous wreck, he was taken there exactly three days after his abdication, placed in a room with the rather ironic number 1, and left alone.

Then for the kaiser, like for King Peter of Serbia in 1916, there began a strange, inclement period with awkward, clumpy minutes and hours which would simply not dissolve in the river of time. For two days the patient just looked through the window, and not a single muscle on his face moved, while the doctors whispered anxiously behind his back. For three nights he didn't think of going to bed, let alone going to sleep, and therefore they decided to adopt a radical therapy. On the fourth day, he was overcome by weariness and fell asleep, which was considered a positive initial response.

His sleep truly was a good sign at first. The kaiser slept deeply and dreamed. He dreamed it was 1914; he was on his throne in Berlin and ruled half the world, unchallenged from any side. Only the war broke out in 1914 in his dream, in that first night of sleep. A short officer took out the royal proclamation and read it with pathos. Still, his voice trembled a little: 'These are dark times for our country. We have been surrounded and are forced to use the sword. God give us strength to wield it as needed and wear it with dignity. To war!'

The next night, Wilhelm of Prussia dreamed of 1914 again, but this time the fire of war had not been ignited. His proclamation did not figure, and no one had to swing a righteous sword; Prussian Germany prospered in 1915, saw unexpected industrial progress in 1916, and went from strength-to-strength in 1917 and 1918. Then the patient in room number 1 woke up in sweat-drenched satin sheets like a butterfly larva in its bedlet. He shuddered and saw the dark house of the sanatorium around him again, his iron hospital bed and the apartment all in white at the end of a long corridor. All around him it was 1918. Germany had lost the war, he had abdicated and handed power to the ineffectual Prince Adolf II. What was there for him to do in that reality other than look out through the window, without a single twitch of the optic nerve, and worry his doctors? Or was it perhaps better to sleep? Yes, the former kaiser would flee from that reality into his dreams.

After just two weeks, Wilhelm made a point of spending as little time as possible awake. He ate almost nothing and declined markedly, but it was his increasingly long hours of sleep which now concerned the doctors. He, whom people still addressed as 'Kaiser', slept and slept and occasionally woke up. His dreams were as lively as reality itself, but he spoke about them to no one. It was 1916 in his dreams, and he saw great industrial progress in the Empire, and in 1917 one success followed another. Then the important patient woke up, and around him it was harsh and inhospitable 1918 again. What was reality, and what a dream? As time passed, the deposed kaiser believed the dreams ever more. Everything nice was reality, he thought, and everything nasty a bad dream. He woke up, but when was he awake? He slept, but when was he asleep? It would be just one more week until he entered another world altogether.

He laughed a carefree laugh as he ate black grapes. His left arm was no longer shrivelled, and he reached for the grapes with it. In the distance, through the window of his palace, he saw Berlin's brown houses, which looked to have been made of chocolate bricks. He ruminated and thought he would be the happiest ruler in the world if only he could get over his bad dreams: dreams in which Germany lost the Great War and he was secretly moved to a sanatorium on the Dutch-German border, where he dreamed the same terrible dream every day.

THE AUTHOR

Aleksandar Gatalica, in short

Born in 1964 in Belgrade, Aleksandar Gatalica graduated from the Department of General Literature with Classic Sciences in 1989. He has published five novels, with the most significant being '*The Lines of Life*' (Linije života) in 1993 (winner of "Miloš Crnjanski" Award and "Giorgio la Pira", Italy), '*The Invisible*' (Nevidljivi) in 2008 (winner of "Stevan Sremac" Award), and '*The Great War*' (NIN award, "Meša Selimović" Award, National Library of Serbia Award, Best selling book in 2013 in Serbia).

He has also published five story cycles, with the best known being '*Mimicries*' (Mimikrije) in 1996, and '*Century, One Hundred and One Histories of a Century*' (Vek, sto jedna povest jednog veka) in 1999 (winner of "Ivo Andrić" Award).

Gatalica also translates from Old Greek and has published translations of Aeschylus' '*Prometheus Bound*', Sophocle's '*King Oedipus*' and, for the first time into Serbian, the following Euripides' plays: '*Alcestis*', '*Iphigenia at Aulis and Bacchae*', as well as the last play by Sophocles, '*Oedipus at Colonus*'.

Aleksandar Gatalica has also been active as a music critic and writer. He has written music criticism for several radio programs, and daily newspapers. In his capacity as a music writer he has published six books; among them: '*Rubinstein versus Horowitz*' (Rubinštajn protiv Horovica) in 1999, and '*The Golden Age of Pianism*' (Zlatno doba pijanizma) in 2002.

He is editor of numerous anthologies in Serbian and other languages and his own stories are represented in more than twenty anthologies of Serbian short stories, which have been translated into a number of languages. He is also a regular contributor to numerous foreign magazines and writes entries on contemporary Serbian literature in several foreign encyclopaedias.

Aleksandar Gatalica is married and has one child. He lives in Belgrade, Serbia.

More on www.gatalica.com

THE TRANSLATOR

Will Firth was born in 1965 in Newcastle, Australia. He studied German and Slavic languages in Canberra, Zagreb and Moscow. Since 1991 he has been living in Berlin, Germany, where he works as a freelance translator of literature and the humanities. He translates from Russian, Macedonian, and all variants of Serbo-Croat. His website is www.willfirth.de.